Marvin's World of Deadheads

by

Paul Atreides

World of Deadheads Series

Marvin's World of Deadheads

Cover Art by *Debbie Taylor*

The Wild Rose Press, Inc.
PO Box 708
Adams Basin, NY 14410-0708
Visit us at www.thewildrosepress.com

Publishing History
First Mainstream Fantasy Edition, 2016
Print ISBN 978-1-5092-0863-0
Digital ISBN 978-1-5092-0864-7

World of Deadheads Series

He stood in the living room

and loaded the gun, careful not to drop any bullets on the floor, and returned the box to his pocket. With one more look at the hole on the shelf, he strode to the door of the bedroom. If he took any more time, he might falter in his resolve, so he lifted the gun, pointed it at Jen's sleeping form, closed his eyes, and pulled the trigger.

Nothing. No gunshot reverberated through his ears. He opened his eyes, and a soft snore escaped from Jenna.

"What the… You gotta be kidding me."

He pulled the trigger again, and again nothing happened. It was like something out of one of the movies Tommy always seemed to go on about; one where the main character is repeatedly pulling the trigger of an empty gun. But he knew this gun was not empty, he'd loaded it not three minutes ago.

He fumbled with the gun in his hand to study it, but it was just a little too dark to make out the details, increasing his fury. Light from the streetlamp poured through the window, which in the past had always kept him awake and was why he made Jen sleep on that side of the bed. He went to the window and brought the gun close to his face for a better look. A deafening roar issued from the gun. Something burned through his right ear. He fell backward and spun around in a complete circle. "Ow! God*dammit.*"

The bullet lodged in the crown molding above the sleeping Jenna, and a soft sprinkle of powder dusted her hair.

Praise for Paul Atreides

"At the heart of it all, this is a love story that not only keeps the reader involved on a deep emotional level, but asks them questions of morality not grounded in black and white. [*MARVIN'S*] *WORLD OF DEADHEADS* is a welcome surprise!"

> ~*John Daryl Winston, author*
> ~*~

"…a great entry into comedic literature."

> ~*22nd Annual Writer's Digest*
> *Self-Published Book Awards*
> ~*~

"…a humorous romp through the afterlife."

> ~*PW Select, a quarterly of Publisher's Weekly*
> ~*~

"In this comedic romp through the hereafter, author Paul Atreides gives us a main character with a strong voice and sardonic wit. [*MARVIN'S*] *WORLD OF DEADHEADS* kept me engaged from page one until its unexpected…and highly spirited…end."

> ~*Carrie Ann Lahain, author*
> ~*~

"A fun fantasy and dark comedy."

> ~*Tom Keller, author*

Dedication

For F.B. Premie,
who keeps waiting for someone
who has passed on to stop by
and let her know there's life on the other side.

Chapter 1

"Oh, shit!" were the last words Marvin spoke.
The last thing Marvin heard was *Thump.*

****

Marvin stood, dazed from the impact, and inspected his clothes. They didn't seem to be any worse for the wear; no dirt or grease stains, no tears, not even a scuff on his shoes. He looked himself over, all six-feet two-inches, and didn't see any blood, but he knew one thing for sure: Marvin Broudstein, "Marv" to his girlfriend—no, that wasn't right—fiancée, Jenna, "Brody" to certain friends and co-workers, was dead.

He knew it because he saw his body lying halfway under the bus, and his face looked like it had slammed into the nose of a 747. He knew it because a dirty imprint of the bus grille showed smack in the center of the light tan shirt. He knew it because he watched the driver, who slammed on the brakes, cut the engine, and scrambled out looking like a woman with apoplexy (though he wasn't entirely sure what that was, but thought it sounded right). She bent down to touch two fingers to the bloody neck, turned a scrunched-up face away, and opted for a splayed out arm instead, and then shook her head.

He knew because he heard Jenna, who knelt over him, wail like a banshee. "No. No." She punched him and screamed, "Get up, Marvin. Come on, Marv. Get up."

He knew because after the EMTs arrived, they didn't rush medical equipment to him. Instead, after dutifully checking for a pulse, they grabbed him by feet and armpits, plopped him onto the gurney, crammed it into place in the back of the ambulance, shut the back doors, and drove off; without the benefit of lights or siren.

Goddammit. How could this happen? In all his twenty-eight years, Marvin had never done anything so stupid. He sensed the onset of one of his well-deserved rants, but knew it wouldn't help or change a thing, so for the first time in months, he took a deep breath and held it until the urge dissipated. It was all Jenna's fault.

And there she stood, staring at the back end of the ambulance as it drove away, lipstick all smeared (though that could have been from him bumping into her in his rush out the door) and mascara running down her face in a river of non-stop tears. He wanted to tell her she looked like shit right now. But he figured it would just piss her off and trigger another tirade like the one she'd been on when he left. That and, well, he wasn't sure she'd hear him anyway. Being as he was dead and all.

Neighbors streamed en masse back into the building. He regretted not getting to know any of them better like he'd planned. Mrs. What's-her-name, the old lady from the condo across from theirs, wrapped an arm around Jen, led her up the stairs and into the building, saying soothing things that obviously didn't register with Jenna.

"I'm sorry, Jen," he called out, but since it got no discernible reaction, he figured she definitely couldn't hear him. His voice softened. "I really am."

"Oh, man. Bummer, dude."

Marvin turned around to see a kid, about eighteen, maybe twenty, with long, sandy blond hair that looked like it last saw a comb sometime in the 1960s. He stood about three feet away wearing old sneakers, frayed jeans, and a Grateful Dead T-shirt.

"I saw the whole thing, man. What a bitch, huh?"

"Are you talking to me?" Marvin asked.

"Yeah, man. Who'd you think?"

Marvin looked around the area. There were people still standing nearby—the cops interviewing the bus driver and several others who interjected into the fray of questioning; a few men staring at the pool of blood on the pavement; still more who drifted away, off to wherever their hectic lives took them every day.

Then, as if a mist lifted, he noticed some people who were there, yet not entirely. They were a trifle transparent; not quite solid, living, breathing creatures. He could see items *through* them: the traffic, which had begun to move again, storefronts of the buildings across the street, people standing on the corner at the intersection a half block away now cautiously waiting for the light to change in their favor. It seemed weird.

He really wanted to launch into one of his rants, to curse the rotten luck, but the small pragmatic streak in him burst through to the forefront of his brain. *How can you fix being dead?*

"So, what are you, the Welcome Wagon or something?" Marvin finally asked the young man standing behind him.

The kid laughed. It was a clear, tenor tone that made Marvin smile. "Um, or something." The kid put a hand out in greeting. "Tommy. Tommy Kincaid."

"Marvin Broudstein." Marvin shook his hand, surprised it didn't slip right through like he'd seen in the movies. He could actually feel it.

"I know. Nice to meet you."

"You knew my name? What, because I bought the farm there?"

"Nah, nothin' like that. I heard the girl—Jen?—tell the cops."

"Oh. So…" Marvin shrugged. "Now what?"

"Nothin', really. Just, whatever."

"'Just whatever'? Where do I go? What do I do?"

"You do whatever you want. No more punching the old time clock, huh? You go wherever you want."

"Isn't there a check-in, or something?"

"For what?"

"I don't know. For being…you know." Marvin spread his arms.

"Don't be silly. What'd you think, you were gonna stand in line for wings?"

Marv heaved a sigh. "So—Tommy, is it?"

Tommy nodded.

Marvin didn't know for sure right away, but then decided maybe he would like to see his boss, Crowley, the *schmuck*, handle today's meeting without him. That could be quite entertaining. Instead, he asked, "So, what do *you* do for fun around here?"

"All kinds of stuff. Watch people; mess with them. Oh, and movies. I really like going to the movies."

Marvin nodded. A little off-kilter, he pushed his palms against his temples, careful not to mess up the executive cut of his brown hair, and sat down on the curb. When he lifted his face to say something to his new friend, a knee banged through the back of his head. He uttered a quick "Ow! What the hell was that?"

"Oh, yeah. They—people, that is *live* people—they can't see you. So you gotta be careful, or they'll be smacking into you all the time. And the bitch of it is, they know they've bumped into something, they just can't figure out what. Actually, it's pretty funny to watch them gawk around with the same look on their faces you just had on yours."

A confused look crossed Tommy's face as he paused.

"What?" Marv asked him.

Tommy shook his head. "Nothin'. I was just thinkin'. You want to go see a movie? The early show starts in an hour."

"Actually, I'd like some coffee. Can I do that?"

"Sure. Come on, I'll show you how this works."

Marvin stood up to follow Tommy and explained, "I wore mine this morning, instead of drinking it."

"What happened? Your lady get pissed and throw it at you?"

Marvin snorted a laugh. "Nah. Jen snuck up on me, scared the bejesus out of me. Where to?"

"There's this great little deli around the corner on Forty-Fifth." Tommy hooked a thumb over his shoulder.

"Yeah, yeah…Epstein's, right? I love that place. Best pastrami this side of Pittsburgh."

"Yeah, I go in there all the time."

"You do? You Jewish?" Marvin's brows knit in doubt. "You don't look Jewish."

"No, but what exactly does Jewish look like?"

"Like me, ya schmuck," Marvin said, chuckling

and slapping Tommy on the back of the head.

"Don't mess up the coif, man."

Marvin followed him the three blocks, being careful to avoid the resultant buzz of bumping into any of the living, though he got plenty of enjoyment watching Tommy stand stock still while some guy walked right through him. The look on the guy's face as he wondered what the hell just happened—Priceless. Laughing like a school kid on a playground, Tommy turned to see Marvin's reaction.

In the deli, Tommy told him, "Now, here's how it works. You walk around the counter, grab a cup, pour your coffee and enjoy."

"Won't someone see the cup and carafe move, or anything?"

Tommy glanced around until he picked out a target. "Watch."

The brunette waitress in a short black skirt and white blouse carried a tray with an empty cup and a carafe of coffee across the small restaurant, weaving through the crowded tables. The tag over her left breast read TINA in large letters and under that in small print, *I'll be your server today*.

She approached a professional-looking woman sitting alone at a small table for two, placed the cup down, filled it to almost overflowing, pulled a menu from the pocket of her apron, and dropped it on the table.

"I'll be right back to take your order," Tina said, and strode off.

The woman mumbled something under her breath. Before she picked up the cup, her cell phone rang. While she rummaged through her purse, Tommy grabbed the coffee. He turned back to Marvin with a grin.

Amused, they stood and watched as the woman replied to a question from her caller, nodded, made a grab for the cup, and swiped air. Confusion passed over her face when she looked and found nothing more than a menu lying on the table. The woman glanced around the deli, shook her head as if to clear it, then said into the phone, "Hang on a minute, Sal."

She waved Tina over. "Do you think I might get some coffee while I look at the menu? Would that be too much trouble for you, *hon*?"

From experience, Tommy told Marvin, he knew Tina didn't like people like this. Especially rich-bitches, dressed in their Jimmy Choo shoes and Donna Karan power suits, copping attitude. Tina visibly struggled to contain her anger.

"I know I—um, sure thing, *hon*." Tina turned on her heels to fetch the requested order.

"It's easier to go somewhere that has DIY-slash-free refills, but this is much more fun, don't you think? Here." Tommy held the cup out to Marvin.

"Am I going to be able to hold that? I mean, don't I have to learn—you know, like what's-his-name, uh…Patrick Swayze in *Ghost*?"

Tommy rolled his eyes. "That was a *movie*, this is life. Well…sort of. Over here, like if you lean against a wall, or sit on a bench, those things are grounded in *their* world. But if you pick something up and hold it, they can't see it until you put it down."

"So no one will see the cup in my hand? It's not just floating in the air?"

"Nope. Not until you put it down. Awesome, huh?"

Marvin accepted the coffee as he laughed and slapped Tommy on the shoulder. "Oh, I am going to have some *fun* with this."

Chapter 2

The morning of November 30th—a few hours before Marvin died—had begun like any other day. Marvin woke with the alarm ringing in his ear. He opened an eye to see Jenna slap the snooze button and try to roll over. She ran right into him and growled.

He felt the punch as it landed right into the solar plexus. The air expelled from his lungs. He grunted loudly as he doubled up and moved to his own side of the bed.

"What was that for?" he demanded, finally able to catch his breath.

"For hogging the bed again. Jesus, Marv, it's a king size bed, and you can't seem to leave me enough room to wiggle a foot."

"You couldn't just nudge me?" he asked tumbling off the bed and heading for the bathroom.

He caught the reflection of her raised middle finger as she giggled. "Yeah, like that ever works."

Marvin had just finished brushing his teeth when Jenna sauntered in, yawning and stretching the hem of the shirt—she always wore one of his T-shirts to bed as a nightgown—up the length of her thighs. He gave her a sexy wink and a smile.

"In your dreams, cowboy. Put the rope away and get ready for work."

He shrugged and spit in the sink. "Can't blame a

guy for tryin'." He turned on the shower and stepped in, closing the glass door behind him.

Jenna took her toothbrush from the holder and went to shove it under the faucet. "Gross. Why can't you rinse the sink out when you're done?"

"Sorry. Got distracted."

Jenna paused in the middle of her typical loud brushing and spitting.

All Marvin heard was "eh, own or-et r un eeting oo-ay" and it pissed him off. She was always doing that to him; mumbling with a toothbrush in her mouth, talking into her closet, or saying something as she walked away from him. Then she always got pissed off when he either, 1. didn't respond at all, or 2. responded with "Huh?" or "What?" This morning, as payback for her plunging a fist into his chest, he pretended he didn't hear a thing. By the time he'd finished soaping up and rinsing off, he heard her gargle and spit. He lathered up to shave.

"Marv, did you hear what I said?" She climbed into the shower stall that was barely large enough for the two of them.

"No, what?" Marv asked and let loose an aggravated sigh. Another thing that bothered him: She'd get into the shower with him on a work day, rub against him, which always—always—started a stir in his groin and then elbow him away. Today, he decided to ignore both the elbow and the sprouting erection.

"Lunch today. Don't forget," she reminded him and pushed her way under the spray.

"Um, about that…" He paused while he swiped the razor across his Adam's apple. "Can't this wait?"

"Marvin! No. Not again. We've talked about this."

The waves of her tamed, dark hair sprang into natural curls, which delighted him right now because she hated it, and shampoo bubbles ran down her wet body.

"I know, I know. It's just that, um…Crowley is insisting that I go to this meeting with him today."

"Bullshit, Marv. Since when does he need your help landing an account?"

"I don't know, Jen. Maybe since this is *my* client?" His exasperation mounted. First the punch in the gut, then mumbling at him, now the pecking and nagging; the day was one heartbeat away from turning to shit.

"You're just trying to postpone the whole thing, aren't you? Or are you trying to cancel completely?"

"Cancel? No. Of course not, honey." He hedged again. "Move over, let me rinse off."

He pushed her aside, hung his razor on the holder stuck to the wall, and stood under the spray. He deliberately took his time while she stood there, her arms wrapped around her small breasts trying to keep warm, all wet and *goddamit* looking sexy as hell doing it. He finally pushed the door open, stepped out, pulled his towel from the bar, and started vigorously drying himself. The palm of her hand hit him square between the shoulder blades as she shoved him. His left arm shot out against the wall to keep from landing on his ass.

"Damn. Kill me why don't you."

"Close the door. You're letting air in and it's cold."

He turned to face her with a sly grin. "Yeah? Show me."

For the second time that morning, she flipped him the bird. "Close the f'in' door."

Marvin closed the door, finished drying off, and hung his towel neatly in place. He used a washcloth to wipe the steam from the mirror and combed his hair, "mmhmmm-ing" in response to her running commentary. He finally said, "Jen. Please. Give it a rest," and walked out to get dressed.

But she didn't. The entire time he was getting dressed, he heard the drone of her voice, which he did his best to ignore. She still rambled on about the wedding as he walked out of the bedroom.

He stood on the small balcony overlooking Broad Street. Her voice carried to him from the galley kitchen.

"Are you looking for a way to postpone again?"

"No. I don't know where you get that idea. Come on, Jen. Stop it, already. Can't we talk about this later?"

"It's always later for you, isn't it Marv?"

"No, honey." He tried to use his soothing voice. "I just…"

A swan dive into the pavement looked good right about now. He wondered, not for the first time, or even the hundredth, why, oh why, he had proposed. At times like this, he wanted to stuff a rag in her mouth. Though, in the back of his mind, he knew he'd miss the verbal sparring. After all, it had been the spark of attraction in the first place.

"Then why do you keep finding excuses?"

"*Me* finding excuses. How many times have *you* been the one to weasel out? Who canceled the last five—count 'em, *five*—lunches because of work?"

"That's different."

"That's bullshit, Jen, and you know it. My job is just as important as yours."

"I didn't say it wasn't. But you don't have to work at it as hard as I do."

It was true. Marvin had moved up faster than

12

anyone in the advertising company of Saxton and Crowley; his own boss, Martin Crowley, included. Crowley treated every employee with the same amount of disdain, yet Marvin not only withstood the diatribes, he excelled in spite of them.

Jenna, with no formal training, started out in the roving secretarial pool of a law firm, and it had taken hard work and long hours to prove her worth. Her ability to spot inconsistencies and holes in the briefs she typed got her noticed. It could only be sustained if she continued to be diligent; there could be no room to slack off. "You're just trying to avoid it, that's what I think."

"Avoid what, for God's sake?"

"Planning our wedding."

Marv jumped at the closeness of her voice, spilling coffee down the front of his pants. "Jesus H… I've asked you not to sneak up on me like that. Dammit. It looks like I pissed myself. Thanks a lot. Now I have to change."

She didn't back off the argument as he squeezed past her to get back into the apartment. "Well, maybe it serves you right."

"You can be a petulant bitch sometimes, you know that?" Marv shot over his shoulder.

"Yeah? Well, you can be an arrogant prick."

Marvin rolled his eyes, shook his head, and kept on walking. He didn't have time for a fight right now. He kicked his shoes off, removed his pants, took wallet, keys, and change, and tossed it all onto the bed. As he stripped the black leather belt off, the end flew free of the last belt-loop and snapped him right in the nuts.

Bent over, grabbing his crotch, he howled in pain.

"Goddammit. Son-of-a-bitch. This is turning out to be a day from fucking *hell*."

He dropped his wet trousers on the floor in front of the closet and carefully pulled on a clean pair of khakis, threaded and cinched his belt, slipped on the shoes, and grabbed his things off the bed. He stuffed his wallet into his back pocket while he strode out of the bedroom. He planned to holler "Later!" from the hallway and keep on going. Instead he ran right into her as she applied lipstick in front of the small mirror on the wall.

"Oof!" Jen caught herself before her nose smacked the wall. "Marvin, I swear to God," she warned as she checked her makeup, "if I have to redo everything, I'm going to kick your ass."

"Sorry. I didn't expect you to be there. I gotta go, I'm late already and Crowley is gonna be pissed." He pecked her on the cheek and literally ran out the door.

"You better—" was all Jenna got out before the door closed behind him.

****

Jenna stood there, stunned, but only for an instant. She recovered quickly, walked through the condo and out onto the balcony. She waited for him, determined that nothing would stop this lunch date. As soon as she recognized the toe of his shoe when it emerged from the small portico at the front of the building, she hollered again.

"Marvin? Marvin!"

He waved a hand over his shoulder as he walked at a quick pace and checked traffic to his right.

"Marvin, you better not screw this up again. Lunch. Today. At one-thi—"

Marvin stepped off the curb into the street. Jenna's breath caught in her throat. Her knees buckled, and she screamed, "Marvin, no!"

He glanced up and his stunned, "Oh, shit!" drifted to her.

Chapter 3

On their return to the condo, Marvin pointed Tommy to the door marked 2-F in nickel-finished characters toward the end of the carpeted hallway. "This is it. It's a small building; only six units on each floor. The F stands for Front—you pay extra for the street view." He hesitated and stood digging through his pockets.

"Are we waiting for something?"

"I'm trying to find my keys. I don't know what I did with them; I had them when—"

"Marvin, you ain't gonna find 'em, bud. They're in your pocket—at the morgue. But, you don't need 'em anymore." Tommy walked through the closed door.

"Oh. Right. Does it hurt, walking through stuff?"

Tommy answered from inside the apartment. "Nah, you'll just get a little buzz, a tingle really. Like, did you ever stick one of those nine-volt batteries to your tongue?"

"Yeah, when I was a kid."

"It'll feel like that. You get used to it."

Marvin pushed a hand through, waited for the sensation to register, then smiled and walked in. The dead quiet of the place surprised him. He thought Jen would've been home, on the phone to notify friends and family, looking like hell and feeling much too distraught to even think about funeral arrangements. It disappointed him that she wasn't there.

"Nice pad," Tommy said from the bedroom.

"Mmm, yeah. Thanks." With a job secured, he'd purchased the two-bedroom, two bath condo right out of college. The graduation gift from his folks covered the small down payment. In the heart of the up-and-coming urban area, the pseudo-brownstone appealed to him and reminded him a little bit of the row houses where he grew up in upstate New York.

"My place isn't nearly as nice. And the old lady that moved in after I died snores like a gorilla."

"So, what you're saying, if I understand, is I can still stay here?"

"Of course. Most of us find it, um…comforting, I guess, to stay where we lived. 'Specially younger ones, like us, when we—how did you put it earlier—'bought the farm' so early. Some just wander around until they decide to 'go into the light' as the living world likes to think of it. But, I'll tell you that's *nothing* like you see in the movies. Older folks tend to gravitate to the parks and coffee shops, wherever they spent lots of time. Unless they left a spouse behind, then they tend to want to mess with them as much as possible." Tommy snorted a laugh, spreading his arms out to indicate the apartment. "I'm kinda hungry. Got anything to eat?"

"We usually did take-out, but there might be something. Look around," Marv said from the balcony in the exact spot Jen had witnessed his death. He could see a pool of his blood still on the pavement. "Jesus, don't they clean that stuff up? It's kind of creepy."

Back in the kitchen, Tommy rattled pans. Marvin went in to sit at the table to watch. The smells made him aware of the hunger pangs that stabbed at his stomach. Tommy wrestled up a mean brunch: bacon and eggs, toasted bagels with a *schmear* as Marvin's mother used to call the plain cream cheese, big glasses of orange juice (which Marvin didn't realize Jen had stashed in the fridge, or he would've grabbed some that morning along with his coffee), and small bowls of fruit cocktail mixed in plain yogurt.

"Quite a spread, Tommy. Thanks for doing the cooking."

Tommy shrugged. "I was one of the short order cooks at Epstein's."

"Really? How come I never saw you in there?"

Tommy laughed. "It was years ago."

Marvin contemplated asking how many years but nodded instead and dug into the plate of crispy bacon.

"Bacon? I thought you said you were Jewish."

"You've heard of Jack Mormons?"

Tommy nodded.

"Well, just think of me as a Jack Jew."

They ate in silence, and when they finished, Marv got up, washed everything, put it away, and even emptied the trash per Tommy's instructions: "If you leave things in disarray, it'll spoil the fun later on."

After Marvin inspected the kitchen to make sure it was spotless as always, they went into the living room.

"Daytime TV," Marv said picking up the remote. "What's that all about? Is it still all soap opera crap?"

"Not if you have cable. You do have cable, right?"

Marv looked at him as though Tommy had just asked if he wanted a blueberry bagel with strawberry cream cheese, which as far as Marv was concerned was akin to sacrilege. He'd stick to plain or onion bagels, thank-you-very-much, and don't even get him started on flavored cream cheese. He tossed the remote to Tommy. "Whatever you want. I'm new to the scene."

Tommy flipped through the channels much slower than Jenna had ever done. For some reason, when Jenna got control of a remote, her inner man reared his head as if her testosterone levels had suddenly surged and she blazed through channels; it always aggravated him. Somewhere around the thirtieth click, Tommy landed on a baseball game and turned to wait for Marv's reaction. Marv shrugged indifference. Two more clicks and there was Bruce Willis in a wife-beater, all dirty and grimy, with his Beretta at the ready.

"Ah. *Die Hard.* I love this film. Have you ever seen it?"

"Can't say as I have. But ask me about any musical and I can give you a blow by blow." Tommy smiled at Marv's grimace. "What can I say, man, I'm a sucker for musicals."

"Turn it up. It may not be as awesome as something like *Twister*, but the explosions will rattle your cage with the surround sound."

****

At precisely two-thirty in the afternoon Mrs. McClaskey stepped out of her condo across the hall to check her mail as she did every day. She heard music and a man's voice say very loudly, 'Yippie-ki-yay, motherfucker' from inside Jenna and Marvin's unit. The sound was up awfully high. '*Don't damage your ears, and they'll serve you for a lifetime*' was a motto she lived by. She tried to spread the wisdom, though the kids of today often laughed and ignored her advice. She knew one day they would finally understand, though it would be too late.

She tapped her knuckles on the door, "Jenna? Jenna, dear, are you home?"

She waited several seconds and, when she got no response, went down the stairs to get her mail. On the way back up, music and gunshots drifted through to the hallway, but thankfully no cuss words. Not that swearing bothered her, as a retired librarian, words were just words to her. She'd heard them and read them all before, but still, she believed young people overused such things, perhaps to a point the words almost lost all effect. She tapped on the door again and waited.

With no response, Mrs. McClaskey went back into her place.

Chapter 4

Jenna stood at the door to the condo and fumbled through her purse for keys. Did she smell bacon? It was the weirdest thing. They hadn't cooked that morning because, as usual, Marv had been in such a hurry to rush out the door. The smell reminded her of all the times Marvin had taken her to Epstein's for breakfast, or even a quick cup of coffee before they headed off in different directions to work. The memory made her cry again.

"You son-of-a-bitch, Marv," she said through sniffles and opened the door. "How could you do this to me?"

"It's your fault." Marvin stood from where he'd been sitting on the arm of the sofa. "You made me spill my coffee. You badgered me until I wanted to run out the door just so I wouldn't have to listen to it anymore."

Tommy nudged him with an elbow. "You know she can't hear you, right?"

"I know. It makes me feel better though."

Jenna tossed her keys and purse on the small table in the foyer and made her way to the kitchen. Nothing seemed out of place; it was spotless as always. They didn't cook very often, though when they did it had always been together and a lot of fun. Marv had learned quite a set of kitchen skills from his mother, who'd insisted her sons learn to take care of themselves

21

because God only knew when 'a decent woman' would come along. Having lived in a series of foster homes, Jenna had learned nothing about cooking. Each subsequent family told her what she'd learned was wrong, and consequently, nothing sank into her brain. The aroma of sizzling bacon was stronger in here and made her stomach grumble. She opened a drawer, took out a spoon, and reached into the cupboard for a can of fruit cocktail that was no longer there. She threw the spoon to the counter in a fit. "Goddamit, Marv. When did you eat that?"

"This afternoon, when you weren't looking," he taunted.

She opened the fridge looking for the small container of yogurt she bought the day before. It was nowhere in sight. Thinking she was losing her mind, that maybe she had eaten it last night, she peered into the wastebasket for the empty carton. Not there. Maybe she hadn't bought any after all.

"Shit. Is there *anything* left around here?" Jenna opened cupboard after cupboard until she spied and settled on some stale Saltine crackers.

"You know, maybe if you'd paid attention and cooked once in a while there'd be food in the house," Marv told her.

Stuffing two in her mouth, Jenna took a can of diet Pepsi from the refrigerator. She popped the top and the resulting *pfssst* reminded her of the hydraulic brake system on the bus. It had made that same noise after the bus stopped in a screech of tires. And her tears ran in a fresh torrent. She grabbed the box of crackers, plopped into the only chair in the living room—Marv's chair— and, in the dying light, dejectedly stuffed crackers in her mouth followed by gulps of soda.

"What the hell is this? No eating in the living room. You *never* let me eat in here. What, we have new rules now that I'm dead?"

Jenna looked to the ceiling. "I know I never allowed this, but you know what? Fuck the rules."

Marvin looked at Tommy in surprise. "I thought you said they couldn't hear us."

"She can't. I know it's strange, but sometimes they'll pick up on thought patterns or something."

Jenna jumped, startled by the phone. She picked it up on the third ring just before it went to the answering machine; she couldn't handle hearing his cheery voice right now on the recorded greeting. "Hello?"

"Jenna, dear, are you all right?"

Jen snuffled and wiped the tears from her eyes. "Yeah, I'm…I'm fine."

"Are you sure, dear? I tapped on the door this afternoon. I heard the TV going but didn't get an answer. Did you fall asleep with the television on? Oh, you poor thing. The strain probably has you exhausted."

"I'm okay, really. I had to go to the morgue and pick up Marvin's things and run some other errands. I didn't get in until twenty minutes ago. Are you sure the sound came from here?"

"I told you it was too loud," Marvin told Tommy.

"Sorry, dude. You're the one who said to turn it up. You said the neighbors were at work."

"Oh, right. Well, I forgot about old Mrs…What's-her-name over there." He waved a hand in the general direction of the place across the hall.

"Well, I am getting up in years… But I could swear it was your TV."

"You know, Mrs. McClaskey, maybe it filtered through the vents. From downstairs?"

Marvin slapped himself in the forehead. "McClaskey. Right. Hey, Tommy, do you think now I'll get a better handle on people's names?"

"Sorry. It is what it is, when it ain't no mo'." Tommy laughed at his own joke.

"What's that supposed to mean?"

"It means, things don't change over here on this side. Your hair, your nails, your weight, nothing. It all stays the same. So, it probably goes to figure, man, your brain won't change either. It's a real bummer, I know, but…" Tommy lifted his hands as if it were explanation enough.

Mrs. McClaskey sighed. "I suppose so. Well, I just wanted to offer my condolences again. Remember, dear, if you need anything, anything at all, I'm right across the hall."

"Thank you, Mrs. McClaskey, I appreciate that."

"You're sure you're all right now?"

"Positive." Jenna mustered a weak smile for an empty room.

"All right, then. Get some sleep, dear. Take something if you have to. Don't be too proud to admit when you need help."

"I will, and I won't, Mrs. McClaskey. I promise. And thank you."

"For what, dear?"

"Being there. Caring enough to call."

"Oh, go on. It's my pleasure. You're a fine young lady. Why, I think of you as my own daughter."

"That's sweet. Thank you."

Marvin bent over in mock agony, two fingers stuck

in his mouth. "I think I'm going to barf."

Tommy laughed.

"Good night, dear."

"Good night, Mrs. McClaskey."

Jenna hung up the phone and sat in the growing darkness, mindlessly eating. She turned on the TV and flipped channels, not finding anything that would engage her brain, to make her stop thinking about Marvin. The scene from the balcony replayed through her mind again and again, in slow motion. It wasn't what she wanted to watch, but it was all her brain managed to project.

"Stop already. You're making me nuts with the channel surfing," Marvin yelled.

"Dude—"

"I know, I know. She can't hear me."

The TV went off, and the room turned dark. Marvin sighed in relief. Jen pushed the scroll button and stared at a blank screen. Click. Click. Click.

"What the *hell* is she doing?"

"How should I know? I just met her—sort of. Anyway, it's gettin' late, man. I think I'll wander on home. The old lady is probably rattling the windows by now." He shrugged. "At least I can shower."

"You shower? Does everyone after they...you know."

"Probably not. What for? Eh, I mostly do it out of habit, I guess. You'll find we do most things out of habit. And I like the feel of the warmth."

"Oh." Marv looked down at the floor. He had things he wanted to know, things about this new existence. "Before you leave, can I ask you something?"

"Anything, man. My brain is full of useless information, just for the taking. Ask away."

"What about...other things."

"Like..."

"Uh, you know. Personal things."

Tommy laughed. Marv saw it move down to Tommy's belly and spread until his entire body shook. Marvin stood stone-faced.

"Oh, sorry, man. I can't help it," Tommy said through fits of laughter that threatened to turn to giggles. He settled down with forced control even though the broad smile never left his face. "Marvin, my man, I am a child of the flower power generation. You know: Drop out, tune in, turn on." He waited for some recognition to come to Marvin's face, when it didn't appear he continued, "The late sixties? Hippies, communes, free love?"

"Ah," was all Marv responded with. At least now he knew how many years it had been since Tommy had flipped burgers, figuratively speaking of course, at Epstein's Deli.

"So, we're both guys here. Ain't nothin' you could ask that's gonna shock me, or embarrass me. What you wanna know?"

"What about... Well...like, what if I need to take a leak? Do we do that?" Marvin wasn't sure why he was fidgeting and acting like a twelve-year-old kid, because he'd had plenty of "guy" conversations with his co-workers, that schmuck Crowley not-withstanding, but maybe it could be due to Tommy being a recent acquaintance.

"Well, we drink don't we? Ever wonder why some folks swore they could hear running water, but when they check, it turns out to be nothing? They think they imagined it? It's usually because one of us showered or flushed the toilet. Me? I normally do *that* kinda thing in large restrooms."

"Like at the movies," Marvin stated to prove he got it.

"Like at the movies," Tommy confirmed. "Or in a restaurant. You know, I just can't bring myself to take a whiz on the street like some do."

"You're kidding, right? That's gross."

"How many times have you walked down a street and seen a small puddle, or noticed the side of a building is wet in one spot?"

"I guess I always assumed it was someone's dog."

Tommy shrugged. "Well, it is mostly bums. You know, homeless men. Guess old habits die hard."

Marvin paused for a moment before he asked his next question. "What about sex?"

"With ours or theirs?"

Marvin splayed his hands. "Whatever."

"Not with them." Tommy nodded toward Jen. "Never with *them*. Unfortunately, for me anyway, it ain't any easier on this side than it ever was over there."

"What happened to all that 'free love' you mentioned." Marvin made quotes with his fingers.

Tommy shook his head. "I never said *I* got much after leaving the commune."

Marvin sighed. "So, just suffer huh?"

"'Bout the size of it." Tommy walked to the front door. Just before he stepped through, he turned back and said, "'Course, you could always flog your log, as we used to say. Catch ya later, dude."

Tommy's laughter rolled down the hallway.

Marvin turned his attention back to Jen, who hadn't moved from the chair but still sniffled frequently and ran the back of her arm against her cheeks to swipe at the tears.

A while later, he followed her to the bedroom, where she pulled her clothes off, dropped them in a pile on the floor, and in a sudden burst of anger, kicked the entire heap across the room. "You know, I hope you can hear me, you—you *asshole*. I am so pissed off at you right now."

"Jesus H, Jen. Now what? I'm dead, and I *still* can't do anything right."

"You did this on purpose, didn't you?" she asked with a catch in her voice. "I knew it. I knew you'd do anything to get out of it." She pulled on one of his old, cast off T-shirts and flopped to the bed.

"Oh, yeah, I walked in front of a bus just to get out of marrying you. What're you, nuts or something?"

"Why? *Why?* What am I supposed to do now, huh? What am I supposed to *do*?"

She sounded so forlorn, he wanted to help, but he didn't have an answer. No one had ever died on him. His entire family was still alive and kicking. He chuckled at the way his mother always implored, always pleaded, always worried over silly things, over such...*nonsense*. He looked in the direction of upstate New York, "Well, Ma, at least you don't have to worry about me anymore. Now, you can concentrate on David. And David? Sorry bro, I feel for you, but you'll have to pick up the slack on that end."

Jen got up and went to the closet. She yanked one of his dress shirts from a hanger, put it to her face and breathed in deep; the scent seemed to calm her. She balled it up and hugged it close as she went back to bed.

Marvin climbed in and wrapped his body around hers, like he had done every night of their life together. Of course, when he was alive, it was because he hoped he would get laid. And he had to hand it her: most times, he did. This was different though. This time he just wanted to be close to her, hold her, comfort her. He sensed the buzz and tingle of contact with one of *them*, as Tommy had put it, a live person. He whispered in her ear, "Jen, I wish you could hear me. I am so sorry. I wish I could fix it. I wish I could help you, but I'm not sure how I can."

Jen brushed at the tickle and let out a little sigh. "Oh, goddammit, Marv..." She cried herself to sleep.

Chapter 5

"Marvin. Hey, Marvin. Marvin, wait up. Dude, where ya goin'?"

Marvin turned to find Tommy struggling to maneuver around the other pedestrians along Broad Street and catch up. "Following her to the funeral home." He pointed to Jen, who was about a yard ahead. "She's got an appointment at eleven o'clock."

"Bummer."

"I want to make sure she does this right."

"Did you have everything laid out? I mean, in writing—a will and all that?"

"No, why?"

"What do you expect her to do then?"

Marvin considered this for a minute. "I don't know. I'm sure we talked about this kind of thing at some point. Didn't we? I mean, wouldn't we?"

"You're asking me? Dude, we just met yesterday. How do I know what you did or didn't talk about with your wife."

"Not my wife. Girlfriend—I mean, fiancée. She better do me right, that's all I can say. She doesn't know my mother."

They followed Jen as she turned left on Thirty-Eighth Street, walked another half block, and stopped in front of a building. The small, discreet black sign, with gold lettering read Davis Funeral Home, Leonard

Davis, Proprietor. She nodded and stepped to the entrance. She opened the heavy door just far enough to let her slight frame slip in and it shut behind her, cutting Marvin in half.

"I don't believe this. She let the door slam in my face. How do you like that?"

"Marvin, you're dead. She didn't know you were there."

"Don't go making excuses for her, Tommy," Marvin protested, until Tommy's words actually registered and he let out a deep sigh. "Sorry. This dead thing is going to take some getting used to."

An older man in his mid-sixties dressed in a black Armani suit, silver hair perfectly combed, approached Jenna. "Mr. Leonard Davis, Proprietor of Davis Funeral Home, how may I help you, young lady?"

"How do you like this guy, Marvin? Holy crap, gold and diamond cufflinks for God's sake."

"He's Jewish anyway; that'll make my mother happy."

"How do you know he's Jewish?"

"The cufflinks—Star of David."

Jen put her hand out and expected to shake his. "I'm Jenna Wilson. I called earlier?"

Mr. Davis held her hand in a gentle grasp. "Yes, Ms. Wilson. Of course. The unfortunate accident of your, fiancé was he? We're sorry for your loss." He bent slightly at the waist and planted a light kiss on the back of her hand.

Marvin watched with his brow creased and imparted a grunt through pursed lips. "I'll bet. This is a chunk of change in your pocket. You're probably so happy to see her, you could soil your silk underwear."

Tommy laughed and walked around to Mr. Davis's back. "Silk, huh? Want me to find out?"

Marvin laughed but shook his head.

They all followed Mr. Davis into an exquisite, but showy office. A monstrous mahogany desk with leather inlay and a big executive chair done in Italian leather sat at the far end of the room. Closer to the door two comfortable chairs, but not too comfortable—Mr. Davis didn't want people lounging half the afternoon, after all—and a matching brocade sofa surrounded a large mahogany coffee table that was strewn with pamphlets on the grieving process. He gestured toward the sofa, "May I get you something to drink?"

"A nice stiff shot of scotch would be great. And make it the good stuff. I know you've got it in here somewhere," Marvin said for Tommy's benefit and looked around the office. "Let's see…bottom drawer of the desk? Nope. The credenza, over here beneath the window? Bingo!" he announced, when he lifted it out.

Tommy chuckled. "I'm gonna leave you to your fun and explore the rest of the place."

"A bottle of water would be nice, thank you," Jenna said.

"Coming right up." Mr. Davis walked to the desk and stopped short.

Marvin got a kick out the man's befuddled expression at the open credenza, though he didn't scan the room in search of the missing bottle. "Yeah, you wouldn't want to take a stiff nip now, would you? That might imperil a lucrative transaction."

Davis pushed a button on his phone. "Liz, could you bring a water in for Ms. Wilson please?"

"Right away, Mr. Davis."

"Thank you, dear." He pushed the button again to release the intercom. He shut the door on the credenza, walked over, sat in a chair, and picked up a file from the table. Opening it, he continued, "Now, Ms. Wilson, what were you thinking of for your fiancé?"

"Please, call me Jenna."

Mr. Davis smiled. "Jenna, then. Did you want a viewing of the deceased? Are you planning on burial, or cremation?"

"Oh, just cremation, I guess."

"Are you kidding? That's what you think of me?" Marvin took a swig of scotch. "You're just going to toss my body into a furnace? I'm gonna kill her."

"Well, that's certainly most economical," Mr. Davis replied to Jenna, as he scanned her off-the-rack couture. "Something to think about in these dreadful times. We do have quite a nice selection of urns for you to choose from. Now, for the viewing, we have rental caskets... You *were* thinking of a visitation, were you not?"

"I don't know. That seems awfully...morose; depressing."

"Never mind," Marvin said, hoisting the bottle toward Jen, "My *mother's* gonna kill you."

"Besides," Jen continued, "I don't think anyone would really want to look at him, if you know what I mean."

A light tap on the door interrupted them. Liz opened the door enough to stick her head in and waited for Mr. Davis to wave her in. She placed the bottle on the table in front of Jenna, crept back out, and closed the door softly behind herself.

"I see... Now, your fiancé was of the Jewish faith,

wasn't he," Mr. Davis inquired.

"Yes, well, we're both Jewish, but we didn't attend services or anything like that."

"Does he have any immediate survivors?"

"Oh, yeah. His parents. And a brother. They all live in upstate New York."

"But, certainly, they'll want to travel down for…well, to pay their last respects?"

Marvin saw Tommy come back into the room. "Either this guy isn't half bad and I take back what I said earlier, or he's trying to up the ante."

Whatever the man was thinking, Marv knew his mother would wail loud enough to be heard in Jerusalem if there wasn't a proper Jewish burial, in a proper Jewish cemetery, with the proper length of mourning. My God, his mother, miss sitting *Shiva*? Miss a week's worth of moaning and crying, and feeding the masses? Unthinkable.

In the end, Jenna agreed to two days of visitation, proper burial in the King David Cemetery across town, and had picked out a decent enough casket, even though Jewish tradition called for a wooden box. Overall, Marvin was satisfied. At least he wouldn't have to listen to his mother moaning more than the occasion required.

Marvin and Tommy hovered over Mr. Davis's shoulder as he tallied up the damage, whispering each item as he checked it off on the invoice. "Casket, visitation room, preparation of the body for *closed* casket, Rabbi for the services—one at the Temple, one graveside, obituary notice for three days' publication, cemetery plot, ceremonial shovel, flowers for visitation, which will transfer to gravesite, hearse, limousine for procession…" Chalking it up to discretion, Marvin made no comment as Davis skipped over the transfer of the body from the morgue; it wouldn't do to upset the client. However, he evidently noticed one missing item. "What about a headstone, Ms. Wilson?"

"Oh, right. Yes, of course."

"The standard now is actually a stone marker of sorts, very low to the ground for maintenance purposes. What would you like on it?"

"His name of course… Well, Mr. Davis, though I am Jewish, I wasn't raised in a Jewish home. Do whatever is customary for the faith."

"Of course." Satisfied, Mr. Davis slid the invoice and a pen across the desk to Jen, "That comes to a total of twenty-three thousand, four hundred, seventy-six dollars and thirty-five cents. I'll just need you to sign here"—he pointed to a line on the top page, flipped it to point to another line on page two—"and here."

Jen leaned forward, her brow creased. This was more than their combined savings, and Marvin didn't know where she would find the rest. She squinted one eye as she often did when mulling over a decision. If she made it more affordable, like, say twenty-five percent of the current total, there just might be enough to cover things. But he had no idea how she could accomplish that and make it everything he figured he deserved.

"Ms. Wilson, is there a problem?"

"Uh…that's an awful lot of money. I wonder if we could trim some things."

"Don't you dare. Don't you *dare*." Marvin warned.

Jen shook her head and picked up the pen. "No. Never mind, Mr. Davis. This'll be fine." She scribbled her name in the appropriate places, pushed the paper back across the desk, and stood up, hand outstretched to shake his hand.

"Now then, how would you like to pay for this? Check, credit?" Mr. Davis waited with a furrowed brow.

"Um, I'll have to…I didn't think it would be this much. I guess I can put some on my credit card, but I'll have to pay the rest later."

After a minute's hesitation, while he summed her up, Mr. Davis took her credit card and ran the deposit amount through to the tune of ten thousand dollars. He stapled one copy to the signed contract and placed that into the file folder.

"Excellent." Mr. Davis handed Jen copies of everything, returned the credit card, and rose to escort her out. "We'll see you in two days, then. And, don't worry about a thing, Ms. Wilson, we'll handle everything with utmost dignity."

Marvin put the bottle of scotch back into the credenza and as an afterthought, just to screw with the guy, left the door open again.

"Thank you, Mr. Davis, I'm sure you will."

"Again, we're most sorry for your loss."

"Yeah, and your mind is jumping for joy at the payday," Marv accused.

"Bye," Jen said, as she slipped out the door.

"Good day, Ms. Wilson."

Outside, Marvin and Tommy stood pressed against the building to keep people from bumping through them and watched Jenna head toward home.

"Wanna catch the one o'clock at the CineDome?"

Marvin shrugged. "What the hell. What else do I

have to do?"

They walked back to Broad Street and hopped the bus headed west.

"Another perk, Marvin," Tommy indicated the bus. "Free transportation."

Marvin smiled. "Tommy, it seems to me, it's free everything."

When the bus came to the stop at Eighty-Fourth Street, they patiently followed other passengers off, walked north across the parking lot, and cut through the shopping mall. The CineDome sat another quarter mile across a shared parking lot.

Once inside, Marvin suggested the new James Cameron film would be good and kill a fair amount of time to boot, plus it had what's-her-name in it—the chick from *Alien*—and she was one hot number. Tommy wanted to see the new one with Meryl Streep.

"How could you *not* want to see a Streep film? She is by far the best actress of this generation. Dude, she's Hepburn times four. She's awesome."

Marvin gave in easily, so they headed into Theater 6 and sat in the last row. On a weekday afternoon, they pretty much had the place to themselves, except for the handful of senior citizens, if you didn't count all the others who greeted them with nods and waves. If you did consider them, it was a full house.

"I have to admit, I enjoyed it. It was funny," Marvin said afterward, as they exited the CineDome and headed for the bus stop.

"I told you, man, Streep is a sure bet. Say, you wanna grab a bite to eat somewhere, Marvin?"

Marv considered for a second. "Tommy...I think you should call me Brody. My friends call me Brody."

Tommy's face broke into a grin. "Far out. Thanks. So, what do ya say—dinner? It's my treat."

"'Far out'? I might have to rescind my offer."

"Sorry, man. I try to keep up with things, but the lingo of the sixties creeps back in along the way."

Marv laughed. "You're forgiven, but I'll take a pass on dinner anyway."

"Gonna go home and mess with Jenna's head?"

"She's got a lot to do here now; relatives to call, blah, blah, blah. I gotta make sure she keeps this real for me."

Tommy whistled and shook his head. "That funeral's gonna cost her a bundle. Did you guys have that much put away? Or did you have insurance that'll cover it?"

"Mmm...there's some savings. No life insurance though. No, wait...I think the company has a policy."

"Does she know about it?"

"Maybe." Marvin shrugged in ignorance. After all, money sure as hell wasn't his problem anymore. That was for the poor *schmoes* who, day in and day out, still had to rush from home to work, work to home, and off to do a hundred other things that, it turns out, really aren't important. They rode in silence again, until Tommy stood up when the bus made a stop at Fifty-Ninth, tossed a casual "later, dude" over his shoulder and jumped through the side of the bus to the sidewalk.

Marvin realized too late he had no idea where Tommy lived—if that was the right word—and didn't know how to find him. He wondered if maybe it was some astrological, *Wizard of Oz*, wishing-made-it-so kind of thing—you know, close your eyes, click your heels together three times, and repeat 'There's no place like Tommy's.'

"Whatever," he said to the elderly gent sitting across the aisle and up one row. "But I'll tell you one thing, I'm not gonna wear any goddamn ruby slippers, that's for sure."

The elderly gentleman continued reading his evening paper.

What Marvin heard as he went to push his body through the door at home stunned him and he stopped halfway: one arm and leg in the foyer, the others in the hallway; the door cutting him in half from crotch to crown. Jenna was talking, but the sound emanated from across the hall, from Mrs. What's-her-name's place.

"...Maybe I should sell those stupid baseballs of his. The way he fusses over—sorry, *fussed*," Jen changed to past tense and her eyes teared up, "fussed over them—did you know, he's got them sealed in glass?—well, they have to be worth *something*."

"I'm gonna kill her!" Marvin howled. He stormed through the door and took an angry stance, cross-armed and threatening in front of her.

"I don't know Mrs. McClaskey," Jen continued, sighing loudly. "I just don't know."

Marvin slapped his forehead when Jen said 'McClaskey,' then shook his fist in Jen's face. "Do you know, do you have any idea what it cost me to get those balls? No way. You can't sell those. I about killed myself lunging across the bleachers for that Barry Bonds ball. And, you were with me the night I snagged the Griffey. And the hours I waited to get them signed. How could you even *think* about selling those?"

"Well, have you asked them, dear?" Mrs. McClaskey asked, placing her teacup gently down on the maple table next to her, on a coaster, of course. *'Don't wantonly ruin what you have, and you'll never want for more'* was one of the mottos she lived by.

"What do I say? 'I really hate to ask Mrs. Broudstein, but we didn't have an insurance policy so could you pay for his funeral? Oh, and by the way, it'll be about twenty-four thousand.'?"

"Nope, I take it back again. My mother's definitely gonna kill her," Marv said with certainty, and he sat on the couch next to Mrs. McClaskey.

Mrs. McClaskey let out a quiet sigh. "These are uncertain times, aren't they? I never thought I'd live to see such days again. It's bad enough for us old fogies, but I really worry about all you young folks. Now, I don't mean to seem…insensitive, dear…but, why did you arrange for such extravagance?"

Marvin turned to study her during the conversation and wished he had gotten to know her, rather than know *about* her; she seemed like such a nice old lady.

"You know, Mrs. McClaskey, Marv may have talked a tough game, arguing with him was part of the fun of being with him. But he was funny, and smart, and kind. He was one of the good guys. No matter how much we might have argued about something, in the end he never denied me anything. I loved him. He deserves whatever I can give him—and then some."

"Well, then," Mrs. McClaskey said, as she rose from the couch. "He should have it. I believe what goes around, comes around. In fact I live by it. Run along home now, Jenna, and let me think this over. If your Marvin was all you say, something will turn up to help."

Jen stood up, reached for the empty glass she'd

drained completely dry of iced tea, and took a step toward the kitchen to put it in the sink.

"Now, now, just leave it there. I'll take care of it. What else does an old lady have to do?" She smiled and wrapped an arm around Jenna, leading her to the door.

Jen felt a little bit like she was being kicked out, summarily dismissed as it were, but instantly regretted thinking that of such a sweet woman. "Thanks for listening, Mrs. McClaskey. And thanks for the tea."

"My pleasure, young lady. Now, you go and get yourself a good night's rest."

"Good night, Mrs. McClaskey," Jen said, stepping across the hall to her own door.

"Night, night, dear."

Marvin slipped through both doors as they stood open. It wasn't that he minded the buzz or tingle of walking through objects, but why do that when he had not one, but two lovely ladies holding them open for him.

He waited for Jen in the living room, since she announced, as she did so many times when they would walk in the door together, "I have to powder my nose." Her comment made him realize how many things people do each day that simply become habit and how those routines had a calming effect. He was sitting in his chair when she came out, already changed into one of his T-shirts, and sat right on top of him in the chair. This buzzed and tingled too much for him. He stood and turned to face her.

"Hey, do you mind? I was sitting there. Jen, you're in my chair. What're you doing in my chair? You hate that chair. How many fights did we have over that thing, and now you're sitting in it?"

Marvin had lived in the condo for a few years before he'd met Jenna. After he proposed and she'd moved in, Jenna wanted to add her own flair to the décor. Marv went along with some of the more subtle suggestions like repainting, some new artwork, and curtains, but drew the line when it came to the furniture.

"Sorry, Marv. I hope you don't mind, but for some reason, I like sitting in this ugly thing. I'm glad you refused to throw it out." She pulled her legs up under her body and snuggled into the high back.

Jenna hadn't seemed to be affected by sitting in him; there was no surprised look on her face or anything like Marv noticed when people had walked through Tommy. She just looked tired and sad. He wondered if maybe she was immune or something. He would have to remember to ask Tommy about that.

"You know, you look like shit right now," he told her in a soft voice and smiled down on her. Her eyes were all red and puffy from all the crying. He followed the gaze of her eyes as they flickered over to the baseballs sitting on the shelf of the entertainment center. "If you don't stop leering at those baseballs with dollar signs in your eyes, I swear I'm gonna kill you."

Chapter 6

Marvin needn't have worried about how to find Tommy, because he burst into the apartment waving a newspaper in his hand. "Marvin, look."

"Shhh." He was listening in on Jen's phone call with his mother. The conversation had started out with his mother bellowing through sobs, 'Morty. Morton... It's that *woman*... The one who killed our son, what other woman is there?' and had Jen in tears within seconds.

"What's going on?"

"It's my parents. Well, more precisely, my mother. They're staying at the Hyatt."

"Yes, I promise, Mrs. Broudstein," Jenna said, still trying to control her sobs. "I'll pull his suit out of the closet now and meet you at the mortuary. Yes, a shirt and tie as well. Yes, Mrs. Broudstein."

She hung up the phone and pulled a tissue from the box that had been ensconced on the table next to Marv's chair for the last two days. "Why has that woman never liked me; what did I ever do to her?" she asked, in between blowing her nose and wiping her eyes, and then headed for the bedroom.

Marvin laughed. "You thought you were good enough for me. For my mother, that's all it takes."

Tommy spun Marv around by the shoulders, held him at arm's length, and shook his head in a dour

43

appraisal. "Do you have more than one suit?"

"No, why?"

"We have *got* to get you some clothes. You cannot go to your funeral looking like this. Trust me, man, I went to mine in ratty old fatigues. Very embarrassing."

"I understand why my mother wants me in the suit, even though it's closed casket because of the," Marvin made a circular motion around his head, "well, you saw my face; she's my mother. If I didn't have a suit and the relatives found out, she'd die of embarrassment. Outside of that, who's going to care what I'm wearing?"

"Believe me, the place'll be packed."

"I don't have that many friends or relatives, and they certainly won't see me."

"Oh, no. Not them. *Us.* You wouldn't believe how many show up."

"You've got to be kidding. Why?"

"I'm not sure, exactly. With closed casket it's even worse; they show up in droves. Maybe they just want to see what you look like. And, with as far out as this shindig is going to be, you cannot go dressed like this."

"All right, if you say so."

"I definitely say so."

Marvin jutted his chin out to indicate the paper Tommy had tucked under his arm, "What is it you were waving around when you came in?"

"Oh, dude. Your obit. Very nice."

Marv took the paper from him and saw his name, first on the list, and read aloud.

"'Marvin Eugene 'Brody' Broudstein,'...Why did she put that in there? She knows I hate my middle name...'born in Westchester, New York, on May fifteenth, nineteen eighty-one, passed away suddenly on Monday, November thirtieth, two-thousand-nine.' " He turned to holler to Jen, "Yeah, I passed away suddenly all right. You pushed me in front of a bus."

"No man, I saw the whole thing. She wasn't even there."

"Yeah, well…she may as well have shoved me under it. If she hadn't been nagging me, I wouldn't have been so eager to rush out the damn door." He went back to reading, "'After graduating from Harvard, he worked as an assistant manager and account rep for Saxton & Crowley Advertising until the time of his death.' Felt like a hundred years working for that schmuck," he interjected to Tommy, who was now huddled over his shoulder reading with him even though he'd read it on the way.

"What are you grousing about? Mine should've been half that nice."

"You didn't have a decent obit?"

"Well, if you consider 'Thomas Sinclair, age nineteen, died on—whenever it was. No services scheduled.' decent, then yeah, I guess I did."

"Sorry." Marvin went back to reading. " 'He is survived by his parents, Morton and Gertrude'—my mother's gonna kill her, she hates that name. She always went by her middle name, Madelyn. 'He is survived by his parents, Morton and Gertrude Broudstein, brother David Broudstein, and longtime fiancée Jenna Wilson. Visitation will be at Davis Funeral Home on blah, blah, blah. Graveside service at King David Cemetery.' *Longtime* fiancée? It was only eighteen months. I swear, Tommy, I'm gonna help my mother kill her."

Chapter 7

Later that night, when they stood in the empty parking lot of the mall, Tommy said, "You don't strike me as a Walmart kind of guy. They wouldn't have anything classy enough for this 'do' anyway. So, what should it be? Macy's? Dillard's? Nordstrom's?"

"Shouldn't we stick to a rental place? I mean we can't just walk out with new stuff."

"You ever hear retailers mention budgeted loss?"

Tommy led him into Macy's first. The men's suits were in a little corner at the back of the store. "It's a nice selection," he mused. "Anything pop out at you?"

Marvin gazed around. He didn't quite know what to make of this whole midnight (well, it was more like late night—very late night) shopping thing; he'd never not paid for something and it seemed wrong to him, though he saw plenty of other 'deadheads' as he'd begun referring to them, with apologies to groupies of the Grateful Dead. *'Course, if you considered the doped-up ones, it may be closer to the truth than any of them might want to admit.* They were thumbing through racks of clothing, trying on shoes, and looking through accessories like belts, wallets, and even underwear.

He was thinking a nice black pinstripe, but all he saw were grays and navy blues.

"Maybe we should try Nordstrom. If I'm going to walk out with a suit, it may as well be a good one." On the walk through the mall, it occurred to him to ask, "What the hell do I do with it after the funeral? I sure as hell don't want to walk around in a monkey suit forever. And what do I do with the clothes I have?"

"It's no problem, man. The clothes you have on, you carry out with you and leave in a dumpster out behind the mall. And when this whole shebang is done, we come back, you pick out something comfy, and we leave the suit hanging on the returns rack."

Marvin felt a little better about the foray knowing he could bring back such an expensive suit; his mood brightened and he stepped livelier. Again, they had to make their way to the back of the store. Retailers weren't stupid. Women did more than ninety percent of the shopping, and they left nothing to chance; all women's items were up front to assail the female senses as soon as they walked in the door. Though he figured black was the appropriate thing under the circumstances, a nice charcoal-gray pinstripe about jumped off the wall at him.

"Now, that's a nice suit," he said, pointing to the mannequin on a stand, high on the wall. "In fact, the whole thing looks great."

"It should," a voice said from behind a rack of dress shirts. "Dolce and Gabana. You have good taste."

Tommy stood on his toes to peer over the top. "It's for his wake."

"Well, in that case, you need to look your absolute best. Perhaps I can be of assistance," the man offered as he came around the end, hand outstretched.

"That would be terrific, dude. I'm not exactly a, what-do-you-call-'em—a fashionista." Tommy smiled.

"I'm Davy. And you are?" He offered an

outstretched hand to Marv.

"Marvin," he said, shaking the guy's hand. "This is Tommy."

Davy ogled Tommy when they shook hands, but evidently dismissed the thought as quickly as it entered his brain when the smile disappeared. "Nice to meet you. Now, Marvin, what size are you?" he asked leading them to the racks of suits, then turned to look carefully. "You look to be…oh…I'd say a forty-two Long jacket. Waist: thirty-four. Inseam: thirty-four. Am I right?"

"Everything but the inseam. I'm a thirty-two."

Davy glanced down at Marvin's feet. "No. You're a thirty-four. The drape of a pant should break just slightly above the shoe." He thumbed through the rack and within seconds was holding a hanger in front of Marvin. "Voila! Try this one."

Marvin took the hanger and glanced around looking for the men's fitting rooms. "Where are the—"

"No need for that. It's just us chickens around here tonight," Davy told him.

Still, Marvin wasn't sure he was the kind of guy to strip down to his skivvies in public, even if it was a bunch of dead people. "Are you sure? I mean…"

"What's wrong, are you commando?"

"Even if you are—honey, trust me, we've seen it all before."

"No, I'm not commando. Jesus H., Tommy, what do you take me for?" Marvin held the suit out for him to hold while he kicked his shoes off and shed his pants. He slid the suit pants on, and Davy helped him into the jacket. "What do you think? Is it okay?"

Tommy liked it immediately, but Davy stood

looking at him in a critical stance: one arm across his chest, his chin resting in one hand. "Mmmm. Nope, I don't think so. The cut doesn't drape properly around the, um...package, if you'll excuse me for noticing." Davy looked over at Tommy. "No, this one would be better suited for you. Don't you need to dress for your friend's occasion as well? For you, I'd say, thirty-eight Regular, Waist: thirty, Inseam: thirty-two," he said, as he pulled one off the rack and handed it to him.

"Now for you, Marvin... Let's see," Davy mused, with a slow gawk around. "Yes. I've *just* the thing. Kenneth Cole. *Kenneth* knows how to dress a man. And nothing says masculine these days more than a vest. This is going to be the hottest new trend."

He held up a pair of black pants with dark gray pinstripes and a black jacket. He slid a leather-front vest inside the coat, then disappeared into the shelves of dress shirts, flipped through them and came back carrying a light pink shirt with pearlized buttons.

Marv put the shirt on, tucked it in and pulled on the vest and jacket.

"Lovely. Turn around for me," Davy told him, one finger pointed to the floor and the hand making a circular motion. "Yes, that is going to do nicely, I think. Stay right here, don't move. I'll be back in a few minutes."

"Whoa. Very groovy, man." Tommy stood in his new suit, looking at Marvin.

"Very groovy yourself. *What* is he doing?"

Tommy shrugged. "Help me find a shirt and tie while you're waiting."

Ten minutes later, Tommy had completed his new look. He'd even included a new belt and shoes. They

49

stood another five waiting for Davy, who finally showed up with an armful of items.

Davy held his prized finds up one at a time, as if he'd been on the treasure hunt of his life. "Black and silver tie, with just a *hint* of pink. Black leather shoes with nickel trim on the strap. A leather belt with a brushed nickel buckle. Brushed nickel cufflinks with quarter carat diamonds, watch and bracelet to match. All Kenneth Cole. Oh, and black silk briefs, white silk undershirt, and black and silver pin-stripe socks."

Tommy and Davy waited patiently. When the look was complete, and his old clothes were in a pile on the floor next to him, Marv turned to face them with his arms held slightly away from his sides and a questioning look on his face.

"Oh, honey, you look good enough to eat. You're perfect."

"Good enough to eat, huh? I wish someone would've convinced Jenna of that when we were getting ready for work the other morning. Maybe I'd still be alive," Marv said, though he smiled.

"Dude… Yeah. If she could see you in this, it wouldn't be on for long."

Davy turned to look at Tommy. "And see there. Don't *you* clean up nice. You two are going to turn heads when you walk in, let me tell you. Now, just let me get Leo to come out."

"Leo? Who's Leo and what do we need with him," Tommy wanted to know.

"Leo will need to tailor, of course. It'll only take a few minutes. He's very good and quite fast, especially since you'll be bringing it all back afterward."

Within thirty minutes Leo had adjusted both suits

to his satisfaction and was off to another part of the store.

"Now what?" Marv glanced around the store.

"We gather our old clothes, pitch them in the trash, and head out," Tommy said.

Marv consulted his new watch. "Holy shit. It got late." He turned to Davy and held out his hand. "Davy, is it? I don't know how to thank you."

"No thanks necessary. I enjoyed it, believe me." Davy shook their hands.

Marv bent over to pick up his old clothes. "Oh, just leave those, I'll get rid of them for you. Hand me yours, hon." Davy held a hand out for Tommy's heap.

They were just rounding the corner of the casual clothes when Davy called out to them. "Um, gentlemen. Do you think... Well, I'm just so...proud of my work here. I'd like to see the reaction. Might I join you this morning?"

Marv stopped and looked at Tommy who shrugged. Marv figured what the hell, if there would be a full house as Tommy had projected, one more deadhead wasn't going to bust the building at its seams. He waved acceptance. "It would a pleasure to have you attend my funeral, Davy."

Chapter 8

At the Davis Funeral Home, Davy rushed to the room ahead of them, stood in the doorway and announced with a grand sweeping arm gesture and a bow, "Ladies and gentlemen, may I present Mr. Marvin Broudstein."

Marv whispered to Tommy, "He pronounced it wrong, but how the hell did he know my whole name?"

Tommy laughed and pointed. "Maybe from the sign on the stand over there?"

To Marvin's astonishment, the room was filled with living and dead and a crowd of people applauded amid a storm of murmurs. It reminded him of the response to brides at their weddings as they started the march down the aisle, and it was odd to be the center of attention. The live ones all looked morose and weepy except that schmuck Crowley. He was as stone-faced as ever. The deadheads wore smiles of appreciation and offered a chorus of welcoming comments.

When Marv spotted Jen, his heart melted and he walked toward her. She sat with shoulders hunched and head hung, dressed in a black suit, sitting in a folding chair at the front of the room all alone, unless you counted Mrs. What's-her-name—Marv slapped his forehead until he remembered—*McClaskey*, sitting with Mrs. McClaskey.

A beautiful young woman dressed in an elegant

ivory gown smiled suggestively at him as he passed. He heard her call out to Davy.

"Davy. How nice to see you." She held out her hand to be kissed. "Doesn't he look scrumptious? One of yours, I suppose," she asked with disappointment.

"Diane, how nice. Yes, I *can* work miracles, can't I? But, sad to say, he's one of yours." Davy nodded toward Marv who was now standing close to Jen. "And, sadder yet, it appears he's still too fresh for you."

Everyone heard the commotion at the back of the room. All heads turned to look: Marv, with an expression of no-less-than-expected, Jen cowering in sheer terror, everyone else with expressions of who-would-make-such-a-commotion which then turned to a look of understanding, and suddenly, Marvin was no longer the center of attention at his own funeral.

Supported between her husband and her son, David, Mrs. Broudstein, at the first sight of the coffin which was placed on a dais in a small alcove front and center, wailed with a sound not unlike that of a wounded walrus. Surrounded by wreaths, the casket gleamed under the can lights and the flickering of candle flames standing to either side. A single picture of Marvin had been placed on top. Under the din of people—both living and dead—came the mournful sounds of music; sad and moribund.

"My boy... My little boy... What has she done to you? Hold me, Morty, I don't think I can make this trip alone."

"Madelyn, get hold of yourself and stop making a scene," Morton whispered. "Or I'll dump you right here like a sack of flour in the bakery."

Madelyn wailed once more for effect, buried her

face into David's arm, took a deep breath, and stood with her head held high. It certainly was not that Madelyn didn't truly grieve the loss of her son, Marvin knew, she simply believed she had to give the people what they expected of a mother in mourning. "David," she commanded, "take me to your brother."

They made the trek of fifty-five feet seem like five footballs fields; David doing his best to act the loving, supportive son, his mother doing her utmost to garner as much sympathy from the crowd as possible, his father behind them shaking his head in disgust at the scene he knew his wife could make.

When they reached the front row of chairs, Marvin's mother glanced to her right where she already knew Jen sat in fear, as if searching for a place to sit, then nodded to the left. "Over here, David, where *family* sits."

Marv stalked over to stand in front of his mother. "Knock it off, Ma. Don't treat her that way. She's a nice girl. You'd know that if you'd give her a chance."

"You're a good son, David" She patted his hand. "You take care of your mother. You don't move hundreds of miles from home and take up with…" She jerked her head in Jenna's direction. "With girls like her."

"Ma, don't. Marvin wouldn't want you to be this way. She's probably a very nice woman."

"She killed your brother, David. Nice women do not kill their boyfriends."

"Ma. She did not kill me—well, not literally anyway. She's a good woman, and you'd know that if you'd ever given her a chance. Now, come on, be nice."

"Madelyn, that's enough," Morton told her in a

gruff whisper. "How do you think she feels? Look at her, you can tell she's devastated. David, go talk to her. Bring her over here. She should be with the family."

When David stood up to obey his father's wishes, Marvin's eyes were drawn up, and he noticed someone at the back of the room he thought he should know. The guy looked familiar. It appeared he was hanging with the deadheads, and Marv couldn't remember anyone he knew who had died, but then again, he was pretty terrible with names. In short, slow steps he wended his way through the crowded room, being cautious about bumping through bodies. About half way back, the guy waved to him. "Brody. Hey, Brody."

Well, that pretty much settled the question: he was dead, and he definitely knew Marv. Now all Marvin had to do was remember what the hell the guy's name was.

"How ya doing, Brody? Mike. Mike Hamilton, remember? From Harvard?"

"Mike. Sure," Marv said. He mentally slapped himself on the forehead and shook Mike's hand. He and Mike had quite a number of classes together over the four years of school and had even hung out a few times at the bars.

"It's good to see you, man. Sorry about your joining us though."

Marv nodded. "Yeah, thanks. It takes some getting used to, but I guess you know that. So, what happened? I mean, it's okay to ask that, right?"

"Oh, sure. You remember the flight that ditched into the Hudson earlier this year?"

"Yeah. You were on that flight?" Marvin asked. Then his face scrunched up in confusion. "I thought they said nobody died on that flight."

Mike laughed. "Nobody did. But when I mention the flight I did buy it on, nobody remembers. I was on the commuter puddle-jumper flight that hit the 'burbs in Buffalo right after that."

"Oh, Jesus, sorry Mike. That must've been bad."

"Eh, probably not any worse than you. What about you?"

"Bus. Nose to nose. Didn't feel a thing."

"Neither did any of us. We shit our pants on the way down, but the actual impact? Nothing." He laughed and gave Marv a pat on the arm. "You're looking good though, Brody. You must've done well for yourself, huh? Who's your tailor?"

Marv had to stifle a laugh. The idea of Crowley paying well enough to buy expensive suits would bring anyone who worked for him to fits of laughter. "Borrowed for the occasion—Nordstrom. Davy—see the guy over there with the gray silk suit standing with the blonde in the gown?—he helped me."

"Very nice. Is that your wife up there?"

"Fiancée."

"Wow. She's pretty. Must be tough leaving *that* behind."

Marv wouldn't have had time to answer that even if he wanted to, which he didn't, but was never-the-less formulating his opinions on the subject, because just as he opened his mouth to respond, his mother did her impression of a walrus again. He swiveled around to see what brought this one on. She stood looking at a display of photos: Marv at the beach, Marv in college (though he had no idea where Jenna found those), Marv at the office, Marv with David, Marv with friends at a bar, Marv with Jen, and then it hit him. There wasn't a single picture of him with his mother.

"Oh, Jesus H! my mother's gonna kill her."

"You see, Morty? You see how she treats the mother of her fiancée? In all this...*drek*"—she waved a hand around the room—"what do I get? *Gornisht*—nothing. See, not even a picture of his mother."

"Oh, shit," David whispered under his breath. "No... Ma, that's my fault. I'm sorry. She called and asked for pictures. I forgot to bring 'em in from the car."

"She called and asked?"

"Yeah, Ma."

"And you have them in the car?"

"Yes, Ma. And Ma, look around, it's not shit; she did very nice for Marvin."

Madelyn glanced around the room. "Well, okay, so the flowers are pretty. It's a nice coffin. The candles are a good touch. The Hebrew prayer on the card...and she did use a very nice picture of him for that." She paused as she considered everything. "And she called you for pictures?"

"Ma, I promise. Now will you be *nice*?"

Madelyn turned to Jenna, who cowered behind Morton. "So, Jenna"—she offered a hand in truce—"have you met my son, David? He's a good boy."

Marv's jealous streak surged without warning. "I'm gonna kill her."

Tommy rolled his eyes at what he figured to be Marvin venting his frustration and asked, "Jenna again?"

"*My mother.*"

Chapter 9

That night, watching Jen go through her nightly ritual in silent tears, Marv longed to reach out to her and enfold her in his arms like he'd always done when she was sad over anything. She walked into the living room and sat in his chair, heaved a sigh, and for the thousandth time, Marv heard her utter his name. He watched closely. To her credit, she didn't once glance at his baseballs.

"Marv, I miss you so much. Are you really gone?"

"I'm right here, Jen. Dammit, I wish you could hear me and see me so you would know I haven't abandoned you. I would never do that. I can still see you and talk to you and touch you. Well, sort of. I miss you, too."

"Why did you have to go and jump in front of a bus? I would've waited to get married. You know I would have waited. All you had to do was tell me you just weren't ready."

"Well, I didn't exactly jump. But, what was with all the pushing and prodding? I'm sorry. But, I was so aggravated by the time I walked out of here, I just wanted to escape. You've got to know I didn't do that on purpose. I wouldn't do something like that to you. I couldn't."

"Your mother seemed to warm up a little bit today. A fat lot of good it does me now."

"Ma can be a bit of a drama queen, can't she?" Marv chuckled.

"What's with the pushing me toward your brother? Does she think all I cared about was landing a man and getting married? And it didn't matter who the guy was?" Jen paused with sudden comprehension. "Oh, shit. Marv, is that what *you* thought? That I only wanted to get married? Is that what kept scaring you off? It's not true. I swear it's not true."

"Well it's a little late to be figuring that out now. Are you shitting me?" Though he was just getting fired up, Marv stopped when he heard Jen's voice through his tirade.

"Marv, I loved you," she said, soft but emphatic. "I loved you so much."

"I know. You have to know I love you too. Ahh, goddammit Jen..."

Chapter 10

The next day things were a little calmer around the funeral home, and it could have been attributed to the fact that pictures of Marvin's mother had indeed been placed alongside the others. There weren't as many deadheads hanging around, but it was just as full. Marv glanced around the room and realized the entire firm of Saxton and Crowley had shown. He wondered what was up. *It sure as hell isn't like Crowley—the schmuck—to close down the whole place for anything less than his own death.* He also noticed the only people there in support of Jenna were one of the partners in the law firm that seemed to suck out her life's blood, her boss JoAnne, and Mrs. McClaskey.

Morton huddled in a corner with a sobbing Jenna then hugged her and whispered something. He led her to a chair in the front row between David and Marvin's mother and then approached Mr. Davis. "Uh, oh."

"What," Tommy and Mike asked in unison as if on cue.

Marvin nodded toward his father who had just signaled to the funeral director for a word in private. "It looks like Mr. Davis is about to get talked to. I'll be back, guys. This could be interesting."

Marv followed the men into the overdone office and couldn't imagine what the problem might be because, as far as he could see, everything Jenna chose and the mortuary had supplied seemed to be quite nice.

"Please, have a seat Mr. Broudstein. Can I offer you something to drink?" Mr. Davis motioned to one of the chairs.

"There's some scotch in the credenza, Dad. It's the good stuff, too," Marv urged his father who of course didn't hear him.

"What have you got?"

"Water, soda, coffee?"

Morton gave a small grunt. "That's it? Come on, a guy like you," he said glancing around at the expensive furnishings, "doesn't have a bottle of something good on standby?"

"I see." Mr. Davis retrieved two crystal rocks glasses from the credenza and poured two fingers of scotch into each, carried them back, and settled into the opposite chair. "Now, then, Mr. Broudstein, what can I help you with?"

Marvin's father took a studied sip of the scotch, nodded, and glanced over the rim of his glass in silence. It was a silence Marvin had witnessed many times until Morton was sure his opponent was sufficiently unsteadied by the awkward lull before he spoke. "I'm a businessman, Mr. Davis. I understand making a...presentable profit," he said gesturing around the room with the glass of scotch, to which Mr. Davis blanched. "You know Ms. Wilson is not in a financial position to pay for all of this," Morton paused long enough to make him squirm, "so I'd like to pay the bill."

"Very good, Mr. Broudstein." Mr. Davis nodded confidently, but the redness that crept along his ears betrayed him without his even knowing. "It's generous of you to think of young people just starting out in life, especially in these hard economic times. All of us are suffering, you know."

"Yeah, we see how you're suffering. Armani suits, twenty-five-year-old scotch," Marvin said, hoisting the bottle for a swig, "and probably a new Mercedes every year, too."

"I'm sure you're right. Now, Ms. Wilson tells me the total comes to twenty-four thousand dollars. I'd like to go over the invoice before I pay," Morton said, as if it were not a suggestion. "If it won't cause too much trouble," he added in a near perfect accusatory tone.

"Oh, this is gonna be fun. I haven't seen him do this in years." Marvin thought Tommy might enjoy watching his dad in action and hurried out to the visitation room, bottle in hand.

"Certainly." Mr. Davis' ears turned a deeper shade of red as he rose from his chair to retrieve the folder from the active file. He did a slight double-take at the open door of the credenza. He inspected the shelf inside for the Scotch. He glanced at the table near Morton. Then he closed the door. His words came with a halting lack of confidence, which was certainly not normal for a man of business, as he handed over the invoice. "I'm sure you'll find…everything is…is in order."

"Watch this," Marvin said to Tommy and Mike, who had followed him back to the room. They all leaned against the gray silk-papered wall to enjoy the show.

Morton held Davis in a steady gaze longer than necessary then turned his attention to the numbers on the pages. He took his time, looking off to different corners of the room as if to add things together. His alternating nods and scowls served to elicit more noticeable squirms.

"See the little bead of sweat on Davis' forehead? That's what my dad's been waiting for."

"It looks to be in order, Mr. Davis."

The funeral director, who looked like he'd been holding his breath with a mixed air of arrogance and nerves, straightened in the brocade chair, reached out for the invoice, and attempted to ignore the perspiration on his brow.

"But a little excessive, don't you think?"

Mr. Davis paled a shade and the sweat on his forehead couldn't be ignored any longer. He removed a handkerchief from an inside pocket of his jacket and patted his brow dry.

"These few items here," Morton said, folding the paper in three and handing it back. "I think you could adjust them downward a bit. Say, by about fifteen percent? And I think the rental fees for the bier and the hearse could be eliminated altogether. I'm sure you agree."

Mr. Davis accepted the sheets of paper in hands he couldn't stop from trembling. Glancing down at the invoice, his mouth dropped open the slightest bit, but he nodded.

"I'll also want to see the charges on Ms. Wilson's credit card reversed," Morton added handing his own card to Davis.

"Certainly, Mr. Broudstein."

"Huh. That was too easy. This guy's not nearly as tough as he acted with Jen the other day. Look—my dad's even a little disappointed. He loves a good debate over price," Marvin told them before he led them back to the crowd in the other room and left poor Mr. Davis to wonder why the credenza doors were open again after he was positive he'd closed them moments ago. And how the four fingers of scotch he'd poured had managed to bring the level of soothing liquid so near the bottom of the bottle.

Back in the visitation room, Marvin thought he better stop to thank Davy again for dressing him. "Davy. Thanks for coming again today. And thanks again for making me so…"

"Spectacular, I believe is the word you're looking for, and you're entirely welcome, honey."

"You do look scrumptious in that suit. I can see why your girl is so upset. I'm Diane," the woman standing with Davy said, and held her hand in position to be kissed.

Marvin took her hand in his and shook it. "Nice to meet you. Well, I have friends to greet. We'll see you graveside. Yes?" With that, he walked off.

"Oh Davy, I think I've changed my mind." She waved a hand at Marvin's back. "A bit of a boor, don't you think?"

"Sorry sweetie, I can dress them up, but I'm not a charm school."

"Well, then. I'm sure we'll see each other soon." Diane turned on her three-inch heels, ivory gown in a swirl, and left.

Marvin made his way over to Mike and Tommy and positioned himself to keep an eye on Jenna, who now stood talking to Crowley and nodding in agreement to whatever was being said.

Several minutes later Marvin's father and Davis showed up, the music slowly faded out and the lighting brightened. Mr. Davis glanced toward Jenna and nodded.

David, Morton, Crowley, and another of Marvin's associates made their way to the dais. With subtle prompting from Mr. Davis, they swiveled the bier around and took their proper places: David and Morton at the head, leading the procession of mourners out of the mortuary.

"Crowley? *Crowley?* You asked *that* schmuck to be a pallbearer?" Marvin marched over to Jenna and followed her to continue his rant. "I can't believe what I'm seeing. Did you ever hear a single thing I said? I knew you never listened to what I was saying. What, you were too busy thinking about our *farkakte* wedding?"

With the casket loaded into the hearse and the family, including Jenna, which Marvin found intriguing considering his mother's long-suffering demeanor, comfortably seated in a limousine, the procession began the long ride across town to the cemetery. Marvin sat sandwiched between David and Jenna just in case his brother got nudged enough by their mother to crumble under pressure and give too much attention to Jen. Marvin laughed when David reached out once to pat Jenna's arm and yanked it back as if he'd stuck his finger in an electrical socket after it bumped through Marvin's chest. Tommy and Mike were up front alongside the driver, with Tommy sitting shotgun. He played enough with the dashboard and console buttons to make the driver question his own sanity by the time he pulled to a stop at the cemetery.

When the proceedings went so far as Crowley beginning a eulogy of sorts, Marvin went into a rant that woke the attending deadheads from the boredom of hearing yet another new inductee overindulged in death. Though now it made perfect sense to him why Crowley had closed the office; his ego wouldn't allow him to let the staff off the hook for one of his speeches. Though as far as Marvin was concerned 'speech' might be too kind a word, since Crowley made twice-daily strolls through the offices to deride and berate the employees. And one never got called into his office for a dressing-down; it was done in front of the entire staff. Marv's rant increased when, after the ceremonial shoveling of dirt had ended and the mourners were drifting out to resume life among the living (deadheads included), Jenna, being egged on by his mother, folded an arm around David's to be led back to the waiting limousine.

"What the hell is this? I'm not even cold in my grave, and you're taking up with my brother?"

"Dude, I hate to break it to you, but you're about as cold as you're ever going to get."

Marvin paid no attention to Tommy. "And you, Ma. What, she wasn't good enough for me, but suddenly she's a perfect match for my little brother?"

"Come on, Brody." Mike slung an arm around Marv's shoulder and headed in the opposite direction. "I know it's tough, but she's still on the other side."

Marvin shouted over his left shoulder in the direction of the departing limo, "She won't be there long if she keeps this shit up."

Chapter 11

Marvin went back to the apartment that evening after going with Tommy to return the borrowed suits. Of course they both had Davy help them pick out new clothes, though Marvin couldn't for the life of him understand why he needed new clothes when he still had a closet full at home. The only excuse he could conjure up, and not seem like a fool to ask what might be considered a stupid question, was to keep Jenna from noticing that clothes had somehow disappeared. He slipped through the door, greeted by the sight of Mrs. McClaskey sitting in his chair. He remembered her name again without having to slap himself in the forehead and made a mental note to remember to mention this to Tommy, who had told him his memory with this sort of thing wouldn't get any better.

Jenna paced the room in agitation. "And do you believe this? Mr. Crowley, Marvin's boss, told me the company held a life insurance policy for all the employees, but since we weren't married yet, the money would go to Marv's parents."

"That seems proper, don't you think, dear?"

"No, Mrs. McClaskey, I don't. I'm sorry if I sound greedy, but Marvin and I were together a long time. I thought the least he could have done was make me the beneficiary of one lousy insurance policy."

"Lousy? I'll have you know that policy is equal to

a year's salary," Marv said, leaning against the archway to the kitchen.

Jenna hugged herself and shrugged. "I thought I would use the money to pay for the funeral expenses. When Crowley told me, I started to sob. I can't tell you how scared I got. When Mr. Broudstein asked what the trouble was, I just blurted it out. And that's when he told me not to worry, he would take care of everything."

"There now, you see, dear? I told you something would come along to help you. All you needed to do was have a little faith." Mrs. McClaskey took a careful sip of tea and looked for a coaster to set the cup down. "A coaster, dear?"

"Oh, I'm sorry. We don't have any. Just set it on the table. It's not a big deal. It's not like it's good furniture or anything."

Marvin bristled. "Hey, it's not cheap shit either, you know."

Mrs. McClaskey tsk-tsked softly. "We'll have to see about a remedy for that."

"I just thought it was very sweet of his father," Jenna replied, either not hearing or choosing to ignore Mrs. McClaskey's issue with coasters. "And Marvin's brother was very attentive today. He's a nice man. Not at all like Marvin."

"Just what the hell is that supposed to mean?" Marvin stood upright away from the wall.

"And his mother was so nice today. What changed in one day? I don't know. But I'm not about to question it."

"I'll tell you what changed," Marvin told them. "She wants her only son married now, is what happened. She wants grandkids."

"Good thinking, Jenna, and I'm glad today was a little better. Well, dear, I best be getting home," Mrs. McClaskey said, rising and moving to the front door with Jenna close behind. "It's late, and I never was much of a night person. You know, early to bed, early to rise, et cetera. I believe that, you know."

"Thank you for going today, Mrs. McClaskey. I really appreciate it."

"Think nothing of it. I'm happy to have been of help." Mrs. McClaskey unlocked the door to her apartment. "Sleep well, dear. I'm sure we'll talk again tomorrow."

"You too, Mrs. McClaskey. Goodnight."

"So," Marvin started in when Jenna closed the door. "The furniture is garbage, and my brother is nothing like me because *he's nice*? I swear, you are just cruisin' for it, aren't you?"

Jenna pulled on the usual T-shirt and slipped into bed without a word. She wrapped Marv's dress shirt in her arms, held it tight against her chest, and let out a sorrowful moan. A minute later, she sat up in the bed. Tears streamed down her cheeks. "I have nowhere to go, and no one but the old lady across the hall. Damn you, Marvin. What am I supposed to do now? Would you please tell me that, you son-of-a-bitch."

"I don't know. I don't know. But I'll find a way to take care of you, don't you worry about that," Marvin told her, though a slight tinge of menace colored the melancholy tone.

Sitting in his chair in the living room after Jenna cried herself to sleep, Marvin pondered the situation further. The more he thought about it, the more he started to think he had an excellent idea; though he wasn't sure of the consequences and would have to find a way to broach the subject with Tommy without rousing too much suspicion. At least not at first. He figured maybe he could talk to Mike Hamilton about this too, and perhaps, if it seemed feasible, recruit both of them into his plans. He certainly needed assistance, especially when dealing with something he knew so little about.

His mind reeled with possibilities, but he had to be sure that, number one, it was possible, and number two, he wouldn't be thrown to Hell, if there was a Hell. After further contemplation, Marvin was almost positive there must be something like it because he hadn't seen any rapists, or murderers, or child molesters among the deadheads. Well, none he could recognize as such anyway. If he ended up in Hell, his mother would never forgive him when she came over and found out.

"So the question is," Marvin wondered aloud, "what are the consequences of these acts if you're already dead when you commit them? There can't be jail. I mean, you could walk right out, couldn't you?"

Chapter 12

It took Marvin several days to muster up enough courage to start the conversation. They had begun what would become a daily ritual, meeting at Epstein's for coffee at mid-morning to avoid the early crowd of workers jostling for position at the take-out counter and tables.

"I think a little tour is in order," Tommy said, handing Marvin and Mike cups of coffee he'd just poured from the fresh pot, to the obvious dismay of TINA-I'll-Be-Your-Server-Today, especially after she'd just promised a table more was brewing and she'd be right back with it. He slid into the booth across from them.

"A tour of what?" asked Mike, who had just shown up and missed the beginning of the conversation.

Tommy nodded toward Marvin. "Marvin here wants to know what happens when a criminal dies."

"Well, what more harm can they do? They're as dead as we are."

"Mike, think about it. We all waltz into a store and take what we want," Marv said gesturing at their clothes. "What's to stop a bad guy from doing worse?"

Tommy chuckled. "You two have a lot to learn. I kid you not, there are bad guys here just like there are anywhere."

"And if someone was to, oh...I don't know,

say…steal a huge amount of money by walking through a vault wall, what would happen to him?" Marvin looked down into his cup attempting an air of innocence.

"Brody, what would be the point? We get whatever we want. Nobody here pays for anything." Mike lifted his cup and indicated the other deadheads in the deli.

"Or, say forging some documents?"

"Those are pretty minor crimes, Marvin," Tommy told him in a tone to indicate he had begun to catch on. "The *really* bad guys? Forces keep them contained. Don't get me wrong, once in a while one gets loose and wreaks some very serious havoc. I mean, you've both seen *Amityville Horror*, right?"

Mike whistled low. "That was for real?"

"Dude, you have no idea what some of them are capable of. And I'd suggest you don't want to find out. But, back to the issue: what are you thinking Marvin? Spill it, man."

"Um…" Marv stalled and took a sip of coffee. He wanted help and hoped Tommy would be willing. It seemed like the kind of thing he'd think of as fun, after all. But to be honest, Marvin didn't know either of these guys well enough to know for sure they would be up to the hi-jinx rolling around in his brain. "I found out the firm did have a life insurance policy."

"Brody, that's a given. Any firm the size of Saxton and Crowley would do that for its employees."

"Well, the thing is, Mike, because we weren't married, the money goes to my folks. I want it to go to Jenna."

"Why didn't you change it when you got engaged?"

"You heard my mother bellow at the funeral home?" Marvin paused for the nods. "That, my friends, was nothing compared to the noise she would've made if I'd left insurance money to a woman before I was married. And knowing my mother, possibly even before the first grandchild."

"So, you want to break into the firm and change the forms?" Tommy asked. When Marv nodded Tommy burst out laughing. "This is a piece of cake, Marvin. When do we go?"

"Wait, wait, wait." Mike shook his head. "Isn't that kind of thing computerized now? I know our firm did all that shit on computer. You'll have to print the consent form, change the beneficiary, forge your dad's signature, scan it, and then get the digital file into the system. Can you access that?"

"Maybe there's a file with a hard copy somewhere. We could take it and change that, right?" Tommy suggested.

"They keep all the personnel files locked up when the office is closed," Marv told him when he saw the expression on Tommy's face. "And Christine locks it when she goes to lunch, too."

"Dude, who cares?"

"What do you mean 'who cares'? How do you propose we get into the files if they're locked? I can't stick my head into a drawer to read the files. Besides, I'm not *that* near-sighted."

Mike laughed at the image. "Brody, I think what Tommy's trying to say is, we can walk in and watch where she puts the keys. Hell, we can hover over her shoulder while she logs onto her computer and snag her password."

"Duh…"

Marvin sipped his coffee as he contemplated breaking into the office files, thinking not only could they achieve the goal but he could have some real fun screwing with Crowley's mind by moving his computer files and changing presentations. Besides, Marv figured it would serve the bastard right after bawling out staff members for not remembering what they'd done with an old file. He smiled. "Okay then, let's go."

After a short bus ride, they followed Christine into the building as she returned from lunch. Tommy hit the call button for the elevator just as Christine approached it, causing her to stop short and look over both shoulders. Tommy and Mike both enjoyed the look of confusion on her face when she realized no one was within twenty feet of her.

"Tommy, don't screw with things. She might catch on," Marv said.

"Sorry, Marvin. Force of habit," he lied and winked at Mike.

Up on the fourth floor, Christine stopped in the ladies' room before heading to her office. Tommy almost followed her in and was stopped only when Marvin grabbed the back of his shirt.

"Come on, we can go wait in her office," Marv said leading them through the maze of cubicles.

Tommy and Mike immediately started to rummage through things. Marvin stood in the doorway to play lookout and watched for the secretary's red curls to appear bobbing over the walls of cubicles.

"Hey, Marvin. This folder has your name on it. Should I open it?"

Marv snatched the folder. "No. What're you,

dumb? There's personal shit in there. Hand it to me."
He leafed through his personnel file looking for the
insurance forms. Seconds later he told them, "Nope.
Not in here. You think she already processed it?"

"Brody, did Jenna get all the death certificates and
give one to your boss at the funeral?"

Marv took a moment to think about that, going
over the day in as much detail as he could. Finally, he
shook his head. "I don't think so."

"What about Crowley's office? Wouldn't he have
to sign something in order for anyone to send the claim
in?"

"Shit, here she comes. Tommy, why don't you stay
here and get her computer logins. Mike and I will go
check out Crowley's desk," Marv said.

He and Mike headed down the hallway to
Crowley's office and Marvin hollered, "And don't
screw with her, Tommy. She freaks easily."

"Purely professional today." Tommy raised his
right hand. "I swear."

Mike and Marvin walked through the tall wooden
door into the sparse office and saw Crowley sitting
behind his desk.

"Shit. He's usually gone a couple hours for lunch.
Christine always made it a point to beat him back here.
Now what?"

"I think we have a Bingo, Brody. Look there."
Mike leaned over the front of the massive desk and
pointed to a form sitting to Crowley's right.

"Now how do we distract him?"

Mike held a finger in the air, then walked back to
Christine's office where Tommy had just completed
scribbling a login and password on a pad of sticky-

paper.

"Tommy. We've got it. We need to distract Crowley so we can swipe the papers. What's the extension number on her phone?"

Tommy leaned over the girl's shoulder. "Um, two-three-one."

Christine brushed at her ear.

"Thanks. Now all I need is to find someone— Aha! Tommy, hand me that memo pad from the table back there. And the pen you have."

When the pad Tommy had written on flopped to the desk near her right elbow, Christine gave out a yelp pushing her chair away from the desk and looked frantically around the room. "What the hell?"

"Oops. Sorry. Here ya go, Mike."

Mike took a second to glare at him, then looked down the row of offices and scribbled a rapid message. Handing the pad and pen back and turning to leave he said, "And Tommy?"

"Yeah?"

"Don't put it down where she'll see it appear like some fairy godmother just made a deposit."

"Mike…Man, I said I was sorry," Tommy said to the empty doorway.

Within a few minutes Mike was back after he dropped a note on a clerk's desk. "Now what?" Tommy asked him.

Mike stood with an index finger poised in the air. When he sensed the timing was right, he pointed at the phone. An instant later, it rang.

"Yeah," Christine barked into the phone before it got to her ear. She listened for a minute, then said, "I don't need to see that. Just send it to him… Yeah,

76

okay... Fine. Just a minute." She hung up the phone. When she walked to the door of her office, she went right through Mike and stopped short. She shivered as if a draft of chilled air conditioning had blasted over her. She shook her head slightly and walked away.

"I love it when they do that." Tommy laughed.

"Now we push the intercom button for Crowley," Mike told him. The indicator light next to Crowley's name lit up. "And we wait."

"Yeah?" Crowley waited for a response. "Christine? Christine. What the fuck?" He disconnected. Just as Christine approached the door to her office, Mike pushed the button again. "Yeah. What?"

"Sir?"

"You called me."

"No sir, I didn't."

"Yes you did."

"There must be something wrong with the system then, Mr. Crowley, because I didn't call."

With that Crowley, who hated interruptions, especially by the endless stream of inept, stupid secretaries the idiots in Human Resources kept hiring for him, slammed a finger on the button to disconnect, rose from his chair, and strode out of his office. As he did so, Marvin grabbed the forms off the desk with a twinge of guilt and sorrow for the ass-chewing the poor secretary was about to get, and followed him out the door.

"Now all I do is cut out the line where I put my father in, make a clean copy, print in Jenna's name and social, and put it back on his desk."

"Don't we need to forge your mom and dad's

signatures? Mike and I can do it."

"Nah. That's only if I'd filled out a change form."

Mike and Tommy stood beaming at their ingenious success.

Though Marvin didn't mess with any of the computer files as he'd considered doing earlier for fun and havoc, he did enjoy the copier room: employees wondering why the copier had left sleep mode, spitting out paper. One intern did a real double-take while passing by. He stood in stunned silence as one of the cupboard doors suddenly opened and the scissors disappeared from his vision, then reappeared on the countertop. Goosebumps spread over him. When the scissors vanished a second time, reappearing on the shelf of the cupboard, he grabbed at his crotch as if his privates had shriveled. A moment later he ran for the men's room in obvious terror; one hand squeezing at his butt cheeks.

Just as Marvin wondered aloud and asked about what shenanigans they'd have to go through to put the altered form back, Crowley walked through Tommy on his way down the hall without missing a step.

"Huh, how do you like that," Tommy said. "He didn't even flinch. It's like he didn't feel it."

"That self-important bastard? He has no feelings," Marvin told him. "I don't think he'd feel a hand pulling on his pud if someone told him it was there."

Mike and Tommy laughed and followed Marvin back to Crowley's office, where he laid the form on the desk with a sigh. "When my mother hears about this, especially after they paid for the funeral, she's gonna kill Jen."

Chapter 13

"Look, Jen, I'm sorry. We're all…you know, sad that you lost Marvin. But you've already used more than the company allows for a death in the family," JoAnne said as mildly as she could muster. After all, her own supervisor was putting pressure on her.

"Jo, I'm sorry," Jen sniffled. "I'm trying. I really am."

"I know. But you're going to have to try a little harder here. Since you two weren't married, the firm has already been more than generous in even allowing you the same benefit. And your vacation balance is in the red."

Jenna started crying again. "I know. Look, it's not just that he died, you know? I'm having to deal with the banks and mortgage, and all that stuff too."

"Jenna," JoAnne stated in a firmer tone, "we all understand that. But—and I don't mean to sound like a total bitch here—you're just going to have to come back to work. Things are piling up, and everyone is swamped. We need you here."

"I can't sit there blubbering. It'll—"

"We know you'll have your moments, okay? We get that. Just tell me *right now* you'll be in on Monday morning."

"…Okay."

"Promise me."

"Promise."

"Good. Thank you. Now, try to spend the weekend gearing up for it, and I'll see you then." JoAnne hung up before Jenna could respond.

Jenna put the phone back into its charging base, flipped the bird at the silent receiver, and said, "Gear this up!" and cried for almost an hour. It probably would've been longer if Mrs. McClaskey hadn't rapped softly on her door and invited her to go out for dinner. 'My treat, dear.' she'd said and Jenna knew she couldn't refuse such a sweet old lady.

On Monday morning, Jenna slapped the snooze button on the alarm too many times. Marvin looked around the room for something, anything he could use to rouse her from her mourning. He was tempted to throw something at her, but he was afraid it would scare the shit out of her and then, even though he'd arranged for the insurance to come to her, she'd be tempted to sell the place. Then where would he be? His brain finally kicked in when his eyes landed on the alarm. Just in case she might actually be awake, he double checked to make sure Jenna faced away from the clock so it wouldn't vanish from her vision, picked it up, moved the time two hours ahead, reset the alarm for a minute later and waited.

Jenna reached for the alarm when it buzzed, thinking *five more minutes* until her eyes focused on the time. "Holy fuck-a-duck." She jumped out of bed, showered, and dressed faster than she'd done anything before in her life. She stopped at the mirror in the hallway to put on her makeup and glanced at her watch. "Shit. If I don't go, I'll miss the bus and have to wait another fifteen minutes."

She raced out and headed down the hallway. As the door slammed closed through Marvin, his head and shoulders poked through the wood. When she disappeared down the stairs, he pulled his head back into the apartment. Her keys were lying on the table under the mirror. He grabbed them, yelling for her to stop, but of course she didn't hear him. He chased after her. She tripped over a toy left in the foyer by one of the kids who lived in the building, uttered a quick vulgarity, and continued on her way. Marvin sprinted behind her as she made her way down to the next block just in time to jump into the northbound bus to her office.

"I might as well save my energy, there's no way I'll catch up now. Eh, maybe after coffee at Epstein's I can take a trip to her office and slip them into her purse." On the way back into the building, he noticed the toy.

"Goddamn kids. How many times have I told those idiots their kids have to stop leaving toys in the hallways? Mrs. What's-her-name"—he slapped his forehead—"McClaskey? Yeah, that's right." He smiled for remembering. "Mrs. McClaskey could fall and break a hip."

He grabbed up what turned out to be a Hot Wheels car, a Classic Camaro circa mid-sixties if he was thinking right, and took it up the stairs. He stomped down the hallway, pushed his arm through the door of the unit, and tossed the car. A woman screamed and he laughed.

"Serves ya right. I hope you think the place is haunted and you sell. Dumbass."

After a more than an hour of chit-chat at the deli,

Marvin drained the last of his third cup of coffee. "I'm gonna head out. I'll see you two later."

"Anything special, Brody?"

"Nah, not really. Jen left her keys at home this morning. I'm gonna take them to her."

"See you later then," Tommy said, as he headed for the coffee pot. He stopped in his tracks and shouted, "Hey. Hey, Marvin."

Marvin stopped at the door and waited.

"Dude, we were thinking, Mike and I, we're thinking we'd go catch a flick today if you want to join us."

"Depends. What film?"

"Not sure yet, man. Whatever strikes our fancy when we get there."

"Eh, maybe. I'll see how I feel."

"Cool. Two o'clock in the lobby."

Marv nodded, walked out, and hopped on the bus headed toward Jen's office.

"You left your keys at home," he told her in a matter-of-fact tone. She kept on typing away. He looked around for her purse and didn't see it. Though he'd never heard her say anything about where she stashed it, he figured she must put it in one of the drawers of her desk and waited for his chance to look. He stood patiently and watched the comings and goings of the office, a run-of-the-mill personal injury law firm where they banked on quick, out-of-court settlements and usually realized more than the victim once fees and expenses were deducted from the compensation.

He yawned and glanced at the time on the menu bar of her computer and realized he'd been there for almost an hour. "Dammit, come on. My God, you're always so damned focused. I don't know how you do it. Don't you ever have to go take a leak? Get up, get out. Go…make a copy or something."

Jen typed away.

"Oh, by the way, I saw you trip over that toy. Don't worry, I took care of it so you won't trip again when you get home tonight. Those stupid kids. Stupid parents. You know one of these days somebody's going to fall and get hurt. Maybe your firm could get the lawsuit. And, think about it, if poor old Mrs. McClaskey fell, she could break a hip. You know a lot of old people die after breaking a hip. I shit you not, if those kids don't knock it off, somebody's going to get killed."

Jenna pushed the save icon, rose from her chair, and walked out, to finally go pee Marvin presumed. He sighed with relief. "It's about time."

As soon as she was out of earshot, he rummaged through her desk drawers until he spotted her purse dumped into the bottom one. He opened it and went to drop the keys in, but he had no idea if she had a special pocket for them. Some women could be absolutely rabid about that shit. Women like his mother for instance. When he was growing up, she would holler and moan to the point you'd think her life depended on finding whatever it was one of them had borrowed from her. In the end, he just dropped them in the centermost compartment.

With that mission accomplished, he stopped in the men's room to rid himself of the morning's coffee. He flushed, washed and dried his hands, all the while being highly entertained by the smart-ass lawyer, in his three-thousand-dollar suit, who stood gaping with his fly open as the urinal flushed, the water in the sink turned on and off, and the air dryer turned on by itself. Marv chuckled and headed to meet Mike and Tommy at the movie theater.

Chapter 14

Marvin, Mike, and Tommy sat enjoying the hot corned beef sandwiches Tommy had made. Tommy had explained how much he liked being in the deli after hours. Sometimes, with the customers all gone, the live ones anyway, and the staff finished cleaning and left for the night, he would enjoy heating up the grill and being a short-order cook again. Or on the occasional Sunday morning, when the restaurant was closed. But he was careful not to do it too often and never served too many at once. And he always scrubbed the grill and cleaned up before stepping out through the door. He didn't want the old man who owned the place getting suspicious or thinking anyone on the staff was pilfering product. Moe was a good guy, though he was getting up there in years. Tommy knew the man would never retire and wondered what would happen to the place when the old guy joined them.

While Marvin continued to spend nights "at home," as he still considered it, wrapped around Jenna as she slept, it suddenly occurred to him that Mike was from somewhere in the New England area. Why was he still hanging around Dayton? "Where are you living?" Marvin asked, though it still bugged him to use the word when they all knew they weren't *living* anywhere.

"Oh, I stay in the penthouse suite at the Hilton. I figure it's empty, why not?"

"Cool. You think maybe I should dump the apartment and that tired old lady who's living there and follow suit?"

"Do whatever makes you happy. Me? I'm staying put. Right where I am, nice and close where I can keep an eye on her."

"Brody, don't you think… I mean, what happens when she moves on with her life?" Mike stuffed another French fry into his mouth.

"Yeah. What happens when she brings a guy home?"

Marvin stared at Tommy, drilling holes right through his forehead. Mike, sitting next to Tommy, elbowed him hard.

"What? I'm just askin' man. It's only natural. You know it's gonna happen someday. Dude, you can't change the rotation of the earth."

Marvin decided he would change the rotation of Tommy's head if he didn't shut up about it. The last thing he wanted to imagine was some other guy in his, well, what he still thought of as his, bed—or his anything else for that matter. Especially his *anything else*. So, he took another bite of his sandwich and changed the subject. "What's it like, Mike? Living up there. Does anyone ever bother you?"

"Nah. The maids come in and spread the dust around once in a while. That's about it. It's cool though. Big LED television, nice stereo."

"Shit, all the old lady has is a tiny color TV that's probably as old as she is. She leaves that thing on all night. Between that and her snoring," Tommy complained, shaking his head. "Drives me batty."

"Well, come stay with me sometime," Mike

offered. "We'll watch some movies on Pay-per-View and you can bunk down in the other bedroom."

"Pay-per-View?" Marvin looked at him. "How do you pay for it? I mean, it's not like you're a paying guest."

"Ah, screw 'em. Let them figure it out. Actually, it's kinda fun watching the manager pull his hair out when he sees movies charged to an unrented suite. At first he blamed the night staff. Accused them of going up and using the room and shit."

"What changed his mind?"

"The hallway security cameras." Mike laughed. "He reviewed the tapes from a few nights and didn't see a soul coming or going. Hmm, imagine that. Oh. One time I was in taking a shower when one of the maids showed up. You should've seen the look on her face when she saw the water being splashed around with no one under the spray. Hilarious."

"It is so much fun to dick with people. Did she run off?" Tommy was enjoying the mental image that cropped up.

"No. That was the funny part. She just turned it off and went out to the living room area. When I turned it back on to rinse off, she came back with a strange look on her face. She crossed herself—guess she's Catholic or something—and ran for the hills. I had turned it off and was lying on the bed by the time the maintenance guy showed up. He looked into the bathroom, mumbled something about ditzy broads, and left."

Tommy got up and paused. "You guys want anything else? Refill on drinks?"

"I'm good. Thanks though, Tommy. This was a real treat."

Marvin gave Mike a smile. "I told you he was a good cook. Hey, yeah, Tommy, I could use some more soda."

"Comin' right up."

"Thanks."

"No problem, dude," Tommy told him before turning to the small crowd he'd allowed in that night and raised the volume. "Okay, people, last call. Time to clean it up."

To Marvin's amazement, there was a flurry of activity. Everyone pitched in collecting dirty dishes and busing them to the dishwasher. Ketchup and mustard squeeze bottles were being filled along with salt and pepper shakers.

Mike and Marvin got up and grabbed wet cloths to wipe down tables. Tommy noticed them when he brought Marvin's drink out. "No, no, no. Sit. Let the others do that. You two are guests tonight. Our treat, our pleasure."

"You sure? It's no problem, you know. We don't mind doing our share," Mike offered.

Tommy waved a hand at them and went to get place settings for the clean tables. "Absolutely not. You sit and enjoy yourselves. Catch up on old times or somethin'. The place will be put back together in no time."

When Tommy was out of earshot, Mike leaned in to Marvin. "Come on Brody, spill it."

Marvin tried to put on his innocent 'what are you talking about face.'

Mike laughed. "Did that shit ever work with Jen?"

"What shit?"

"That lame look."

Marvin sighed. "Never."

"Doesn't work on me either. You've been distracted the entire week. What's got you bugged? The insurance papers worked, right? Everything's taken care of?"

"I'm just curious about…things, that's all. Trying to learn the ropes of this…" Marvin paused for a sip of his soda, "this…life, I guess you call it."

"All you gotta do is ask, Brody. All you gotta do is ask."

They sat silent for a while, watching the deadheads finish up, and fade through the walls and windows, like something out of Star Trek, tossing shouts of "thanks" and "later" to Tommy as they left. When everyone was gone and Tommy was hanging up his apron, Mike turned to Marvin.

"So?"

Marvin opened his mouth, then paused before he said, "Well, remember last week when I… Nah, never mind. It's nothing."

"What's nothing," Tommy wanted to know as he slid into the booth again.

"It's gotta be something, Brody. Come on, we're your friends. Ask."

"Dude, you need something? You want something? What is it?"

Marvin sat with a hard look on his face. "Uh…"

"This isn't about sex again is it?"

Mike smiled. "Somehow I don't think that's it, Tommy. I knew him in college and sex was the last thing he ever needed to worry about."

Marvin's mind turned again to the consequences of being a deadhead and what happens in this world if you commit a crime. Not the forging-of-documents kind, the deadly kind. Though he tried, he still couldn't quite steel his nerves enough to ask, and then asked himself, *if I can't muster the balls to ask about it, are they big enough to actually do it*? He had to know and putting it off hadn't made the question go away, it just made his stomach churn even more. In a rush, the words burst from him. "What would happen if one of us, a deadhead, killed someone? I mean, come on, seriously. What could anyone do, call the cops? They gonna put me on death row? Kill me?"

Tommy settled a deadpan stare on him even as he nudged Mike under the table for a little bit of help. "Marvin... Are you serious about this?"

Marv just sat and waited.

Mike stood and stretched. "Although I'd love to hear about this, I'm tired. I'll see you two tomorrow, and you can tell me all about it."

"Is it okay if I come with you? I'd like to experience a night without the sound of the old woman's buzz saw competing with the television."

"There's another bedroom. Sure."

Tommy jumped at the chance to avoid the discussion. "Cool, thanks, dude. So we'll see you tomorrow, Marvin."

Marv stood to follow them. "Fine. But I'm not letting you off the hook on this."

Chapter 15

"What're you doing for the holidays, Brody?" Mike asked a few days later as they headed out of the deli.

"Nothing. Jews don't celebrate Christmas, remember?"

"Some do," Tommy argued. "I knew a family when I was a kid; they did the whole nine yards. Tree, lights, presents. They figured why miss out on all the fun just because of a little thing like religion."

Marv shrugged. "I suppose. I'll admit it, after Jen and I moved in together, that first Christmas when she bought a little tree and put a few decorations up was kinda fun. But at home," he shook his head, "even though my folks weren't exactly temple-every-week people, Christmas was just another day of the year. My dad even went to the bakery as usual. Not that there was any business, he didn't open for customers, but he took care of other shit."

"You guys want to come to Buffalo with me? My family always does it up royal. A real feast, decorations everywhere, and piles and piles of presents."

Tommy made a last visual sweep of the tables inside. "That sounds like a blast. Count me in."

"Brody?" Mike looked at him over the rim of the glass of soda he'd carried out with Tommy's permission.

"Nah, thanks anyway, Mike. I think I'll just stick around here."

"Has she done anything around the place yet?"

"Like what?"

"Decorations, tree?"

"Nah. I doubt she'll do anything this year."

"Why? You said she liked Christmas."

"Tommy, I've only been…gone for four weeks. She comes in the door from work at night, gets dressed for bed, lies down, and cries herself to sleep. I feel terrible, but what can I do?"

Mike nodded in understanding.

Tommy shook his head. "That's a drag. You should do something."

"Such as…" Marvin left the phrase dangling.

They stood in silence. Marvin stared down the street at nothing. He knew Jenna had always enjoyed the holiday season and he couldn't help feeling as if he'd ruined it for her this year.

"I've got it. Dudes, we need to do the place up for her."

"Tommy, did you get your hands on some grass? Or did someone score you some 'ludes?" Mike asked him.

Marvin snorted. "LSD is more like it. He's hallucinating."

"No, seriously. We could do this. Come on Marv, maybe it would cheer her up a bit."

Mike looked at Marvin for a minute. "Maybe it would cheer you up too, Brody. You look like you need it."

Marv rolled the idea around in his head, and then said, "It's preposterous."

"Oh, come on Marvin. Please?" Tommy pleaded. "It'll be fun."

Marvin looked from Mike to Tommy and tried to make up his mind. Then he thought maybe it would be fun to see her freak out when she got home from the office and found the place all spruced up. Maybe he could even get her a present and leave it under the tree. "Oh, Jesus H. All right, why not? It's something to do."

"Far out. Thanks, Marvin. Okay, tomorrow morning after our coffee, we go back to your place and set everything up. This is gonna be a blast." Tommy and Mike started up the street.

About forty feet separated them when Tommy turned back. "Marvin. Hey, Marvin."

"Yeah?"

"Do you need anything? I mean, like a tree or any shit like that?"

"Nah, I think she's got everything. Either in the storage locker or in the closet in the extra bedroom."

"Okay. Cool." Tommy turned to walk away again but halted when Marvin called out to him.

"Oh, hey, Tommy. I gotta warn you. We aren't gonna have a lot of time. They close the firm at one o'clock on Christmas Eve. That'll put Jen home no later than two."

"It's cool, man. No problem. We'll make it quick, won't we Mike?"

"You bet, Tommy," Mike said just before they turned to hop the bus to the hotel. "See you tomorrow, Brody."

****

Jenna dropped her purse on the table in the hallway in stunned silence. She was almost too stunned to cry, and forgot to take off her coat. Someone had snuck in and put out all the Christmas decorations.

"Oh my God," she whispered and placed her hands over her mouth. "Oh, my God." She wandered through the entire apartment and stopped to stare at each thing. She laughed even as tears streamed down her face, the first happy ones since Marvin had died. "Who did this? This is so nice, it's so beautiful."

Tommy stood beaming at Marvin. "See, Marvin? I told you she'd like it, man."

"I wonder... Mrs. McClaskey... No, she doesn't have a key. I don't believe this. Oh, my God. Marv, look...even the little Star of David ornament you gave me is on the tree."

"Looks like you hit a home run here, Tommy," Marv said as Jenna grabbed the phone and dialed a number.

"I think we done good," Mike told them while he surveyed the completed decorations. "Yeah, not bad for a bunch of guys, right?"

"Right on." Tommy reached out to Mike and Marvin for high fives.

While Jenna interrogated Mrs. McClaskey about who snuck into the place and babbled about how beautiful it all was and how nice it was of whoever had done it all, Marvin slipped over to the tree. He tied a tiny gift box into the crook of a tree branch. He'd experienced the tiniest bit of guilt when he'd taken the jewelry from the store case, but for him the expression on her face when she opened it would be worth it.

"Okay, let's go, you two," Marvin instructed as he turned back to face the guys. "Let her revel in whatever it is she's reveling in."

"Mrs. McClaskey, it's just so…nice. Whoever did this, I couldn't thank them enough. It's like Marvin himself snuck home from work to surprise me," Jenna said. "I wonder if maybe he paid the maintenance guy months ago to do this."

"Did you hear that, Brody?"

Marv nodded but didn't say anything. Mike and Tommy went through the door. Marvin hung back for just an instant and whispered "Merry Christmas, Jen," and followed them out.

"See, Mrs. McClaskey? I told you, deep down inside he was one of the good guys." Jenna started crying again. "I miss him so much, and yet it's still so hard to believe he's gone. I wake up, and I'll actually start to tell him something before I remember."

"That's quite normal, dear. Why, when my Patrick passed, it took me months. And, if you can keep a secret, I'll tell you something."

"What's that?"

"Sometimes, I still talk to him," Mrs. McClaskey said with a chuckle.

Jenna let out a light laugh. "Well, I better get out of these clothes. I'll speak with you later."

"All right, dear. You have a good night."

"You too, Mrs. McClaskey." Jenna pushed the end call button and stood gazing around the room. She wasn't sure how the woman had accomplished this, but if someone pressed her for an answer, her best guess would be that Mrs. McClaskey talked the maintenance guy into it. Jenna decided the responsible culprit had to be her neighbor.

Jenna put the phone back on its base and tried to think of what she could do in return. She knew a woman that age couldn't possibly want another flower vase, or jewelry, or any other such unnecessary stuff. Plus, she remembered, when she'd been over there she didn't notice a lot of knick-knacks of any type; only pictures of family members graced tables and wall space. Then it hit her: Tea.

She grabbed her purse and went out the door headed for the mall. She knew she could buy an assortment of teas at one of the specialty shops. And she would have them wrap it in the best paper and prettiest bows she could pick out.

****

It was early the next morning when Marv snuck into the kitchen and brewed a small pot of coffee, poured himself a cup, and sat in his chair waiting for Jenna to wander out. He remembered how excited she always was on Christmas morning and how she would search through the tree for the jewelry that was always there.

The room was still dark when she emerged. She headed straight for the kitchen, fixed a cup, and took it back into the living room. As she plopped down in Marvin's chair, he scrambled out and sat on the floor to watch her. She lifted the cup, inhaled the aroma, and mumbled, "Mmm, coffee smells so good."

After a few minutes, she reached over and flipped the switch to turn on the tree lights. As the twinkles cast rotating shadows over the room, she took off on a running commentary. "I don't remember setting the timer on the coffee pot last night, but I'm glad I did. Remember how we'd sit here like this on Christmas mornings, Marv? 'Course, you'd be in your chair. I can't believe how comfy this ratty old thing is. No wonder you never wanted to give it up." She snuggled further into it. "I don't know if you can hear me, Marv. It's not going to be the same without you. But, isn't it amazing what Mrs. McClaskey did? The tree and all the decorations and everything."

"I'm here, and you're right, it's not the same. It's never going to be the same, kiddo."

"I hope you don't mind, I gave all the stuff I bought you to charity. Well, at least I didn't have to sneak behind your back to do it this year."

"What's that supposed to mean?"

"I really didn't like doing it, you know—buying things for charities at Christmas and hiding it from you—but you always bitched about budget."

Marvin smiled. "I knew you gave stuff to charity every year. But what the hell, Jen? You know, I harped on sticking to a budget because, with you growing up without a real family, I know how easy it is for you to get carried away. Actually, I loved that soft spot you have for the underdog."

"I didn't finish shopping, what was the point? But the tree looks bare with nothing under it."

"Look inside the tree, Jen. It's there like it always was."

Jenna sighed and wiped her face with the sleeve of her robe. She placed her cup on the table next to the chair and went to pick up the lone gift under the tree. "I hope Mrs. McClaskey likes the tea. It doesn't seem like much, but I didn't know what else to do for—" Jen caught a glimpse of something hidden in the tree, then shook her head. "Couldn't be. I mean, could it?"

"It could and it is. Pull it out and open it."

She leaned in to get a closer look then fell on her

rear end, her hands covering her mouth. "How? I mean, okay, you could've bought something before you"—she took a breath—"before you died, but how would it get in the tree? Who would know where it was hidden and where to put it?" It dawned on her when she noticed it was loosely tied to a branch—she'd finally discovered Marvin's hiding place for her yearly gift. The one place she'd never go into: the tree in the storage locker.

She reached out tentatively and grasped the box in her hand and gave a gentle tug. She held it close and inspected the silver wrapping paper and tiny gold bow.

Marv's excitement grew, and he scooted across the floor to sit opposite her. "Don't just sit there and stare at it. Open it, for Christ's sake."

Jen removed the paper from the box as if she were a surgeon, each flap was opened so the paper didn't tear. Marvin wasn't sure why, but for the first time he wanted to reach over, grab the box out of her hands, and rip it open for her. This year her usual slow precision made him crazy, maybe because he knew he couldn't do a thing about it.

Jen peeked under the lid, let out a gasp. "Oh, Marv… It's…" She opened the lid, slipped the necklace on, and jumped up. Marvin followed her to the hallway mirror, where she stood twisting her torso to admire the blue and white sapphires as they gleamed. And he beamed.

"Well, I better get a move on. I promised Tommy and Mike I'd meet them at the deli. Tommy's cooking up a special breakfast for everyone. Then I guess we're hopping the train to Buffalo." He slipped through the door, and a moment later his head popped back in and he smiled. Jen still stood before the mirror, her eyes fixed on the glittering stones, admiring the reflection. Laughing, he walked to her and kissed her on the cheek.

Jenna thoughtlessly brushed at the stray hair on her cheek and continued to admire the gift.

"Merry Christmas, kiddo," Marv said, and left.

Chapter 16

After a somewhat botched four-day holiday with Mike's family in Buffalo, where Tommy's usual exuberance failed to materialize because of the overt bigotry on display, they had all looked forward to getting back home.

New Year's Eve celebrations happened all over town, but Marv wasn't exactly a partier, he never had been. So, when Mike asked if he and Tommy would want to spend the evening in the hotel suite drinking champagne and watching the festivities on the big screen, he accepted. But before he went, he wanted to know what Jenna would be doing. He really didn't want to think of her sitting all alone. Not that he'd be any real company; it seemed he never was. He always talked to her, but of course, she never answered.

At seven o'clock that night, Jenna finally came in from work muttering under her breath. She looked exhausted. She dropped her purse in its usual spot on the table in the entryway, hung her coat, and headed into the bedroom. She plopped onto the bed and sighed. She was just drifting off to sleep when the phone jarred her awake.

She fumbled for the receiver on the nightstand. "Hello?"

"Happy New Year, Jenna dear."

"Oh, Mrs. McClaskey." Jen put on a bright voice,

but her expression didn't match the tone. "Happy New Year to you, too."

"I don't mean to bother you. I just wanted to catch you before you went out on the town with your friends."

"Oh, you didn't have to worry about that. I'm not going anywhere."

"Oh, my, a young woman like yourself? Not going out to celebrate the new year?"

"It's not that I didn't have invitations. There were plenty of them, believe me. And I know they meant well, you know—"

"Well, of course they did, dear. No one likes to think of the people they care about being alone on nights like these."

"I know. It's just..." Jenna paused. It struck her, Mrs. McClaskey might actually be referring to herself being alone. "Are you going out anywhere?"

"Me?" She giggled. "An old woman? No. No, this is a night for you young people."

"Nonsense. Besides, you're not that old. So, we're two single women without dates on New Year's Eve. What should we do?"

"Oh, now, don't be silly, Jenna. I'm fine here. I've spent so many of these at home by myself since Patrick passed on. It's nothing new for me, but..." she paused, "if *you* wanted to do something—something where an old lady could keep up, I'd be happy to join you."

"I had thought I'd just stay in. But, you know? I remember seeing an ad for a show—a dinner show. I could call over and see if they still have tickets left. That is if you think you'd like to go. Do you like plays?"

"A play?" Marv asked. "Jen, have you been smoking pot? Since when do you like going to the theater?"

"You know, I haven't been to a play in years. Patrick wasn't the type of man to enjoy those things."

"Neither was Marvin. But I used to like going. Sometimes, when he had to travel for work, I would go to the ballet or theater."

"The ballet? Theater? I would've gone if you'd asked."

"So, is it a date?"

Mrs. McClaskey was silent for a moment. "It's a date."

"I'll get myself freshened up, and I'll come knock on your door."

"I'll see you in a little while, then."

Jenna put the phone back and sighed. Then she went to the bathroom, splashed some cold water on her face, reapplied her makeup, smoothed the wrinkles in her skirt, and headed into the kitchen. While a small amount of coffee brewed, she pulled the newspaper, found the ad, and called for tickets. She poured her coffee, tossed a couple ice cubes in it to cool it, and slugged it back.

Jen looked in the mirror to check her makeup again.

"You look gorgeous, as always." Marvin smiled.

"It may not be what I planned, but I haven't been to a play in months. And she's been so good to me." She looked back into the apartment before she closed the door and said quietly, "Happy New Year, Marvin."

"Well, okay then," Marv said. "Happy New Year. I'll see you later." He walked through the door, crossed the hall, and popped his head through Mrs. McClaskey's door as Jenna stood rapping on it. "Happy New Year, Mrs. McClaskey."

But she didn't answer him.

Chapter 17

In the ten weeks Marv had known him, Tommy never displayed more seriousness than he did right now. "Can you see them, Marvin? The deadheads walking around?"

"Yeah, so?" Marvin moved the boat closer.

Tommy reached out and grabbed Marvin and yanked his arm backward. "No. Don't ever get closer than we are right now. I know it seems stupid, but I'm telling you. Those there are some really bad folks you don't *even* want to get mixed up with."

Mike peered into the haze that shrouded the island in Lake Superior. "The smog is horrible out here. Jeez-Louise."

"It's not smog." Tommy pushed Marvin out of the way and took over the steerage position. He maneuvered the Starcraft another ten yards away from the edge of the rocky shore that jutted up out of the murky water.

Marv and Mike looked at him waiting for the full explanation.

"It's the field that keeps them contained. They can't see it," Tommy explained, by *they* he meant the living.

"Where are we? I mean, are we still in the States?"

"I don't think so, Brody. The lake is split between the States and Canada. I think we're past the border."

"Mike's right. The lake isn't evenly split, but the island is in Canada. See the pier down at the far end? Picnickers use that. The lighthouse and one outbuilding, those are the only structures. The island is safe for them during the day, but at night…"

"Well, it's daytime, so why can't we go ashore?"

"Marvin, listen dude. I said it's safe for *them*—the live ones. For us, no. Once you get on, you can't get back off. Or, at least that's what I've heard anyway."

Marvin wondered if Tommy was just bullshitting since, after all, if moving through solid mass was possible, how could there be some invisible force keeping deadheads confined to one place. "So how bad can any of them be? Give me one example of who's being held there. Someone I'd know about, or have heard of."

"The worst of the worst, Marvin. The real dregs. We're talking nasty, drag-your-soul-to-hell types. Not very nice. These aren't bank robbers, burglars, and the like. These are *not* nice people."

"Who, though, Tommy? Give us a couple names," Mike prompted him.

"Um… Let's see. Jeffrey Dahmer, of course. John Wayne Gacy, Gary Ridgway…"

"Who's that?" Mike asked.

"Green River Killer. Killed over ninety women, mostly prostitutes," Marvin answered.

Mike whistled. "Whoa, I remember the moniker, but I didn't know his real name. Who else?"

"Donald Henry Gaskins. He confessed to killing one hundred and ten people. Andrew Kehoe. He killed fifty-seven kids. Like I said Marvin, these are not nice people."

"But if this is in Canada, how come all of our killers are here? Do they keep everyone here? Wouldn't they run out of room?"

"The U.S. shares this with Canada. There are places like this all over the world. I'm sure Hitler is in one someplace."

"Yeah, probably. Probably somewhere in Europe, huh?" Marvin said seriously. Then he added, "Playing Gin Rummy with Mussolini or Vlad the Impaler," and laughed.

"Marvin. This is no joke," Tommy warned. "Mike, make him understand."

"Look at it this way Brody, we didn't make the trip all the way up here for nothing. And, look at Tommy, look at his face. I think he's on the level."

Tommy nodded solemnly.

Marv scowled. "I think you're yanking our chains, Tommy. What, does some archangel come swooping down from the sky, grab them by the scruff of the neck, and whisk them away, dropping their asses in the middle of that island?"

"Where did you learn this Tommy? Who told you about this place?"

"Guys, I've been a deadhead for a long time," Tommy said, falling easily into using Marvin's word for the dearly departed. "People talk. I mean, why don't you see any of these guys," he jerked his thumb over his shoulder at the island, "anywhere around? Do you think they've suddenly changed, now that they're dead they've mended their ways?"

"But you're talking about serial killers, psychotics, child molesters."

"Well, think what you want, Marvin. But, dude,

I'm...I swear to you. Now, will you stop threatening to kill Jenna?"

Tommy stood and waited for Marvin to answer.

Marvin stood and stared out over the island.

Mike sat and tried to wait it out...and bit by bit lost his composure; a slight smile that broadened and turned into a chuckle.

Within minutes his laugh grew louder until his whole body shook.

When Marvin asked what was so funny, Tommy's face split into a grin and then broke into laughter. "Aw, goddammit, Mike. We were doing so well..."

Marvin looked from one to the other, realized he'd been had, and broke into a smile—right after he smacked Tommy upside the head. "Ya schmuck. You brought me out to the middle of fuckin' nowhere in the dead of frickin' winter to bust my balls?"

In between peals of laughter, Mike and Tommy tried catching a breath. Each time they looked at one another, fits of giggles broke out again.

"You gotta admit, Brody, we were doing pretty good. Tommy had you starting to believe it."

Marvin nodded and laughed. "We're a good twelve hundred miles from home, on a stolen boat out in the middle of Lake Fuckin' Superior on a Wednesday afternoon. Just so you two could pull this stunt?" Marvin looked over his shoulder at the island. "What is that place then?"

"Michipicoten Island. We're in Ontario right now. The island is part of their park system," Mike told him, as he regained control of his laughter.

Marvin shook his head. "You two jokers are something else, you know that? Well, now what?"

Tommy and Mike shrugged.

"What time is it?" Tommy asked.

Marvin consulted his watch, "Four-thirty-three, if we're still in the same time zone."

"To be honest, Brody, I don't have a clue. It doesn't matter what time zone we're in because it doesn't really matter what time it is. What else do we have to do? You got some where you need to be Tommy?"

"No, just gettin' hungry."

"Well, let's go to Sault Ste. Marie and see what we find," Mike offered.

"Shouldn't we take the boat back where we picked it up? I mean, you guys don't want to end up on that island, do you?"

Mike rolled his eyes.

"Okay, lame joke," Marv admitted to them. "But, seriously, this is a pretty swanky water ride. Whoever owns this thing is gonna be mighty pissed that it's gone."

Tommy fired up the twin engines and headed due southeast. "They'll get it back. They'll find it. We'll coast into the marina. It'll be dark by the time we get there, and we can even gas it up for them. How's that? We got to use it, they get a nice little cruise taking it home. No harm, no foul."

"Do you think we'll be back home sometime tonight," Marv asked.

"Dude, seriously, you need to learn to chill out, man."

"Yeah, Brody. Come on, live a little. We can hop on any train we choose, any time we choose, and go any*where* we choose. Relax, have some fun. Jenna will be just fine without you."

"Yeah, that's what I'm afraid of."

Chapter 18

They walked out of the restaurant after having seen a Friday Night Fright-Fest of *Salem's Lot* and, for complete contrast, *Love at First Bite*. "So, seriously, what happens to the bad guys?" Marvin asked.

"My God Marvin, are you still obsessing over that?" Tommy shook his head. "I thought you were over it three months ago, after we took you on that excursion."

"Well, I can't help it. Seeing a film like that, what with all the immortal beings, got me thinking about it again. I mean, they're dead, right?"

"Brody, it's a *movie*."

"I know that, Mike. I'm just sayin'. Do you think maybe we don't have souls, you know like the vampires in the film?"

"Marvin, look around. Do you see any of those guys we mentioned when we took you to the island? Do you ever hear anyone talking about them?"

"No. But I'm not talking about *them*. I'm talking about us—you, me, or any other *deadhead* who kills a live person."

"Maybe it's just one of those mysteries of life, Brody. Something we'll never know about."

"Mysteries of life." Marvin gave him his best deadpan stare. "We're dead."

Mike laughed. "You know what I meant."

"Dude, why don't you just stick with the usual stuff, like turning on lights and moving things, shit like that?"

"Well, I'll admit it's been fun messing with Crowley. I think I've succeeded in driving him nuts. Did I tell you, I think he's actually started seeing a shrink?" Marvin laughed remembering how he'd moved files on his old boss' computer, or stood pushing the power button to shut it down while the schmuck was in the middle of typing one of his egomaniacal memos to the staff.

Tommy leaned across the table. "So, that's not enough for you? What about Jen, have you been messing with her?"

"Mmm... No, not really. I've thought about it."

"Why not, man? Maybe it'll cure your boredom."

"Mike, it's just that... Well, I don't know." Marv knew perfectly well why he didn't screw with her. He didn't want to frighten her. He wanted Jenna to think about him and miss him as much as he missed her, even though he could see her and hear her. It was the bantering back and forth that he missed. The fun they would have taunting one another, sometimes getting angry and then making up. The making up was always the best part for him. He missed all the time they spent together out on the balcony with glasses of wine, hand in hand; time they would just enjoy being near one another. But he didn't feel he should admit such a thing to these two.

"You miss her, don't you Brody," Mike stated. "I kinda understand, but killing her isn't gonna win you any favors, you know?"

"Why are you two always trying to talk me out of

this?"

"Marvin, we're not trying to talk you out of it. I mean, not really. Are we, Mike?" Tommy nudged Mike to get some assistance.

"No, not at all. So, then what's your plan Brody? What can we do to help?"

"I don't know. I have to think about it. I'll see you guys tomorrow." Marvin jumped into the bus.

Tommy stood with his mouth open, staring at Mike.

"What?"

"*What can we do to help?* Dude, *that* was not the kind of help I was looking for there."

"The guy's hurting, Tommy. We should help him if we can."

"And what happens if we succeed?"

Mike shrugged. "What do you mean, what happens? She joins us. Is that so terrible?"

"Oh, please, we do not need some chick tagging along. If we wanted that, there're plenty of them here for us. But you know that's not what I'm asking. I'll help with silly stuff, things that can mess with her. But I will *not* get involved in anything that will get her killed. Because, I'm telling you, there're consequences."

"Oh, come on, Tommy. You don't know what happens any more than the next deadhead," Mike said. They walked in silence for a block before he offered up a thought. "When I walked away from the plane after the crash, there was no line forming in front of a man with a long white beard in flowing robes to check us through pearly gates. There wasn't any scary-looking guy with a sickle. I mean, really, what authorities do you see on this side? Do you see some sheriff riding around on a white steed; is there some Head Grim Reaper waiting to dole out some ultimate punishment? And if there *is* one we don't know about—one we can't see—as Marv said before, we're dead, what're they gonna do, kill us again?"

Chapter 19

Marvin fidgeted on Mrs. McClaskey's couch. "Here I was actually beginning to like you. Maybe I was all wrong to think you were an innocent old woman."

"Well, Jenna dear, I'm not sure what more advice I can give. Can I freshen your tea a bit?"

"A little more would be nice, if I'm not keeping you from anything."

"Now, now, you just relax. I know how difficult things have been for you since Marvin passed." Mrs. McClaskey topped off Jenna's cup. "I have all the time in the world, and I'm always happy to help where I can, you know that."

"Thanks. Thank you," Jen corrected herself, knowing how Mrs. McClaskey could be about being proper, especially when it came to grammar.

"You're quite welcome."

"Anyway, it's been almost six months. But I just don't know what to do. I'm so torn. I mean, I loved Marvin, you know? But, this guy is kind of cute. He's nice too. How long is sufficient, or appropriate before I start dating?"

Marvin shook a fist at Jenna. "I'll tell you how long—never."

"You're a young woman, Jenna. You have a whole life ahead of you. I know times have changed. In my day a woman would have to wait at least a year before she could even *think* about entertaining a gentleman caller again. Why, any sooner and the neighbors would place a scarlet letter on your chest." She giggled about the last part.

Jenna laughed, thought, *Maybe Mrs. McClaskey owned a scarlet letter herself, however faded it may have become over the years*, and turned serious again. "Part of me just thinks, it's only dinner and I'm going to eat anyway. Then the other half of my brain tells me I shouldn't, I can't because…Well, *because*."

"And my mouth is telling you, *you better not*." Marv punched at the couch cushion for emphasis and his fist drove right through.

"Why, for goodness sake, you two weren't married, but you were living together as if you were. Of course you miss him, of course you loved him, but take a good look at me. Someday, and a lot sooner than you'd imagine, you'll be old. So, I guess what I'm saying to you is this: You're a beautiful young woman, don't let life pass you by. If you want to see this new young man of yours, I say do it."

"Don't you dare. Don't you *dare*." Marvin stood and warned Jenna. Then he turned his glowering face to Mrs. McClaskey, "Here I thought you were a *nice* old lady."

"Well, I've taken enough of your time. It's getting late, and I have to get up and go to work in the morning." Jenna rose from the couch and leaned down for a hug, but the old woman rose from her chair and enfolded her. "Thank you, Mrs. McClaskey. Sleep well. I'll see you tomorrow," Jen said as she headed to the door.

"You too, dear."

"She'll sleep well all right. How does permanent sleep sound?" On his way through the door, Marvin turned and pointed a finger at the old woman. "I'll deal with you later." He crossed the hallway behind Jen.

Marvin followed Jenna through the apartment and out onto the small balcony where she lit a cigarette, a habit she'd reacquired after Marvin died. She recalled the day she knew things were getting serious between them.

Marvin had gently pulled the half-smoked cigarette from her lips, stubbed it out in an ashtray, and looked directly into her eyes. "I don't want you to do that anymore."

"Why Marv? I enjoy it."

"Because it'll take away from the time I have to spend with you. And I want all I can get," he'd said and kissed her softly.

She held the lit cigarette up and inspected it. "You wanted all the time you could get with me. Yeah, well, that was short-lived wasn't it you son-of-a-bitch," Jenna said in level tone.

"No, no, go ahead. I changed my mind. Smoke up a storm."

"Shit." Jenna let out a long sigh. "Mrs. McClaskey is right, I might as well go for it. I mean, what the hell, you're not coming back. I still have a life to live."

"Not for long, you don't," Marv roared and ran at her. He rushed right through her, went over the brushed steel railing of the balcony, and fell to the sidewalk below. He looked up to see Jenna standing there, looking out over the neighborhood as calm as ever. He pounded a fist to the concrete and an unintelligible frustration rushed out.

An instant later, Marvin yelped when a smiling young couple, arm in arm, with all the time and without a care in the world, walked right through him; the woman's heel found pavement directly through his groin. She glanced over her shoulder as if she'd tripped on something.

"Goddammit," Marvin swore as he got up, brushed himself off, and growled at the old man who stood across the street shaking his head. "What?"

"Dat ain't no way for a young'un like you to be actin'"

"What the hell do you know about it?" Marvin shouted, getting up from the pavement, and stalked off down the street.

"Mo'n you could know, chile. But you keep it up and you's gon' fin' out."

Chapter 20

Mike and Tommy howled with laughter as Marvin recounted the story to them during coffee the next morning at Epstein's Deli. Even the other deadheads within earshot turned to listen and laugh. If the live customers could have heard it, they would have thought it was open mic night at a comedy club.

"Goddammit. It's not funny," Marv said, yet knew he sounded like a grumpy old man.

"Oh, but it is, Brody. It's hysterical."

"You have much to learn yet, Grasshopper," Tommy said, making reference to an old television show.

Marvin flipped him the bird as he visualized the entire episode and could see the humor of it, at least from the deadhead perspective. "I got some new clothes out of it anyway."

"I was wondering why you were dressed different when you walked in."

"Well, the pants got shredded at the knees when I skidded on the sidewalk. I figured I might as well change the shirt while I was at it." Marvin glanced at Tommy, "Davy says hello by the way."

"He remembered me? Far out, I may have to go over tonight and get something different. I'm kind of tired of the khaki's thing. I miss my button fly jeans and T-shirts."

Leaning away from him, Mike turned to look at Tommy, who sat next to him. "Far out? Did you just say 'far out?' What decade are you *in*?"

Tommy smiled. "Sorry, sometimes that shit just slips out, you know?"

"Who's Davy?"

"The guy that dressed me for my funeral, remember?"

"Oh, right."

"So here's a question for you then, *Sensei*," Marvin said, with a bit of a sneer.

"That's *Karate Kid*, Marvin. In *Kung Fu*, Po was the student's master."

"Whatever," Marv expressed his frustration. Marvin had wondered about this since the first day, when Tommy had shown him he could walk right through a door or a wall and after his episode last night he had to ask. "Since I have so much to learn, explain to me why I didn't go through the concrete instead of having some bitch spike my balls with her high heels?"

"Brains." Tommy tapped the side of his head with a finger.

"I'm just guessing here, Brody." Mike paused for a minute. "But I think it's because we alter our physiology…our matter. When we're going through solid matter, we think about it. We see the wall, or whatever, and imagine melding into it and emerging on the other side."

"Yeah, Marvin, otherwise, I think we'd experience the *China Syndrome*. You know, we'd fall—"

"I know what the China Syndrome is! Tommy, my friend, I think you've watched too many movies."

"No, think about it Brody. Maybe he's right; we'd

slip through the earth too."

"But, wait a second. The door at the funeral home sliced me in half length-wise once, and I wasn't thinking about going through it."

Mike shook his head. "You didn't think about it, but maybe your brain did."

Marvin believed he was being handed another crock of bullshit. It must have registered on his face, because Mike continued, "The brain makes millions, maybe billions, of calculations a second, Brody. You can't be aware of all of them. We'd probably go insane if we were cognizant of every synapse up there."

Marvin sighed and drained his cup. "Well, I think you two are full of crap, and you don't know how or why any of this works the way it does. And you're making my brain hurt right now. God, I'm tired."

"No sleep last night?"

Marv shook his head and didn't know if he wanted to get into it completely. The guys knew about his issues: still not accepting what happened, and not happy at all with Jen contemplating moving on with her life. But it sure was good to have friends to talk to, to help him sort things out. He didn't always agree with the advice his old college acquaintance, Mike, gave him. And the suggestions of a pothead, who had actually spent time living on a commune, and probably screwed anything that walked on two legs—in groups no less—was certainly suspect when it came to matters of the heart.

"You are seriously bummed out about this, aren't you Marvin."

"Five months ago, she's nagging me to such distraction about the wedding that I walk in front of a bus. Now she's gonna start dating? So, yeah, *dude*, I'm bummed out. What? You think I'd be happy about it?"

Tommy and Mike stayed silent. Marv figured maybe they just didn't want to fuel his dark mood, but it didn't keep him from expressing it.

"Shit. How do you go from in love and wedding plans to dating this fast? *I* couldn't. I *haven't…*I'm not even really sure who the guy is. Probably one of the young hot-shot lawyers at the firm." Marvin slumped in his chair.

"Come on, Brody. Don't get depressed. It'll get better. It just takes a little time, that's all. We know you loved her. We know it's tough to leave her behind, but really, what choice do you have in the matter?"

Marvin understood it was a statement, not a question. But it didn't make it any easier to accept. *I'll do something about it or I'll die trying.* Then he laughed out loud. *Ha. That's stupid; I'm already dead. Okay, one lesson learned: life's habits are hard to break and typical human reactions and emotions aren't left behind.*

Instead of going to a movie or bumming around the city like he usually did with Tommy, or sitting around the pool at the hotel with Mike, Marvin decided to go back home. He knew he just wasn't fit for human consumption. The depression had lifted a bit after a nap on the couch. To help him wake up, he went into the kitchen and made some strong coffee. He sat in his chair, sipped on the steaming drink, and mulled over the situation. Jenna startled him when she bounced through the door and tossed her keys and purse onto the little table in the foyer.

He forgot about his cup of coffee on the end table

and followed her around the place. It seemed she was moving with more spring in her step than she'd exhibited since…

"I died," he said aloud. *There, I said it.* Maybe that would help him to get used to the fact.

Jenna stopped and sniffed at the air on her way through the living room. "That's weird. I swear it smells like fresh brewed coffee in here." She shook her head and proceeded with her usual home-from-work routine.

"I still like watching you undress," Marv said as the skirt slid down her legs to the floor. She hung it in the closet and reached for one of his shirts.

"Well, I might as well make use of them until I have the Salvation Army pick it all up." Jen walked back to the living room, wearing nothing but her bra, panties, and his shirt.

"You wear them all you want. You look pretty good like that," Marv told her. She settled into his chair. He panicked as she reached for the phone. He lunged for the coffee cup he'd left.

"Son-of-a-bitch." Jenna jumped up from the chair. Coffee splashed against the wall, ran across the top of the table, and splattered onto the carpeting in a puddle. "Jesus Christ, Marvin is gonna kill me if I ruin…"

"Oh, Jesus H! What're you stupid?" Marv berated himself. "Look, Jen…I'm sorry. I didn't mean…I didn't know it got so late. I would've made sure things were put away."

She ran to the kitchen to grab a large handful of paper towels and stopped dead in her tracks at the sight of the half-full coffee pot. "What the hell? I didn't even have coffee this morning." She placed the back of her hand against the glass carafe. "It's still warm. Why is there warm coffee…"

She went back to the living room and looked at the puddle of amber liquid, and her body trembled when she realized Marvin drank his coffee black. She backed up until her knees buckled against the seat of the couch and she slid to the floor.

Shaken with fright, Jenna tried to calm herself. "Don't be ridiculous. You made the coffee yourself. That has to be it. I made it myself, poured it, got a case of scatter-brain, and put the cup there without thinking. And I left for work without turning the warmer plate off."

She stood on wobbly legs and retrieved the roll of towels from the holder, grabbed the wastebasket from under the sink and stared at the wreckage. "That has to be it. That has to be what happened," she told herself as she moved forward.

Marv hovered over her shoulder. "Did any spill on the chair? Jeez, I hope not. All the years I had that and not once did I stain the leather."

"Well, at least nothing hit his chair, thank God," Jenna said, poking a finger into her ear and wiggling it against the hair she thought had tickled her. "He would've been so pissed."

Marv watched her from the safety of the couch as she cleaned up the mess. There was nothing else he could do. He figured if he tried to help she'd see the dripping coffee disappear from the walls, or the puddle on the table dry up as if by magic and would freak out again.

When Jenna finished cleaning up the mess, with whatever phone call she had intended to place forgotten, she opened the dinner she'd purchased, sat in Marvin's chair, and stared.

"Jesus, turn on the television or something. It's too quiet in here. How can you stand it?" Marv asked her.

Jen didn't answer him. She sat and stared at the blank screen eating her cold pastrami sandwich.

Marv stood up and headed toward the door. "Well, I can't handle it. Sit here in dead silence if you want." Marvin considered the innuendo of that statement and laughed. "Dead silence. Now there's a misnomer if I ever heard one. I'm going to the Hilton to see Mike. At least there I can turn on the TV for some noise if nothing else."

Chapter 21

Jenna sat in Marvin's chair balancing her plate of food when the phone rang and startled her. Most of the potato chips and the dill pickle landed on the carpet. "Shit." She grabbed for the phone with one hand as she scooped errant food back onto the plate.

"Hello? Hello?"

"Just a second, I dropped something," Jen called out. "Okay, sorry about that."

"No problem."

"David, hi. How are you?"

"Doing okay, I guess. You?"

"I'm...getting better."

"Yeah, me too. I miss him though, you know?"

Jen's eyes started to tear up. "I know. Me too. Gosh, I haven't talked to you since..."

"Yeah, it's been a while, huh? So, I thought I'd give you a call and check in. See how you're doing. See if you needed anything."

"Thanks, I really appreciate that. But, I'm okay. Really. How're your folks?"

"Dad's fine. I know he thinks about Marvin all the time. We all do. Ma's...well, Ma's Ma. You know how she is. It doesn't take long to figure her out, does it?" David laughed.

"No, I guess not. But she still scares the crap out of me."

125

"Eh, don't let her bother you. It's all for show. She doesn't really mean it, any of it. So, listen, Jen…I was wondering…"

Jenna waited. She smiled as she remembered how Marvin would call out "Ten-Second-Rule!" after food landed on the floor and took a bite of the pickle.

"I was wondering if I could come by some day. You know, to see you. And, um…I…Jen, do you think I might pick out a few things of his that I could have? After Marv graduated, my mother made him clear everything out of his old room. Guess she was trying to make him feel guilty for moving so far away."

"Oh, of course. I should have offered long ago. How stupid of me."

"No, don't say that. You've been… This has been a rough time for you and I'm sure you would have offered…"

"What about your folks? They must think I'm rude and callous."

"No, of course they don't think that."

"David," Jenna said in a flat tone, "you don't—"

"Okay, so Ma's bitched. But it's just her, you know?"

Jenna let out a small laugh. "Well, any time. It would be good to see you again, and I know Marv would want you to have some of his things. And maybe you can find something for your parents too."

"Cool. Thanks. Would this weekend be all right?"

"Sure, I don't have any plans. How about Saturday morning, around ten?"

"Perfect."

"Good, I'll see you then."

"Bye, Jen."

Jenna's eyes wandered the room until they focused on the baseballs. All they did was collect dust and remind her of how much Marvin had fussed over them, which pissed her off all over again. He would polish the glass and stare at them for an hour before he put them back on the shelf. She knew they could be worth a little bit of money, perhaps even increase in value with time—particularly when the players died—but, with the surprise of the insurance policy, she didn't need the money. She decided they would be the first things she offered to David. And she was positive Marvin would like it that his prized baseballs went to his little brother.

Chapter 22

Marvin came through the door to the apartment. It seemed quiet for a late Saturday afternoon. This had always been Jenna's time to vacuum and dust and nag him about helping. Where had she gone? Maybe grocery shopping, or out to meet a girlfriend for lunch. He took a swig of the beer he carried from the deli, where he'd had lunch with the guys, and went out onto the balcony to wait.

The view still mesmerized him, and he couldn't decide if the blood stains he saw were actually there, or if it was his imagination. But for reasons that escaped him, he would stand here in this spot, the spot where Jenna had seen him get flattened by the bus, and just stare. He caught movement out of the corner of his eye and turned to see her walking toward the building, hands loaded down with shopping bags.

He went into the foyer, stuck his head through the door, and waited for her to appear at the head of the stairs. When she came into view and strolled the hallway, he could tell she certainly hadn't been grocery shopping. "Macy's? Nordstrom? What the *hell* is all this?"

He pulled his head back into the apartment while she unlocked and opened the door. Her keys and purse got tossed in their usual place on the table in the foyer, and she went straight into the bedroom without missing a beat. The bags dropped onto the bed, and she took the items out and laid them down as if she were putting an ensemble together. In all, she bought a short black skirt, a red and white print blouse, a white silk scarf, red high-heeled shoes, and a purse to match. She stood back and studied her handiwork, her head tilting from one angle to another. Then with a nod of satisfaction, she walked to the living room to get the phone.

Marvin spotted his chance and rummaged through the bags for receipts. "Holy mother of Mary." He stuck his head around the door frame as Jenna dialed a number. "I changed that insurance policy so you could pay the mortgage on this place. We didn't break into Crowley's office so you could squander it on shit like this. What the fuck were you thinking?"

"Hey, JoAnne. It's Jen." She returned to the bedroom. "Can you give me a call when you get this message? I need an opinion on something."

"I'll give you an opinion. You need to take all this shit right back where you got it." He waved the receipts at her.

Jenna pulled a small bag from one of the larger ones and removed two boxes from it.

"More? There's more?"

She opened the larger box first, arranged a braided gold necklace across the blouse, and placed gold and ruby earrings, one on either side.

"Wait a minute, wait just a… Have you lost your mind? Gold jewelry? And rubies for Christ's sake."

Jenna opened the final box and laid a braided, tri-color gold bracelet on the bed and smiled.

Marvin blew a gasket. "How do you think you're going to pay for all that? We don't have the money for this. I'll bet you put it on a credit card again, didn't you?"

The phone rang and broke his tirade. After she answered the phone, he followed Jenna through the kitchen where she stopped for a can of diet Pepsi and continued her conversation describing her new purchases as she walked out to the balcony. "This stuff better be for the office, that's all I gotta say."

"No, Jo, it's for tonight. Do you think he'll like it?"

"Does she think *who* will like it?" Marvin butted in and leaned closer to listen in until Jenna put the phone into speaker mode.

"I think you'll look hot. If he's like any other man, he'll be all over you. If he's the gentleman he is in the office, his eyes will be all over you. Either way, you win." JoAnne told her.

"You're going out with some wienie intern from the office, aren't you?"

"Well"—Jenna giggled—"good. I need to feel..." She shrugged. "I don't know...sexy again. Does that make sense?"

Marvin's blood pressure rose. "Sexy? What, I didn't make you feel sexy?"

"All the sense in the world, girlfriend."

Jenna let out a little sigh, though a smile spread over her face. "I just haven't felt, well, you know, attractive, since Marvin died. I kind of miss the way he leered at me sometimes."

"I'm leering right now, but I'm not sure you'd like the tone of it," Marvin said, walking through the glass door. He reached into the refrigerator, took the last can of soda, popped the top, and headed back out to the balcony as he emptied half the can.

"No, we're meeting at the restaurant at 7:00 tonight. Jesus, I'm nervous. I haven't been on an actual date since Marvin and I moved in together."

"Oh, bullshit. I took you out on lots of dates. How many times did we go to dinner, or to a movie to see some lame chick-flick? Or both? You know, you are just *cruisin'* for it, aren't you?"

"Oh, relax, Jen. Just be yourself. Have fun. Pretend you're just meeting a buddy for drinks or something, you know—no pressure."

"Well, I'm not looking for anything serious. But, still…I don't want this to be a disaster either." Jenna's eyes opened wide. "Oh, geez. What if he asks me back to his place? What do I do?"

"You slap his face and walk out is what you do," Marvin told her.

"What do you *want* to do, Jen? If you want to get laid, go."

Jenna gasped. "Oh, shit…I don't know. Marvin and I were together for so long, I'm not even sure I'd know what to do."

"Know what to do for what?" Marvin wished there could be a few more perks to this existence, like reading minds maybe. "You better not be thinking about going out and better not *even* be considering having any sex with this blowhard, whoever he is."

"Jenna, listen. You're a grown woman, you'll remember. I'm not trying to push you into anything, but you'll know when you're ready. When you do, start out slow."

"Well, I guess. But the thought of sex with someone new makes me nervous."

"It damn well better, if you know what's good for

you," Marv threatened and thrust the can in Jenna's direction.

"But, at the same time, it's exciting to think about. I don't know, maybe I'm putting the cart before the horse. We haven't even had dinner yet. But something tells me, if he makes a move, I think I might jump at the chance."

"Oh, no you don't. No you don't." The mercury in Marvin's thermometer broke through the top, and he hurled the can of soda.

It soared past Jenna's face, and she let out a scream. The can landed in the gutter across the street exploding in a splash of dark amber liquid and left a swath of wet spots splayed across the sidewalk. A man stopped in his tracks, looked up at Jen, and flipped her off, and grumbled, "Stupid fuckin' bitch."

"What? What? Jen? Honey, what's wrong?" JoAnne's voice came loud and clear through the receiver.

Jenna stood frozen, speechless.

Marvin heard JoAnne and responded. "I'll tell you what happened. This bitch is going down," he yelled. He rushed toward Jenna and attempted to throw his arms around her in a vice grip. His momentum carried him through her, through the railing, and he landed on the sidewalk nose first. He screamed with his face buried in the concrete. Lifting his head, he noticed the old man who leaned against the building directly under the balcony, shaking his head and tsk-tsking. "Shit."

Chapter 23

It took JoAnne a long while to calm Jenna down enough to get any verbal responses. "I'm telling you, Jenna, it had to be a bird. It swooped in a little close. Too close for you to actually see what it was."

"Then where did the exploding can come from?" Jenna's voice was still filled with fear.

"I don't know. Maybe someone dropped it out of a window from that building."

"I watched it fly across the street, Jo."

An exasperated JoAnne gave up. "Fine. It was a can of soda. Maybe someone in the building next to you hurled it at the guy walking down the street."

"I don't know…"

"Is there anyone there with you, in the apartment?"

Jenna looked over her shoulder into the kitchen. "…No."

"Then it had to come from somewhere else, didn't it?"

Jenna heaved a sigh. "Okay. You've got to be right. Wherever it appeared from, it sure flew damn close to my face. And if I find out who did it, I'm gonna kick someone's ass."

"Now, go relax. Have a glass of wine, take a nice long shower, take a little nap, and then get your sexy on, girl."

"Thanks. I'll call you tonight."

"No you won't. You'll call me tomorrow morning and tell me whether he's as talented as that bulge in his crotch makes him look."

Jen cheeks flushed and she laughed. "You are *so* bad."

"Listen, honey, at my age I should only be so lucky. Now go get 'em, girl." JoAnne hung up.

Late in the afternoon, Jenna put the last touches on her make-up and checked her hair one more time. Marvin came through the front door as she picked up the new purse from the top of her dresser and walked into the living room.

"Ho—lee—shit!" Standing in the archway, Marv could only stare at her in lust and appreciation. "You look fantastic," he said as Jen walked through him.

A shiver ran down her spine, and she hesitated for a brief second, but she passed it off as nerves before the date. She opened her purse to make sure she had everything she needed. Satisfied, she picked up her keys, walked out, locked the door, and gave it a couple of good yanks to be sure. Though she tried to tell herself otherwise, she still wasn't entirely convinced someone hadn't been in the place. Missing cans of soda, the spilled coffee, the cooking smells, and a few times the shower walls were wet and one of the towels had been damp to the touch.

Marvin followed her to the restaurant. When she was shown to the table, he slid into one of the chairs and didn't even care if anyone saw it had moved. A young server came to fill her water glass and offered her a menu.

"Oh, I'm waiting for someone. There'll be two of us tonight."

"Three actually," Marvin corrected her.

"Very good, ma'am," he responded with a broad smile, and his eyes swept across the front of her blouse.

"Hey, hey. Put the eyeballs back in your head, asshole," Marvin told him.

"I'll be right back with another menu. Can I bring you something to drink from the bar? A glass of wine, perhaps?"

Marvin smiled up at the waiter. "A scotch, neat. Four fingers. This could be a long night."

"Um, sure. How about a glass of Zin?"

"Red or white?"

"Red."

"Yes, ma'am. I'll be right back." He tried to make a subtle adjustment to his crotch as he turned to leave.

"You better tame the snake, ya punk, or you'll be right back—right through the back door to the alley." Marvin got up to follow the guy. "I guess I'll have to serve myself, since you don't seem to care about *everyone* at this table."

He went behind the bar, took a glass from the shelf, and looked at the selection of bottles. "Well, it's not the best, but if it's all you have, Johnny Walker Black Label it is." He changed his mind and tossed a few ice cubes into the glass, then poured the tumbler to the brim. He laughed at the reaction of the woman sitting at the end of the bar. For sheer entertainment, he watched her changing expressions of horror and dismay when he replaced the bottle on the shelf. She leaned in and squinted, shook her head as if to clear it, and took a large gulp of her drink. He lifted his glass in salute, "Cheers! I hope that's as bad as your night gets."

Marvin took a detour to the men's room. By the

time he returned to the table, Jenna's date was seated across from her. Yep, one of the interns from the law firm. Marv couldn't remember his name, but he recognized him from the frequent visits to the office over the months. Visits Marvin made just to spend time with her, to be near her. He scowled at the guy and sat down again.

He supposed the man was okay-looking, but he sure didn't like the fact that, through the entire dinner, this schmuck couldn't seem to focus his eyes on anything but Jen's boobs. Marv kicked a foot through his leg and smiled when the guy twitched.

Jenna and her date ordered dessert. "Oh," Marv encouraged, "order two or three. Maybe you'll gain some weight and this bastard will lose interest." Now on his third glass of scotch, he was beyond caring if people saw things move by themselves or disappear. In fact he wanted people, at least certain people, to freak out; like this horn-dog sitting across from his fiancée, for instance.

Marv pushed the guy's water glass over the edge of the table at the same moment the waiter placed his crème brûleé, and laughed. "That'll cool you down where it counts, won't it?"

Jenna let out a little screech, and her date jumped from his chair with soaked pants.

"I'm so sorry, sir."

"No, it's okay. Don't worry about it."

"Oh, Larry, are you…" Jenna left her question hanging in the air.

Marv slapped himself in the forehead. "That's right, Larry."

"I don't know how that happened, sir. I didn't see

the glass, honest." The waiter tried to dab Larry's wet pants with a napkin, and Jen stifled a giggle

Larry backed away from him. "Hey. Hey. I think I can clean myself up. Jesus, man, it's just water and a little ice."

The waiter blushed and handed Larry the napkin. "Of course. I'm truly sorry. I—"

"It's no big deal. Really."

"The dinner is completely on the house, sir."

"No it's not. Don't be ridiculous. It's just a little water and ice. It'll dry."

"I'm very sorry. Sir—"

Larry raised his hands to stop him. "Just... Don't you have other tables to take care of?"

"Yes, sir. I apologize again."

By this time Jenna was in stitches. Larry glared for a minute and then found his sense of humor again. "Well, that'll dampen things and cool me down," he said as he raised his brows suggestively.

Jen laughed but blushed with delight. "Do you want to go? That's got to be very uncomfortable."

Larry squirmed in his chair. "It is, a little. Should we go then?"

Marv, who up until now found the entire episode rather funny, frowned in confusion. "What? Wait a minute."

"Yeah. You need to get out of those wet pants." Jen pushed her chair back.

"No. No, no, no, no. This is not what you're supposed to do."

Larry stood to signal the waiter, who rushed over. "Management insists the evening is on the house. I apologize again for my clumsiness and please, I hope you'll come back?"

Larry pulled his wallet out and slipped a one-hundred-dollar bill into the waiter's hand, winked at him, and smiled. "We'll be back. And even better? I'll be sure to request you."

The waiter looked down at the money and stared after them as they left the dining room.

Just as a man at a nearby table was about to dig into his steak, Marvin grabbed the knife from the table. A loud, low growl issued from his throat. He lunged for Jenna and stabbed at her over and over, swiping air, and howling like a dog banished from the pack. He didn't notice the small tear that sliced the hem of her skirt when he lost his grip on the final swing, and it winked back into view of the living.

Jenna glanced over her shoulder toward the floor behind her to see what bumped the back of her leg. Then she and Larry walked out the door, hand in hand.

In frustration, Marvin marched back to the table where the man waited for another steak knife, picked up the plate of food, and hurled it across the dining room with a very loud "Son-of-a-*bitch*."

"Shame, shame on you. You gon' give *all* us a bad rap, you keep that up," said the old man who had appeared next to the reservation podium and shook a finger at Marvin.

"Screw you!" Marvin yelled and rushed out the door without looking at him.

Chapter 24

Mike looked up from the section of the morning paper. "Hey, Tommy, listen to this.

"Pandemonium broke out last evening in Mr. C's Italian Bistro and Steakhouse when, apparently, a man's steak dinner flew across the room of its own accord and smashed against the wall.

'I swear I didn't touch the plate. In fact, I was waiting for a steak knife. Mine had disappeared. Right in front of my eyes.' explained the customer who wished to remain anonymous.

The scene didn't start there, though. Darlene Bartholomew, a frequent customer of the bar area, claimed to have witnessed a tumbler flicker from view just before 'a bottle of Black Label scotch disappeared for a minute and showed right back up. But I could tell there was less in the bottle, a *lot* less. It kind of freaked me out.' Another witness described seeing a steak knife drop out of thin air as a young couple walked out of the dining room.

It was like the place is haunted, or something,' reported one employee, who insisted on not being identified.

The management refused to comment for this article, except to assure the public this kind of commotion has never happened in their establishment before. 'We aren't haunted, and it's really a very quiet and safe place to dine.'

Mr. C's is located on Bennett Street and has been a local favorite for over twenty years."

Tommy shook his head when Mike finished reading the short article from the Dayton Daily News. "You know? It's assholes like that who give us all a bad name."

"I know. What are they thinking?"

Tommy got up from the bed and stretched. "You want some coffee before we meet Marvin at Epstein's? I can make a pot."

"Nah, we better not. The maid is scheduled to come up here this morning to scatter the dust."

" 'K." Tommy pulled on the jeans and shirt Davy had helped him pick out. "I suppose that means we should straighten up the beds."

"I guess so. You do that, and I'll get rid of the paper and trash." Mike got up, pulled the scattered sections of the Sunday paper into a single pile, and carried it with him while he emptied the trash cans from the bathroom and kitchen of the penthouse suite, then walked through the door and out into the hall of the hotel.

"Jesus H, Mike. Why don't you put some pants on before you go wandering around the neighborhood."

Mike looked down the hallway toward the elevator. "Oh, hey, Brody. We were just cleaning up before we headed over to the deli to meet you. Go on in, I'll be back up in a few minutes."

"Tommy's here, huh? He's been staying here a lot lately," Marv remarked when they passed each other.

"Yeah, I guess so. I think he got tired of the old lady's snoring."

Marvin went through the door. He called out when he didn't see Tommy. "Hey, hippie. Where are you?"

"Hiya, Marvin. In here, making up the beds so the maid doesn't have a heart attack."

Marv followed the sound of Tommy's voice. "Does he walk around like that all the time?" Marvin asked, poking a thumb over his shoulder in the general direction of the hallway.

"Yeah. We both do actually. Why?"

"I've never seen either one of you walk around out there in the buff."

Tommy laughed. "He went to take the trash out in the nude? Man, that's funny. But, then again," he shrugged after he thought about it, "who's gonna care? It's not like any *people* will see him."

Marvin shook his head. He didn't think he'd ever understand it. Though he had to admit he slept butt naked. "What about other deadheads? We don't count? Besides, isn't it a little cold to be walking around like that?"

"It's warm enough; it's the end of April already." Tommy scowled at him. "Geez, Marvin. Lighten up a little."

"Lighten up. I don't want to lighten up."

"Okay, spill it. What's wrong?"

"Nothing."

"You know, you're a very bad liar, dude." Tommy walked out to the living area and through the kitchen to inspect everything. He didn't care about it being spotless, he just didn't want to leave obvious clues the suite had been used.

Marv followed him, the sour look on his face increased when Mike came back.

"What's the matter, Brody? Everything okay?"

"Yeah. Fine. Jesus H. Christ, will you go put some pants on?"

"Yeah, yeah. I'm going, I'm going." Mike tossed the comment over his shoulder and walked into the bedroom. "What's your hurry? Are you that hungry?"

"It embarrasses him, Mike," Tommy hollered to him.

"It does not embarrass me. It's just—"

"Oh, for God's sake, Marv," Mike yelled back, "it's not like we didn't see each other when we were kids in college."

"Mike, in case you hadn't noticed, we're not kids. And we're not in college anymore."

"Marvin, in case *you* hadn't noticed, we really aren't in *anything* anymore."

"What the hell is that supposed to mean?"

"I think what Mike is trying to say is, we aren't over there. We aren't kids, students, doctors, or," Tommy pointed to Marvin, "advertising agents anymore."

"Then you tell me: what exactly are we?"

"Entities in a parallel world. Plainly put, Brody, we're ghosts." Mike pulled his polo shirt over his head on his way back out of the bedroom, which effectively ended the conversation.

"Thank you."

"You're welcome." Mike aped Marvin's sour tone and studied him for a minute. "Okay, come on, Brody. Why are you upset? What's got your panties in a bunch?"

"Nothing."

"I call bullshit."

The phrase made Marvin look up and smile. He remembered how his group of college buddies would call each other out when they suspected someone was lying. "Ahhh. It's nothin'. Nothing I can't get past. Really."

Tommy came up to him and looked him in the eyes with mock sympathy. "There, there," Tommy told him and patted his shoulders, "it'll be all right. Come on, son, you can tell me. Tell your Uncle Tommy all about it."

Marvin laughed. He could always count on these two jokers to bring him out of a funk. "Come on, let's go. I'm hungry for one of your famous omelets. I'll tell you both all about it when we get there, but…"

"But what?" Mike asked, slipping his shoes on.

"Only if Tommy doesn't open for everyone this morning."

"Why, dude?"

"Because you schmucks're going to laugh at me again," Marvin said, though he knew they could just as well get really pissed off over the situation.

Mike and Tommy looked at one another.

"You thinking what I'm wondering?" Mike whispered as they dropped a few paces behind Marvin on the way to the elevator.

"I heard that," Marvin said, and they all laughed.

The packed-in crowd of Tommy's loyal customers applauded as the three of them walked through the side wall of the deli, and Marvin heaved a sigh of relief. Maybe it would be his chance to brush off the real explanation Tommy and Mike seemed determined to pull out of him.

Tommy bowed to his audience. He called out to the

kitchen, "Glen, are we fired up and ready to go?"

"All ready, boss. Hit me with it."

Orders were taken and put up on the spin rack, drinks were made and served as Tommy and Glen cooked.

During the whole meal, the place buzzed over the tiny article in the morning's paper. Multiple copies were spread out on more than a few tables as everyone tsk-tsked over the scene one of their own caused in public. Marvin feigned ignorance of the affair and asked to borrow someone's section. He wondered how anyone would have even noticed it, buried like it was in the middle of Section D, or why anyone paid attention to it. But then he had to remember who he was having breakfast with. To blend in with the crowd, he interjected his own comments of disbelief over such blatantly inappropriate behavior from a deadhead.

Marv was relieved when the topic of conversation finally shifted gears. When it came time to clean up, he pitched in to clear tables and refill condiments. Once everyone had left, he offered up a silent thank you when Glen decided to stick around and join the three of them for coffee. Tommy and Mike seemed to have forgotten about his moodiness of the morning.

Tommy flopped down in the booth. "Whew, that was intense today. We went through a lot of stuff. Anyone up for a midnight grocery run tonight?"

Marvin and Mike both volunteered.

"Glen, are you in?"

"You know it."

Chapter 25

After helping to restock the restaurant, Marvin went home. Jenna was sound asleep. To him, she looked so peaceful and beautiful, especially the way she always slept curled up with one of his shirts hugged to her chest. He wanted to curl up around her and stay there for eternity and it's just what he set out to do. His arm slid around her shoulder and entwined a hand into her hand. An empty hand.

"Huh. So what's the deal here? You go out on one date and all of a sudden I'm out? Out of sight, out of mind? Is that it? Come on, Jen. Don't do this. Please don't do this. You can't fall for some other guy. I couldn't take watching that happen, it would kill me to have to see that."

In spite of his hurt feelings, he lay down next to her. She adjusted her position, as if she knew he'd wrapped himself around her body. He lay there for a few minutes and then took a deep breath. Something was different, but he couldn't quite put his finger on what it might be. He sat up and leaned over her and sniffed her hair. "No, the shampoo is the same." He moved his nose down her body and it hit him. "What's with the new perfume? I liked the other stuff better."

He got up off the bed and went into the bathroom to survey the counter where the bottles and atomizers were lined up. He spotted a new one, picked it up, took a whiff, nodded, and opened the bottle and emptied it down the drain. "There," he said as he dropped the bottle into the wastebasket. "That takes care of that."

Jenna stirred but didn't wake. Marvin stood looking at her.

"You know, I'm not sure if the new stuff was just because you liked it, but I have a sneaking suspicion you bought it for that creep Larry. I'm sorry, but ya know what? Larry can go fuck himself."

Marv realized he wouldn't get any rest with that offensive smell invading his nostrils, bringing images to mind he didn't want to see. *I might as well do something constructive.* He went to the kitchen, grabbed a handful of paper towels off the roll and the bottle of glass cleaner from under the sink, and walked into the living room. He stopped dead in his tracks.

On the wall opposite the archway to the kitchen, a noticeable gap in the series of framed photographs glared at him.

"What the hell did you do with my diploma? I worked my ass off for that degree. What other stuff of mine have you dumped?" His eyes swept the room, and there was an empty space in the entertainment center. A *very* glaring empty space. He couldn't believe he hadn't noticed it earlier and the cleaning supplies dropped to the floor in his rush across the room. His hands glided across the bare surface of the wood, and he wailed in anger and frustration.

"Not my balls! What have you done with my *balls*?"

Marvin's anger increased as he rummaged through the cupboards and drawers of the entertainment center and found nothing. He stormed into the bedroom and stared at Jenna, fists balled up at his sides. "You...you...*bitch.* How could you do this? I could see getting rid of crappy photos of people you didn't know. My music, my movies... I could even understand dumping my clothes. Those things I could forgive. But this? My balls? Never. You'll pay for this, I swear to Jesus H. *Christ*, you're gonna pay for this one."

Marvin stormed out of the apartment not sure of what to do or where to go. He ran through the streets of the city, swearing at every person he came in contact with, live or dead; kicking at anything that landed in his path. An hour later, still angry and frustrated, a store across the intersection caught his attention.

Inside, eyes adjusted to the dim light, he looked through the glass cases until he spotted what he hoped would do the job: a .357 snub-nose revolver. Marvin glanced around the shop, worried the gun wouldn't come through without breaking the glass, or an alarm of some sort might be rigged to go off. He reached in, took a firm grip on the handle, and slid his hand back to freedom as gently as he could. A smile spread over his face when the gun slid right through along with his hand as if butter had been slathered around his wrist. He shoved the gun into the waistband of his pants. After a quick look toward the street, he scanned the shelves for the correct ammunition. He walked to the shelf he was sure contained the right bullets, grabbed a box, shoved it into a pocket, and walked back out the glass and security bars of the front window.

By the time he climbed the stairs of the building at home, his anger had subsided and he felt a little silly. But it threaded itself right through his brain again the instant he looked at the empty spot where his prized baseballs should have been.

He stood in the living room and loaded the gun, careful not to drop any bullets on the floor, and returned the box to his pocket. With one more look at the hole on the shelf, he strode to the door of the bedroom. If he took any more time, he might falter in his resolve, so he lifted the gun, pointed it at Jen's sleeping form, closed his eyes, and pulled the trigger.

Nothing. No gunshot reverberated through his ears. He opened his eyes, and a soft snore escaped from Jenna.

"What the… You gotta be kidding me."

He pulled the trigger again, and again nothing happened. It was like something out of one of the movies Tommy always seemed to go on about; one where the main character is repeatedly pulling the trigger of an empty gun. But he knew this gun was not empty, he'd loaded it not three minutes ago.

He fumbled with the gun in his hand to study it, but it was just a little too dark to make out the details, increasing his fury. Light from the streetlamp poured through the window, which in the past had always kept him awake and was why he made Jen sleep on that side of the bed. He went to the window and brought the gun close to his face for a better look. A deafening roar issued from the gun. Something burned through his right ear. He fell backward and spun around in a complete circle. "Ow! God*dammit.*"

The bullet lodged in the crown molding above the sleeping Jenna, and a soft sprinkle of powder dusted her hair.

The sound of the gunshot didn't penetrate the world of the living; Jenna snored lightly. Marvin turned toward the window and twisted the barrel to catch some streetlight for a better look at the safety when the gun went off again. The glass shattered as the window exploded outward. Small, diamond-shaped shards rained to the alley below. The bullet ricocheted off the next building and buried itself in the wood framing of a window in the condo below theirs.

Jenna sat up screaming, turned on the bedside lamp, and stared at the near-empty window frame. A very frightened Marvin muttered a single "mother-fucker," ran out with gun in hand, and forgot about the glass cleaner and paper towels on the floor.

Jenna ran for the phone and dialed 911 as lights turned on in several apartments. She sat in Marvin's chair shaking as she waited for the police to show up.

She heard a loud tapping on the door. "Jenna, dear, are you all right?"

"Oh, Mrs. McClaskey." She ran to open it and immediately buried her face against Mrs. McClaskey's shoulder.

"Dear, what's wrong? I heard you scream. What happened?"

"I don't know. I don't know. The bedroom window…it's shattered."

Mrs. McClaskey hugged her tight and tried to calm her down. "Did you break it while you were cleaning it?"

Jenna broke the embrace and stepped back to allow Mrs. McClaskey in. "No. I wasn't cleaning anything, I was in bed, sound asleep."

"Well, dear, you should've put your cleaning things away. Why, you could've tripped on this and hurt yourself," she warned, and picked the items up.

"Now, where do they belong? I'll put them back for you."

Jenna stood looking at the paper towels and glass cleaner, confusion planted across her face. "I don't understand... How did those things get out here? I swear they weren't there when I went to bed."

Mrs. McClaskey settled a questioning look on her face. "Well, maybe...maybe you've been doing things in your sleep. You have been under an awful lot of stress since your Marvin passed on. It would be understandable, dear."

Jenna hesitated for a minute to conjure up a response. "I guess you could be right. Because I sure don't remember cleaning anything before bed."

"So?" Mrs. McClaskey shook the bottle of cleaner.

"Oh. Um, under the sink."

Mrs. McClaskey went to take care of the wayward items, there was a sharp rap on the front door, and a man's head poked into the foyer, "Hello? Ma'am? Police."

Jenna let out a yelp.

The officer pushed the door wide. "Oh, sorry, ma'am, I didn't mean to scare you. The door was open. Is it all right if we come in?"

Mrs. McClaskey peered around the corner and moved back into the living room. "You called the police? Why?"

"I was scared. I thought someone was trying to break in."

"Oh, of course. I apologize. How silly of me. Forgive an old woman's addled brain."

"Mrs...?" The officer left his question hang.

"Oh, um, no. It's Miss. I'm not married. Jenna.

Jenna Wilson. Thank you for coming officers, but it appears I wasted your time."

A decidedly female voice issued from behind the patrolman. "Are you sure?"

"Oh, sorry. This is Officer Dent. I'm Officer Gentner."

"Do you mind if we take a quick look around, just to make sure?"

Jen gestured. "Suit yourself."

Dent did a slow walk through the entire place and paused to peer into each nook and cranny. She yanked on the sliding door to the balcony to make sure it was locked and opened closets to ensure no one was hiding in them. From the master bedroom she called out, "Clear."

"I told you. I'm really sorry."

"But, Gentner? I think you better come in here."

When the patrolman entered the bedroom, followed by Jen and Mrs. McClaskey, his partner was pointing at the ceiling above the bed. A small hole in the crown molding and small spider-web cracks spread out along its edges. "Yeah, and?"

Dent's arm lowered and her finger pointed to the gypsum powder on the pillow. "It's powder from the wallboard. But, look at the window. It got blown *out*."

"I don't get what you're driving at, Officer...Dent, is it?"

"Yes, ma'am."

Gentner understood. "Do you own a gun Miss Wilson?"

Jenna shivered. "No. I don't like guns."

Mrs. McClaskey wrapped an arm around Jen. "Now, officers, I know you mean well and you're trying to do your job, but don't frighten the poor girl any more than she already is."

"I'm sorry, ma'am, but that up there," Dent pointed to the molding, "is a bullet hole. And the only way the window would've shattered outward, to the street, is if a bullet had been fired from inside."

Jenna's legs weakened, and she almost fell to the floor. When Mrs. McClaskey lost her tenuous grip, Gentner lunged and caught Jenna and led her to the bed. "Here, Miss Wilson, I think you better sit."

"Oh, my, God. Mrs. McClaskey, I haven't been imagining things. Someone has been in here. Someone's trying to kill me." Jenna burst into tears.

Officers Gentner and Dent shared a knowing glance.

"Ms. Wilson, are you sure there are no guns here?"

"I told you, I don't like guns."

"Well, then, does anyone else have a key to your unit?"

"No…No."

Gentner gently lifted Jenna's arm. "Why don't we go into the living room, and Officer Dent will take your statement and fill out the report." He guided her to Marvin's chair and then turned to Mrs. McClaskey. "May I speak with you, ma'am? In private."

"Why, of course, young man. I don't know what I can tell you." Mrs. McClaskey smiled as the policeman squired her properly to the hallway and then into her own unit. "I wasn't in there when the accident happened, but I'd be happy to help Jenna in any way I can. She's a lovely young woman, and she's had a very tough time of things since her young man died."

"Have you known Ms. Wilson long, Mrs…"

"McClaskey, Mrs. McClaskey, dear. Oh, let's see... I believe it's about three, perhaps four years now."

"Has Ms. Wilson been unusually upset lately?"

"I wouldn't say so, no, not really."

"You mentioned someone died recently. Has she seemed despondent at all?"

"Well, her fiancé passed just about five months ago. She grieved, as any normal woman would, of course. But it would seem the fog is beginning to lift a bit."

"How's that?"

"Well, she just went out on a date with a new young man. She seemed to be in high spirits again."

"So, you don't think she may have tried to...you know," Gentner drew a finger across his throat.

"You mean kill herself? Oh, for goodness sake. My heavens, no."

Gentner took a long minute to study Mrs. McClaskey's face and then nodded. "Okay. I apologize, but I had to ask."

"What on earth for?"

"Well, ma'am, to be honest—"

"I expect you'd better be, young man," Mrs. McClaskey cautioned him.

Patrolman Gentner smiled. "The only way that window could break like it did—out?—would be from a bullet coming from inside the bedroom. There are no signs of forced entry, nobody else has a key, and no one else was in the place with her, then it stands to reason she had to have fired the gun."

Mrs. McClaskey scowled in puzzlement. "Oh, my... I just don't think Jenna would." She stood silent for a moment. "So, what do you suggest we do, Officer?"

"If she's suicidal, we can't let her stay here. We have to take her to a hospital."

"I simply don't believe that's the case. How can we make sure though? I certainly wouldn't want to see such a beautiful young lady…"

"I think you can help us. Do you think you could convince her to go to your place while we search hers? It won't take long, I promise."

Mrs. McClaskey patted his arm. "Of course."

She followed Gentner back across the hall. Jenna's hands wouldn't stop shaking, and she attempted to apologize. "I'm afraid my writing may not be too legible."

"Now, dear, don't you worry about that. In fact, why don't we take this over to my place? I'll fix you a nice cup of that lovely tea you gave me for Christmas. It'll help to calm your nerves. You just tell me what to write, and I'll fill out the form, how does that sound?"

"Oh, I've disturbed your sleep enough. I just need to take a few deep breaths."

Mrs. McClaskey leaned down and pulled Jenna to her feet. "Nonsense. Now I don't want to hear another word. We'll go across the hall and allow these nice young officers to inspect every nook and cranny for your safety. When they're done, they'll come and bring you home. Won't you?" She hesitated at the door and turned to get a nod from Dent.

In less than thirty minutes Dent knocked lightly on the door, which Mrs. McClaskey had left open a few inches. "All clear. If you're finished with the report, we'll sign it and give you your copy, and we'll be out of your way."

Gentner nodded in response to Mrs. McClaskey's questioning look, held up a single bullet, then spread his arms in a gesture of surrender. "I sure can't explain it, except to think it had to be a stray bullet. It may have ricocheted off the other building. The way the glass blew outward is weird, but I guess stranger things have happened."

Jenna signed the bottom of the form and handed the pen to Dent. "I'm really sorry. I guess I just panicked."

"Don't give it another thought, Ms. Wilson. Really. It's what the police department is for, ma'am; to investigate things." She signed and put the date and time in the appropriate places, ripped off the copy. "If you need anything else, you call anytime. I know how tough it can be for a woman living alone."

"Thank you. Both of you. You're shining examples." Mrs. McClaskey showed them out. She turned back to Jenna after closing and locking the door. "Now, I think we need to get you tucked in. The bed in the spare room is old, but it's comfortable."

"I couldn't possibly put you to any more trouble. I can sleep in my own bed."

"Nonsense, dear. How can you sleep in a room with a broken window?"

"I can sleep on the couch. I'll close the door to keep the bugs from invading the entire place."

"No, you absolutely will not. I won't hear of it. I'll be sure to wake you in time for work."

Jenna managed a weak smile and stood in surrender. "All right, you win. I'm too exhausted to argue. Lead the way. I'll call the office first thing in the morning to tell them I'll be in after the window is repaired."

Mrs. McClaskey turned the light on in the hallway and gestured to the open door. "I'll get it done for you, Jenna. Don't worry about anything."

Jen wrapped her arms around the old woman and gave her a gentle hug. "I don't know what I would do without you, Mrs. McClaskey. You've come to my rescue more times since Marvin died than I can count. You're a real gem, and I have no way to ever repay you."

"Oh, go on." Mrs. McClaskey waved her hand and blushed. "The truth be told, my life has been too quiet since Patrick passed on. It's nice to have someone to look after again. Now, get some sleep, and I'll wake you in the morning."

"Good night, Mrs. McClaskey. Sleep tight."

"Thank you, dear. You sleep tight as well." Mrs. McClaskey closed the door.

Chapter 26

Marvin wandered the streets talking to himself. "How could I be so stupid." His heart still pounded, and he feared he'd die of a heart attack if he wasn't already dead. He wondered if Jenna was okay; he hoped so. He'd heard her screams when he ran out and remembered about the cleaning supplies too late. "Well, it's not like I could go back and grab them up; things disappearing right in front of her face after I shattered the window would've sent her over the edge."

He pulled the gun out of his pocket and stared at it. "Now what the hell do I do with this?"

He checked the street signs to find out where he'd ended up, gestured, and muttered, "The store should be two blocks that way." He didn't exactly believe in God, didn't really know who he might be talking to, but he turned his eyes to the night sky. "Should I take it back, or dump it somewhere?"

"I'd done take it back where I done foun' it."

Marv spun around to see an old man standing across the street, dressed in a dingy-white dress shirt and red bow-tie, wrinkled tan pants under an ill-fitting tan trench coat, and old dirty sneakers. The man's gray, wiry hair poked out from under his brown tam hat in frizzy tight curls. The guy looked vaguely familiar, but Marv couldn't remember if they had met or where he may have seen him before. What struck him the most, even with the distance between them, was the brightness and intelligence in the deep-set eyes.

"You're probably right. Don't know what I was thinking. Thank you." Marvin turned to start toward the store.

The old man raised his voice. "It don't make no sense for a young'un like ya'll to go messin' wit stuff like dat. Dat dere's some dang'rous thang you invitin' in. You not careful, they's gon' make you fade. A bit of darkness 'roun you already."

"What do you m—" Marvin turned back to an empty street. He peered into the dimness, squinted, and looked harder, but the old man was nowhere in sight. "Huh."

Marv made his second foray of the night into the store and slipped his hand through the glass as gingerly as he'd done it earlier and dropped the gun back into the case. He looked for the hole on the shelf and slid the box of ammunition in, then walked out.

He wanted to check on Jen, just to make sure she was okay, but was so ashamed of himself he couldn't gather the gumption to go anywhere near home. Instead, he went to the hotel to hang out and try to get a little sleep on the couch. "That is, if I can sleep after all of this. Holy mother of Mary. What a night. Broudstein, you are such a schmuck."

An hour later, on the couch in Mike and Tommy's hotel suite with the sun filtering in through the window, sipping a cup of coffee, Marvin wondered about the old man and what he'd meant.

Tommy wandered out from his room, yawning wide. He poured some coffee and went to sit in his usual chair, evidently awake just enough for his brain to register someone sitting on the couch. "Oh, hey, Marvin. What's up? You're out and about early today."

"I've been wandering around. Couldn't sleep."

"Mmm. Sorry about that, man."

"Tommy, do you see anything different about me?"

"Dude, give me a couple minutes to let the fog burn off."

"Sorry."

Marvin waited and stared at Tommy, studying him. Marv didn't grasp what the old man meant at all; Tommy looked like Tommy. After a while, not really sure what he should be looking for anyway, Marvin gazed down into his own coffee cup.

Mike made his appearance as Tommy drained his cup, gave a "good morning, buddy" to Tommy and then greeted Marv. "Hey, Brody. What're you doing here this early?"

Marv scowled. "Don't you two ever wear pants?"

"Well, good morning to you, too." Mike filled his cup and went back into his room shaking his head. He emerged a minute later wearing briefs and a T-shirt. "Happy now?"

"Thank you."

"You're welcome. Now, what bug crawled up your ass this morning that you're in such a foul mood?"

"I don't want to talk about it."

"Suit yourself, Brody." Mike situated himself on the opposite end of the couch, put his feet up on the table, and sipped his coffee. "What's the plan for the day, Tommy?"

"I don't know…" Tommy stood and stretched. "Let me get some more coffee down."

Marv winced at the sight. "Get some pants on

while you're at it."

Tommy flipped him off and went to refill his cup. "You need to get over yourself. Chill out."

Marvin returned the salute and mumbled, "Jesus H…"

"Don't antagonize him, Tommy. It's too early for that shit. Let him wallow in whatever muck it is he's rolling around in this morning."

Marvin got up from the couch and went to the window. He questioned if there might be some significance to the old man he'd talked to but, at the same time, it could be nothing more than another deadhead yanking his chain, pulling some stupid prank; that is, if he'd actually seen and talked to anyone. He was beginning to doubt his own sanity. When he turned back toward the room, Tommy had pulled on jeans and sat in the chair with his legs pulled up under him. Marv let out an ironic chuckle. "Sorry. I don't know what my problem is. Really. Maybe I suffered some kind of trauma as a kid; saw my dad naked or some shit."

"Whatever, dude. Far be it from me to upset you, 'cause God knows it's all about you, isn't it?"

"What the hell is that supposed to mean?"

"It means, Marvin, that you only seem to be concerned with yourself."

"Bullshit."

"Bullshit? Really, Marvin? 'Cause from where I've been sitting, you don't seem interested in anything but feeling sorry for yourself over an early death. An early death," Tommy chortled, "can you imagine that, Mike? Like he's the only one."

"Jesus H. you're so full of—"

Tommy stood to face him. "How old am I, Marvin?

What do you know about my family? How did *I* bow out early? Do you know what happened? I got shot late one night during a robbery at the deli."

Marvin stared at him for a moment and didn't know what to say other than, "Sorry, Tommy."

"There's a lot you don't know about me, Marvin, because you've never bothered to ask. You're too wrapped up in your own misery to think about anyone else."

Mike nudged Tommy with a toe. "Can't you see he's had a rough night, Tommy? Cut him a break."

"No. No, it's all right, Mike." Marv stood silent for a minute and looked at Tommy. "He's right and I probably should have worse than that coming to me. I'm sorry, Tommy." Marv headed for the kitchen. "Really. I mean it. I don't know what my problem is." He sighed quietly. "Maybe I need a vacation or something. I'm bored." Marvin drained the last of the coffee from the pot and held the empty carafe aloft. "Should I make another pot?"

"I call bullshit, Brody. You miss Jenna, you love her, and just don't want to admit it to us. And, no, no need to make more. Not for me, anyway. Tommy?"

"No, thanks." Tommy smiled at Marvin as he passed by on the way back to the couch. He looked from Mike to Marvin and back again. "Dudes, I got it. I know what we can do. Maybe it'll take your mind off things for a while, Marvin."

"What're you thinking?"

"Just get dressed Mike. And we'll need to straighten the place out a bit," Tommy stopped in the doorway to his room, "'cause, we're gonna be gone for a few days."

Mike rose from his perch on the couch and headed for his bedroom with Marvin close on his heels. "What the hell does he have up his sleeve now?"

"Beats me, Brody," Mike answered with a wide grin. "But it's always entertaining, whatever it is." Mike pulled on his pants and shoes. "Here, help me put the bed back together. We wouldn't want the maids getting in trouble if someone actually wants the suite."

Marv helped straighten out the bed and then went back out to the living area where Tommy had already cleaned up the coffee maker and wiped down the sink.

As Mike walked into the room, Tommy took a look around and hoisted up a small bag of trash and gave Mike a questioning look. "Ready?"

"Ready. You can close the bag, no trash from in there."

"Let's go then."

"Where are we going?"

"Marvin, just follow along for once, okay? Trust me," Tommy told him and walked through the door.

Marv hung back for an instant, raised his eyes to the heavens. "Trust him he says. A nineteen, twenty-year-old pothead says trust me. I think we're in for some trouble."

"I heard that." Tommy laughed. "And you know what? Personally, I think it might do you some good to get into a little trouble."

"I may have already."

"Now what did you do, Brody?"

"Long story. Wait'll we get wherever he's taking us," Marvin said. "Do we have time to check in on Jen?"

Tommy stopped in his tracks so quickly that Mike

walked right through him. "Whoa." Tommy shook his head. "Head rush. Dude, don't *do* that."

"Sorry, I didn't know you were going to stop."

"No, Marvin, we do not have time to check in on Jenna. You need to forget about her for a couple days. Now, come on, get with the program." Tommy waited for a smile and got none. "Or do you need Uncle Tommy to give you a big, warm hug to comfort you?"

Marvin held a serious look for effect but laughed when Tommy threw his arms wide and came toward him, the bag of trash swinging from his hand. "Okay, okay. Anything but that. Let's go, ya schmuck."

The trip to the airport took a couple hours as they transferred from route to route. Before the bus came to a complete stop at Passenger Dropoff, Tommy announced, "End of the line, folks. Everybody off," and jumped through the side to the curb. He turned and waited for Mike and Marvin to join him.

Mike stood on the curb, stared at the doors to the terminal. "Uh…Tommy, do we have to do this?"

"What's wrong, Mike? You don't look so good. Like maybe you've seen a ghost." Tommy laughed at his own joke until Marvin slapped the back of his head.

"Ya schmuck. Did you forget why we took a train to Michigan?"

"Ohhh, shit. Mike, I'm sorry. Really. Come on—"

"No. No, no… You know what? It's stupid, right?" Mike said, but stayed glued to the spot, unable to move.

"Dude, really. I feel like an asshole. We can go somewhere else. Somewhere we don't have to fly."

Mike took a deep breath and started for the doors.

"Are you sure, Mike?" Marvin called out.

"Come on, Brody. Before I change my mind.

Besides, if *this* plane drops out of the sky what's it gonna do, kill me?" Mike replied and walked through the doors.

Inside, Tommy studied the Departure screens until he found what he was looking for. "Okay, this way. Gate A-12."

"You know what, guys? This is the way to travel," Mike commented as they hitched a ride on the back of a cart that was taking an old couple through the airport. "No standing at the ticket counters; no security bullshit…"

"No credit card bills waiting for you when you get back," Marv finished. "So, where is it we're going?"

"Miami."

"*Miami*? Good Christ almighty, I swore as a Jew, originally from the state of New York, I would never go there."

"Why?"

"Too many old Jews, like these." Marvin pointed a finger at the couple up front. "I swore I would never become one of them."

"Well, you can calm your fears, Marvin. You've already accomplished that feat. It's only a pit stop, anyway."

"To where?"

"He said trust him, remember Mike?"

At the gate, Tommy got even more excited as they walked through the locked security doors before the gate agents started to board the live passengers, strode down the gangway and stepped into the plane. He looked to his right, then to the left, and turned to Mike who stood directly behind him. "What do you think? Coach, or first class?"

164

Mike hooked a thumb to the left.

"First class, it is." Tommy stepped into the cabin and stopped. "Well, crap."

"What? What's up?" Marvin craned his neck to look past Mike.

"It's full already."

Tommy strode to the front of the cabin. "Okay, folks. We got a new—well, fairly new, anyway—inductee. He really needs some pampering. We need three seats; who's gonna move for us?" He waited.

"What're you doing? We can sit in the back."

Tommy shook his head. "Marvin, you need this distraction." He looked around the cabin again and waited. A minute later he took a firm stance and crossed his arms. "I know there's got to be three people here who remember what it was like when they first crossed."

Mike shifted his weight from side to side. "Tommy, come on, nobody's going to move. Let's either sit in coach or wait for another flight."

"Wait a minute," a voice called out from one of the middle rows. "You look a little familiar. Are you the guy from the deli on Forty-Fifth?"

"As a matter of fact he is," Marv replied before Tommy could say anything.

A man stood up and peered at Tommy. "By God, it is." He looked around the cabin and focused on certain faces. "You, I know you've been in there a million times. Up. Out. And... You, too. I know I've seen you in there. Go on, go."

A handful of deadheads stood up, looked directly at Tommy, nodded, and moved out.

"Thank you. Thank you, folks. We appreciate it.

We'll see you at Epstein's," Marvin said as they passed by.

"Extra bagels and lox next time," Mike added. Marv elbowed him. "What?"

"Are you crazy? Do you know how much good lox is going for these days?" Marv whispered.

"Brody, are you paying for it?"

"That's not—" Marvin stopped and sighed. "Sorry, habits learned from my old man."

While they waited for the flight to leave, Tommy went to the galley and opened mini-bottles of champagne. He gave one each to Marvin and Mike and then took three back to the people who'd given up their seats and moved to coach. Later, during the flight, when the steward finished serving meals, Tommy stood up and hollered, "Hey, I think you missed some folks." He went to the galley, found the remaining meals, which the steward had set aside for the crew, passed them out until they were gone, and got a thunderous round of applause from the deadheads.

A short while later, Marv went to the head and, as he passed the galley, heard the steward grumbling as he stood checking the paperwork. The man gazed into the empty warmer, then looked at his manifest again. "Shit. I know I put extra in there. First class passengers my ass; first class pigs is more like it. Well," he slammed the warmer door shut, "forget extra drinks you assholes."

Marvin told Tommy about the steward's grumblings when he returned to his seat. "Now look...the real passengers are going to suffer. That's not right."

"No worries, dude. I'll take care of it." Tommy

kept an eye on the crew. When they settled into their assigned jump seats, he went into the galley again, pulled out a couple handfuls of minis. The tiny bottles of booze dropped like manna from heaven into the laps of the passengers. A couple of delighted squeals as bottles fell out of nowhere were all the crew heard; but Tommy got another round of applause from the deadheads. He kept enough alcohol flowing for the rest of the flight to calm Mike's nerves.

The three of them stood curbside at the line of waiting taxis until Tommy heard what he had been listening for. He pointed to a cab. "That one."

Tommy and Mike jumped into the back seat and dealt with the tingling of sitting in live passengers.

Marvin sat in the front next to the driver. "Holy shit! Watch where you're going. You're gonna kill us driving like this. What a maniac."

"Aw, can it, Brody. At least you don't have to deal with all this buzzing. Are we going far Tommy? 'Cause, man, this is weird for long periods of time."

"Shouldn't take long. The docks are about fifteen minutes from here."

Chapter 27

In her dream, Jenna heard glass shatter. She woke with a start and let out a scream. Someone had tried to shoot her. The door to the room flew open and light from the hallway flooded in.

When Mrs. McClaskey burst into the room, she found Jenna upright with the covers pulled to her chin. She rushed to envelope her. "It's all right dear. I'm sorry."

"Oh, my God. I dreamt someone tried to kill me; to shoot me with a gun and the bullet shattered the glass in the window."

"Shhh… Shhh. Calm down, everything's fine."

Jenna looked at her. "How…"

"How what?"

Jenna glanced around the room. "I forgot…" She shook her head. "Never mind, it's not— I'm just being stupid."

"Nonsense. You're still shaken from the events of last night. It's understandable. I'm sorry you woke in such a manner. An old woman's feeble strength, I'm afraid. I tried to get too many things out of the cupboard at once and broke a few glasses."

"Oh my gosh. Are you— Did you get cut? Are you bleeding?"

"For heaven's sake, I'm fine. See?" Mrs. McClaskey held up her hands and lifted the arms of her robe. "Now, you go back to sleep. I'll wake you when breakfast is ready."

"What time is it?"

"About five-thirty I should guess."

"I might as well stay up." Jenna got out of bed and put her robe on. "Do I have time to shower and dress?"

"You take as long as you need. Just tap on my door when you're ready, and we'll have a nice breakfast together. How does that sound?"

"It sounds terrific," Jen said as she cracked the door to the hallway between the units.

"I'll have a nice cup of tea waiting for you when you get back. Do you like bacon and eggs?"

"Bacon and eggs would be perfect, thank you," Jen answered with a smile. She promptly went into her own kitchen and flipped the switch to start the coffee maker. She'd set the automatic timer on the brewer before going to bed, but it wouldn't start for another hour. "How anyone can function in the morning without coffee is beyond me. Especially after a night like that."

She opened her bedroom door an inch to peer in, and it looked to be free of winged or six-legged critters; well visible ones anyway. "To quote you, Marv: Jesus H, what a fucking night." She stared at the broken window from across the room. "I sure hope the insurance will cover this. Oh shit. I paid the premium, didn't I? Dammit, Marvin. Why did you do this to me? Why did you leave me alone like this?" It was the first time since he'd died she didn't tear up when saying those words.

She showered, dried, and styled her hair, put on her make-up and pulled on a jogging suit until it was time to dress for work. After checking the time, she sat on the balcony with her coffee and a cigarette. She reminded herself to brush her teeth again before she went back to her neighbor's for breakfast so she wouldn't get a lecture about the dangers of smoking.

They ate in relative silence until Jenna refilled their tea cups.

"I took the liberty of researching some window repair shops while you were gone. I hope that's all right."

Jen smiled wide. "Mrs. McClaskey, I couldn't imagine anything you'd do *wouldn't* be fine. Thank you."

"Well, I try my best to be helpful. As I've said, it's such a pleasure to have someone to look after. Perhaps it's I who owe you thanks."

"For what? You're the one who seems to be doing everything."

"For making an old lady feel needed again."

Jenna laughed and mimicked her neighbor with the wave of a hand. "Oh, go on."

"Anyway, I've found one who will be here at eight o'clock to replace the glass for you. Now, don't you worry. I made sure he's licensed and insured and all of those things you young people seem to have to worry about these days."

"That's great. I'm sure he'll be fine."

"Isn't it a shame though? What's happened in the world that you can't trust folks now-a-days? Why, you know, in my day, when a man gave his word he was good for it. He did a good job; one he'd be proud to lay claim to."

"It sure is a different time, isn't it?"

Mrs. McClaskey clicked her tongue and shook her

head in agreement as she took a sip of tea. "Was breakfast all right? I hope you liked everything."

Jenna got up and gave the woman a hug. "Everything was pure perfection. Just like you."

Mrs. McClaskey waved a hand at her. "Oh, go on."

They looked at one another for a moment and laughed.

"Now, you go off to work, dear. I'll make sure the window gets fixed as good as new. Don't worry about a thing."

"You'll call me if there's a problem?"

"Of course. Now scoot. Off you go so you're not late."

Jenna stopped in the open doorway. "Thank you. Oh, I'll leave a signed check on the kitchen counter. Just fill out the amount and you can leave the receipt. And then, tonight, when I get home I'm taking you to dinner."

"Now, dear, there's no reason to make a fuss."

"We'll go to any restaurant you want, and you can have anything that strikes your fancy. I mean it now. No arguments, young lady."

Mrs. McClaskey giggled. "No arguments."

The window repairman parked in front of the building as Jenna walked to the corner bus stop.

Chapter 28

Mike whistled. "Wow. It's huge. I mean, I knew the cruise ships were big, but when you see one up close and personal like this..." He shook his head.

"Tommy, are you serious?"

"What's wrong, Marvin? You don't want to go? Come on, man, it'll be a blast."

Marvin pointed to an old couple waiting for the gates to open so they could board. "Recognize them? It's the same couple we hitched the ride with at the airport back home."

Tommy shrugged. "So?"

"And," Marv continued, "do you remember what I said about Miami? Well, the same thing goes for cruises."

"Dude, believe me, it's fantastic. Really. I've done this before. You're gonna love this."

"What would you prefer instead, Brody?"

Tommy didn't wait for Marv to answer. He walked across the boarding plank. "Besides, this is just for the connection to the main attraction," he said once they'd caught up.

"And what would that be, pray tell?"

"Marvin, you're sounding pretty grumpy again. Lighten up, man. According to the schedule I snatched from the gate, this ship will stop in St. Maarten. We hang out there until one of the tall schooners comes in, then we hop on that."

"What makes them so special?" Marvin asked.

Tommy pointed to the old couple. "They won't be there." And laughed. "No, seriously, the schooners attract a much younger crowd, they sail to small islands these behemoths can't get to. And the parties they throw on them are incredible."

Mike stepped onto the main deck and stopped. "Okay, let's see. Where's the presidential stateroom? You know I expect to travel in style, Tommy."

Tommy consulted a map of the ship he swiped from the purser. "One deck up and all the way fore. There're two, actually; one starboard, one port."

Mike headed toward the elevator. "Well, let's go before someone else lays dibs."

"What if someone's reserved it? I mean...you know what I mean."

"So what, Marvin. It could be fun messing with them," Tommy said, but did a turn-around when Marvin scowled. "They won't even know we're there."

"*I'll* notice *them*."

Mike slugged Marv on the arm. "Then sleep in a deck chair, Brody. Me? I plan on taking advantage of everything."

"Oh, and wait'll you get a load of the food they lay out. All day long, anything you want, anytime you want it. It's a good thing we don't gain weight, huh?" Tommy laughed as they walked out of the elevator on the next deck.

They'd walked the length of the ship and slipped into the stateroom by the time the gates opened to the passengers.

Mike stood and gaped around. "Wow. This is *nice*.

Damn, I hope no one has booked this. It would be a shame to have to share it."

"Oh, sorry," a voice said behind them. "Looks like you beat us to it."

Marvin, Mike, and Tommy turned around to see three deadhead couples standing just inside the door.

"There's one on the other side." Tommy pointed to the wall dividing the staterooms.

"Mmm. We know. That one's booked; we checked the manifest."

"Sorry," Mike offered.

When the couples turned to leave, Marvin said, "Hey, wait." It wasn't right for the three of them to hog the place, especially since they were only staying for the first leg of the cruise. He turned to Mike and Tommy and pulled them into a huddle. "Tommy, how long 'til we get to where you want to jump ship?"

"Day after tomorrow."

"So why can't we just share until then?"

"I'm game, Brody."

They both looked to Tommy who nodded, and broke the huddle.

Marv turned to the couples. "Um, if you don't mind sharing for two nights, we're jumping ship at…" he looked to Tommy and waited for an answer.

"St. Maarten."

"Up to you," Marv finished.

The deadheads traded glances and a few shrugs.

Over the next two days, it was rare for the nine of them to be in the cabin at the same time. The three couples did everything the ship had to offer together. Mike spent most of his time either lying on a deck chair or standing at a rail looking out to sea. Tommy hung around the buffets and visited with other deadheads, and watched the ninety-minute rendition of *Chicago*, "but, it was pretty lame in production value."

Between stops at the various bars where he helped himself to a variety of liquor, Marvin wandered every corner of the ship. He knew Jenna would've liked this. They had spent many evenings on the condo balcony sipping on wine while he'd tried to convince her to take a vacation.

"Come on, Jen. Two weeks."

"Marvin, I told you. The case is too important. I can't just up and leave the other girls to pick up my slack—they have enough work of their own."

"One week. Just one week." When she tried to cut him off, he blurted out, "I don't mean now; when the case is over."

The disparaging look left her face. "We'll see."

Marvin couldn't shake the disappointment. So many times and it was always the same excuse. It almost reached the point he could mouth her responses word for word as she spoke. *Now look where we are*, he thought, *I'm embarking on a long-awaited vacation and where are you? Probably sitting at your desk pounding the keyboard for yet another 'make or break case' for a firm of litigators who don't even bother to toss you a lousy little bonus at Christmas*. That thought led him to his all-time big question: *How would you have been able to plan a wedding and go on a honeymoon when you couldn't even leave work behind for one lousy week?*

The wait for one of the schooners at St. Maarten was short. Mike bitched about the lack of any time for sightseeing, but once on board the three-mast clipper ship, he was like a kid at an amusement park. He ran from bow to stern and climbed up the mainsail to the crow's nest. Tommy kicked back in a hammock strung between the rails of the bow.

On the third day of the cruise, from his perch in the hammock, Tommy nudged Marv with the toes of a bare foot. "Now, isn't this better than lying around the pool at home?"

"This is incredible. I don't think I'd ever get tired of this." He stood at the bow and a light sea mist splattered his face. Marvin had been bored on the huge ocean liner; in his opinion, they may as well have been in a huge hotel in Las Vegas.

"I told you, didn't I? Wait 'til we get to the island. That's the best. Food, drink, lying on the sand, snorkeling. And we'll have the entire thing to ourselves."

Marvin turned to look at Tommy in amazement. "Really?"

"Have you managed to tally up how many of *us* are on the ship?"

"I think I counted four more; one guy who's by himself from the looks of things, and three girlfriends." Marv replied, looking back out to the vastness of the ocean.

"Cool. Any of them float your boat?"

"What?"

"Do you *like* any of them?" Tommy clarified.

"How should I know, I haven't met any of them."

"Dude…Turn around and look at me." Marvin followed his instruction. "Get busy."

"With what, ya schmuck?"

Tommy rolled his eyes. "Introduce yourself."

Marv heaved a heavy sigh; for him it was simple—nobody could replace Jenna, but he didn't think Tommy, or Mike for that matter, would be able to understand.

"Marvin, why do you think I brought you here? Now go." Tommy waved a hand in the direction of the main deck. "Distract yourself. Have some fun."

Mike sauntered up. "Who's not having fun? This is terrific. Why didn't we do this during the winter?" He looked over the starboard rail. "Holy crap, would you look at *that*? Brody, do you see them?"

Marv looked down at the bow's wake to see six bottlenose dolphins riding the white-capped water. "Yeah."

"Yeah? Just 'yeah?' " Mike moved to Marvin's side and nudged him. "Aren't you enjoying this at all?"

"Sure."

"It doesn't seem like it."

"Why? Because I'm not climbing the mast? Or running from one side of the boat to the other?" Marvin teased.

"Not boat. Ship," Tommy corrected him. "A boat is what we borrowed on Lake Superior."

"Boat, ship, whatever."

Mike clapped a hand on Marvin's shoulder. "Brody, you are on a *serious* downer."

"Yeah, you're becoming a real bummer, dude."

Mike looked over at Tommy. "Tommy, do me a favor, would ya?"

"Sure thing. What d'ya need?"

"Never use bummer and dude together in a sentence again. Never, ever, ever, ever."

"You can't be serious, man. Bummer of a request,

dude. But it's okay; far out, man. It's cool." Tommy laughed and kicked Mike's backside. In return, Mike grabbed the main rope of the hammock, gave it a hard swing, and Tommy went tumbling to the deck.

A shipmate nudged his companion. "Geez, look at that. We must be moving pretty fast, the hammock is spinning in the wind."

Laughing, Mike and Tommy launched into a wrestling match, wet bare feet sliding along the polished wood. They both lost balance and grip, and tumbled toward the cabin; a malformed ball rolling through people. If they'd been alive, they would be knocking them down like bowling pins.

The tussle caught the attention of the other deadheads, and they all gathered to watch. Marvin laughed at their antics and began to comment to the others. Tommy paused with Mike pinned beneath him and nodded toward the group.

Mike acknowledged him. "Okay, okay. I give. I give."

"Say bummer, dude."

Mike started to laugh. "Never."

"Say *bummer, dude* or I won't let you up."

Mike's laughter digressed into a giggle. "Uncle. Uncle."

"Not until you say it." Tommy waited, with a laugh that turned infectious. "Say it."

Mike tried to speak through gasps for breath. "Uh-uh...Unc..."

"No, not uncle. Say bummer, dude, and I'll let go."

The group of deadheads, Marvin included, joined in a chant. "Say it. Say 'bummer, dude.' Say it."

"Buh...bum." Mike laughed harder. "Oh,

crap…I…I can't bre…I can't breathe…"

"Say it, say it, say it."

After a titanic effort to control his breath, Mike blurted it out. "Bum…bummer, dude."

The group around him applauded and cheered and Tommy rolled off to his back, still laughing. "Far out!"

Mike swung and slapped Tommy's arm. They looked at one another and burst into renewed fits of laughter just as the captain announced the imminent arrival to the private island owned by the cruise company.

While the crew made the required adjustments to anchor and prepared to haul the food, drink, and other equipment ashore, some of the more experienced passengers dove into the clear water and headed for the beach.

The group of deadheads made introductions and followed suit. Their wet footprints mingled with those left by the living and went unnoticed. The palm trees and grasses waved in the breeze, and from the top of the rise near the southern end, smaller neighboring keys could be seen. A flock of gulls floated on the wind currents above already eagerly awaiting any scraps left behind when the schooner sailed after dusk.

"It's so beautiful. And peaceful." Nancy stood to Marvin's right near the northwest end of the island, a hand shading her eyes from the glare of the sun.

"That it is. I'm glad those two," Marv nodded toward a small expanse of white sand where Mike and Tommy sat, "dragged me out of the city for this."

"They're a couple of characters, aren't they?"

Marvin chuckled. "That would be an understatement."

"How did you meet them?"

"Tommy—the one who still hasn't rid himself of all things hippie-commune—saw the accident and helped me get through the initial stage of being...you know...dead. I met Mike in college. He showed up at my funeral. What about you? Where did you meet the others? I assume you all know each other, right?"

"Yeah. I met Connie and Mel—Melissa—at a club in Manhattan—"

"Ah, a city girl, eh?" Marv interjected.

"A transplant from the west actually. I figured if I could be anywhere I wanted, it may as well be where I could find some excitement. And we met Dennis at the airport on the way down here."

"So, where in the west?"

"Boulder, Colorado. You sound like you're from New York."

Marv nodded. "Upstate; Westchester. I ended up in Dayton. An offer from an advertising firm," he explained when he noticed her quizzical look. "I have a suspicion, those two jokers will be happy to find out none of you is involved with Dennis."

Nancy laughed. "Oh, I'm thinking they're going to be disappointed anyway."

"How's that?"

"Connie and Mel are a couple. They've been partners for a lot of years."

"That must've been bad news for Dennis."

"Why?"

"Well, if the three of you are gay... What?" Marvin asked in response to her laughter.

"I'm not a lesbian. What gave you that idea?"

"Ah, Jesus H. I'm such an idiot. I'm sorry, when

you said they're gay and you met them at a club I just thought…"

Nancy put a hand on Marvin's arm and a jolt traveled through his body. "It's okay, don't worry about it. Oh, and as far as Dennis goes?"

Marvin nodded and decided he best wait before he opened his trap again with another stupid statement.

"He's going to be more interested in you and your friends than any of us."

"Ahhh…"

"And he'll be especially let down when he finds out the three of you are straight. He's been watching you guys ever since he saw you. Poor guy. He hoped he'd find someone during this trip."

Marv smiled and wondered if he should tell her about Tommy's sex-capades when he lived on the commune; he might not be so far out of reach for Dennis as Nancy imagined. He decided discretion would be the best route and kept it to himself. A second later they both turned toward the beach as they heard a "Whoo-hoo" and a simultaneous "Yeah, baby" to see two bare asses running into the waves.

"So much for discretion…" Marvin mumbled to himself.

"What?"

Marv shook his head. "Nothing. Well, should we go back and see if things are set up?"

A man stood directly behind Marvin peering out at the water. "Damn it. Looks like someone beat us to it. But I don't see anyone out there, just clothes laying on the sand."

Marvin and Nancy got a chuckle out of the statement. "Someday you'll see them just fine," Nancy assured the guy, who didn't respond.

"I don't see anyone. Besides, who cares? Come on, let's go," the girl with him responded removing her top and starting down the small hill to the water.

"Cover your eyes, Marvin." Nancy giggled and tapped him on the arm.

Marvin felt a rush again, and while he couldn't be sure because he didn't know if it was even possible, he thought he may have blushed. He laughed and put his hands up to his eyes as if they were binoculars.

"We can join them if you'd like."

"Nah. No, I'm getting kind of…thirsty, actually. Let's go back."

As they turned to leave, Mike yelled out to them. "Hey, Brody. Where you two goin'?"

"Yeah. Come on in, the water's great."

Marvin waved to them as Mike pointed to the topless girl and added, "The view's not bad either" and let out a wolf howl.

Nancy gave them a wave. "He says he's thirsty and wants to get something to drink. Later, okay?"

Tommy gave her a thumbs-up. Mike signaled okay with thumb and forefinger.

Marv and Nancy started the walk back to the main beachhead at the southeast end where the crew put the finishing touches on the temporary party site. A few large canopies to offer shade from the harsh Caribbean sun lined the sand just above the tide line; the weathered structure used as a bar displayed bottles of liquor and mixes; several very large coolers held ice; a row of buffet tables twenty feet long displayed the banquet of food; three volley ball nets straddled the dunes, with balls nestled into pockets of sand, waiting for a friendly game to begin; fins and snorkel gear sat piled at the water's edge. It promised to be quite a festival.

Mike and Tommy waded up out of the water and picked up their clothes. A man's voice carried over the sound of the waves, "Holy shit, Sandy. Did you *see* that?"

"See what?"

"Look—the clothes that were on the beach; they're gone. I mean, just like that." He snapped wet fingers. "Poof. Gone."

The girl laughed. "I think you've had too much sun already." She jumped onto his back, and the man returned his attention to her. Mike's and Tommy's loud howls of laughter could be heard by deadheads half way round the isle.

Marvin spotted Mike and Tommy when they appeared at the crest of the tiny ridge and walked toward the crowded beach. "Oh for the love of Christ. What's the matter with you two?"

"What, Brody?"

Tommy nudged Mike, pointed a finger at Mike and then to himself. "It's the whole pants thing again."

"Oh, for God's sake, Brody. Who gives a rat's ass?"

"In case you haven't noticed, there are ladies present. Don't you think you could show a little respect here?"

Mel and Connie let out a sigh, Dennis laughed as he stared at the feast for his eyes; Nancy said, "It doesn't bother any of us at all, guys. Pants or no pants, we don't really care. Do whatever makes you happy." Marvin caught her gaze as she said, "God knows we put up with enough rules like that when we were alive. Now? Now we should enjoy."

"Thank you, kind lady." Tommy bowed at the waist. " 'Tis wondrous fair to meet a damsel such as thou."

"Oh, can it, Shakespeare." Marvin laughed. "All right, I give up. Go around flapping in the breeze all you want."

Chapter 29

Later in the day, Marvin and the rest of the deadheads sat in their own little group eating and drinking what they'd pilfered from the bar and buffet. Tommy glanced over to watch two couples sitting in the sand not far from them. One of them reached into a backpack, pulled out a small baggie, waved it at his friends, and nodded toward the other side of the hill. Heads turned toward the main gathering of passengers, swiveled back and indicated agreement.

Tommy who had watched it all with an apparent great deal of interest, elbowed Mike and jutted his chin toward the activity. Mike smiled when Tommy leaned in and whispered, "I'm gonna score some. What d'ya think, wanna join me?"

"I think it would be perfect. Get two. Maybe we can get Mr. Tightass over there," he whispered back with a nod toward Marvin, "to loosen up."

Tommy giggled. "You got it."

"What're you two jokers cooking up now?" Marvin asked.

"Just a little, um, entertainment for later, Brody."

Tommy kept an eye on the baggie. When the small group disappeared over the sand dune, Tommy stuck his hand into the bag and pulled out a closed fist.

"What did you do, wipe the poor guy out?" Mike asked him when Tommy opened his hand enough for a peek.

Tommy stashed three joints in his shirt. "Dude, I got *nothin'* on this guy. He's got enough doobies in there to last me a month."

Dennis broke a long pause in conversation. "The sun's starting to dip. Means they'll start packing up soon."

Mike gave a smile around the group. "How long do you think we have?"

"Mmm. Two, two-and-a-half hours maybe. Why?"

"Tommy and I would like to invite everyone on a little trip."

Tommy laughed. "Nice choice of words, Mike. I couldn't have phrased it better myself."

"Where would you take us on this tiny spit of sand we haven't already been?" Mel piped up.

Tommy rose and headed for the dune with Mike close behind.

"Follow us to never-never land, me mateys," Tommy hollered. "We'll lead you to the treasure, arrrgghh."

"Does he always steal lines from films?" Connie asked.

"Always," Marv replied and stood to follow. "I told him he's seen too many."

"He's a bit of a goofball, but he's cute." Dennis commented as the men marched up the tiny rise; Tommy pretending to walk on a peg-leg.

The rest of the group caught up, and with the lowering sun, but no ship's crew or fellow passengers in sight, they stopped and sat under a copse of palm trees.

Tommy pulled the joints from his shirt pocket.

"This, my friends, is treasure indeed. Who would like to share in the bounty?"

"Better yet, who's got fire to get them started?" Marvin reached out to grab one.

"Really, Brody? You're up for this?"

"What? I'm not that much of a *tight-ass*," Marv said, to let Mike know he'd heard the earlier comment. "Did you forget some of the frat parties we both attended? Now, who's got a light?"

Nancy pulled a lighter from her bag and handed it to Marvin, who did the honors and took the first two hits. The joint got passed around the circle of new friends until Tommy burned his fingers.

"Ow! Damn, we need a roach clip to finish this off properly." He passed the glowing nub to Marv. "Mike, help me look around—there has to be something we can improvise. Maybe a shell or something."

"Wait." Nancy again opened her bag and dug through it. "Aha! I knew I had something in there." She held up a paperclip and was rewarded with cheers, laughter, and applause.

Marvin leaned over and planted a kiss on her cheek, which did not go unnoticed. He put the clip in place, took a hit and passed it on. "Tommy, hand over another one."

"No problem." Tommy pulled one from his pocket. "You know, Marvin, it appears you are actually enjoying yourself for a change. I don't think I've heard you talk or laugh this much since you crawled out from under that bus."

Marv gave him the finger as he lit the joint and everyone laughed. He took a hit and went to pass it to his left. "Where did Dennis go?"

"On a manly errand." Mel took the offered treat and pointed to a clump of high grass, where Dennis had his back turned to the group and his stance made the mission obvious.

Five minutes later Dennis settled into his spot tossing a volleyball between his hands. He shrugged in answer to the questioning looks. "I get a little fidgety."

"Toss it here." The minute it touched Mike's outstretched hands he batted it to Tommy.

The ball and the joint made the way around the circle amidst chatter and laughs. After the third doobie was stuck into the paperclip, the raucous group took their volleyball game closer to the water on the east stretch of sand.

The two couples who snuck off for their own pot party were on the way back to the main beach when one of them pointed down at the bottom of the dune. "Good Lord, that's some kind of weird wind funnel."

"Where?"

"Down there. Look at the volleyball. It's bouncing all over the place."

The four stood as if mesmerized for a good ten minutes in their marijuana stupor.

"And look how it blinks out of sight every few seconds. Wild, huh?"

The ball flickered out of sight for a brief second then bounced through the air again. When the ball hit the ground and rolled to the water's edge, where a wave caught it and took it a few yards out, they turned away and headed back to the ship.

Tommy yelled, "I'll get it." He pulled his shirt off and tossed it to Mike, dropped his pants, and ran into the waves.

When the sight of Tommy's bare butt made Marvin laugh, Mike poked him in the side. "Brody, is that you in there?"

Then someone yelled "All in!" and when Marvin turned toward the sound, everyone had dropped their clothes and was running for the water. Marvin looked at Mike, shrugged, and stripped, leaving his clothes in a heap.

Mike's chuckle rolled into a full laugh. "Tommy. Would you look-it here? Do you believe this?"

Tommy's infectious laughter started up. "Far *out*. I am so proud of you right now, I could kiss ya."

Marv flipped them the bird with both hands, let out a yelp, and ran into the waves.

An hour later, still laughing after a water fight, the sun flashed its green flare on the horizon. The group of deadheads sloshed out of the water and fell to the sand. Except for the occasional chuckle and sigh, they lay there in silence and waited to dry off in the light breeze.

Mike lifted his upper body by the elbows. The sky faded to pinks and ambers. He nudged Tommy and tilted a nod.

"For real?" Tommy whispered after he noticed Marv and Nancy lying side by side, hands entwined. "Very cool."

"Cool?" Mike fixed Tommy with a stare. "No, I'd say it's about flippin' time."

Tommy let out a quiet chuckle and nodded.

Dennis rolled to his side, looked at the watch lying on top of his pants. "Oh, shit." He jumped up and pulled his pants on, slid into his shirt, and slipped the watch onto his wrist. "Come on. We're late. They'll leave without us."

Marv turned his head to Nancy and smiled. "I think I could just stay here."

Gathering up his clothes, Tommy said, "That would be cool if we'd taken enough stock to hold us 'til the next schooner shows up."

Nancy turned her head. "And how long would that be Tommy?"

Tommy laughed. "I have no idea."

Dennis stood at the top of the dune and turned back. "Guys. Come on. Hurry up, everything's gone and the skiff is shoving off."

The group scrambled to their feet, grabbed clothes, and pulled them on as they ran for the main beach. Of course the crew didn't hear their shouts of "Wait." or the peals of laughter that chased them. By the time they reached the tide line, the ship's crew hit water deep enough to engage the oars.

A fellow passenger made the oarsman pause and turn to follow the pointed finger. "Do you see them? The crazy waves? What's causing them, do you know?"

"A school of fish, maybe." The crew member plied his oars enough to keep the boat from being carried back to shore by the waves. "It's interesting though, because the surface disturbance doesn't seem to be diminishing as the school moves this direction into deeper water. But there's not enough light to tell what kind of fish would be this close to the surface."

Marv shouted, "The dead kind, buddy."

"Come on, me mateys. *Swim*, ya lazy scurvy." Tommy yelled at his friends. "Or ye'll be findin' yerselves in Davey Jones's Locker right soon. Arrrggghhh."

They laughed harder but renewed the effort to

catch up to the skiff. Tommy latched onto the tail end and reached a hand back for Dennis who was close behind. Mel grabbed one side of the boat, Connie the other. Mike grabbed onto Dennis. Marvin and Nancy brought up the rear.

The paddles dipped into the water again in earnest. "My God. Must've hit a small rip current...There's a little bit of a drag."

Water splashed into the small craft when Tommy threw a leg over the side.

"What the hell..." A guy swiveled around on his seat and threw a dirty look at the crewman rowing, though the oars were deep in the water.

The boat rocked from side to side with the waves, and Mel and Connie tried to hoist themselves up, water splattering the passengers.

"These are the weirdest waves I've ever seen," a young man commented.

Mike moved up a bit and swung a leg over the side, and a female passenger let out a scream when a sopping wet piece of kelp landed on the brim of her hat. "Don't freak out folks," he announced, "it's just a few dead people tryin' to hitch a ride."

Marv, Nancy, and Dennis floated in the water until the boat pulled alongside the schooner. They waited their turn to climb up the rope ladder and joined the rest of their group at the tail of the ship.

Dennis pulled his shirt off. "Watch this."

To live folks, it looked like a faucet being turned on and off as small streams of water fell from nowhere and splattered against the wooden planks. One by one, the deadheads shucked their wet clothes and wrung them out onto the deck. A woman looked up at the crow's nest and unfurling mast, then back to the clothes that had appeared soaring through the air and landed on the ship's rail. "Where... Whose clothes..." Her question went unfinished when she spotted a few people from the last load of the skiff from the island removing wet clothes.

"Do you think we're being too mean?" Mel asked the group as they all settled to the deck floor.

"Nah." Tommy paused to chuckle, then looked to the rest of the group. "Do ya think so?"

"Hey," Mike addressed his question to everyone. "What's the worst thing you've done?"

"Dead or alive?" Dennis asked him.

Tommy elbowed him. "Dead of course. For instance, Marvin here tried to push his fiancée off a balcony."

They all turned to look at Marvin. "You didn't. Did you really think that would work? That's hilarious."

"Not only that," Marvin stated and broke into fits of laughter, "I actually tried it a second time."

"Dude..."

"Brody, you didn't."

"I did. Didn't work that time either."

By the time Marvin had finished regaling them with his latest exploits: the knife in the restaurant and how the tale ended up in the newspaper, to which Mike interjected, "I knew it. I *knew* that was you." and the story of how he shot himself last week when the gun accidentally went off after the first seven or eight pulls on the trigger hadn't worked, he had everyone but Nancy rolling on the deck and gasping for breath.

Tommy slapped Marv on the shoulder. "Marvin, dude, you are in serious need of assistance."

"Isn't that what I've been trying to tell you, ya schmuck," Marvin said as he slapped Tommy on the back of the head, which made everyone laugh again.

"Is anyone else hungry?" Dennis asked the group. "I am, like, ravenous."

Howls of laughter erupted from Tommy and Mike in the midst of a chorus of 'me too.' "The stoned munchies have hit. Come on, Dennis, we'll help you raid the galley."

"You really want her dead, Marvin?" Nancy asked.

The question made Marvin sober up a bit and he thought for a minute before he answered. His eyes lowered and the words came out in a whisper, "I do. I miss her something awful." Then he looked up. "Come on, who's next? I'm not going to be the only *schlemiel* to fess up."

One by one, while they chowed down on the fruit and bag of shrimp the foragers brought back, they swapped anecdotes about the things they'd done to the living: stolen items, things moved, the usual bag of tricks to mess with people. After a while as they slowly sobered up the stories didn't have the same sense of hilarity.

Dennis yawned and stood. "I'm tired. I need to hit the rack." He pulled his dry clothes down from the rail, slung them over a shoulder, and went below deck.

Mel and Connie went next. Tommy left to find his perch in the hammock at the bow; Mike followed soon after. And Nancy chose to make her move on Marvin as he helped her up from the deck.

Marv placed a hand on top of hers. "I'm not so sure that's a good idea."

She ran finger down his bare chest. "So, get sure."

Marvin studied her. He tried to deal with the conflict of thoughts: one part of him wanted to throw all caution to the wind, as it were, the other longed for the day he'd be with Jenna. In his college years he wouldn't have hesitated at all, *but* he told himself, *I'm not a college kid, I'm a grown man.* He wondered if it would be fair to this woman who seemed…nice, *but* he thought, *she isn't Jen.* "It's just that… I mean, you're gorgeous and all, but when we get back to port…"

"I have no delusions, Marvin." Nancy took his hand.

"Still…"

"It's obvious you really do care for her."

Marv nodded. "I do. Well, truth be known, I love her like crazy. I miss her even more than that. And I want us to be together again. I can't help it. Is that stupid?"

"Look at me, Marvin."

When he looked into her eyes, he saw a familiar, deep intelligence. He knew he'd seen someone with similar features, but for the life of him he couldn't remember where, and he fought against a sense of falling, slipping from reality.

Nancy smiled. "It's okay. Let's just go. We'll talk. There're…things I'd like to know."

They pulled their clothes from the ship's rail, and she led him to her cabin.

Up at the bow of the schooner, Mike shook Tommy. "Slide over, man."

"Mmm. No prob, dude. Where's Marvin? I thought he'd be up here to stand at the bow like some honorary masthead."

Mike raised his brows suggestively and jerked a

thumb over his shoulder.

"You're joking. He didn't."

"He did."

"Wow…"

After a short silence Mike snickered and asked in a low voice, "Hey Tommy, if we're dead and we have sex, what do you think, does that make us necrophiliacs?"

Chapter 30

"You seem preoccupied, Jen. You've made some stupid mistakes this week. What's going on?" JoAnne looked across her desk at a silent Jenna. "Come on. The last couple weeks you were finally showing some life. Now all of a sudden, you're nothing but gloom again." When Jenna still didn't respond, JoAnne leaned across the desk and fixed her with an intense stare. "Did something happen with Larry?"

"What?" Jen scrunched her brow in confusion. "No. No. We've been having a good time. Dinners out, a couple of movies. And Saturday morning we're gonna go golfing." She gave a weak smile. "Well, he's golfing; I've never been."

"Okay. Then why the long face? What's distracting you?"

"Look, I'm sorry. I don't know. I'll…I'll pick it up. It's nothing." Jenna straightened in her chair and put a forced smile on her face.

"I can't give you any major time off, not with the Pratt case in our laps. But, look, if you need a couple hours to shake this thing so you can concentrate, go for it. Walk over to the café and get your game on. This case is too big; a lot is riding on it, and Robb will have our asses on platters if we screw up. And any thought of that promotion gets flushed."

Jenna stood and smiled. "You know what, Jo? I

think I just need an hour or so to catch my breath. You want me to get you something?"

"The only thing I want you to bring me is a good brief at the end of the day. Deal?"

"Deal. Thanks, Jo." Jenna left her boss's office and headed straight to the Dayton Coffee Mill café across the street from the law firm.

****

That night, when Jenna and Mrs. McClaskey sat in Applebee's for their weekly outing, Jen hoped her friend could help figure out what might have thrown her off keel.

"I just don't know why, but it's been," Jenna shrugged, "odd in the house for the last week."

"Odd how, dear?"

"Quiet. Too quiet. Like there's something… missing." Jen shook her head. "I just don't know how to explain it. I can't quite put my finger on it."

"Is work going well? What about this young man of yours, this Larry? Perhaps your interest is waning?"

"We're very busy at the firm. I'm on a huge case, and a few weeks ago, JoAnne hinted if I do my usual miracles, as she put it, they might bump me up to paralegal without the two-year degree. The days fly by." Jenna laughed. "If Thursday wasn't our date night, I'd forget what day it was."

"Well, that's positive." Mrs. McClaskey paused for a sip of her iced tea. "I don't mean to make you feel bad, but do you think it's the date?"

Jenna looked at her dinner partner, confused. "Why? What would the date have to do with anything?"

"It *is* around the time Marvin passed, isn't it? Why, after my Patrick passed each month I would feel a bit down for a while."

Jenna sat stunned. "Oh, my God. It's *May* thirteenth, isn't it?"

"It is. I thought perhaps it was the date that had you down, but perhaps not." Mrs. McClaskey straightened in her chair. "Perhaps I'm just being a foolish old woman."

"Oh, Mrs. McClaskey, of course, you're right. That's got to be why I've been in such a funk. But, it's gotten worse the last few days, and I think that might only be a part of it."

"Well, for goodness sake, what else could there be?"

"Saturday is Marvin's birthday," Jen uttered in a soft voice. "He'd be twenty-nine if…" Her voice trailed off, but once again, sadness produced no tears.

"Oh, Jenna…I apologize, dear." Mrs. McClaskey signaled the waiter for the check. "We'll go home. Let me fix you a nice cup of chamomile tea. It'll soothe you."

Jenna looked up, annoyed. "Is that your remedy for everything? A cup of tea?" Mrs. McClaskey stammered, but said nothing coherent, which made Jenna immediately regret the outburst, and she reached a hand across the table. "I'm sorry, that was stupid of me."

The two grasped hands and Mrs. McClaskey managed a smile. "Not at all. I suppose I resort to it for lack of anything else. What if… Now, feel free to say no, or to tell me I'm just a foolish old woman. But, what if we celebrated his day with a dinner? You bring this new young man of yours; I'd like to meet him. I'll cook up a nice meal, and the three of us can raise a toast to Marvin's memory. How does that sound?"

Jenna mulled it over for a moment and then smiled brightly. "I think it's a capital idea. I'll call Larry tonight. I'd love you to meet him. He's a nice guy, I think you'd like him." They walked to the cashier where Jenna insisted it had to be her turn to pay. "Besides, if you're going to trouble yourself with making a birthday dinner for Marvin on Saturday, this will even things out."

Mrs. McClaskey laughed. "I didn't know we were keeping score. Now, what was his favorite? What should I make?"

"Well, Marvin said when he lived at home his mother always made a nice corned beef brisket and potato latkes. But when he moved here he resorted to knishes because he said there was no such thing as a decent latke in Dayton. I have to confess, I'm not much of a cook. I cheated." Jen laughed. "I always bought it all at Epstein's Deli."

"I'll see what I can do. I know I can get a good Jewish corned beef. Patrick loved it; in fact it was his favorite, too. Except he always wanted the standard Irish boiled potatoes, cabbage, and green beans. But if Marvin liked potato latkes, that's what we should have."

"If memory serves me right, I tried making them. Once." Jenna rolled her eyes and chuckled. "If you'll pardon the language of a young person, they're a pain in the ass. All that peeling and grating and frying. It took hours."

"Then perhaps I could try my hand with the knish?"

"I highly recommend against it. I think they're

even worse to make. How about this: How about I buy them from the deli? It'll be my contribution to the dinner."

They hooked arms and strolled toward the parking lot where they'd left the fifteen-year-old Buick Patrick had doted over and Mrs. McClaskey rarely drove but kept maintained.

"I wonder if we shouldn't be discreet about the real purpose of the dinner."

"Why would we do that, Jenna?"

"Well, what if Larry— I mean, don't you think Larry might get upset we've invited him for a dinner to celebrate Marvin's birthday?"

"If you'll pardon my asking, if he gets upset is he worth keeping? He should understand you were with Marvin for a long time, and just because someone passes, it doesn't mean we forget about them."

"I know, but...men can be so— What's the right word? I don't know," Jenna tilted her head to think, "silly, childish, about these things."

"Competitive, perhaps?"

"I think you've hit it. I would hate Larry to think he's competing with a dead man."

"I think I see what you mean, dear. Even in my day a girl needed to be quite demure in these kinds of affairs. It's a deal. Now, what kind of wine did your Marvin like?"

"Wine? Nope. He wasn't a wine drinker. Marvin's choice of poison was scotch. I can ask Larry to pick up a bottle if we'd like to raise a glass to Marv."

"Oh. No need for that, dear."

"Mrs. McClaskey." Jen turned and gave her companion a big smile. "And here I thought nothing stronger than tea ever passed those sweet old lips."

Mrs. McClaskey blushed. "Oh, go on."

Chapter 31

"Brody, you're looking jaunty this morning. Any interesting, uh...*news*...you'd like to share?"

"Mike, a gentleman never kisses and tells."

"That leaves you out, dude." Tommy laughed at the middle finger Marvin showed him.

"Like we don't know anyway." Mike nudged an elbow into Tommy's side.

"Yeah, well... All I remember is...or, are, her eyes, those deep amber eyes." Marv scowled and headed to the bow of the ship.

Tommy rolled off the hammock. "I'm starved. Marvin, did you notice if breakfast had been laid out on deck yet?"

"I think so."

"Anybody else hungry?"

"Come on, I'll go with you." Mike jabbed a thumb over his shoulder. "He's surly again this morning."

"Yeah, a little."

"Maybe last night didn't go as well as we thought."

"Nah, I know he spent the whole night." Tommy lowered his voice. "I think I know what the problem is though."

Tommy and Mike made their way to the bar area where a crew member was serving an assortment of morning libations. Dennis, leaning against the far corner, smiled and hoisted his cup in greeting when he saw them emerge from around the deck cabins.

"Morning, Dennis. How are you?"

"I'm good. A little groggy from last night, but I'm good."

"You want coffee, Mike?" Tommy waited for Mike's nod, then bellied up to the edge of the bar and smiled big. "I'll have a double-mocha-venti-leaded-with-a-shot, hold the sprinkles, and one large leaded-no-frills."

Dennis laughed. "What the hell is that?"

Tommy chuckled. "I have no idea." The guy behind the bar stood there and stared vacantly out at the wake of the ship. "Guess it must be self-serve." Tommy walked behind the bar, grabbed a cup, filled it from the large urn, and held it out. "Here ya go, Mike. Should we take one up to Marvin? Maybe the caffeine would put him in a better frame of mind."

"There's nothing wrong with my frame of mind," Marv said as he rounded the corner. "But I'll take some anyway."

"Then what's wrong? The look on your face... You don't seem happy." Tommy came out from behind the bar with two cups of coffee and turned to Marvin, arms outstretched. "I think someone needs another hug. Dude, do you need a hug?"

Marvin managed a brief smile. "If I need a hug, I'll let you know." He took the coffee from Tommy and walked back to the bow of the ship.

"Whoa, he is grumpy. Not even a thank you." Tommy yelled out, "Not even a thank you to your Uncle Tommy?"

Marv's voice drifted over the breeze. "Sorry. Thanks."

"I heard someone say we pull into the final port today. Maybe he's bummed out over that," Dennis offered as a reason.

Mel, Connie, and Nancy all surfaced from below-deck at the same time. Mel walked around the bar and poured three cups of coffee and passed two over the counter to Connie and Nancy. "Who's bummed out?"

"Brody, who else? I thought this trip would get him to lighten up, but... Tommy, got any theories on this we can explore?"

"No exploration needed, man. It's his birthday."

"He's bummed about a birthday? Why? They don't mean diddly-squat to us."

"Maybe not to us, Dennis. But it's his first since he 'joined the club,' so to speak."

Nancy shifted to head toward the bow. "Well, let me go see what we can do to cheer him up."

Tommy stopped her. "Got it covered already, Nancy."

Mike threw an arm around Tommy's shoulder. "You are an amazing friend, you know that?"

"Yeah, I am, aren't I?" Tommy broke into a wide smile.

"So what's your plan?"

Tommy peered around to make sure Marv wasn't lurking about within hearing distance. "Just before we pull into port..."

Within sight of Bluebeard's Castle, the schooner dropped her sails in the middle of Magen's Bay. A crew member walked around the deck of the ship banging a wooden spoon on a metal pot. The noise was enough to rouse anyone. "Listen up mates! Gathering on the aft deck. Gathering on the aft deck."

The passengers and crew looked on as the captain stood on a crate and led everyone in an off-key rendition of Happy Birthday. Marvin poked his face around the corner of the cabin. "...happy birthday, dear Marvin, happy birthday to you..." and a big cheer went up from the crowd.

The captain yelled over the heads of the small crowd. "Come on up, Marvin! Blow out your candles."

No one moved.

The captain looked around at the faces. "Where are you, Marvin? Come on, you can own up to this. Twenty-nine isn't that old." Everyone laughed but stood waiting, looking from one to another.

A bewildered group looked around waiting for the birthday boy to come forward and claim his cake. A beaming Tommy waved Marvin forward. "Well, go on, Marvin."

"You mean to tell me this whole thing is for me?" Marv shook his head, but the smile that spread over his face told the true tale. Without the slightest bit of breeze in the air, the passengers stood in wonder when the little flames of the candles flickered and went out. Marvin took a bow to the applause of the deadheads. "Did you do this, hippie?"

"Did you really think I'd forget, Marvin?"

"How did you pull this one off? Wait a minute, I don't care how." Marvin threw his arms wide. "Come here, ya schmuck. I think I need a hug."

"Well, go ahead, be shy," the captain called over the heads of the crowd. "We'll divvy it up and enjoy it anyway."

The deadheads expressed their good wishes and Nancy gave Marvin a quick kiss as the crew handed small plates around. None of their fellow passengers took notice or mentioned the seven plates of cake that winked out of sight and didn't get passed on.

Marvin slung an arm around Tommy's shoulder. "This was nice. Thank you. In fact the whole idea was terrific. It's been a great week. I'm sorry to see it end."

"Dude, it doesn't have to, ya know. We can stay for a while."

Mike shuffled his feet and his gaze swept along the calm water and pristine beach. "This may surprise you two. It's been a blast, but I'm ready for home."

"You know every year Jen'd have dinner ready for me. I wonder if she remembered…" Marvin's melancholy voice trailed off.

Nancy nudged him. "From a woman's perspective, Marvin, let me promise you: a husband's birthday is not something we tend to forget."

"Oh, no. We hadn't gotten married yet."

Connie collected their plates and plastic forks to toss them out. "You sure made it seem that way, Marvin. Pardon me if I come off sounding…bitchy, I guess, but your constant moaning over this woman certainly made one think you'd been married for quite a long time."

"Really?" Marvin asked. He looked at Mike and Tommy. "Is that true?"

Mike rolled his eyes. "Brody, I've seen hang-dog looks on people, but yours take the cake. You mope better than anyone I've ever met."

"Well, what can I say? Sorry. Hope I didn't ruin anyone's vacation."

Mel pinched Connie and gave her a now-look-what-you've-done glare. "You didn't ruin anything,

Marvin. How long had you been with her?"

"About five years. We had the date set a few times, but things kept getting in the way."

The sound of the engines coming to life signaled the final approach to the marina, and the crowd gathered along the rails to watch. The crew busied themselves with the last minute preparations to arrive in port.

"I'm sure you have every reason and right to miss her, Marvin. It's perfectly understandable. This," Nancy swept a hand around the circle of new friends, "dying thing can be tough to adjust to. Anyway, I repeat, I'm sure Jenna remembered your birthday. You'll get back to Dayton and find out you missed the party."

Marvin laughed. "Damn. If there's one thing I hate, it's missing parties. Especially if they're in my honor. Well, what do you say, hippie? Are you ready to head home?"

"I'm cool with whatever, man."

"Home it is. Besides, I have this burning need, and you're the only one who knows how to serve up a good corned beef." Marvin's knuckles scrubbed the top of Tommy's head. "This guy is the best chef in the region."

Tommy beamed a smile. "Thanks, man."

The ship's engines shut down, and she slid alongside the dock with a tiny bump and scrape, the first mate tossed the bowline to the pier, jumped the rail and secured the line as the gangplank hit the deck.

The group stood on the dock saying their goodbyes, jostled by the departing passengers bumping through them. Marvin turned to Nancy. "You should come to Dayton sometime."

"I just might do that." Nancy gave him a hug and kissed him. Then she held his eyes in a serious gaze. "You be good now, Marvin."

Mel, Connie, Nancy, and Dennis, who had talked about staying on St. Thomas for a few more weeks, walked in the direction of the beach. Mike, Marvin, and Tommy followed the crowd to a line of waiting taxis. When they neared the curb, Tommy walked backward, turned to the departing deadheads and called out, "What do you say we do it all again this same time next year?"

The four stopped and waved. "Deal" drifted over the sounds of traffic and waves.

"Far out, man." Tommy put an imitation phone to one ear. "Have your people call our people."

Chapter 32

Other than the typical pranks Tommy loved pulling on the living, the trip back to Dayton proved uneventful. On the bus from the airport, he invited Marvin and Mike to the deli.

Mike checked his watch. "He's still open, though, Tommy."

"So what. It won't be any tougher putting together a birthday dinner for Marv than it is getting our bagels and stuff every morning. Besides," Tommy looked out at the lowering sun, "it should be getting pretty slow by the time we get there."

"I know it was my idea, but if you don't mind, Tommy, I think I just want to get home now. Can I have a rain check?"

"No problem, Marvin." Tommy scowled and rolled his eyes. He knew Marv's intent was to hurry back to check on Jenna but decided to let it pass and looked to Mike. "What about you? You want something to eat, or do you want to head back to the hotel?"

Mike tried to stifle a yawn through his answer. "I'm hungry, but I'm really bushed. You'd think after such a relaxing week, I'd be rarin' to go. I wonder if it's the air in the planes that does this…Anyway, let's just go home."

"Whatever. I'm easy. So, tomorrow morning as usual?"

The bus slowed for a red light, and Marvin got out of his seat. "Well, this is as close as I'll get." He stepped through the side of the bus when it came to a complete stop and waved a hand in goodbye. "See you two jokers tomorrow."

When the bus pulled away, Tommy swiveled in his seat to face Mike. "So. Do you think he had fun? Does he realize *that* woman isn't necessary to an enjoyable existence?"

"Hard to tell," Mike mused through another yawn. "Guess we'll find out."

"Jeez, I've never seen the likes of him before."

"How so?"

"Well, at first he seemed to take the transition in stride, you know? The shopping for the suit, her making the arrangements. The funeral itself. But then... I don't know. What do you think happened?"

Mike sat silent for a while. "Maybe it's just what he said, maybe he misses her. Isn't there anyone you miss?"

"Dude...I live in the present. The past is so...past. My folks taught us that on the commune."

"You mean, 'live for the moment' kinda shit?"

Tommy nudged Mike to signal their impending exit from the bus. "No. Live *in* the moment. Big difference."

Mike followed him off the bus. "For the moment, in the moment. Whatever. My moment right now is to get back to the suite and sleep the sleep of the dead." Tommy laughed. It took Mike a few seconds to realize what Tommy found funny. "Ah, the truth shall set ye free. Can I have an Amen, brother?"

"Amen, brother."

In the hotel room, they shucked their clothes and fell onto the bed. Tommy kept tossing and turning.

"Tommy, if you can't sleep, go watch some TV."

"Sorry." Tommy propped his pillow against the headboard and sat up. A few minutes later he got out of bed, turned on the shower.

Head tilted back, eyes closed, he jumped when Mike touched his side. "Sorry, didn't mean to startle you. Turn on the side heads and slide over a little. Let me get under the water."

Tommy turned the valve and adjusted a shower head, moved to give Mike some room and closed his eyes again. The two stood side by side under the cascade. Tommy broke the silence in a whisper. "I do, you know."

"Do what?"

"Have people and things I miss." Tommy choked back a sob. His tears ran freely down his cheeks, mingling with the water. He turned toward Mike and buried his face into a shoulder.

Mike wrapped his arms around his friend. "Hey... Hey, I didn't mean...I mean, we all do. And, Brody'll be okay. Some of us just take a little longer to adjust, is all. You know that, don't you?"

Tommy lifted his head a bit and nodded. "Sorry... It's..." He leaned back into his own space. "The odd thing is, I guess, he reminds me of my brother. He's older than me, like Marvin, and he was always smacking me upside the back of my head, making fun of me and stuff too. But he always made me laugh. Like Marvin. I heard my folks say he cried like a baby when he heard about me getting killed in the robbery at the deli. I didn't know what to do for him, how to help him.

So, I guess it just bothers me to see Marvin unhappy, and I don't know what I can do to make it better."

A lot of Mike's questions were answered in those few words. Tommy had been a deadhead for so much longer than he or Marvin, and Mike sometimes had to remind himself Tommy was younger; though nine or ten years may not seem like a lot, a guy goes through significant emotional growth during his twenties. He wrapped a hand around one of Tommy's and squeezed. "Would you like to go see your brother? We can you know."

Tommy shook his head. "No… I promised to help Marvin. I can't do that if I'm out on the west coast."

"You've done a lot for Brody. It'll get better. *He'll* get better. He'll figure this out. So, if you want to see your brother, we should go."

"Dude, no. Really. I—it's better if I stay. It's been such a long time; I'm sure Gene is fine now. I can still help Marvin, though, and that's what I'm going to do."

"Okay, then. Come on," Mike pulled him close and hugged him, "let's dry off and get some sleep."

Mike turned off the water, pulled a towel from the rack and draped it over a motionless Tommy, dried himself off, then pulled Tommy's towel and patted him dry. He dropped them both into a damp heap on the marble tiled floor, led his friend to the bed, and tucked him in. Minutes later they were both fast asleep.

****

It didn't surprise Marvin to hear Jenna's voice coming from Mrs. McClaskey's place as he walked toward the condo. She'd been spending a lot of time with the old lady. Well, when she wasn't chained to her desk writing briefs for lawyers who reaped the benefits of her skills without having to pay the higher wages of a paralegal. Marv went through the door to what he still considered his condo and rummaged through the cabinets looking for the bottle of scotch he knew should be there.

"Dammit. Jesus H., Jen, where the hell is my scotch? You never drank much of that stuff... What'd you do, give it away?" He grabbed a beer from the refrigerator and crossed the hall to the old lady's place. Laughter rolled through the room.

Jenna, Mrs. McClaskey, and Larry sat around the dining room table. A hunk of corned beef on a platter dominated the center, a lonely looking half of a knish remained on a rack beside Larry, and a half full bowl of green beans with slivered almonds was situated between Larry and Jenna. The aroma of the corned beef still hung in the air and Marvin breathed it in with appreciation. "God, that smells good."

Larry sighed, wiped his mouth and leaned back in his chair. "Thank you. That was really excellent. Kudos, Mrs. McClaskey."

"Oh, you're quite welcome." She studied them both for a moment. "But, please—you should address me as Colleen. That goes for you as well, Jenna. I feel as if we've become good friends, family really. And it's silly to keep being so formal, don't you think, dear?" She didn't wait for an answer and scooted her chair back to stand. "Now, why don't we retire to the living room and have that small sip of scotch."

"Let me clean up for you a bit and put the leftover food away, Mrs. McClaskey."

"My heavens, no. Jenna, just leave it there. I'll take care of it all later. And, dear? Honestly, I want you to call me Colleen."

Jenna nodded. "On one condition."

Mrs. McClaskey bristled the smallest bit. "And that would be?"

"You let us," Jen gave Larry a meaningful glance, "both of us, help you clean up before the end of the evening."

"Oh, go on," came with the smile and wave of a hand, and Mrs. McClaskey led them into the other room where the bottle and three glasses waited on a silver serving tray.

Marvin stood in the corner and watched the three of them abandon what was left of his favorite meal. He couldn't decide if he wanted to follow them and filch a glass of scotch, or stay and eat. His hunger got the better of him, and he piled everything onto one platter, leaned against the edge of the archway as he devoured the food, and listened to the chatter.

"Now, you never told me how the golf outing went this morning. Did you enjoy it, dear?"

Larry scowled at Jenna. "We missed our original tee time." Then a smile broke across his face. "But she's almost a natural."

"I wouldn't say that."

Marvin's ears pricked up. "You golfed? Since when do you golf?" He shoved the last bite of corned beef into his mouth, put the platter on the table next to his can of beer, moved into the other room, and sat on the couch next to Larry.

"Shooting under one-hundred on a par seventy-two course your first time out, that's pretty damned good, if you ask me," Larry stated.

"Why did you miss your tee-off, if you don't mind

me asking?"

"Well, Mrs.—Colleen," Larry corrected himself as the scowl returned to his face, "it seems Jenna felt she *had* to go into the office."

Marvin laughed. "You may as well get used to it because that's not about to change any time soon."

"I had to make some changes on the Pratt brief. Robb needs it for court first thing Monday morning. What was I supposed to do?" Jenna asked in defiance.

"Robb has a whole pool of paralegals at his beck and call."

Jenna opened her mouth to make a retort but was interrupted before she could utter a single word.

"Now, now, it's water under the bridge, as we used to say. There's no need to argue about it now." Mrs. McClaskey sighed softly.

Marv chuckled. "Damn. I was enjoying that. You should've let them keep going. Maybe this creep would back off a bit."

"My, how things have changed since my day," Colleen continued. "But, I realize it's important for young ladies to be able to support themselves. Just think, what would have happened, where our girl would be right now, if she wasn't capable of supporting herself. Besides, Jenna, didn't you just tell me something about a promotion?"

Larry turned to a smiling Jenna. "Really? How come I didn't hear anything about this?"

"Because JoAnne didn't want anyone to know. Evidently, Robb said if the brief is good enough to convince the judge to allow this new evidence, I become the newest paralegal in the firm."

Marv sat stunned, his mouth hanging open. "Holy

shit. No kidding. I think that deserves a toast." With the focus on Jenna, he quickly pulled a glass through the door of the corner china cabinet and poured a good amount of scotch. The only evidence of his pilfering was a barely detectable sloshing of the amber liquid after he set the bottle back onto the tray.

"That's terrific. And the income to go along with the new title?"

Jenna beamed. "As far as I know."

"Well, this calls for a toast." Larry held his glass up and waited. The three clicked the tumblers together and held them in place. Other than a slight tingling in Larry's left side he blamed on his golf swing, they didn't know Marvin's glass was right up there with theirs. "To our brightest star. Congratulations."

Mrs. McClaskey stopped short of drinking. "And a Happy Birthday to Marvin. Wherever you are right now, I hope it's a good place."

Jenna flinched.

Larry shot her a quick look. "Is this his birthday? Was all this for *him*?"

Jenna nodded and tried to prepare for Larry's poor reaction.

Mrs. McClaskey put a hand to her mouth. "Oh, dear. I'm afraid I just let the cat out of the bag, so to speak." She looked at Jenna. "I'm sorry, dear. I'm such a fool of an old woman."

Marvin smiled and hoisted his glass toward Jenna. "You remembered! Just like Nancy said you would. And you two did this for me? I hoped when I saw my favorite meal, but...thank you." He leaned into Jen, kissed her on the cheek, and hoped Larry would stomp out in anger.

Jenna looked at the floor and rubbed a hand against her cheek to brush away the stray hair that had tickled her face.

Larry frowned for a split second and quickly recovered in a smile. "No. You know what, I think it's great. It's nice you remembered him. You should. He was a big part of your life for a long time, and I hope you'd do the same for me if the situation were reversed." He raised his glass and waited for them. "Happy birthday, Marvin."

"Son of a bitch." Marv lowered his glass to his side. The three raised the toast to Marv while he glowered and then turned to Jenna. "I don't believe this. He's actually a nice guy? Dammit. Well, don't think for a minute I'm willing to let this go on."

"Come on, Larry. It's getting late. Let's help Mrs.—Colleen—clean up, and then we should be going."

"Now, there's no need to rush out of here. Honestly. I enjoy the company."

"I know it's still fairly early, but I've had a long day. I'm afraid if I don't get to bed soon, I'll nod off right here." Jenna moved directly into the kitchen and stood in front of the cupboards. "Where will I find containers for the leftovers?"

"What leftovers?"

"Come on, Larry, don't eat that stuff just because it's there. Let Colleen have it for her lunch tomorrow."

"Now, Jenna, don't chastise him. He's a growing young man, and I'm glad he liked it."

"Jen, hon, I'm not eating a thing. I'm saying it's all gone."

"Hey! Don't call her Jen," Marv threatened.

"That's what I called her. And you certainly may *not* call her 'hon.' Keep it up, buddy, and I might take you right along with her."

Jenna walked into the dining room and stared at the empty dishes. She gave Larry a questioning look and noticed the beer can on the corner of table. "Now, where the heck did that come from?"

"Oh, crap." Marvin snatched the can from the table, and it disappeared from sight.

Jenna shook her head and mumbled. "Maybe I'm more tired than I realized."

"Why do you say that, dear?" Colleen asked, gathering the dirty dishes.

"I could've sworn there was still food left and…for an instant, I swear I saw a beer can on the table. I must be seeing things."

"A beer? God, you *are* tired. I better get you home and into bed fast." Larry winked at her and Jenna smiled.

"I don't think so." Marvin threw a punch that swiped right through the left side of Larry's face.

Larry flinched and a strange look came into his eyes. "Unh." He rubbed his temple. "Damn. What the hell was that?"

Jenna turned to him, concern in her voice. "What? What's wrong?"

"I don't know. It's… There was just this odd tightness, a tingling. Just for a second. I'm fine now."

"Oh, my. Perhaps you better sit down. Go sit in the living room. Jenna and I will have this cleared in a jiffy, and then we'll be in to join you. We can have a final night cap before I send you two scurrying across the hall."

"No, I'm...I'll be fine. Really."

Marv took another swing, this time into the solar plexus.

"Oof." Larry pressed a fist to the sudden tightness in his chest and walked out of the room. "You know maybe I will sit for a minute."

Jenna scurried after him. "Larry, are you okay? Should we go now?"

"No. No, I'll be...I don't know what the deal is. Maybe it's indigestion. Go help Colleen clean up, I'll be fine. Really."

Marvin glowered in front of Larry. "You won't be fine if you keep it up. I should plant a foot in your ass. Or, better yet, right in the nuts. That'd knock the wood right out of your dick in a hurry, wouldn't it?"

Jenna studied Larry for a minute. "You're not faking to get out of—" She peered at the sweat beaded across his brow, muttered "never mind," and went to the kitchen.

"Listen up, you schmuck," Marvin said. "I might be stuck over here, but it doesn't mean I've left her. I'm gonna warn you right now, don't get attached. I'm not leaving her there with you. She belongs with me, and that's exactly what's gonna happen." He poked a finger in Larry's direction and mumbled, "As soon as I figure out how."

Chapter 33

At the deli, Tommy handed Marv his coffee, and they slid into the booth in their usual spots with Tommy and Mike across from Marvin. The smile on Marv's face should've told them everything they needed to know, but Tommy asked anyway. "So, how was Jenna last night?"

"Fine. Fine." Marv took a sip of coffee and grinned.

"Come on, Brody, spill it. What's with the grin? You look like the proverbial cat."

"Yeah, dude. You look like you've been to Wonderland with Alice."

Marv laughed. "They had a birthday party for me. Can you believe it?"

"Who had a party?"

"Jenna, the old lady, and," Marv frowned, "the guy Jenna's been dating from the law firm."

"Seriously?" Mike asked. "The guy was part of the celebration?"

"Yeah, but I don't think he knew it from the get-go. The old lady slipped. I noticed a quick look on the guy's face, but he recovered quite nicely. He raised his glass and wished me a happy birthday. The schmuck."

"Brody, come on. I think that was nice of him."

"Oh, get real, Mike. The guy's just trying to get into her pants. He'll do whatever it takes, but I'm not about to let that happen. I knocked the wind out of his sails."

Tommy scowled at him. "Marvin, what did you do?"

"Ah…nothing brutal." Marv looked into his cup. "I punched him in the face. Once."

"And?"

"And nothing. He rubbed his temple a bit, and he was fine." Marvin shrugged and took a swig of coffee without looking at either one of his inquisitors.

"Brody."

"*What?*"

"You're not telling us everything." Mike prodded.

Marv stalled. Tommy *had* said they'd help. "Well, okay…so, I sucker-punched him, too. Big deal."

Mike and Tommy laughed, leaving Marvin to glare at them in defiance.

"Dude, how do you sucker-punch one of *them*? I mean, he couldn't see the fake."

"I guess you got a point." Marv's knitted brow smoothed. "But I landed one right above the diaphragm. And told him I'd kick him in the balls if he didn't knock it the hell off."

"You still got it bad for her, don't you?" Mike asked.

Tommy sang, "I got it bad and that ain't good…" He stopped but smiled anyway when Marvin kicked his shin under the table. "Ow! Not cool."

Marvin's mood brightened again. "But you should've seen the spread they put out. Corned beef, knishes, green beans with almond slivers. And Jenna broke out the scotch for the toast."

"This was at your place, then?"

"No, across the hall at the old lady's. Oh, and get this, Jen's taken up golf. At first I figured it was because of this guy, Larry, but then the old woman lets it slip Jen might have a promotion coming." Marv paused for a second. "Maybe all the long hours she put in over the years are gonna pay off, so I figure the golfing is a way to schmooze with the partners."

"And this Larry guy didn't know about it?"

"Guess not, Mike."

"Well, that's good then, right? I mean, if she was at all serious about him, she'd have told him, don't you think?"

"Yeah. Tommy has a point there."

Marvin decided it shouldn't change his plans. As far as he could figure it, Jenna belonged with him, plain and simple, and he was determined to go through with things; however that could be accomplished. "Yeah, and so? It doesn't change a thing."

"Well then, let's get on with it. I, for one, am sick of watching your tired ass mope around moaning over this woman. So, let's get a plan together here and do it."

Marvin looked at Tommy in surprise and then turned to Mike with a silent question.

After Mike studied Marvin for a minute, and a quick glance to Tommy, he nodded. "Okay, I'm in."

A loud sigh of relief escaped from Marv, and he smiled. He hadn't been sure they would actually carry out the promise they'd made while basking in the afterglow of the cruise. Now, he just needed to get them to help him figure out how to accomplish it.

"So then Brody, how do you want to do this?" Mike asked.

Marv shrugged. "I don't know."

Tommy ticked off the failed attempts on his fingers as he recounted them. "Okay, let's look at this. You tried pushing her off the balcony—which I found to be very funny, because, man, you should've *known* you'd go right through her. Then, like a real dumb-ass—"

"I'm new at this. What do I know?"

"—you tried to grab her and take her over with you," Tommy continued. "*That* didn't work for the same reason. What else have you tried?"

"There was the gun episode," Mike offered with a snicker.

"Oh, yeah. Right. The gun episode; where you shot yourself instead of her. And let's not forget the night in the restaurant when you tried to stab her. Dude, your batting average is not good so far."

"So, hire Jen's law firm and sue me. What d'ya want from me? I don't know how all this being dead thing works."

Tommy chuckled. "You know, it gets tiresome trying to teach this shit. I swear I should put a handbook together for newbies. I'll steal your phrase, Marvin, and call it The Handbook for Deadheads."

"Terrific. Start on it when Jenna's with us; she can do your typing," Marvin said in droll response.

"Look, we need to think linear here. There are certain things, like pushing or stabbing, that won't work. I'm not in favor of guns, dudes, for obvious reasons. But tell me this: where did the bullet end up?"

"I have no idea. I got the hell out of there when the gun fired and the window busted."

"Well, contrary to what your actions may lead us to believe, it's not lodged in your head."

Tommy laughed at Mike's witticism, but Marv

didn't quite see the humor. "Ha, ha. Very funny, Mike."

"Wait. Brody, didn't you say the window shattered? And that's why you ran out of there?"

"Mmm…yeah."

"No. No guns," Tommy insisted. "I don't like guns."

"I'm not thinking a gun, Tommy. But I might have an idea, something that could work."

Marv waited for Mike to explain, but all Mike did was focus on something out the window. When he couldn't stand the suspense any longer, Marvin prodded for an answer. "Which would be…"

"Let me mull this over a while. I'll let you know tomorrow."

Chapter 34

The phone rang as Jenna put the key in the lock. Marvin walked through her and the door, strode to the living room to stand next to his chair, and waited for her to answer it.

"Hello?"

"Jenna?"

"Yes?"

"Hey, it's David."

"David. I didn't recognize your voice. Hi. How are you?"

"David? My brother, David?" Marvin moved closer to the phone.

"I'm good. I'm good. You?"

"Okay, I guess. Doing a little better, anyway."

"It sounds like you're out of breath. Did I disturb something?" David asked in an insinuating tone.

Jenna laughed good-naturedly. "No. Not at all. I just came in the door."

"Good. It's nice to hear you're doing well."

"And you're calling my fiancée, because..." Marvin wasn't sure he had blood pressure, *but* he thought, *whatever we have, it's rising.* "Ma isn't at the bottom of this, is she?"

"What's been happening? Are your folks all right?"

"Yeah, yeah, they're fine."

With the initial niceties taken care of, Jenna went

to the point. "So, to what do I owe this pleasure?"

"Well...I don't know. I was just thinking about you. Wondering how you were doing. Kinda surprised we hadn't heard from you in a long while."

Jenna picked up on the *we* and realized David had called on his mother's behalf. She listened hard and could tell Madelyn was there, her voice barely discernable in the background. "Oh, David. I'm sorry. Really. I've been so busy at work, which I think just might be paying off."

"Really, how's that?"

"If the judge agrees with the opinion of my latest brief, I get promoted."

"That's terrific. Ma's gonna love hearing that."

Marv laughed. "Yep, I knew it. That woman is like a pit bull. She gets an idea and clamps her jaws down on it; you aren't going anywhere until she's satisfied."

Jenna smiled. "She's actually interested in me now? Why?"

Marv looked at her in disbelief. "I told you months ago. You never listened to a word I said, did you?"

"Oh, you know... She never *didn't* like you."

"Could've fooled me, David. But, anyway..."

"Listen, I'm going to be coming down there next week. Um, can I interest you in a drink, or um, maybe dinner?"

"Dinner? A drink?" Marvin's blood pressure ratcheted up another notch, and he leaned closer into the phone. "You listen to me you little bastard. Brother or no brother, she's not available."

"Did I just hear..." David's voice trailed off.

Jenna rubbed the side of her face to brush at the fly, or the strand of stray hair that had just tickled her cheek. "That'd be nice. Depends on when, though."

"Uh, next Sunday? Maybe a nice brunch?"

"Mmm. No. I can't, I already have plans."

Marv looked at her, surprised. "You have plans? For what?"

"Oh. Well, then, how about an early dinner on Saturday?"

"Well, maybe. I have golf at eleven."

David's voice carried a tone of surprise. "Golf? Really?"

"Yeah. I thought it might help me."

"It'll help you with the job all right. You may not realize it yet, but it's also going reel that creep, Larry, in further," Marvin interjected.

"You know, I never realized how much gets accomplished on a golf course, but Larry, he's one of the lawyers at the firm, took me out for a round yesterday. After we played the front nine, we ran into a foursome from another firm, and by the time they were done talking, they'd settled a case. So, I figured, since he asked again, I might as well add golf to the gamut of skills to help advance my career."

David's laugh contained a hint of naughtiness. "As long as that's all you're doing with him. Maybe I should chaperone."

"Okay, little brother, maybe I changed my mind. I like the sound of that."

Jenna joined David's laughter. "You're beginning to sound like your brother. He—"

Marv bristled at the accusation. "What the hell is *that* supposed to mean?"

"—was always wanting to know where I was going and who I would be with. It got on my nerves at times, but it was kind of sweet too."

"And Sunday is out, huh?" David asked again.

"Well…" Jenna hedged. "Maybe I can back out. But I'd feel really bad doing it. I've neglected the place for so long."

Marvin looked around the condo. "It doesn't look neglected to me. Besides, you still have the girl coming in."

"The shelter has called me and called me since Marv died to ask if I'd come back to volunteer again. I finally said yes." Jen sighed. "Let me think about it, okay?"

David and Marv responded at the same time. If Jenna could've heard Marvin, it would've sounded like stereo in her ears. "Shelter? What shelter?"

"Oh. Didn't Marvin ever tell you?"

"Now how could I tell him something I'd never heard about?" Marvin tilted his head in thought, but quickly shrugged it off. "Maybe I forgot."

"I used to volunteer at a women's shelter. I kinda drifted away when Marv asked me to move in. I don't know, I guess I felt like I should put all my efforts toward him."

"Really? No, he never said a word to me, or the folks. I'm sure of it. Something as important as that, I'd remember."

Marv poked Jenna in the ribs affectionately. "All your efforts toward me? I would've liked to have seen that."

Jen flinched. She looked behind her to see what she'd bumped into and frowned at the kitchen chair she'd passed in the kitchen on the way to the balcony. "Well, either he forgot, or he didn't think it was worth mentioning. But, yeah, I put in quite a few hours over there helping out."

"You sound as if you enjoyed it."

"Mmm," Jen managed to get out as she swallowed a sip of the soda she'd pulled from the refrigerator on her way outside. "I did. I mean it was heartbreaking to listen to some of the things those women went through. Sometimes, I'd be on my way home and think I couldn't do it anymore, you know, listen to the brutalities they put up with before they finally found a way out. But I always went back. How could I not? Some of them were so emotionally scarred they needed to know somebody cared about them."

"That's nice, Jenna. You'll move up at least three or four rungs on Ma's ladder for that one."

This was a Jen Marv hadn't met. She sounded soft and vulnerable and caring to a fault. And while he found concern for others commendable, it sure didn't remind him of the girl he met in the bar and found irresistible. He'd seen her from across the room and couldn't stop staring. Besides being beautiful, she looked so put together, so confident in the way she perched on the bar stool and the way he saw her interact with the bartender. He'd finally walked up to her and abruptly asked for her phone number without even a simple introduction.

She'd stared him down without effort, and said, "You're one ballsy son-of-a-bitch," and turned away. He knew in that instant, here was a woman who could hold her own, a woman who could see right through the bullshit, call a spade a spade, take as much in stride as she gave out; he was hooked. He ignored the group of guys he'd walked in with and spent the rest of the night trading barbs with her and fell in love.

Jen let loose a sardonic laugh. "Marv's gone, David. He's not coming back. Tell Madelyn, if she's not close enough to the phone to hear it, she should've thought about her level of appreciation for me while he was still alive."

A broad smile spread over Marv's face. "Now *that's* my girl."

David met the comment with a short silence. "Well, anyway, um… So, where were we?"

"Next Sunday."

"Right. So, uh, I can call later in the week? Maybe you'll change your mind?"

"Sure. I'll let you know what my schedule is then."

David's voice pitched lower and sounded as if he'd stepped into a tunnel. "No, Jen, really. This is *me* asking now. I'd really like to see you."

Jenna lightened her tone. "In that case, I'd be happy to meet you for coffee."

Chapter 35

In the hotel suite, Marvin kept fidgeting in his chair. It grated on Mike's nerves until he couldn't handle it. "Brody, what the hell is bugging you this morning?"

"David."

"David who?"

"David. David. Remember my brother, David? *That* David."

"Okay, okay. Holy shit, man. You don't have to bite my head off. What's the problem?"

"I think he's actually interested in Jenna."

"And this is a problem because…"

"Because it's not right. He's my little brother. It's freaky. And I can't believe he doesn't think that. My mother is the real problem."

"Um, I thought you just said David—"

"I did. But this has my mother written all over it. I'll bet she's nagged him until she's convinced him it's his idea."

"What's your mother's idea?"

"Jenna and David. I told you guys at the cemetery. You didn't believe me, or you weren't listening."

"Well, look, Brody…It's not all bad. I mean, she'd stay a part of the family. You'd know she was being taken care of."

"She's gonna be taken care of all right. So is that

little schmuck of a brother."

"Come on, calm down. You're gonna wake Tommy. Besides, you know how he hates seeing you all worked up."

Marvin took a deep breath. "Well…shit. I'm sorry, but I can't help it."

"So, what do you want to do about it?"

Tommy yawned and stretched on his way out of the bedroom to the coffee pot. "Geez, you couldn't hold it down a little? You have to be loud enough to wake the dead?"

"Sorry, hippie. I didn't mean to wake you. I just got a little worked up."

" 'A little worked up.' Marvin, you never get just a little worked up. I heard Mike ask what you wanted to do about something. What's the problem now?"

"Oh, he's upset. He thinks his brother has the hots for Jenna," Mike interjected.

"Not a chance, dude. No way. Ain't gonna happen."

Marvin's brow scrunched. "What makes you so sure?"

"Marvin. Listen to your Uncle Tommy. She's not interested in him."

"What, you have some kind of crystal ball now?"

"Yeah, Marvin, I've got a crystal ball all right. In fact I got two of 'em." Tommy grabbed his crotch. "Right here."

"Very funny, ya schmuck. Go put some pants on."

Mike rolled his eyes. "Oh, jeez. Are we back on that kick again? Come on, Brody. Every time you get a bug up your ass, your attitude sucks. You know that?"

Tommy plopped down on the couch opposite

Marvin. "Eh, give him a break, Mike. He's upset right now."

"Yeah, give me a break," Marv sneered.

"I'll give you a break all right. Snap out of it, or I'm going to break your head." Mike slapped the air for effect.

"Now, boys. Don't fight. It's not nice. Besides, I'm not awake enough yet to come over there and give you both a hug. Do I need to give you hugs?" Tommy put his cup on the coffee table and went to get up off the couch.

Marv covered his eyes in mock horror and laughed in spite of his foul mood. "Jesus H. Christ. Anything but that right now."

Tommy sat back down. "I thought so. Now, what can we do to calm your little self?"

"I don't know... I need to convince the little squirt to stay away from her. Besides, if we're successful in...well, you know, he'll be hurt and I don't wanna see my little brother get hurt."

They sat in silence for a few minutes until Mike spoke up. "Okay, so what do you suggest?"

Tommy, who had been staring out the window, turned his gaze to Marvin. "We could pay him a visit."

"And do what?"

"I don't know. Mess with him. Go all *Shining* on him." Tommy gave him a sinister smile.

"What the hell is that?"

"*The Shining*? Stephen King? Book, movie..." Mike chimed in.

"I know that, Mike. I'm not a complete ignoramus."

"Well, remember how messages were written in

red on the walls and the mirror? We could do that," Tommy suggested.

"I don't want to give him a heart attack."

"Dude, I'm just tossing things out here."

"What else you got rattling around in that head of yours?"

"Just some harmless fun." Tommy got off the couch and headed for the bedroom to dress.

Three hours later, the three sat in the living room of David's small apartment waiting for him to wake up. Tommy snickered when he saw David sauntering out from the bedroom.

Marvin stood up and his mouth engaged before his brain could remind him he was attempting to communicate with someone still among the living. "For cryin' out loud, David, go put some shorts on. Don't you know you've got company?"

Mike and Tommy no longer bothered to mention his outbursts to the living and allowed it to pass.

David stretched and yawned on his way through the room. At the archway to the kitchen, he stopped and sniffed the air. He turned around to face them. "You're here, aren't you Marv? I smell your cologne."

"He knows we're here?" Marvin asked Tommy and Mike, who sat on the couch.

Mike shrugged. "Maybe he does, Brody. I think some folks are more in tune than others."

"What do you want, Marvin?"

"Seriously?"

Marvin had directed the question to Mike, but it was David who answered. "Seriously." He paused and took in another sample of the air. "Is someone with you? I smell…"

Tommy whistled. "Whoa. I think he really does know. This is far out."

"If he thought he wasn't alone, wouldn't he put some pants on or something," Mike asked and waved a hand toward the naked David. "I mean, *I'd* never parade around like that."

Marvin laughed. "Yeah, right. You two got your own nudist colony going on over there at the hotel. Besides, he's my kid brother. We shared a room until I left for college. What's he got I haven't seen before? What's he gonna *do* I haven't seen before, if you get my drift."

David cocked an ear and an inquisitive look toward the sound, then went into the kitchen. He returned with a glass of iced tea and plopped down into a chair. "Ma's really pissed off, you know. About the insurance money? She thinks Jenna conned you into it."

"What, if you know I'm here ya little bastard, you can't offer your brother a beer?" David didn't answer. "Ah, forget it. I'll help myself. You guys want anything?"

"I'll take a beer, dude."

"Brody, if there's any soda…"

"Coming right up." Marvin went into the kitchen.

"Anyway, it's not helping my cause, you know what I mean, bro? I mean, how can I ever get Ma to accept her, if she keeps thinking Jen's nothing but a piker?"

Marvin didn't believe his brother really knew they were there. He figured David was just talking to the air, trying to clear his own conscience, so he wouldn't feel guilty. He brought the cans to the living room and passed them around. When the tabs were popped,

David's head tilted toward the sound.

"Christ almighty, Marvin, how many beers are you going to drink at once?"

"You little shit. You really do know we're here, don't you?"

"You do have friends with you, don't you? And you let me walk around swinging in the breeze?" David asked, though he didn't move other than to tilt his head and lean forward to sniff the air again. "Eh, we're all guys so I guess it doesn't matter."

"Can you hear me David?" Marvin asked in amazement.

"Anyway, you're probably upset that I'm thinking of…dating Jen, I guess you'd call it. But, I swear Marvin…"

"I guess not," Tommy interjected to David's commentary.

"…it's Ma's idea. You know that, right?"

"I don't care whose idea it is, I don't like it."

"And Jenna—she's, well… At first I didn't think it was cool, you know? Moving in on my dead brother's territory. But it would get Ma off my back. You know how she can be…"

"I put up with her nonsense for twenty-three years until I moved to Dayton. So yeah, I think I know. But, I'm beginning to think it's not Ma at all," Marvin said, his anger rising again.

"But, you don't have to get your Jockey's in a bunch. 'Cause, even if I *was* serious about it, I don't think it would last very long."

"You don't know how right you are, except not for the reasons you're thinking."

"After talking with her on the phone last night, I

don't think I'm really her type. So, you guys don't have to get all *Paranormal Activity* on me, you know? Anyway, I'm sorry Marvin. Hang on a second." David stood and walked to the bedroom.

Tommy let out a soft whistle. "This is weird. I've never had one of them carry on a conversation like this. Your brother's...strange."

"Don't you be dissin' on my little brother, hippie. He's a good kid."

"Dude, I was just sayin'—"

"Well, don't." Marvin pointed a finger at Tommy. "Besides, I think—"

"—if you'd let me finish, I'm *sayin'* it's strange because when *they* can hear *us*, they hear all of us. But, it seems like he can only hear you, and just bits and pieces at that."

"Oh. Well..."

David came back carrying the baseballs. "Thanks for these."

Marvin's shoulders slumped. "Ah, Jesus H. She gave 'em to *you*? Here I thought she sold them. Jeez, what an asshole I was."

"It kinda helps to, you know... I'm sorry you died 'cause I miss you. Whenever I thought I needed someone to talk to, you'd always be my go-to guy. But...I think...now I talk to these. Or Jen, if she'll answer the phone." David shrugged and sank into the chair again. "Oh, Ma's got your diploma by the way. It's hanging on the dining room wall, right next to mine."

Marv walked over, put a hand on David's head, and scruffed his hair like he used to do when they were kids and he was about to leave for a date. "Look, kid, you hang in there. Things'll be…okay." Marv turned to leave. "Come on you two. Let's get out of here."

David smiled and ran his hands through his hair. "Oh, Marv?"

Marvin paused. "Yeah?"

"Thanks for coming by."

"Sure thing, kiddo. Be good."

"Marvin, is that you in there?" Tommy asked after they'd walked through the wall onto the street.

"What d'ya mean is it *me* in there? Of course it's me, ya schmuck." Marvin slapped Tommy on the back of the head.

Tommy grinned. "Yeah, it's you. Just checking."

Marvin smiled and put an arm around Tommy's shoulder. They headed for the bus stop with Mike following close behind. "Come on, hippie. Let's go figure out how to do this."

"About that," Mike said. "Didn't you say she's golfing this weekend?"

Marv turned to look at him. "Yeah. Why?"

"I hear that can be a pretty dangerous sport." Mike raised his brows.

"*Golf?*"

"Oh, dude, you'd be surprised how many folks have died on a golf course." Tommy deliberately failed to mention he knew the bulk of those deaths to be caused by heart attacks and lightning strikes.

Chapter 36

Tommy, Mike, and Marvin followed Larry and Jenna around the golf course. At first the pranks were harmless. They slipped clubs from the bags and put them back, and kicked balls off the tees. On the third hole, Marv took all the extra balls from Jenna's golf bag and passed them off to Tommy "for later."

On the fifth hole, as Larry swung his club, right before the moment of impact, Mike snatched the ball off the tee. It winked out of sight, and the club drove right through him. "Ow. Dammit," Mike swore and rubbed his head. Tommy and Marv went into fits of laughter.

"Smooth move, ExLax," Tommy taunted him.

Mike smiled and flipped him the bird. "Note to self: Do not do that from the same side of the ball as the golfer."

Both Larry and Jenna shaded their eyes and peered out along the fairway to watch the drive and the eventual drop to land. While they searched the empty air over the fairway, Mike put the ball back on its tee.

"Where is it? I don't see it."

"I *know* I didn't slice it."

"Well, balls don't just disappear into the ozone, Larry. Face it, you sliced it. Just hit another one. Don't worry, I'll give you a bye so the stroke doesn't count."

Larry returned to his golf bag and wrested another

ball from a pouch in the shape of a scrotum with "It Takes Balls to Golf" printed on it. He turned to place it on the tee and stopped in mid-bend. "What the…"

The guys—especially Tommy, who really enjoyed this kind of thing—cracked up at the confused look of self-doubt spread over Larry's face.

Jenna didn't intend to be unsportsmanlike or bruise his fragile ego, but stood with a smirk on her face. "Looks like you swiped air."

Larry's demeanor turned sour. "I've been golfing for fifteen years. I do not swipe air."

"Sorry. But, you definitely swung the club and there's the ball, sitting on the tee, right where you placed it."

"Well, I don't get it. But, fine." Larry put the extra ball into his pocket, addressed the one on his tee, and swung again. Two-hundred and twenty-four yards out, it dropped onto the green and rolled to within four feet of the cup. "There." He turned to Jenna with an I-told-you-so look and a challenging smile. "Top that."

Jenna rolled her eyes at his little outburst. She fought the urge to compare Larry to Marvin, but she figured comparisons would be an inevitable process of reentering the dating scene after such a long relationship and pushed the idea aside. She placed her tee and ball without a word, addressed the swing, and momentarily glanced over her shoulder to Larry. "Oh, by the way, no byes on air." She swung.

"Holy *shit*. Did you see that." Marv asked after they'd all watched her ball float through the air, drop to the green and roll into the cup. "How does she *do that*? It's like everything she tries, she's good at. No practice, no nothin', she just goes out and does it."

Jenna turned to Larry with a smug smile. "How's that? That good enough for you? Does that top yours?" she asked and headed down the fairway to the green, pulling her bag cart behind her.

Larry followed silently mouthing her words in a fit of boyish petulance.

Marvin laughed. "See? Now *this* is the Jen I really miss."

"Hey, Brody," Mike called from the opposite side of the tee box, "maybe she'll give us all lessons. We can offer to finish the round with her."

"Yeah, far out. I think I might enjoy this."

"Oh, come on, hippie, since when do you care about anything that doesn't act, sing, or dance?"

Tommy put his hands on his hips and scowled. "Marvin, that was uncalled for. Just because I prefer movies and stuff over watching a bunch of guys beat each other up trying to move a hunk of pigskin down a long, white-striped field is no reason to dis me, bro."

Marv and Mike laughed at Tommy's stance and the delivery. Marvin walked to him, hung an arm around his shoulders, and gave him a noogie on the top of his head. "I'm just teasing ya, ya schmuck. You might get stuck in the pot-headed sixties once in a while, but I love you. You know that?"

"Dude…you touch your Uncle Tommy's heart. You really do." Tommy broke into a smile and wiped a false tear from his eyes. "You like me, you really like me."

Marv gave him a playful punch in the arm. "All right Sally Field, let's get on with this."

Mike and Tommy both stood with stunned expressions for a minute.

"What?"

"You actually recognized that?"

"I'm not a total spaz, Mike. I've been known to read about pop-culture like the Oscars from time to time."

"Son-of-a-bitch. There's hope for you yet, Brody."

Tommy pulled a golf ball from his pocket and tossed it to Mike. "Here, let's see how far you can throw one of these."

Mike yelled, "Fore!"

Only a few deadheads on an opposite fairway of the course cocked an ear toward the sound of his voice. The ball sailed through the air and smacked Larry in the buttocks.

"Ow. What the fuck?" Larry turned to look back toward the tee box but saw no one to cuss out for the offense.

"What? What's wrong? What happened?" Jenna ran to Larry. "Did you get stung by something?"

"No. Some nut job just drove a ball into my ass."

Jenna laughed. "Well, at least he didn't drive it *up* your ass. Come on, tap your putt and let's go."

"Very funny, Jen. It hurts like hell." Larry grabbed the offending ball and limped toward the green while he continued to glance around the course for the guilty party.

Jenna rolled her eyes. "It looks as if you'll live, big boy."

"Not bad, Mike. But your aim is a little off, don't ya think?"

"If you can do better Brody, go for it. Didn't you play ball in high school?"

"Toss one here, Tommy." Marvin studied the

distance and strode down the fairway. At the approximate yardage between a pitcher's mound and home plate, he wound up and heaved. Jenna bent down to retrieve her golf ball from the cup at the exact moment the ball soared past her head and rustled strands of hair out of place. "Shit."

"Ah… The timing was off just a hair. Try it again." Tommy pulled another ball from his pocket. "Here's another one."

Larry hollered as he spun around toward the tee. "You sons of bitches. What the hell is going on?"

Jenna stood up, swiped at the errant lock, and pocketed her ball. "What are you going on about?"

"Don't tell me you didn't notice that. A ball just whizzed past your head. If you hadn't bent down, the guy would've clocked you a good one." Larry spun in a complete circle. "I can't figure out where they're coming from. Do you see anyone?"

Jenna looked back toward the tee box at emptiness. "I don't see anyone within range. Maybe someone's got a wicked slice," she suggested and turned with a shrug to scan the opposite fairways.

Neither she nor Larry reacted to the old man who stood next to the bench under a nearby tree, who shook his head in disappointment.

Marvin caught the toss from Tommy. As he measured the distance required Marv thought he recognized the old guy as the homeless man he'd seen before. Dismissing it as unimportant, he wound up and pitched in one fluid motion. This time he came much closer to the mark, but Larry stepped in front of Jenna and took the hit to his left shoulder blade and went down with a loud grunt.

"What?" Jenna turned to look down at him "Oh, please. Is it your bruised ass, or a bruised ego?" She let out a chuckle Larry cut short.

"Ha, ha. Very fuckin' funny."

Concern tinged her voice. "Wait, did you get hit again?"

"God damn it. Whoever this asshole is…" Larry sat up and tried to rub the area. "Ow. Mother*fucker*, that hurts."

"Are you all right? What the hell is going on?" Jen helped Larry get up off the ground and steadied him. She took another look around the course. "Here, come on." She wrapped an arm around his waist to support him. "There's a bench over there near the next tee. You better sit for a couple minutes."

Determined to succeed, Marvin strode to the golf bags left forgotten at the side of the green. He pulled the five wood and a ball from Larry's bag. The ball popped into view of the living as he tossed it a few feet into the air, then it dropped toward the ground and went flying. Before they reached the bench, it cracked Jenna in the back of the head. She crumpled to the ground, and with the sudden lack of support, Larry fell next to her.

Marvin let out a whoop in celebration and ran toward Jenna. He stopped short, confused when he didn't see her get up the way *he* had after the bus hit him. The three deadheads stood in silence. They watched and listened.

"Jen? Jenna?? Oh my God. Where's my phone? Where's my *fucking* cell phone goddammit." Larry frantically searched his body before he rolled the unconscious Jenna enough to get a grip on her phone and yanked it off the waistband of her pants. He looked around the area for the culprits. "Bastards. Whoever you are, you motherfuckers…" He dialed, placed the phone in speaker mode, and dropped it onto Jenna's chest while he tried to rouse her.

"911, what is your emergency?"

"I need an ambulance at the Civic Golf Course. Near the fifth hole green…"

"Has someone been injured?"

"Yeah, my girlfriend's been hit in the head by a ball…

"Is she breathing? Is there a pulse?"

"Uh, let me check…Yeah. On…both counts."

"Okay, sir. Paramedics have been dispatched, the station is close, and they'll be there in a couple minutes."

"Thank you."

"Sir? I need you to stay on the line with me, okay?"

Jenna stirred and moaned.

"Jen? Jenna."

"Sir, are you with me?"

"Yes. She's…I don't know, she's moaning."

"Don't move her. Do not allow her to sit up."

"Uh, okay. Why?"

"Sir, just follow my instructions until the unit arrives. Can you do that for me?"

"Yes. I'm following your fucking instructions."

"I need you to calm down, sir."

"Oh, Jesus…I see blood. Tell them to hurry."

"They should be coming down the fairway any minute now. Can you see them?"

Everyone, the small group of deadheads that had

gathered around included, turned toward the faint wail of the siren and saw the course ranger on a golf cart headed toward the commotion. Marvin moved closer in an attempt to see exactly how much Jenna might be bleeding.

An elbow nudged Mike. "What happened? Guy clobber her wit da club?"

"What club?"

"Dat one, on da ground dere."

"I don't think so. She got smacked in the head with that." Mike pointed to the ball lying next to Jenna.

The man clicked his tongue, looked in Marvin's direction, shook his head and muttered, "I done tol' him. It ain't right for a youngun like him to be doin' dis kina thang. We's gon' hafta think 'bout what to do wit dis one."

"I think I hear the siren," Larry told the operator.

"Okay, they'll take care of her. I'm going to hang up now, okay?

"Uh, yeah." Larry flipped the phone closed and ended the call.

Mike turned to the old man and asked, "Do what about who?"

"Who're you talking to?"

Mike turned to Tommy. "That old guy over there. Have you seen him before?"

"Who?"

"The one across the fairway, over there." Mike pointed to empty space. "Huh. Guess he's gone. Strange old geezer."

"Why? What was strange about him?"

"If he wasn't a deadhead, you'd think he's a homeless person by the looks of him. But more than that, I'd say there's something about his eyes. Kind of mesmerizing. Oh, well." He shook his head, and they turned their attention back to the paramedics who were about to lift a semi-conscious Jenna onto the stretcher.

"On three. One. Two. Three."

"Can I ride along?"

"And you would be?"

"Boyfriend."

"Boyfriend my ass," Marv corrected.

The inquisitive expression on the medic's face turned sour, and he opened his mouth to speak when Larry blurted, "Co-worker; colleague. Call me whatever you want. Look, she doesn't *have* anyone else, okay."

Marv, incensed by the comment, lunged at him. "I beg your pardon? She's got me, you son-of-a-bitch. If anyone's going, it's me."

Tommy stopped Marvin from throwing a punch. "Marvin! No. Dude, let him go."

"Yeah, come on Brody. It's better if we grab a bus," Mike suggested.

"Why? Why can't we just hitch along in the back of the ambulance?"

Tommy shook his head. "Too crowded. They'd just be bumping through us the entire trip."

The paramedics loaded Jenna into the back. Larry scrambled in, and the ambulance drove slowly along the cart path.

Marvin figured if Jenna was bleeding a lot, maybe if he got lucky, she'd be done for by the time they reached the hospital. Then an idea came to him. "What if she dies on the way there? I mean, how will we find her?"

"Brody has a point, Tommy."

Tommy studied the back end of the ambulance for a moment. "I really don't think you're gonna have to worry about it, Marvin. 'Cause, something tells me you missed your mark again."

"Wait a minute. If she dies, wouldn't she just go home? I mean, that's what I did." Mike glanced at them in turn.

Tommy shrugged. "Probably. But," he looked to Marvin, "if you insist, I see a rear bumper and door handles to hang onto. And side running boards."

The three deadheads exchanged quick glances and ran for the ambulance. Marvin and Mike jumped onto the back bumper and held on using the door handles. Tommy leaped to the passenger running board and grabbed onto the side-view mirror bracket.

The ambulance approached the exit and slowed to check traffic. The driver looked to his right. "Huh. That's weird."

"What?" came the response from the medic in the back of the truck.

"The support bar for the mirror over there is gone."

"You mean the mirror's gone?"

"No, the mirror is there."

"What?"

"Looks like the thing is just hanging there in midair."

"That's impossible."

The vehicle stopped, and the driver turned around in his seat. "Man, I'm telling you. Look for yourself."

Tommy took the opportunity of the temporary stop to remove his hands while the medic in the back maneuvered to get a good view.

"See? I told—"

The medic chuckled. "Danny, either you're working too many shifts, or we need to check the med supplies. Go."

Danny gave his coworker the middle finger, flipped the switch for the siren, and punched the gas pedal.

Tommy almost fell off as the ambulance lurched forward and grabbed for the bar. "Whoo-hoo! This is gonna be a fun ride. Better than Montezuma's Revenge at Knott's Berry Farm."

"What the hell is that?" Marv bellowed, in hopes Tommy would hear him, but Mike hollered in answer.

"One *mean* mother of a roller coaster at an amusement park in California. We'll have to take you some day, Brody."

"I'll pass, thanks."

"Aw. Where's your sense of adventure?"

Marv increased his white-knuckle grip on the door handle. "My adventure is hanging on for dear life right now."

Tommy and Mike burst into their infectious laughter and waved to deadheads who turned toward the loud whoops of excitement as the ambulance passed by.

Chapter 37

Exhilarated from the ride, Tommy and Mike jumped from their perches at the hospital.

"Whoo! Far out, man. That was so groovy I might have to do it again just for fun. What a ride."

Though he laughed at the exuberance, Mike gave him a look of warning. "Hey, what did I say on the cruise about those words?"

"Sorry. I couldn't help it. But, if I recall, you lost that tussle." Tommy winked at him.

"Tommy, my friend, you are one weird-ass kid, you know that?" Marvin struggled to gain enough equilibrium to make his way to the curb and sit while the EMTs wheeled Jenna into the emergency room with Larry limping along behind the gurney.

"Sorry, Marvin. But I got you here, didn't I?"

"Barely in one piece," Marv growled. "What if I'd fallen off?"

"Oh, my God, you think you might have been killed?" Mike gasped in mock horror, then shook his head. "Lighten up, Brody."

Inside, Jenna was transferred to a bed, and the curtain pulled closed around it.

A triage nurse, dressed in green scrubs, stethoscope hanging into her cleavage, and a name tag that read Peggy Mercyman, R.N., approached. "What do we have, Danny?"

"Eh, small laceration on the back of the head, bleeding heavy."

Peggy shrugged. "Typical for a head wound."

"She got her bells rung with a golf ball."

"A golf ball cut through the scalp?"

"I doubt it. I saw a rock sticking out of the ground behind her head when we moved her. Probably hit her head on that."

"Thanks." Peggy waved a hand signal at one of the interns to begin a standard evaluation. "So, how's your day been? It's been pretty quiet in here."

"First call of the day for us." Danny eyed the disappearing end of the stethoscope. "This was an easy break from the boredom."

"You working all day?"

"'Til seven tonight, why?" He glanced down at her cleavage again.

"Care for a quick bite after?" She paused for effect. "You never know what could come up between us."

Danny wanted to grab her right there. He'd had a thing for this one since he transferred to this area of town. He smiled but pretended a modicum of disinterest. "Sure. How's Mr. C's sound?"

Peggy nodded. "Okay. I'll be waiting."

The intern emerged from behind the curtain, signaled to Peggy to follow, and headed for the nurses' station to log his orders.

The deadheads passed Danny as he came through the automatic doors, pumped the air with a fist, wearing a smile. "Yeah, baby."

Marvin stopped to watch Danny retreat. "Looks like someone's gonna get lucky. More than I can say for the way my day's turning out."

"Oh, stop being so glum, Brody. So, we failed today. We'll think of something else, right? Come on, let's go in. See what the damage is."

"Sure. Sure." Marvin stopped in the middle of the E.R. and glanced around. "Where'd they put her?"

"Over here Marv. Behind the curtain."

A few minutes later, the intern parted the curtains and entered, a nurse's aide right behind him drew the curtains open. "Mr. Benton, we're going to be taking your wife up for a CAT scan."

"How bad is it? She's bleeding an awful lot. Can't you at least stop the bleeding?" Larry didn't bother to correct the doctor.

"What the hell is this?" Marvin grabbed at the intern's arm to spin him around, but his hand swiped right through. "That is not the husband. This is the husband, right here."

Mike grabbed Marv's arm. "Brody, calm down. Man. Get a grip."

The intern continued as he and the aide wheeled Jenna's bed toward a set of doors. "It's just a little gash. The blood is typical of even a small head wound. We need a scan to know if there's anything serious. There's a waiting room through the double doors over there." He nodded to the right.

"Can't I go along?"

"I'm sorry, but no. Don't worry, I'm sure she's going to be fine."

In the waiting room, Larry used his cell phone to call JoAnne. "Hey Jo, it's Larry. Listen, I'm at the hospital. Jenna got smacked in the head while we were golfing this afternoon. I kinda have a feeling she won't be in Monday."

"You kinda have a feeling? This guy isn't too smart, is he?" Marvin interjected the question to nobody in particular.

"She's in and out of consciousness, and they've just taken her up for a CT scan. Anyway, call me if you pick up messages before Monday morning, and I'll fill you in as much as I can."

An hour later, the doctor walked into the waiting room. "Mr. Benton, your wife should be fine." Larry opened his mouth to correct the error but let the doctor continue. "There's no internal bleeding that we can detect at this point and no skull fracture, but concussions can be tricky. We're going to admit her and keep her overnight for observation, to watch for any signs of swelling. A neurologist will examine her in the morning and if he's satisfied, he'll release her then."

"Can I see her?"

"They're finding a room now. The nurse will come out to let you know where she ends up. She's been given—" he paused when Larry's phone rang. "Do you need to answer that?"

"Um, no. I'll call them back. Go ahead."

The doctor nodded and continued. "She's been given something to dull the oncoming headache and we don't want her making any sudden movements. I wouldn't expect too much from her right now. I'll check in on her before my shift ends."

"Okay. Thanks."

They shook hands, and Larry pulled his phone to check the message.

"This creep has a lot of nerve." Marvin sensed a good rant coming on and frowned when Mike put a quick stop to it.

"Brody. Let it be. You said Jenna doesn't have anyone. If Larry spills about not being family, she's got no one to look out for her here."

"What do you mean, no one to look out for her? I'm here, *we're* here. We don't need *that* schmuck," Marvin pitched a thumb over his shoulder at Larry, "to do anything but get the hell out."

Tommy entered the fray. "No, Marvin. Mike's right. Don't mess with it."

As Larry dialed JoAnne's number to return the call, Peggy pushed the door open to the room just far enough to stick her head in. "Mr. Benton? Your wife is in room twenty-twenty-one. You can go up now if you like."

Larry waved a hand in acknowledgement as the deadhead trio departed for the room. "Yeah, Jo…"

"Is she okay? What the hell happened?"

"Yeah, she's fine. No skull fracture"

"How'd she get hit in the head?"

"A stray golf ball… Well, more like stray golf *balls*. I don't know where they came from, but one managed to clobber her good. She went down fast and took me with her."

"You weren't able to see anyone?"

"Not a soul. I don't know…it was weird. It was like they came out of thin air."

"So, what's going to happen?"

"They've admitted her at least until tomorrow." Larry explained the doctor's plan, promised to call her later, and hung up.

When Larry walked into Jenna's hospital room and sat in the chair, Mike scrambled to get up. "Nnh. Damn, that arm feels funny. I wonder if I should have the doctor take a look at my back. There's probably a bruise the size of Rhode Island."

After a smirk at Larry's discomfort, Marvin returned his attention to his heated debate with Tommy at the sleeping Jenna's bedside.

"Dude, I'm telling you. She doesn't really know you're here. The mumbling and ramblings are from the injury and the drugs."

"So, if you're right and she's not aware, why couldn't we put a little something-something into her IV and finish the job?"

"You are cold, Marvin. Do you want one of the nurses or orderlies to lose their job?"

"Why would someone lose a job?"

"Listen to your Uncle Tommy, would you? Look, I may appear to be twenty years old, but don't forget I've been here on this side longer than you were alive."

"And?"

"And I'm telling you, the doctor said she's got a minor concussion. They did an MRI…"

"CAT scan."

"Whatever. If she suddenly quits breathing, they investigate. They find the added drugs, and the nurse and orderly assigned to her will get blamed for the overdose. They could go to jail, man. And that's not cool."

Marv let out a deep, loud sigh. "You're right. I'm sorry."

"Besides," Tommy fixed him with a broad smile, "with your current track record, you'd inject her with vitamins. She'd be up dancing on the ceiling in perfect health in an hour."

Chapter 38

The next morning, Mrs. McClaskey heard loud thumps coming from the hallway and opened her door a crack. "May I help you?"

"Um…I had a…date, I guess you could say, with Jenna. She's not answering her door. Do you know if she went out?"

A person couldn't be too careful these days, so she studied the face for a minute. "You look familiar, do I know you?"

"I believe we were introduced at my brother's funeral."

"Oh, yes, now I do remember. It's David, isn't it?"

"Yes, ma'am." David put his hand out in greeting.

She stepped forward and accepted. "Mrs. McClaskey. Nice to meet you, again."

"Yeah, you too."

Colleen scrunched her face into an expression of disgust, practiced to perfection in her years at libraries, at the lack of proper grammar in today's youth, but then smiled rather than correct since the young man's initial response had been proper. *Show respect and you get respect* was one of the mottos she believed in. "Thank you. You say you had a date with Jenna today?"

"Scheduled for an hour ago. I've knocked and I tried calling."

Now that she remembered he was family she felt

bad he hadn't been notified. "Well, I see you haven't heard. I hate to be the bearer of bad news, David, but I received a call from a," she almost said 'new young man,' but caught herself at the last instant, "from a young man she works with. Apparently, Jenna had a tiny bit of an accident yesterday out on the golf course."

"Oh, no. Is she okay? I hope it's not serious."

"According to Larry—that's the young man I spoke of—she'll be fine. But the doctors wanted to keep her overnight, just to be sure."

"Whew. Well, that's a relief."

"I'd suggest you might want to check back in"— she checked her watch—"it's ten-thirty now...I'd say perhaps one o'clock or so?"

"Thank you, Mrs. McClaskey. I appreciate you telling me." David turned to go.

"Oh, David. If you care to leave a phone number. I know you young people all carry those cell phones nowadays. I don't have one myself, though Jenna keeps after me about it. But, if you leave your number with me, I can call you if I hear anything new. How would that be?"

"That would be terrific. I'd like that. It's nine-one-four-four-six-six—"

"Oh, good heavens, wait. I'm afraid this old brain wouldn't remember the number for longer than it would take to go back inside. Give me just a moment and I'll get a pen and paper for you to write it on."

While Colleen and David were having their discussion in the hallway of the condominium, JoAnne laughed with Jenna in the hospital room. Marvin leaned against the window sill, interjecting comments they couldn't hear.

"See what happens when you try to play with the big boys?" JoAnne teased.

"Oh, don't. It hurts when I laugh."

"I'm sorry, but Larry getting smacked in the ass with a golf ball, I like the visual of that. Makes me feel all warm and fuzzy inside."

"Yeah it got me all warm and fuzzy too," Marvin offered. "Too bad it was in the ass instead of the nuts."

Jenna giggled again. "It was kind of funny. But I know it hurt like hell. He limped around muttering all kinds of threats to sue."

"Ah, yes…Lawyers love to do that. But it does my heart good once in a while to find out there's a human being inside. As long as they bleed, we know it's true."

The door swung open. "Ms. Wilson? The doctor has signed your release. Do you need me to help you get up and get dressed?"

Jenna and JoAnne looked at the young nurse, exchanged a glance, and they both broke out into laughter.

A confused look spread across the man's face. "What? What did I miss?"

"Nothing. Really. I think I can get myself dressed."

"She'd rather have you help her get *un*dressed."

"JoAnne."

Marvin laughed along with them. "And you talk about guys being trashy?"

"Well, it's true, isn't it? Sorry,"—Jo looked to the nurse's name tag—"is it Dick?" She fought back a fresh torrent of laughs. "But I call a spade a spade. It's just the way I am."

The nurse took the joke in stride. He cleared his throat, "Well, maybe we could arrange that some time.

Let me know when you're ready." He winked and went out the door. When peals of laughter reached his ears, he popped a blushed face back in, laughing. "I meant let me know when you're ready to *leave*. I'll bring a wheelchair. I'm not allowed to let you walk."

"Sure thing, thanks." When the door closed behind him, Jenna moved to get off the bed. "Ow… Damn."

"What, knowing you can't have that cute little ass of his make your head hurt?"

"Never mind that ass. You've got enough cute little ass right here." Marv slapped his own butt. "It'll be yours for the taking—soon."

Jen grit her teeth against the throb in her head, but laughed. "This is a headache from hell."

It took a while, but with JoAnne's help she finally pushed the call button to summon the nurse.

"Okay. Are you ready to go for a ride?" Dick asked as he pushed through the door. He broke into a wide smile when the women laughed. "I can see I need to watch every little thing I say around you two."

"This one," Marvin pointed to JoAnne and chuckled, "especially. I think she's a bad influence."

JoAnne landed a playful slap on the nurse's backside. "Oh, don't spoil our fun."

"See? What'd I tell you?" Marvin told the nurse. "Though I have to admit, she seems to be getting Jenna back to her normal feisty self and the land of the living, though she won't be staying *there* for long."

The nurse helped Jenna into the chair and handed her a clipboard. "Here's the last form you'll have to sign." When she handed it back, he pulled her copy, placed it into a folder and handed it to her. "These are all yours. Ready?"

"Ready."

Marvin followed the threesome out to the front of the hospital, where Jenna and the nurse waited for JoAnne to bring her car up from the visitors' lot. The nurse helped Jen into the front seat, closed the door, and waved as JoAnne pulled away. Marvin sat in the back, listened to the women chatter, and watched the scenery go by.

Once JoAnne had Jenna settled in Marvin's old chair, she heard a light tap on the door. "Jen, someone's knocking. Do you feel like company, or should I tell them to go away?"

"See who it is first."

"It's the old busybody across the hall, is who it is." Marv told them.

JoAnne opened the door to find Mrs. McClaskey standing there. "Yes?"

"I don't mean to be a bother, I'm just checking to see how my girl is doing."

"Colleen. Come on in. Jo? I'll see you in the morning."

JoAnne let the old woman in and yelled back as she went to close the door. "Oh, no you won't. You aren't going in tomorrow."

"Now, how did you know that?" Marv asked.

"Jo! Stop it. I'll be fine by then."

Marv laughed. "Mmmm, I wouldn't be too quick to make that assumption, kiddo."

"Bullshit. Stay home. If you show up, I'm kicking your ass right back out." Jo closed the door to avoid further argument.

"Oh, dear. She certainly is colorful, isn't she?"

"Ha. What's the old saying? 'You ain't heard

nothin' yet.' " Jenna smiled. "But she grows on you. How are you, Colleen?"

"I'm doing better than you it would seem. Can I get you anything?"

"Thank you, but no. I'm just going to sit here and take it easy for the rest of the day."

"That sounds like an excellent plan."

"Sit down, make yourself comfortable. Can I get you something to drink? I'm afraid I don't have any tea to make, but—" Jenna tried to stand up and grabbed the side of her head.

"No, now just sit. I didn't come to be a nuisance. I simply wanted to make sure you were all right and to let you know if you need anything I'm right across the hall."

"That's nice. Thank you."

"All right then. I'll check in on you later." Colleen walked to the front door and opened it. "Oh, where is my brain? I almost forgot to tell you. There was a young man here this morning."

Marvin looked over at Jenna. "A man? How many guys are you stringing along already?"

Jenna pulled in air in a slight gasp. "David. Oh, geez. I forgot about David."

"He wrote his number down for me. Would you like me to call him and tell him you're home?"

"No, it's all right. I'll call him. I'm sure he's really mad I stood him up."

Colleen took a few steps back into the room. "Not at all, dear. I told him what happened. That's okay isn't it? I thought since he's family, of a sort anyway…"

"It's fine."

"He said you two had a date planned?"

Marvin snickered. "A date? With him, or Ma? Ha! It may as well be both."

"Mmm. Not really a date, date. He's not…well, to be honest, he may be Marvin's brother, but he's not my type. He's too…um, he's manipulated too easily. Marvin never let his mother push him around. Hell, Marv never let *anyone* push him around. David seems much too eager to please his mama for my taste."

"But this schmuck, Larry, is your 'taste'? Come on, Jen, get serious."

Colleen waved a hand. "No, now it's really none of my business. I'll talk to you later. Call me if you need anything."

Jenna called out "Promise." and the door closed.

"So if my brother isn't your type, what's so special about this creep from the office?"

Jenna leaned her head back with a sigh and closed her eyes and mumbled. "God, I feel grungy. I really need a shower and to wash the blood out of my hair. Damn, my head hurts."

"I could make the headache disappear."

"What a crock. Things finally start to get on track and wham."

"Trust me, I know how you feel. That bus did me no favors, you know." Marvin sat next to her on the floor at her feet.

"Shit. I guess I better call David." But her hand didn't reach for the phone.

"It really is all Ma, you know. She wants her only kid married now. She wants grandkids. The sooner the better. And if it's you he marries, in her mind anyway, the insurance money comes back into the family and she would consider that a big plus."

"Why did I even agree to see him?" She let out a big sigh. "I just don't have the energy to deal with that right now. If he gets pissed, he gets pissed, isn't that what you'd always say, Marv?"

"I would indeed."

"It's one of the things I miss about you, you know? Take no prisoners, take no shit. Well...I promise I'll call him later..." and she drifted off to sleep.

"I wouldn't make any long range plans, if I were you. Hell, if I were you, I wouldn't make any *short* range plans." After he heard Jenna's light, rhythmic breathing, he left for the hotel with the seed of an idea.

Chapter 39

"Okay, now, just like we planned it, right," Marvin said when they walked into the building and headed up the stairs to his condo. "We wait for her to go into the bathroom to shower."

"Right on, dude."

"I wonder if the meds they sent her home with have worn off yet. She might be right where I left her."

"Where was that, Brody?"

"Sleeping in my chair—the one she badgered me to get rid of. Now she's in it all the time. Go figure. The only time I get to sit in that chair is when she's in bed."

In the living room, Tommy stated the obvious. "She's not here."

Marvin went to stick his head into the bedroom. "Go check the balcony, Mike."

A few seconds later Mike hollered from the kitchen. "Nope."

"She's not in bed either. Where the hell could she have gone?"

"Maybe to the old lady's place? It is around dinner time," Mike passed the thought as a possibility, then mused to himself, "A little late for my tastes, but…"

Tommy popped across the hall and stuck his head through Mrs. McClaskey's door. He gawked around and cocked an ear, then yelled out as he made his way back, "Nope. Not there."

"Oh, Jesus H. Now what?"

"She's your lady, Marvin. It's your gig. You tell us."

"Bathroom?" Mike pointed in the general direction.

"I don't think so, but…" Marvin left the room and a second later Mike and Tommy heard him say "Bingo."

"So," Tommy sat on the couch, "we wait. It would just be too cruel. You know what I always thought would be one of the coldest things that could ever happen to a guy?"

Mike took a guess. "Dying on the toilet? I'm sure it's happened to somebody at some point or another."

"No." Tommy shook his head. "Well, sorta. I don't remember ever seeing a scene in a film where that happens—you know a guy getting shot while on the commode. But I read a scene in a Stephen King novel once where this guy is sitting there straining and groaning in pain, when all of a sudden an alien thing chews out of him through—"

"Whoa. Stop right there. Spare us the details on that one," Marvin hollered on his way back out of the bathroom.

"Sorry Marv, I didn't know you had such delicate sensibilities." Tommy laughed at him. "Anyway, can you imagine this? You're standing at a urinal with your willy in your hand, minding your own business as it were, and someone attacks you from behind. The ultimate cruelty."

Mike plopped to the floor and stretched out. "Oh, thanks, Tommy, I needed that visual. I swear, I'm not taking you to any more movies. Your brain is fertile enough."

Marv stood in the doorway to the bedroom. "Are you done discussing such disgusting things?"

Tommy nodded. "Why?"

Marv hooked a thumb in the direction of the bathroom. "She's in there."

"Really?" Tommy sprang up from the couch and headed toward the bathroom.

"Whoa." Marvin put his hands against Tommy's chest. They sank half way through before Tommy stopped. "Where do you think you're going?"

"To the bathroom, where else?"

"Oh, no you're not. What're you crazy?"

"How else do you suggest we get this accomplished?"

"Tommy, what Marv is trying to say is, she's naked."

"Oh." Tommy looked at Marvin. "Not sitting in a bubble-bath, huh?"

"Did I say she was in the tub, ya schmuck." Marv glanced at Mike who had gotten up from the floor. "Just cool your engines for a while. God. It feels good to sit in this chair."

Tommy reclined on the couch, and Mike went back to the floor.

"How long do we wait, Brody?"

"Depends. We'll know when she turns the shower on." Marvin reached through the side of the table next to his chair. He unscrewed the cap to the new bottle of scotch he'd stashed and took a swig. "Anybody want a drink?" Two hands waved the question off. "Suit yourselves." When he heard the water come on in the shower, he took another hit, put the cap on, and stashed the bottle. "See? What'd I tell you? Okay boys, here we go. Get ready for some fireworks."

Marvin went into the bathroom to find the hair dryer and curling iron set out, plugged in and ready to go just as he'd expected. He found it interesting how people's daily routines never altered; day in, day out, some things became habits and got accomplished without actively engaging the brain. He picked up the hair dryer and steadied himself. He didn't know what to expect, being dead and all, and took the time to look down to study his stance making sure his feet were firmly planted.

Jenna tilted her head back under the spray, eyes closed, water cascading through her hair, and rinsed out the shampoo. She moved a step toward the back of the shower stall and pressed the pump to dispense shower gel into her palm. Marvin chose that moment to turn his head away, shove his arm through the frosted glass door and turn on the blower. Water rained into the appliance and jolts of electricity shot up his arm. He yanked it back out as his body went into a bizarre dance. He yelled and swore trying to shake loose from the hair dryer, but his hand wouldn't open to let go.

Tommy and Mike, who'd both lagged behind, ran toward the commotion. Mike stopped short of bumping into Marvin and stood stunned.

Tommy looked at the hair on top of Marvin's head as it waved in the air. Through his laughter he said, "Pull the plug…Mike. Pull the plug."

"Holy shit. Brody, are you okay?"

Marvin's body stopped moving, but the vibrations continued pinging off the nerve endings. He dropped the dryer to the floor and tried to shake the numbness from his arm. "Holy mother of Mary."

Jenna jumped at the sound of the dryer hitting the tiled floor and turned toward the door and swiped the fog from the glass. She hugged her breasts and let out a meek "Hello? Is anybody there?"

Mike grabbed the dryer and put it on the counter.

"Hello? Colleen... Mrs. McClaskey?"

"Quick, plug it back in, Mike. I don't think I can move yet."

In the instant Mike's hand came off the plug, the shower door opened a small crack.

Jenna peered out. "Is somebody in here?" She opened the door wider and stuck her head around the edge to look toward the bedroom. "Who's there?"

Mike and Marvin froze in place like two kids caught peeking in a window at a naked lady and Tommy's laugh threatened to turn into a fit of giggles. "Oh, my God. Oh, my God, you should see yourselves. You're hysterical. Two deer caught in headlights. And Marv, your hair. Oh, geez... You should see your hair. It's smoking. I swear to—"

"I'm glad you find us so amusing, ya schmuck. Move. Go!" Marvin started to push through him.

"Ahh, dude. No need to shove like that." Tommy walked directly through the wall to the living room where he waited for the other two to stop stumbling around.

Jenna turned the water off, grabbed her towel to step out of the stall, and noticed her hair dryer smoldering, wisps of smoke rising from the end like a smoking gun. "Well, shit. Goddammit." She looked at herself in the mirror. "What a weekend. It just did *not* turn out the way you'd planned, did it?"

"It certainly didn't," Marvin replied.

"Well... It sure as hell can't get any worse."

"I wouldn't say that. Of course, it all depends on your point of view, now doesn't it?"

Jenna carefully pulled the plug from the outlet, dried off, wrapped her head in the towel, and still nursing a headache, reclined on the bed.

In the living room, Tommy had almost contained his laughter when Marvin appeared and set him off again. "Oh, man... That's funny. You need to tame your mane. Hair is sticking up like you stuck your finger in a light socket."

In a fit of anger, Marv balled a hand into a fist.

"Brody, don't you dare."

"Come on. Look at yourself. You gotta admit, you're a sight." Tommy pushed him toward the entryway mirror.

The corners of Marv's mouth quivered, then turned into a smile. The smile turned into a chuckle and slowly built into a full-on belly laugh. He went to smooth his hair back into place and stopped when he caught sight of the fingers of his right hand; the one he'd held the dryer with. The nails were slightly charred, as if he'd held them over a fire for too long. He pushed his hand toward Tommy. "Holy crap, how long will it take for this to wear off?"

"Eh, it's no biggie. A couple days."

Mike stood in the door to the hall. "Come on, I think I need a drink. Let's go over to Clancy's."

"What about finishing what we started here?"

"Brody, face it, this night's a bust. We'll go over to the bar and plan a new strategy." Mike walked through the front door with Tommy.

"You guys go on ahead. I'll meet you there." Marv

could see Jenna's form through the open doorway and wondered if the whole idea might be one big bust.

"I'm really sorry, I can't help myself, kiddo. I can't get back and I want us to be together, but that can't happen unless you're over here. Maybe it'd be different if you were like David, able to at least sense I'm here with you. But I can't handle this hanging around watching you move on without me. It makes me crazy, and yet I can't bring myself to leave either. I miss you something awful. When we find something that works, I hope you'll understand that I'm doing this for both of us. I love you, kiddo." He shuffled slowly through the door and headed to Clancy's.

Chapter 40

It was a little before seven a.m. when the phone on her desk rang once and Jenna picked up without thinking. "Jenna."

"I knew it, I knew it, I knew it. I *knew* you'd be there. I thought I told you not to go in there today."

"Jo, I'm fine."

"I don't care. You shut that computer down, you grab your shit, and you go home."

"Jo—"

"What do I need to do, call someone to babysit you? What the fuck."

"JoAnne, I'm—"

"I don't want to hear any of your back talk. I'm telling you to go home. Now. The doctor said you were supposed to take it easy for a few days, and that's exactly—do you hear me?—*exactly* what you're going to do. Even if I have to drag you out by the hair."

"Good lord. Calm down. Look, I just got this promotion. I can't screw it up by taking time off."

JoAnne lowered her tone, "Oh, well, then, how does this sound?" and built to another crescendo. "I'm on my way now, and you better be gone by the time I get there. I swear to you, if you're still in that office when I walk in, I will personally go to the associates and have them take back the promotion."

"Aw, come on, Jo, that's not fair."

"I know you think I'm being a bitch. You're right, I am."

"I won't argue with you there."

"Good. Now turn the computer off and go home."

"All right. Jesus Christ, you win." Jenna sighed.

"You're damn right I win. I always win."

Jenna laughed in spite of being ticked off. "What do I tell Larry when he calls me at home to ask about his new case files?"

"I'll handle Larry. Don't you worry about Larry and his case files. He'd have some mighty big balls to expect you to work after what happened. Besides, he's the one who told me you wouldn't be in."

"Will you call me later and let me know?"

"Who's your boss? Besides, have you even *heard* from that asshole since Saturday?"

"No."

"Then what d'you care about what he says?"

Jenna didn't have an answer for that. In fact, she'd been relieved he hadn't called; it would make it easier to put things back into the professional realm where they probably belonged anyway. She knew for certain, when things had gone south at the golf course, that she wouldn't be going out with him again. It had been the way he turned things into a big competition. Marvin used to compete too, but in a fun way. Larry became too much like an eight-year-old, and it only got worse when the first ball smacked him in the ass. So, no thanks.

"That's what I thought," JoAnne said when her question was met with silence. "I'm almost there, Jenna. Another ten minutes. The light better be off, and the door better be closed. Am I making myself clear?"

"I'm going," Jenna said, then hollered before the phone hit its cradle, "Call me later." She'd run out of time to complete her simple will leaving JoAnne her jewelry and splitting what little money there might be with David, who would also inherit the condominium. She jotted a note on her calendar as a reminder to finish it when she returned to work. But based on the weekend events, she printed the Living Will naming JoAnne as the person to make necessary medical decisions, signed it, and dropped it on her desk on the way out of the office. She slapped a sticky-note on top: 'Pls send with other ofc docs for filing. Thx. J.'

Chapter 41

Back home, Jenna didn't know what to do with herself once Colleen had wandered back to her own place, but the silence and doing nothing unnerved and grated on her. She started a fresh pot of coffee and went out to sit on the balcony for some sun and a cigarette.

"I have to find something to do or I'll go stir crazy."

Marvin sat on the other chair and looked out over the skyline. "Will you ever learn to just sit and relax?"

"I hate just sitting around. Shit." Jenna stubbed the cigarette out in the ash tray. "There's nobody to talk to; they're all working. Nobody to visit because they're all working."

"I have an idea. Why don't you go for a little walk? Like, in front of a bus? You could save me and the guys an awful lot of trouble if you'd do us that teensy little favor."

Jenna got up from her chair and went back into the kitchen. She poured her coffee and wandered around the house. The headache eased, and she found herself standing in front of the closet in the bedroom. "Well, I suppose I could clean some stuff out of the closet. It's not like he's coming back and is going to need any of it."

"You could clean it *all* out. It's not like you're going to need anything for much longer."

Jenna heaved a sigh and pulled Marvin's shirts off hangers. She folded each one neatly and added it to a growing stack on the bed. When most of the shirts had been pulled out, she sat on the bed and looked at the pile. "I better get a garbage bag for all of this."

"A garbage bag? Is that what you think of my stuff? It's garbage?"

When she rose from the bed, what seemed a huge empty space along the rod drew her attention away from her intended path, and she tripped over the shoe boxes she'd pulled off the top shelf. By instinct, Marvin reached out to catch her, but his arm cut a swath right through her and Jenna tumbled to the floor.

"Shit." Jen put a hand to the side of her head and sat up, "Ow... You clumsy oaf. You better get your head together, girl, or you'll kill yourself. Ha! And who would even know? You'd lay here dead for days, maybe weeks, before someone called the cops because of the stench."

"It wouldn't be all bad. I'd know. *I'd* be here."

With effort Jen turned her body around to stand, kicked into a shoe box, and the lid slipped off. She peered over to see which pair of Marvin's shoes it housed, but it appeared empty. "This must be for the ones you were wearing." She picked up the box and lid and saw a bunch of receipts. "Now, why would you still have the sales slips in here after all this time?"

Marvin recognized it too late. "Son-of-a-bitch. You just close that and throw the whole thing out. That stuff doesn't belong to you." He tried to grab it away from her, but his hand came back empty. "What the hell?"

"A dirty napkin? You kept a dirty napkin?" Jenna shook her head. "Marv, you were weird."

"I am not. What, you never wanted to keep something to remember an event?"

She went to ball up the napkin and noticed some blurred writing. "The handwriting looks... This is my old phone number. Where did you find this?" Jen asked the empty room.

"Where did I find it? Don't you remember? You gave it to me."

"Oh, wait a minute... This is... Oh, my God. This is the napkin I gave you the night we met in the bar. God only knows why I did that. You were such an asshole that night." She smiled.

"An asshole? If I was an asshole, you were an icy bitch."

"I didn't like you at first, did you know that? I thought, who is this arrogant jerk? But you were so...I don't know... The confident smile on your face. But what really did it, what really got my attention were the eyes." She laughed. "Your eyes gave you away, Marvin. From that day on, I could always tell what you were really thinking. All I had to do was look into those blue eyes and it was all right there."

"Huh. Really? I always thought I had a pretty good poker face."

"All the sparring back and forth, the barbs we threw at one another—wow. It's what made me do it. It's what made me go out with you when you called. No matter what I said, no matter how cruel or condescending I got, you gave it right back. Your eyes gave away what you were really feeling. I'd never had so much fun with anyone. Ever."

Marv laughed. "I should've known you were in the law business in some way right then. I loved the quick wit, the way you stood your ground. Every other girl, all the way back to high school, would get pissed or start to cry. I couldn't believe my luck that night. A woman capable of handling herself and anything that got thrown at her. That's what did it for me, kiddo. I knew it right then."

"Are these tickets from a ball game?" Jenna turned them over in her hand.

"Of course. I didn't think you'd go. Even after we dated for months, I figured you for a typical female, but I had to ask. And you went. You were my lucky talisman that night."

"Oh, geez… I should give these to David. They should be kept with the baseball you caught that night. God! You were like a little kid, standing at the rail waiting for Griffey's autograph." Jenna put the tickets up on the bed for safekeeping and picked up another pair of stubs. "Ballet tickets? Why would you keep ballet tickets? You hated the ballet. You didn't fall asleep like other guys I took, but I knew you were bored."

"I never said anything." Marvin shrugged. "I would've kept going, but you never asked again. Why didn't you just ask?"

She hoisted the stubs into the air as if she'd heard him and knew he sat there in front of her, "Those eyes again." She dug into the box and found a sheath of papers. "Now what the hell is all of this?"

"Uh, oh."

"Looks like a report. From the county foster care administration?

"Dear Mr. Broudstein:

In the matter of Jenna Wilson, we regret to inform

you we have not been able to find..."

Marvin. You tried to find my family? Why would you do that? Did it matter to you who I was or where I came from?"

"Look Jen, I know you said you didn't care, but I thought maybe, if they could find someone you'd...you know," Marv shrugged, "want to maybe meet them. Get to know them. So you could have family at our wedding too."

She shook her head and tossed the papers to the floor. "You became all the family I needed, Marv. What else is in here?" Jenna pushed the tissue paper around and uncovered one last item: a photograph. A grinning David stood sandwiched between them, Jenna held up her left hand to show off the engagement ring and Marvin held the prized baseball. "I remember this. David thought we were nuts. He probably thought you'd lost *all* your marbles—deciding to propose because you caught a baseball." She frowned, her brows creasing together. "Hmph. Your mother definitely thought you were insane. She even said so."

"Well, sometimes Ma's a little slow on the uptake."

"I think this should go to David with the ticket stubs." Jenna grabbed the tickets off the bed. She rummaged through a drawer in the kitchen until she found an envelope, slid the game stubs and photo inside, and placed it on the table in the front hallway for safekeeping. She retrieved bags for the clothes, grabbed the phone on her way back to the bedroom, and pushed the speed dial button for David. "Voice mail, damn... David, hi. It's Jenna. I know you're working but I wanted to call and apologize for missing our brunch.

278

Give me a call later. I'm at home, and well, I ran across a couple things I thought you might like to have. Call me when you can. Bye."

The phone rang before she could set it down on the bed. "Hello."

"Jenna, it's David. Sorry, the voice mail kicked in before I could answer."

"Hi, David. Mainly, I wanted to apologize for Sunday."

Marvin leaned into the phone. "Hey, David."

David paused for a second, a smile came through in his voice. "Oh, come on, no apology necessary. Are you feeling okay?"

"I'm fine, really. A little bit of a headache is all. So, look, I started going through Marvin's things today."

"Shouldn't you be taking it easy? I mean, from what your neighbor told me, that was a pretty nasty knock on the noggin."

"Oh, come on, don't you start in on me, too. I've had enough lectures today. I can't just sit around, David. I'm not the type."

"Sorry…"

"Anyway, I found tickets from the game, and I thought you should have them. It might increase the value of the ball."

"Which one?"

Jenna rolled her eyes. *How could he and Marvin have come from the same gene pool?* "The one that made Marv propose, remember? And there's a picture of the three of us right after he gave me the ring."

"Oh, right. Marvin holding the ball and you—"

"Me with my hand out showing off the ring. I

thought you might like to have that too."

"Are you sure you want me to have the photo?"

"I'd say this wouldn't be one of my favorite moments in time, David. Your mother refused to join us and glared at me while your dad took that picture. She was barely civil to me. I've never been one to keep photo albums, anyway. All the memories I need of your brother I have right here," Jenna pointed to her head, "in my brain. I'll have them forever. They can't yellow with age or be burned in a fire. Not even knocked out with a golf ball."

"Besides, you'll be with me, what do you need with a picture when you have the real thing?" Marvin glanced down at himself. "Sort of."

David knew better than to defend his mother with Jenna and let the matter drop. "Well, okay. Thanks, I'd like to have it then."

"Should I mail everything to you?" Jen prompted. "You'd have them sooner."

"Um, well, I guess, unless you'd have time to reschedule that brunch."

"I'd really like to, but after being out from work...I'm just really going to need to spend some extra time to get caught up."

"Understood. I better get back to work myself or Dad'll be throwing baked goods at me."

"Okay, I'll put them in the mail tomorrow."

"Thanks. I'll see you Jen."

"Yeah. We'll talk soon." She ended the call with a sigh and put the phone on the bed next to her. "Now why do I feel bad for giving him the brush-off?"

"Maybe because he's some small connection to me?"

Jenna grabbed the last bunch of Marvin's shirts from the closet and a gentle sigh escaped and she smiled. An old Tommy Bahama short-sleeved, Hawaiian print shirt in a mad mash-up of color on the front and a woman on the back dressed in a halter-top and grass skirt. The words 'Surfer Girl Hawaii' cut across the graphic. "Oh, my God. You stashed this ugly thing in the back of the closet and kept it. I should've known."

"Just because you didn't like that shirt... I heard what you told me, I never wore it after you threatened to stop going out with me if you ever laid eyes on it again."

Jenna folded the other shirts and placed them into the bag. "I don't know..." She held up the Tommy Bahama to inspect it. "I think I might have to keep this one, Marv." She folded it, hugged it to her face, and breathed deep through her nose. "Yeah, this needs to stay. God..." she moaned as she surveyed the pile of his clothes and turned her gaze to the ceiling. "Marvin, I'm not sure what I'm doing here, but it's time. You know? My career is getting back on track and even though it's not the same anymore, life goes on... I'm sorry, but I have to move on." Jenna got off the bed and turned to the dresser to toss out the underwear and socks and the collection of ratty old T-shirts he'd worn around the house on weekends.

Marv smiled at her. "Oh, don't you worry your beautiful head. With any amount of luck, you'll be moving on very soon."

Chapter 42

Tommy glanced out over the dining room of the restaurant to check if Tina-I'll-Be-Your-Server-Today was paying attention to the empty table they occupied. He waited for her to turn her back before he wiped down a booth and slid the coffee cups to Mike and Marvin. "So, how's our girl doing today, Marvin?"

"She's back at work, of course."

"Good Lord, Brody. Today is Wednesday; that's only three days. Doesn't she know she could be milking this one? I mean a head injury should be worth at least a week."

"Shit, she would've been there all along if her boss hadn't sent her home Monday morning."

"Are you kidding me? She actually went in on Monday?"

"Yeah, and early to boot. They threatened to revoke her promotion if she showed up any earlier than today."

Mike shook his head. "She's a tough one, isn't she?"

"Yeah, she's tough all right," Marvin replied. *It's one of the reasons I was so attracted to her.* "But, she's a work-a-holic. She never could sit still. It used to be tough sometimes to get her to just sit on the balcony with a glass of wine for an evening."

Tommy injected himself into the conversation

again. "Let's assess the situation here. We have one tough nut to crack. But there's bound to be something we can come up with." Then he turned to gaze out the window.

After a long silence, Mike broke into whatever thoughts Tommy may have been forming and interrupted Marvin's gaze through the window with a nudge of a foot under the table. "She still takes the bus back and forth to work, right?"

"Yeah, why?"

"What if we could distract her and get her to do what you did?"

"Get hit by a bus? That's not likely when she'd be standing there waiting for it."

"No, maybe not the bus. But maybe a car, or a delivery truck…"

Tommy shook his head. "Nah, I don't think that'd work, man. What would we use to pull her focus, run up behind her and yell 'boo'?"

"How about a bike? Or a skateboard?" Mike turned to Marvin. "Didn't you say the kids in your building are always leaving stuff around?"

Marv nodded but stayed silent and turned his focus back out to the street. The old guy staring at him from across the way looked familiar: the rumpled white shirt and khaki pants, the dirty sneakers and…the eyes; there was something about those eyes. They were bright and intelligent, yet dark and deep; eyes that held his gaze. Tommy and Mike continued to discuss the latest plan, but none of the words penetrated Marvin's brain, they faded into the background and became unintelligible.

****

The old man studied Marvin and tried without

words to get him to understand. *You's fadin' son. And lookit yo' pals there. They's got a tinge roun' the edge now, too. And you'd see it if you'd stop them shenanigans of yo's and* look *at one t'other*. He wished those who occupied this existence would look at themselves once in a while, because if they did, if they really looked, they would notice the darkness creeping around the edges; the fading sharpness. A heavy sigh escaped him. He was tired, getting too full to hold on to many more. The woman could be there soon. He directed his thoughts toward her and nodded. She would be on her way immediately.

Chapter 43

Jenna never waited for anything with much patience. She stood up from the bench at the bus stop and peered down the street for the first morning run; still no bus in sight. She checked her watch and heaved a sigh. "Damn. Come on, come on. If I don't get this brief done and on Jo's desk by nine-thirty, I'm toast." How fast things change. A week ago she was being threatened if she didn't stay home. Now, despite having spent an entire weekend chained to the computer at her desk, it seemed she couldn't spend enough time in the office to finish everything they'd dumped on her. She paced up and down the sidewalk formulating her strategy on the final argument.

Tommy, Marvin, and Mike watched and waited for something to come along that would inspire them.

Tommy sighed. "It's too early for anyone in their right minds to be out riding anything."

Mike stifled a yawn. "Shit, Brody. He's right. Does she always go in this early in the morning? Christ, the sun has barely even cracked a smile yet."

"Come on, something is bound to—"

"Dude, *delivery trucks* have just started to get out on the street. I didn't even see newspapers in front of doors when you came and got us. Really, Marvin, think about it: we had to walk because the buses hadn't started running when we left the hotel. This is useless."

"Jesus H. What a couple of whiners. All right. Come on, let's go to the deli. We'll have to figure out some other plan."

They turned to start the walk when Marv stopped short and caused Mike to bump part way through him. "Brody. What the fuck?"

Marvin ignored him, turned back, and stood in the line of Jenna's path. Just as she approached him, he kicked a shoe off. It dropped to the pavement and winked into sight a fraction of a second too late. The heel of her shoe caught, and she stumbled and fell to the concrete sidewalk. Her high-heeled shoe came off, her purse slipped out of her hand, and its contents flew in all directions.

"Goddammit." Jenna rolled and stood up, looking around to see what she'd tripped on, but Marv had already slipped the shoe back onto his foot. All she could see was her own black high heel tipped over on its side.

"Now, Marvin, what was the point in that? Just to do something to hurt her?"

"No, ya schmuck. Look." Marvin pointed to Jenna. "Now she's gotta go back upstairs and change. It bought us a little time."

Jenna inspected the damage. She brushed dirt from her skirt and scanned it for rips, looked at her skinned knees, and the scrape on her left palm. She limped around to retrieve her belongings. "Son-of-a-bitch. Woman, you are turning into a complete mess." She pulled out tissues that hadn't slid from her purse, spit on them and wiped at the tiny beads of blood on her knees and hand. "Okay, no big deal. Nothing's broken, skirt's not torn. I've got extra hose in my desk…"

Marvin stomped a foot into the ground. "Oh, Jesus H. Christ. Do you always have to be so damned organized?"

Jenna peered down the street and shook her head, picked up her wayward shoe, and slipped it back on. With the first step she took, her foot wobbled, her ankle bent, and the heel broke off. She took in a deep breath, stuffed a fist into her mouth, dropped her head back, and stifled the scream that tried to break free.

That made Marvin smile. "Perfect."

Jenna hobbled down the street toward home, mumbling, crying, and cursing.

"There, that'll buy us some time." Marvin beamed with pride.

Tommy swung a hand through Marvin's arm. "That was mean. Look, you made her cry, man."

Mike chortled. "Jeez, Tommy, I think she'll get over it. She'll live."

"Bite your tongue." Marv pointed a finger at Mike, and looked at Tommy, "Hey, hippie, you think the deli has coffee made yet?"

"Depends. What time is it?"

Mike looked down at his watch, an accessory he had little use for but felt naked without like some men feel naked without keys in their pocket. "Just about 5:50."

Tommy shrugged. "Mm, maybe. It's usually the first thing to get done after Moe shows up, and they open in ten minutes. Are we gonna have enough time, Marvin?"

"Trust me, if she has to change the shoes, she'll change the skirt. Then, she'll decide she has to change the blouse. And because she changed the shoes, she'll change the purse. Plus, since she's crying," Marvin told him pointedly, "she'll have to take off all the make-up and redo it. We'll have plenty of time to get to the deli, get coffee, and come back."

They walked the few blocks, through the unlocked front door, and snatched cups from the rack next to the brewer. Tommy poured and slipped the pot back onto the burner just as Tina-I'll-Be-Your-Server-Today came around the corner of the deli and glanced in the window.

"So, can we sit for a while, or do we have to head right back?"

"How long's it been now, Mike?"

"About twenty minutes," Mike said through another string of yawns.

"Then we can either sit for a few minutes, or we can stroll back slowly. She moves pretty fast when she has to, but I'm thinking it'll be at least forty minutes."

"No time like the present then." Mike walked out through the front door. He waved and offered a good-natured 'morning' to the incoming deadheads who frequented the early rush. Marvin and Tommy, close behind him, nodded in silent greeting.

The three were a block away from the bus stop when Mike nudged Marvin and pointed to a bicycle leaning against a street pole. "Now, why didn't we see that earlier?"

"Damn, it's chained to the pole," Marv called to him after a quick inspection.

Tommy walked over and took an inventory of options. "Maybe…What if we tried this. Marvin, grab the chain and lock in one hand. See how it fades a bit, gets a tiny bit transparent so we can see through it?"

"Okay, now what?"

Tommy elbowed Mike. "Now, you grab the bike by the seat and give it a pull. The wheel will slide right through the chain like it's—"

Mike's hands slipped off the seat, or rather through the seat, and the chain snapped tight. "Uh-huh. So much for that idea. Now what, Einstein?"

"Sorry. I thought for sure the bike and chain would separate between their world and ours. How about if Marvin lets go and you give another pull on the bike?"

Mike came up empty-handed again. "Nope. Something's got it grounded to the living plane, but I'll be damned if I can figure out what."

A small crowd of deadheads on the way to the deli stopped to watch what they were doing and offered a few suggestions.

"Well, why did you lock it up like this in the first place?" the one in the red polo shirt asked as he helped to pull the chain in the opposite direction.

"We didn't."

"What d'you mean you didn't? It's locked."

"Oh." Tommy shook his head. "It's not our bike. We just need to borrow it for a few minutes."

"You're stealing a bike?" Red Polo Shirt dropped the chain and the others mumbled and backed away. "No way. Tommy, I'm real disappointed in you. You never came across as a crook. What's going on here?"

"Nothing. Really," Marv butted in before Tommy had a chance to open his mouth. "We just wanted to take it for a quick spin. I saw it here and remarked how I hadn't ridden a bike in so many years."

Mike piped in. "Right. Then we got into the old argument—you know how people always say 'It's like riding a bike, you never forget?' So, we thought we'd test the theory and have Marvin here give it a shot."

With each lie, the tinge around their edges darkened a little bit more. Red polo shirt studied them for a few minutes, looked Tommy right in the eye, and shook his head. "I don't believe you. You're all up to something. I can tell just by looking at you." He jutted his chin toward Marvin. "Especially him."

The group of deadheads backed away, then turned and walked off at a brisk pace. Marvin looked at his friends. "What the hell was that about? What did he mean 'especially him'?"

Tommy shrugged. "Beats me. You both look the same as always."

Mike glanced at his watch. "Come on guys, let's go. She's going to beat us back to the bus stop. We'll find something we can use." Mike headed off down the street.

When they rounded the corner, they spotted Jen in a different outfit as she paced and peered down the street. Mike glanced around and took off running. Marvin and Tommy sprinted after him.

Tommy craned his neck to look down the street. "Dude. What is the rush? The bus is still more than a mile away with three other stops to make."

"Over there." Mike pointed to a kid across the street from the bus stop.

Blake Simmons propelled his skateboard along the sidewalk on his way to school. He had plenty of time; his ninth-grade homeroom bell wouldn't ring until 7:20. He laughed at the looks on people's faces as they tried to dodge out of his way. He steered in front of them obviously enjoying the harassment and havoc he could cause when his folks weren't around to yell at him to behave and show some respect for others.

Mike slowed to scoop up a small stone, overtook the kid, and dropped the stone in front of the skateboard. Before Blake could adjust, the nylon front wheels locked onto and scraped the rock along the pavement, and the kid launched through the air. Mike snatched the board as it veered into the street.

People on the sidewalk cleared a path as Blake let out an "Oh, shit." and rolled his body with the fall as he hit the concrete. A man approached and asked if he was okay.

"No prob, man. I'm fine." He brushed the dirt off his pants and turned to retrieve the skateboard. "What the fuck… What happened to my board?"

"Okay, you two," Mike held the board out as he crossed the street, being careful to avoid the traffic, "which one of you knows how to ride one of these contraptions?"

"Don't look at me. I wasn't even allowed to ride a *bike* until I was ten." When he noticed the odd expression on Tommy's face, Marvin shrugged and explained, "She's a typical Jewish mother hen, what can I say."

Tommy took the skateboard from Mike and placed it onto the ground. "I've been on a couple, but that was years ago. They still had steel wheels—"

"Hey. Hey, lady!" The kid yelled as he dodged cars and ran toward Jenna. The man who'd stopped to help him continued on his way with a scowl. "That's mine. I don't know how the fuck it got all the way over there, but—"

Jenna shook her head to clear her mind. "I'm sorry,

what? I wasn't paying attention, were you talking to me?"

Tommy heard the commotion, picked up the board, and it blinked out of sight. Blake stopped for a second, dumbfounded, in the middle of the street, and all the deadheads who'd witnessed this prank on the living laughed. Car tires squealed and horns blared as Blake tried to make his way through the increased traffic.

Frustrated, Blake launched himself the rest of the way across the street. "Okay, bitch, what did you do with it?"

"Excuse me?"

"It was right there next to you. Where did you kick it to?"

"First of all, I am not a 'bitch' and second of all, I don't know what you're talking about, you little shithead."

"Ah. I love it. Don't you love it?" Marv turned to address the deadheads who'd gathered around to be entertained by the living. "That's my girl. Heart of gold, but she takes no shit and takes no prisoners."

"Look, lady. I saw it, right here, damn near under your feet. You had to've kicked it or taken it. What, you got some snot-nosed kid at home who wants a skateboard, and you're too fuckin' cheap to buy him one?"

Jenna advanced on the kid, who appeared to be about twelve years old. "I don't know what you're talking about, you little bastard. But, I'll tell you this much, you better get out of my face before I slap yours silly." The kid backed away with each step Jenna took toward him. "I don't have any kids, and you know why? Because I wouldn't want 'em to turn out like *you*.

Inconsiderate little shits with potty-mouths before they're ten. I think maybe you better run off to kindergarten before you get into trouble."

The kid turned and ran to safety a good fifteen yards away. He stopped to watch the crazy-ass woman who'd been so mean to him, when all he wanted was to get his skateboard back from her. And he watched for the board to drop from under her skirt or to see where she'd go to retrieve it and his chance to wrestle it away from her.

Jenna looked back over her shoulder. The bus was just down the street and approaching. Each step she had taken with every word hurled at her accuser took her farther from the bus stop. She walked swiftly back and regretted the way she'd berated the boy; she'd never talked so nasty to a child before and chalked it up to the stress at work, the earlier mishap, and pushed the incident out of her mind.

Tommy walked into the street with the skateboard under his arm and tried unsuccessfully to dodge traffic. He cussed and uttered groans with each car or truck that rolled through him. "Dammit, Marvin. Dude, you better appreciate what your Uncle Tommy is doing for you here."

"I appreciate it more than you know, hippie. We'll figure out how I can pay you back later. Right now, would you just hurry up and get this done?"

Mike yelled, "Now." and Tommy pushed himself forward on the skateboard, jumped it over the curb, and hopped off. It rolled right into Jenna's path. She caught movement out of the corner of her eye and tried to avoid tripping over the blur of red. She skipped and sidestepped to her right, the toe of her right foot slid down the lip of the curb, and she tumbled into the path of the bus.

Chapter 44

The driver slammed his foot onto the brake pedal and held his breath. The brakes screeched and the hulking metal came to a jarring halt inches from Jenna's sprawled body. He threw the gear into neutral, locked the emergency brake in place, opened the door, and ran to help Jenna. "Jesus, lady, are you all right? I thought I'd hit you."

Jenna waved him off. "I'm fine. Really. I'm sorry."

The driver turned to the voice he heard approaching.

"I knew it. I knew you did it." Blake picked the board up from the gutter and pointed an accusing finger at Jenna. "She stole my skateboard. That bitch stole my skateboard. You deserved to be hit."

The bus driver grabbed Blake by the arm. He tried to struggle, and the driver signaled to a young guy sitting in one of the front rows of his bus. After the man descended, he took Blake by the scruff of the neck. "Hey, whoa. Whoa. Don't you move." Blake continued to wriggle, and the guy lifted his feet off the ground. "I'll let you back down, if you stand still while we get to the bottom of this. Otherwise, I can dangle you for another hour and not break a sweat. You got me, kid?"

Jenna stood and swiped dirt from her clothes for the second time in one morning. "I'm fine, see?"

Blake let out a weak, "Yeah, okay."

Marvin stamped a foot into the sidewalk. "Shit."

Mike slung an arm over Marv's shoulder. "Take it easy, Brody. So, it didn't work. Something will, eventually."

The driver gave her a visual once-over. "Are you sure? What happened here?"

"I don't know. That thing," Jenna pointed to the skateboard, "came out of nowhere, and I tripped over it."

"He says you stole it from him. I think it's more like he rolled it in front of you," the driver threw a glare at Blake.

Marvin's face turned glum, and he sighed. "I'm beginning to wonder if this woman is indestructible."

"Look at it this way, maybe she has nine lives. How many has she used up now? You're bound to be pretty close," Tommy pointed out.

Jenna looked at Blake. "No. It was nothing like that. He didn't do anything. He was twenty yards away, for God's sake. Look, I'm sorry, kid. I didn't take that thing. I'm sorry I yelled at you." She paused and took a deep breath. "It's been one hell of a morning."

Blake's expression softened. "That's okay lady. Sorry I accused you. I don't know what happened. It just...I was across the street when I fell off and when I looked around"—he shrugged—"it was over here next to your feet, then it just...disappeared again."

Jenna nodded to the passenger who still had a tight grip on the kid's shirt. "Let him go. No harm, really. Can I get on the bus now? Can we just get moving so I can get to work?"

The guy let go, watched the driver help Jenna onto the bus, and as he boarded, pointed a finger and shot a warning look at Blake.

Blake backed up to the edge of the sidewalk and sighed in relief. Three adults against the word of a kid could've gotten him into a whole heap of trouble. The bus pulled away from the curb, and he walked in the direction of school, the board tucked securely under his arm.

The crowd that had gathered disbursed. The living shivered with tingling in their bodies and goose-bumps on their limbs when they passed through deadheads, muttering attributions that the weird sensations came from the fact they'd just witnessed a woman almost get killed by a bus. When the deadheads scattered, they gave a wide berth and cast wary glances at Mike, Tommy, and Marvin.

After a long silence, Mike yawned and tapped his friend's arms. "Come on. Let's go back to the deli. I need some more coffee."

The usual morning-rush crowd of the living at Epstein's had thinned already as they walked through the door. "Over there," Tommy told them, "next to the window. I'll get the coffee. Anybody want anything else while I'm back there?"

Mike gave a questioning look to Marvin and then answered for both. "Just one coffee, Tommy."

After Mike and Marvin moved out of earshot, a middle-aged guy—one of the Sunday morning regulars—tugged on Tommy's sleeve. "Your friend there doesn't look so good. Is he all right?"

Tommy glanced toward his buddies. "Which one?"

"The tall one with the dark hair."

"Marvin? Yeah, he's just feeling a little down right now. Why?"

"Looks more serious than that to me."

Tommy studied Marvin. "What's that mean?"

"He looks…different. Dark around the edges, if that makes sense."

"I don't see anything. But I'll check it out. Thanks."

"Tell him to be careful." The guy peered at Tommy for a moment and added, "You *all* better be more careful."

"Of what? What could he have? He's dead." Tommy replied to the guy's back as he watched the man walk out of the store. He snatched three cups from the rack and drained the pot, started to make another for Tina-I'll-Be-Your-Server-Today, and then left the empty pot for the entertainment of watching her confusion when she went to serve her customers. He carried the cups to the table and handed them over, rather than slide them; there were too many live folks still nursing their meals. "Well, that was strange. Here Marvin, I got you one anyway. You looked like you needed it."

Marv accepted the coffee. "Thanks, it'd be better if you could've added a shot of something."

"What was strange?" Mike slid over to make room for Tommy on the bench.

"One of the regulars asked me if Marvin here was feeling all right. Told me he looked 'dark,' whatever the hell that means." Tommy watched Marv for a few minutes. "He doesn't look any different to me. Does he look different to you, Mike?"

"Nope. Looks the same to me as he does every other day of the year."

"Jesus H. stop staring at me, will ya," Marv said

without turning to look at them.

"Are you feeling 'dark' Marvin?"

"Listen up, ya schmuck, I feel dark all right. If you two don't stop staring at me I'm gonna come through the table and smack ya both upside the head. How's that?"

"I think someone needs a hug." Tommy rose off the bench.

"Sit back down, hippie. It ain't gonna work today, not this time."

Mike shook his head. "Come on Brody, lighten up. He's only trying to help."

"I know. But give it a rest, would ya? Just let me suck down my coffee."

"Ah, you always *were* cranky in the morning. Whose idea was this anyway, to venture out so early?"

Marvin flipped him the bird. "If I remember correctly, Mike, it was yours."

"Yeah, well, remind me next time we do not do well at the butt-crack of dawn."

Tommy laughed. "Butt-crack of dawn. That's funny." A minute later he offered, "Maybe we should try at night. We haven't tried at night."

"What?" Mike couldn't believe his ears. "What would nighttime have to do with anything?"

Tommy shrugged. "I don't know. But haven't you ever noticed the ghosts and goblins always seem do to better at night? They seem stronger."

Marvin chuckled. "What are you talking about?"

"Dude, think about it. Like in *Night of the Living Dead* and...um, *Halloween* they're always doing this kind of stuff at night. Maybe we need to try something at night."

Marv rolled his eyes. "Oh for cryin' out loud. Have you been taking him to the movies again, Mike?"

Mike held up his hands. "No. I swear it, officer, I'm innocent."

"Shit. Where did this come from?" Tina snatched his cup off the table, ran a damp rag across the spot. She looked out the window for the culprit who had plopped the dirty cup onto a clean table on the way out. "Why can't people leave things where they belong. They just love making work for others."

Mike watched in surprise. "Damn. She's fast."

Marvin laughed. "See what you get for violating my trust? Now, before you go get another cup, repeat after me: I will not take Tommy to any more movies."

Tommy sat up in a sudden revelation. "Oh, hey! How about concerts. Are concerts okay?"

"I suppose so, hippie. What do you have in mind? The Grateful Dead?"

"Hah, hah, Marvin. Very funny. No. What's today?"

Mike consulted his watch. "Friday."

"I know it's Friday. What date is it?"

"Oh, uh…June thirtieth."

"*Very* cool. Then, pack your bags. That's a figurative pack, of course. We're going to New York."

"For *what*?"

"Who cares, Brody? If it's one of Tommy's ideas, it's bound to be fun."

"You'll see when we get there, Marvin. Come on, drink up. This is a once a year event, and I haven't gone in, oh, I don't know, probably ten years. This is primo entertainment, classic."

"I'm not going anywhere. Just cool your jets."

Tommy wasn't dissuaded and his excitement built. "I'm telling you, I'll bet you've never seen anything like this. It's the grooviest thing I've ever seen in my life." Marvin stared at him. "Okay, let me rephrase that, it's the grooviest thing I've seen since I've been dead, but still."

"No. You go. I'm staying put." Marvin stuck to his guns.

"Dude. I promise you, this is Legendary. With a capital L, man."

"Oh, come on Brody," Mike prodded. "You didn't want to go on the cruise and you enjoyed that, didn't you?"

"Come on, Marvin. Please? Besides, I think we need to take a break and regroup here, figure out a new plan of attack, don't you?"

"Oh, Jesus H. Christ. All right. Stop whining. I'll go, I'll go."

Tommy beamed his approval, drained his cup, and set it on the table just as Tina made another pass through the restaurant. She let out a loud sigh, "Dammit." She yanked the cup off the table and swiped the wet ring with her cloth.

Marvin waited for her to turn away and placed his cup on the table. The three of them walked toward the front door and paused with their backs to the room when Tommy said, "Stop a second. Wait for it…Wait for it…"

"What the…" was all Tina mumbled before she let out a frustrated scream.

They melted through the doors to a chorus of laughter and applause.

Chapter 45

"What the hell happened to you? I thought you were going to be in here early this morning?" JoAnne asked when Jenna trudged by her office.

Jenna let out a groan. "Ask me again after I get some coffee." She dropped her purse into its usual spot in her desk drawer, picked up her cup, and went to the kitchen. "Jesus, what a morning."

JoAnne jumped out of her seat to follow when Jenna passed her office in the opposite direction, "Wait a minute. Stop. You have dirt all over your ass end."

Jenna waited for the slaps and swipes at her backside to stop and continued down the hallway. "Thanks."

"And?" JoAnne prompted.

"Well, let's see…where should I start?" Jenna filled her cup and lifted the pot in JoAnne's direction.

"No, thanks. I have a cup on my desk."

"As Marvin used to say, it's been a fucking day from hell. And it's not even eight a.m."

"I thought for sure you'd beat me in this morning. Bad hair day?"

Jenna leaned against the counter. "Bad hair day…yeah. I wish."

"Well, from the looks of it, I'd say it started out that way."

Jenna put her cup down and leaned over to look at

her reflection in the glass of the microwave door. "Shit." She tried to smooth her hair back into some semblance of order and pulled strands over the small spot where the doctor had shaved the hair away two weeks ago to staple her wound. "I would've been here by six-thirty, but I broke the heel on one of my shoes. I fell"—she pointed JoAnne's gaze to her bruised knees—"shredded the hell out of my hose and had to go back home."

"You went home, but your hair is still a mess and your ass is full of dirt?"

"Oh, please. That was just the first spill."

Jo looked at Jenna with concern. "You fell twice? Jen, maybe you should go see the doctor."

"For what?"

"What d'you mean for what? If you can't stand or walk a straight line, I'd say you have a bit of a problem. It could be from the hit in the head. Are you still getting headaches?"

Jenna shook her head. "No. I'm fine."

"Yeah, you look fine."

"JoAnne, I said I'm fine. I tripped over some brat's skateboard. Okay?"

Her boss looked at her for a minute and then broke out laughing. "How the hell did you manage that?"

"I don't know. It came out of nowhere and I tripped over it." When JoAnne laughed again, Jenna grabbed her cup and strode past her. "Fuck you. You almost get hit by a bus, we'll see how funny it is then."

Jo ran to catch up. "Wait a minute. You got hit by a bus? This morning?"

"I said *almost*. The guy stopped in time."

"Sorry, Jen. Boy, you've turned into a real klutz

here lately."

She waved the comment off. "Yeah, yeah, yeah. Whatever."

JoAnne stopped at the door to her office. "Really, Jen, when you get done with the brief, I think you should call the doctor. Just to be sure."

"I do not need a doctor. There's nothing wrong with me that a good stiff shot of Bailey's in my coffee wouldn't cure." Jenna rounded the corner into her office. "I'm fine, JoAnne, I promise. I'll have this to you in an hour."

"Well, okay, then. But don't come bitching to me if you fall and break something."

Chapter 46

The plane was nearly full, but they managed to find three unoccupied seats at the back and settled in for the ninety-minute flight. The jet lifted off the runway and turned its nose to the northeast. Halfway to JFK International, Tommy went into the galley and dipped his hand into the drawers for drinks.

When he settled back into his seat, Mike asked, "Are you going to tell us what we're going to see?"

"Marvin, just trust me, okay? I promise you'll love it."

"And what if we don't?"

"Well, Marvin... You get five free noogies. How's that?"

Marv laughed. "How about five slaps upside the back of the head along with 'schmuck, I told you so'?"

"Whatever. It's all cool. I'm not worried. Plus, this will be a great distraction for a couple of days while we figure out a new plan. So, kick back and chill out, Marv. Enjoy the ride, man"

Later, after some sightseeing, they dropped by Sardi's for a quick snack and a drink. Someone in the crowd of deadheads in a booth near them leaned over. "Are you boys headed for the concert tonight?"

Marvin rolled his eyes as he answered. "I guess we are. All I can say is, this better be good after coming all the way from Dayton."

The man smiled. "Have you ever seen Judy before?"

"Judy who?"

The laughter caught Tommy's attention and he slid a finger across his own throat in an effort to stop the man from giving away the surprise.

"Judy *who*? Garland. Is there another Judy?"

Marvin turned to Tommy and fixed him with a stare. "You schmuck. You brought me all this way to see some old dead woman my *grandmother* used to listen to?"

"Have you ever heard any of her recordings, Brody? She's pretty good," Mike commented.

The man at the other booth leaned over to get a better look at Mike. "Pretty good? Son, Madonna is pretty good. Judy is phenomenal. Her records don't do her justice. You listen to her sing *live* and—" Loud laughter from the crowd interrupted him and echoed through the room. "Yeah, yeah, yeah…You all can bite me. I'm telling you, you will not be disappointed. That is if you can find room to squeeze in."

At one-thirty in the morning, every deadhead in the restaurant headed out through the doors and walls of the building and poured onto Forty-Seventh Street, walked against traffic on Seventh Avenue, bumping through people and cars. The entry to the Palace was swarming, and Mike and Marvin were amazed at how people were dressed. Long gowns, hair perfect, jewels; some of the women even wore evening gloves. Most men were dressed in tuxedo's; the rest in suits and ties.

"I feel a little under-dressed. Like maybe we should've stopped to see Davy for new duds before we left town," Marvin stated as he scanned the crowd.

"I wouldn't worry too much about it, Brody. I think everyone's more interested in seeing Judy than worrying about what you're wearing."

"You never know, there might be red carpet coverage now that Joan Rivers is over here with us," Tommy teased, and laughed as he pushed his way into the building.

In the dimly lit lobby a steady stream poured through the closed doors to the theater. Mike laughed at the throng of deadheads. "I've heard theaters have ghosts, but this is beyond imagination."

Inside, the house lights glowed at half-power and the grand drape was closed, lit by sporadic beams of light. The entire place hummed, deadheads murmured with excitement. They discovered every seat on the main floor filled and a crowd had already begun to gather at the foot of the stage. Tommy craned his neck to check out the loge and box seats. "Looks like it's already standing room."

Marvin turned to make his way back up the aisle. "Oh, Jesus H. This is ridiculous. I'm not standing for however long this is gonna take."

"Dude. Wait. Marvin."

"I told you I didn't want to do this in the first place. This is nuts. If you want to stay, stay. I'll meet you back over at Sardi's."

"No. Brody, up there." Mike pointed to the far house-left loge. "There's still a few rows empty. Come on. Go. Go. Go."

"From nosebleed country...I gotta sit in nosebleed to listen to some washed up old broad...I can't believe I'm doing this."

"I'd be more careful in here if I were you. You

could piss off a lot of people saying things like that."
Tommy pushed Marvin ahead and leaned down to a
woman in an aisle seat, who had snarled at Marvin's
comment. "He doesn't mean it. He's just a little
overwhelmed right now."

They settled into seats and looked down at the
crowded theater. Not only were the seats full, there
wasn't an empty space left on the main floor.
Deadheads packed every square inch, jostling each
other for position. The house lights dimmed, and the
strains of a full big-band orchestra bled through the
curtain. Thunderous applause filled the theater and the
music built louder to overcome the noise. Thirty
seconds later, every instrument went silent except a set
of drums. When the solo started, the curtains parted and
a strong beam of light hit the drummer. He stood and
bowed as his hands flew, and the crowd roared
approval.

"Oh, my God. Is that..." Marvin leaned over and
squinted in an attempt to focus more clearly, or as if the
figure might appear larger as a result. A big smile
spread across his face. "Holy shit. That's Gene Kruppa.
Mike. It's Gene fucking Kruppa!"

"I know!" Mike yelled back to him. "It's awesome,
isn't it?"

Tommy, who sat between them beamed. "I told
you it would be legendary."

"Did you know about this?" Marvin hollered over
the din.

"No, Marvin. But—"

Marvin grabbed Tommy in a big bear hug. "You
son-of-a-bitch. I take back every schmuck."

The orchestra joined in and finished the overture.

The audience applauded and then went silent for a split second as a small figure tentatively stepped from the right wing of the stage and into a spot light. Everyone leapt to their feet and the sound of applause, hollers, and whistles became deafening.

Judy made her way to the center, brought the microphone to her face, and took a breath. The audience still stood and roared for her. She spread her arms wide, hands held high for a moment; bowed and stood waiting. Five minutes went by though she brought the mic up again and again. "Thank you. Calm down, now. Sit, sit. Oh, my goodness. You're too good to me. I haven't even sung anything yet." The crowd laughed and applauded louder.

The first strains of "Lullaby of Broadway" struggled to be heard over the sound of the clapping, but when she sang the first note everyone settled down. In the middle of the verse, Judy interjected. "Wow. It suddenly got dead quiet in here." She shielded her eyes from the glare of the spotlight and peered into the audience. "Are you all still there?"

The crowd laughed, and the sound of clapping rose and fell as she continued with the song.

Thirty minutes into the concert, she stopped to introduce a few of the band members. Each one brought loud acceptance from a houseful of patrons. "And, finally, I really need to thank my friend and conductor. I think you all remember him, don't you? Tommy, turn around and take a bow. Tommy Dorsey, ladies and gentlemen."

Dorsey turned, raised his baton and saluted. When the decibels of clapping lowered, Judy sang for another twenty minutes. "Word filtered to the stage there's a gentleman here who thought I was a washed up old dead broad his grandmother used to listen to." The crowd booed. "I'm only forty-nine for crying out loud." She peered out into the seats. "Is that old?" The audience replied with audible no's. "As for the dead broad part—well, I suppose that's true, but it's pretty nice once you get over here."

She broke into "Over the Rainbow" amid cheers and another standing ovation. As the music continued she interjected, "It's not all bad. I mean, we're all here, we're havin' a good time—at least *I* think we're having a good time. Are we having a good time?" Her fans roared approval. "I suppose things over here can be hard sometimes, too. But when that happens, I hope you'll all think about this next song." She launched into "Get Happy" to the delight of everyone.

As the applause thundered, Marvin leaned into Tommy's ear. "Was she talking to me?"

"Could be, dude, could be."

"And?" Marvin nudged him, but Tommy didn't look at him and didn't see the darkness around Marvin lift a tiny bit, or that Marv's form became a little sharper again.

After the fourth encore ended with a reprise of "Over the Rainbow," Judy took her final bow and the curtain closed.

The three of them made their way out of the theater amidst the flowing crowd of deadheads and Tommy posed the question, "Was that awesome, or what?"

"It was. And, okay, I take it back, she's not some washed up old broad. Holy shit, she's got some pipes, doesn't she?"

"So, you weren't—" Someone pushed through

Mike. "Hey, lady, watch it. Where're you in such a rush to get to anyway?" He turned back to Marvin. "You weren't disappointed?"

"Hell no. I mean, at first I thought we were headed to someplace like Madison Square Garden."

"To see who? Janis Joplin or somebody like that?"

"Exactly. Maybe more like—"

"Janis doesn't play New York. Sinatra, yeah. Sammy Davis, Jr, maybe. In fact, if you wanted the whole Rat Pack, we could hit Vegas. But if you want to see the likes of Janis, you have to hit the west coast." Tommy drew a large breath and changed his speech as if holding in the hit of a doobie. "And be ready to do some *major* recreational stuff, if you catch my drift."

"Would you stop interrupting me, ya schmuck." Marvin gave Tommy his signature smack. "To finish answering your question, Mike, I'm not sorry in the least. She's awesome." Marvin wondered if Judy would know about *this* comment, but he wasn't in the mood for any of Tommy's instructional seminars and changed the subject. "I wonder how long we'll have to wait for a flight back."

Mike stopped short. "Wait. We're going back already? Do we have to?"

"What else is there to do? It's four a.m. I suppose we could hit an after-hours club."

"Nah, that's really not what I had in mind, Tommy."

"What then?"

"Well…it's just that…"

"Dude, spit it out. What?"

Mike gave them a sheepish grin. "I've always wanted to stay at the Plaza. Can we?"

Chapter 47

Marvin and Tommy leafed through the copy of the *New York Times* Tommy had snatched from in front of the suite across the hall on the top floor of the Plaza Hotel and drank coffee while they waited for Mike to emerge.

"Holy shit, he's sleeping late," Marvin commented.

"Yeah, more often than not, I'm the last one to crawl out. But, it was a late night. Besides, we got nowhere special to be, do we?"

"I guess not." Marvin scanned the room and whistled. "This place is nice. My mother would be jealous. This is the kind of luxury she's always aspired to."

"Coffee's pretty rank by now," Tommy said when Mike wandered out. "Want me to make fresh?"

Mike yawned and stretched. "Nah. I'll deal. Shit. What a night... The guy rolled through me and woke me up three times."

Marvin looked up from his section of paper. "You mean someone was actually in there?"

Mike plopped onto the chair. "Yeah."

"Dude, why didn't you just come into my room?"

"I had the master bedroom, I didn't want to give that up." Mike took a sip of his coffee. "Blech. That is nasty."

"Tommy offered to make a fresh pot for you."

"I know. But I know I slept late. I'll down this, and then we can head back." Mike took another sip, screwed his face into a grimace, and vocalized his distaste.

Marvin waved off Mike's growl. "Tommy, make him some fresh coffee, would you? So we don't have to listen to him whine."

Mike flipped him off. "Look who's talking about whining."

"Chill out, Mike. Relax. Take your time."

"What, don't you want to get home? You're always so antsy to get back."

Marvin took a fast glance at the time display on the microwave in the kitchen. "Don't look a gift horse, as the saying goes. I'm enjoying this. I'm in no hurry. The one o'clock flight is fine with me."

Mike glanced down at his watch, his eyes opened wide and he jumped out of his chair. "Shit. It's past eleven-thirty. We'll never make it."

Marvin launched into a big belly laugh. "Jesus H. Mike, sit down. Don't you know by now when I'm yanking your chain?"

"Coffee should be ready in a few minutes. I only made half a pot. That okay, Mike?" Tommy asked returning to the couch.

Mike went to the kitchen, dumped the burned coffee down the drain, and rinsed his cup. He pulled the carafe from the brewer and stuck his cup under the flow, then swapped again when his cup was full. "Toss me a section, Brody." He held his hand out as he passed Marvin on the way back to the chair.

The only sounds in the room for more than an hour came from the sips of coffee, cups being set back down on tables, and the rustle of newspaper pages.

Tommy folded his part of the paper and set it down as he stood up and stretched. "Well, I think I'll go shower and get dressed."

"I'll follow suit in a couple minutes, just let me finish this article first. You going to shower Brody?" Mike asked, his eyes still following along the text.

"Already did. Is anyone else getting hungry yet?"

"Sort of," Tommy said before he disappeared through the wall to the bedroom he'd used.

"Mike?"

"Hm?"

"You hungry?"

"I guess." Mike folded the section of paper and held it out to Marvin as he stood to head for his shower. "Interesting piece…gives me an idea for when we get back. Page D-six, bottom right. I do believe this just might do the trick. Think about it, between the three of us, we've pretty much tried everything else."

Marvin opened to the page and raised his eyebrows as he read the article. He nodded. The darkness crept back over him, and the definition of his body blurred a bit again. "Maybe… Hell, I don't know why we didn't think of this before."

During the next two days, Tommy led them around New York City, more for Mike's benefit than anything since he was the only one who had never visited. Tommy dragged them to every tourist-y place he could think of, doing his best to mess with the living to keep his charges entertained. Mike laughed at the antics and joined in from time to time. They were too busy having fun to notice the increasing darkness that crept around Marv, who followed along, but was preoccupied with the latest plot to take care of Jenna once and for all. Neither noticed the way more and more deadheads skirted around them giving a wider and wider berth, or the concerned looks that passed over faces the minute they laid eyes on Marvin.

Chapter 48

Mid-morning, three days after the concert while they sat in the deli, Tommy continued to object to Marv's latest plan and tried to map out his line of reasoning. "No. I don't think we should do it."

"Nothing else has worked."

A sensation of dread crept over Tommy. "No, Mike. I don't like it."

Marvin studied him. "What's the problem? This would definitely work, wouldn't it?"

"Too painful. It makes my stomach cramp just thinking about it. Nobody should have to endure that kind of pain."

"What pain, ya schmuck? She'll be dead."

The handful of deadheads in the restaurant got deathly quiet and turned to listen to the commotion.

"Keep your voice down." Tommy glared at Marvin. When the other deadheads turned their attention back to their own conversations, he leaned across the table, pushed a finger toward Marvin, and berated him in a low voice. "Don't tell me about pain, Marvin. Okay? I know pain. You think those bullets ripping into me was fun? It hurt. No, they fucking hurt like *hell*. And the pain didn't stop until I lost consciousness from bleeding."

Mike put a hand on Tommy's arm to draw his attention. "I'm sorry, Tommy. I'm sorry it hurt so much. We didn't know, did we Brody?" When Marvin didn't respond, Mike repeated himself in a stronger tone. "Did we, Brody?"

"No...we didn't. And I'm sorry, hippie. Honest. But look, it's all we have left to try."

Tommy got up from the table. "Go ahead then. But count me out. And don't come looking for my help when it's done."

"What are you talking about? I think it'd be perfect. No one would suspect a thing. Nobody gets in trouble and sent to jail for killing her; everyone would think it was suicide," Mike explained.

"Yeah, see...she's just too distraught over *my* death to go on," Marvin added

Tommy looked from Mike to Marvin. "I told you. You don't believe me. Neither one of you. And maybe I can't actually prove anything, but you just remember, I told you: if you do this, there will be dire consequences."

"Like what? Tommy, you haven't—"

Tommy fixed a steady, wordless gaze on Mike.

Marvin stood. "Wait a minute. Then why did you jump in on the other attempts if you thought there would be nasty consequences?"

"Because I knew they'd end up as stupid pranks, Marvin. Well, at least I thought so at the time. That whole bus incident was stupid of me; I should've refused to help with that because she really could've been killed. I'm backing out now, because this is different, dude; this will actually do it. This is serious shit."

"Fine." Marvin walked toward the kitchen. "Then just tell me where it is. I think I can handle pouring a little drain cleaner into her coffee without your help."

All conversations—the deadhead ones, anyway—again came to a halt. The dead sat glued to their seats, nervous anticipation increased, and the atmosphere in the room became tense.

"Marvin." Marvin stopped and turned around to face him, and Tommy stared directly into his eyes. He waited for a light bulb to turn on; for a sign, any sign, some glimmer of understanding of the gravity of the plan. When Tommy didn't see any glimmer of hope, he continued, "I get it that you love her. I get that you miss her. We all leave behind people we care about. But, she'll die, Marvin. Do you *get* that? *She'll die.* It'll be a very painful death. And what if she finds out it was you, then what? Well, I, for one, want nothing to do with it." He paused, a deep sadness came over him, his gaze fell to the worn floor of the deli and he slowly shook his head. "And if you do this Marvin...I don't think I want anything to do with you." He turned to Mike with tears flowing down his cheeks. "Mike, come on, man. Leave with me. Now. Don't be a part of this. *Please.*"

Tommy waited until he could see a decision on Mike's face and turned to walk out but stopped dead in his tracks.

Mike's momentum propelled him through Tommy. "Ugh. Why'd ya—" Mike halted.

Jason and Nancy stood in the deli just inside the doors. Deadheads scattered to the edges of the dining room. Tina-I'll-Be-Your-Server-Today turned back toward the dining area and stood stunned and confused by all the cups and glasses that appeared out of nowhere.

Marvin stopped near the edge of the order counter and broke into a smile. He moved to cross to the two deadheads who had just entered. "Nancy, I wondered if I would see you again." The smile disappeared when she put a hand out to stop him and shook her head. He halted when the old man standing next to her spoke his name.

"Marvin, I done tried to warn you. Mo'n once."

Marv attempted to turn to Nancy for help, for some explanation, but the old man's eyes, those deep, dark but brilliant eyes, held him immobile.

Nancy turned to the old man, her mentor and teacher. "Can't I do anything to help change this?"

"You done all what you could on that ship."

"There has to be a way."

"You see how he be faded already. He ain't gon' change." The old man gave her a slow shake of his head. "You gon' hafta learnt someday, chile. They ain't *all* worth savin'."

All the deadheads heard his words, except Mike, Tommy, and Marvin, who were held in his gaze. Everyone watched in mounting fear as the old man's form altered. He straightened and his height soared over them all, yet an unfamiliar weariness still furrowed his brow.

Nancy touched his coat sleeve. "You look tired, Jason."

He filled his lungs with air, and let it out in a slow, deliberate breath. And his speech pattern changed. "I'm just getting full. Why do you think we need more like you? The centuries are catching up with me."

"Then save yourself the effort and the room."

"What do you suggest?"

Nancy looked over at Marvin, who stood stock still with eyes wide just like every other deadhead in the place. Tina muttered to herself and bustled about to prepare for the lunch crowd.

After what seemed like hours to the deadheads, Nancy leaned toward the old man with her eyes still on Marvin. "Show him."

Startled, Jason moved a step away from Nancy and turned her to face him. "It's never been done. It could be more dangerous than leaving him here."

"How? What could be the harm?"

Jason nodded toward Marvin. "To him, plenty."

"Why? How?"

"It could make him very unstable."

"But it might not. You said it's never been tried. How do we know unless we try?" Nancy's voice took on a pleading tone.

"And what if it doesn't work, what if he can't handle it?"

After quick consideration, Nancy replied with resolve, "Then we take him."

The old man turned away from Nancy. He took a small step in Marvin's direction. "Marvin, you come over here now." The crowd of deadheads, with the exception of Tommy and Mike, who were still under Jason's firm mental grip, left the building running in all directions.

Marvin stumbled and Mike tried to reach out for him but he couldn't move; his arms remained pinned at his sides. Marvin made his way, shoulders slumped, to stand before Jason and attempted without success to avert his eyes to the floor. With each step closer, the edges of his body blurred more and faded to black.

Tommy and Mike watched in fear. Suddenly, as if they both received some silent signal, they turned and fled.

When Marvin stood before him, Jason spoke. "You made quite an impression on my replacement. She's a remarkable being, wouldn't you agree?"

Marvin only nodded.

"I'm old, Marvin. Older than you could possibly even guess. I've seen things that would curl your toes; perhaps send you running, crying and babbling like a baby. I wonder..." Jason paused and gazed out the window, though his eyes never focused on any one thing. "If she's to replace me one day soon, I wonder if she should be the one to take you. I wonder if she's strong enough yet." He returned to face Marvin and his size diminished.

Nancy blew out a soft sigh of relief. Jason had come to a decision.

"Look at me, Marvin. Here. Right in here," Jason pointed to his eyes. "I want you to see. I'm going to show you something. Something no one else has ever witnessed. Look deep. I want you to see what you've wanted to see, what you've wanted to know for so many months."

Jason's eyes grew huge and ever more deep.

Marv had never seen such eyes. He was sucked inward; falling, drowning in darkness so deep, and so thick, he might suffocate. Cries of anguish, sorrow, and woe floated up from the dankness. The sounds were faint at first, but the further he became enveloped, the deeper he fell, the higher the decibels grew. His hands clutched his ears, fingers clawing at them to stop the sound from penetrating. He heard screams of anger and

321

pain; suffering of such indescribable depth. Voices cried out in apology and pleaded for forgiveness; begged to be saved, to be released from the prison of misery and eternal night. There came insistent words of a penance paid, innocence of crimes, and misunderstood intentions. Others laughed with such utter cruelty and maniacal hatred he couldn't escape from the sound of them fast enough.

It was the pain they had inflicted on others being exacted upon them in turn. In time he could make out images.

Men and women of different races and skin color appeared in clothes that represented vast centuries. He became aware of soldiers who carried swords and the crosses of the Crusades; armies of men in togas; mobs of both men and women, naked, who wielded clubs fashioned from tree branches and bone. He stood in the presence of despots and dictators, rapists and murderers, child molesters and torturers, abusers, and sadists.

Tortured faces swam up from the black ink, legs flailed and arms reached out toward him, to grab him and hold him forever in clutched fingers. His attempts to scream became whimpers through his constricted throat. He tried to break away. No matter which way he turned, no matter where he ran, he met more faces of rage and outrage. A tightness gripped his chest, and his mind reeled. His breath burst from his lungs in heavy panting, his limbs ached with a soreness he'd never known could exist, his stomach cramped up in agony until he cried out, in terror and weary anguish, for help.

Marvin feared his mind would explode. Tears streamed from his face, and for a while, the crying turned to the sounds of crazy, uncontrollable laughter of a lunatic. He recoiled from it and sobbed in fear of what he'd become.

After what seemed a lifetime, light crept back into his vision. When he came back to consciousness and glanced around, the deli was closed; the lights were all turned out, the doors locked, and he stood in front of Jason and Nancy alone. Outside, the street was empty, and lamplights glowed through halos of mist.

"This is what happens. This is where 'the bad guys,' as you put it, are contained. *This* is how we police the world and our own. Do you understand now, Marvin?" Jason asked him.

Marv gave a slow, definitive nod. His body beyond exhausted, a sadness threatened to devour him.

Nancy recognized the change that crept over Marvin and saw the spark had gone from his eyes. She turned to Jason. "Will he be all right?"

Holding Marvin in his gaze, Jason responded with a tentative nod.

"What do you think will happen to him?"

"He'll eventually ask to leave, like all who grow weary here. When he does, Teresa, or others like her, will come to him, welcome him, offer him the peace he seeks."

Nancy let out a soft sigh. "I wonder sometimes why I couldn't have been chosen to be one of them."

Jason gave her a gentle smile. "Because we need strong ones like you; strong enough to hold what can never be freed, never allowed to be set out in the world again."

"Did you show him everything? Did you show him…"

"No. Do you think he deserves that favor?"

Nancy nodded. "I do. There's such *good* in him, Jason. There's love, pure and genuine; I've seen it. Without hope, it'll dissolve." She waited for him to respond. "Can *I* show him?"

"Isn't that something for Teresa to provide?"

"Everyone deserves at least a glimmer of hope."

Jason held Marvin locked in his stare though he spoke to Nancy. "You're a whole new breed of Keeper, aren't you, girl? I suppose you can try. Maybe it could be a better way."

Nancy walked to Marvin and tried to look him in the eyes. But when she came between him and Jason he turned his gaze to the floor. She put a hand under his chin to lift his face and he shut his eyes, turning away. Tears flowed down his cheeks.

Marvin's entire body trembled. "I can't. Not again."

Her voice came to him in soft tones. "Marvin, look at me. I promise there will be no pain this time."

Marv raised his head and opened his eyes, an expression of fear and concern swept across his face.

Chapter 49

Marvin wandered the streets for hours after Jason and Nancy left him standing alone in the deli. The sadness lifted, but the fear remained. Visions and sounds that he couldn't shake still clouded his mind.

It was noon when he found himself standing in front of his building. Upstairs, he undressed and stood under the hot spray of the shower until the water ran cold. He took the towel from its hook, the one Jenna had kept laundered and at the ready as if she still expected him to come home from a business trip. He rubbed himself dry, hung the towel, and threw his clothes under the bed just in case he slept too long and Jenna came home from work. He opened the closet, took one of her blouses from its hanger, and laid himself down on the bed, the blouse clutched in his grip.

He closed his eyes and begged sleep to take him. The sights and sounds Jason had subjected him to would not leave him alone. He fought against them, forced himself to think of other things; trying to focus on the things Nancy had shown him, because from what he could recall they seemed pleasant, and the only specific thing he could remember was an image of a truck, lying upside down with its wheels spinning.

It wasn't until his mind wrapped around memories of an evening with Jenna that the horrors eased away. It had been shortly after she'd moved into the condo. One that became more and more rare—much too rare as far as he'd been concerned. They sat on the balcony, holding hands in silence, sipping on glasses of wine, enjoying the masterpiece of the setting sun. She turned to look at him with a gentle and loving smile. And he drifted off to sleep.

Complete darkness had set in by the time he woke. Before he even opened his eyes, he smiled; he could smell Jenna and knew she was lying next to him. He sat up and watched her sleep for the longest time before he pulled his clothes on. He hung her blouse back in the closet exactly where it belonged, then stood in the doorway of the bedroom. "Okay, Jen...I'll see ya soon, okay?" He turned to leave but hesitated once more. "I love you, Jen."

Chapter 50

Mike came out of his bedroom at the hotel, a big yawn forced his eyes shut, and stumbled his way to the kitchen.

Marvin, caught up in some mental exercise or reverie, noticed him but didn't say anything until he heard the rattle of cups and smelled the coffee brewing. "Hey."

Mike almost dropped his cup. "Marvin." He put the mug down and ran to the living room. "Holy shit!" He pulled Marvin up off the couch and gave him a bear hug.

Marv endured it as long as he could. "All right, all right. Enough already." He pushed Mike away. "What was that for?"

Mike laughed and slapped Marvin on the shoulder. "Goddam, Broudstein, we were beginning to think you were a goner."

"What the hell are you talking about?"

Mike studied Marvin's face. "Are you kiddin' me, Brody?"

"Uh…" Marv spread his arms in ignorance.

"Don't you remember being in the diner when Nancy and that old man came in?"

Marvin shivered. "What, you think I can't remember as far back as yesterday?"

"Um, Brody, that was like…five days ago."

Marvin screwed up his face in disbelief. "It couldn't be..." His eyes glazed over for a moment. "So, what day is it?"

"Saturday."

"Holy Mother of Mary." Marv fell back to the couch and looked up at Mike, who stood there with a concerned expression. "Really?"

"Really. You look stunned, Brody. Here." Mike headed for the kitchen. "Let me get you some coffee."

"Yeah. Thanks."

Mike returned with the coffee, sat on the chair opposite Marvin, and leaned in. "So, what happened? My God, Tommy and I went back every day. No other deadheads would even go near the place. The three of you just *stood* there, looking at one another. No one moved a muscle, not even the twitch of an eye, man. It was like, I don't know, like you were all made out of granite or something. And you kept fading."

"I was fading?"

"Yeah, it was weird. You got...I don't know...blurry and dark. I swear, we thought you..."

"What?"

"Well, on Tuesday night, you were so...*black*, I guess...we thought you would disappear completely."

"Black, yeah." Marvin shivered again at the memory of the darkness that had almost consumed him.

"So, what...what was it? What happened?"

"Where's Tommy?"

Mike nodded toward the bedroom. "Still sleeping. Last night was the first time he's slept since Monday. He was really worried about you. Then when we went back to the deli last night and you and Nancy and the old guy were gone, he really lost it."

"He sees we're all gone, he loses it and *sleeps*?"

"You didn't let me finish. So, then, he looked out across the street and saw the old guy staring at him. Two seconds later, he was the old Tommy with a big grin on his face. He wouldn't say anything about you except, 'he's okay.' He couldn't—or wouldn't—tell me how he knew. He just kept insisting you were fine now."

Marvin smiled and nodded.

"Brody."

"What?"

"Tell me what happened."

Marv looked down at the floor. "Let's wait for Tommy to get up. I can only do this once."

Mike placed his cup on the table, stood, and hollered as he headed for the bedroom. "Tommy? Tommy." He stopped in the doorway, "Tommy, get your ass up. Come on, haul it out."

"Ah...let me sleep," Tommy barked.

"Marvin's here."

Tommy moved so quick, Mike wasn't able to get out of his way fast enough to avoid Tommy running through him.

"Damn." Mike pressed his hands to the sides of his head. "Don't do that."

"Sorry," Tommy hollered moving in Marvin's direction. With arms outstretched, he jumped into the air, yelled "Marvin," and landed on Marv so heavy, he sank right through him and ended up with his face in the cushion.

Marv tried to roll out from under the entanglement. "Hey, watch it, ya schmuck. What the hell are you doin'? Get outta me."

Tommy came up in a fit of his infectious giggles. Neither Marvin nor Mike could stop themselves from joining in.

"Marvin. Dude. Whew. I wondered how much longer it would be. I mean, the old guy didn't really *tell* me anything. And Nancy was nowhere to be found. I mean nowhere. She fled the scene before I knew it."

Mike came back out of the kitchen and held out a cup of coffee. "Here Tommy. You look like you could use some of this. You know, you don't seem awake enough yet."

Tommy accepted the cup with a laugh and quick thanks and sat on the couch next to Marvin. "Okay. I'm ready. Spill it."

The smile disappeared from Marvin's face. He hesitated, inhaled as deep as he could and held it for a moment. "I don't know how much I can tell you, really. I mean without getting myself into some deep shit. And believe me, I do *not* want to go through even a little taste of that again."

Mike couldn't take Marvin's pause any longer, "Well, just tell us what you think is okay."

Marv looked directly at Tommy. "All I can say is, you were right. There are consequences. And I know what happens if... Well, let's just say, I know where they keep the bad guys now."

"Can you tell us where it is, Brody?"

"In *him*. In Jason—that's the old man's name."

"*In* him? Dude...that is heav-ee."

"Well, in ones like him; there are other...keepers. I think that's the term they used."

"Why was Nancy there? Did she explain what she was doing with him, Brody?"

With a nod of his head, Marvin answered Mike's question without looking at him. "She's going to be one. She's going to replace him." Marvin mused more to himself than to his friends. "I wonder if that's why she was on the cruise in the first place; to size me up. No wonder she told me then that she harbored no illusions."

"So, let me understand this, Brody. She was there to help Jason?"

"I guess... You know, she showed me..."

Tommy prodded for him to continue. "What, *what* did she tell you?"

Marvin lifted his face momentarily unable to speak. "Huh, that's strange... You know, I don't know. I can't remember exactly, I just remember something about a truck. Weird, huh?"

"Wow... That is far out, man." Tommy let out a low whistle. "What happens to the old man? Where's he going?"

"I don't know. They didn't explain that, and I didn't ask. I don't think I want to know. I learned more than I ever wanted to; more than I should have."

"So, what happens now?"

"With what?"

Mike shrugged. "Jenna. I mean, now what?"

"Nothing. She lives, she works, life goes on. And *we* go on."

"That's it? You've finally come to your senses?"

"Look, I... Don't get me wrong. I'd be more than thrilled if she was, uh, here. But Tommy, you were right: If I had succeeded, she would be here, and I'd be gone. And what would be the point of that?" Marvin stayed silent for a second and amended his statement.

"And if it wasn't for Nancy, I'd be gone anyway just for trying."

"Oooo. How so?"

"I think she talked him out of it. Did you hear him when he first told me to walk over to him?"

Mike shivered. "Yeah, it was creepy. Who would've thought that big voice could come out of a guy that old?"

"Did he seem to get any taller or bigger to you?" Marv looked from one friend to the other.

Tommy laughed. "Holy crap, are you kidding? That's when everyone else scattered. You should've seen them all turn tail and run. One guy ran right through the hot grill. That musta warmed his buns."

Marv didn't laugh. "Yeah, and then what were you able to hear or see?"

"I know his size started to dwindle down a bit, but really? All I could see was you getting fuzzy and dark. Scared the living shit outta me. Reminded me of a really bad acid trip I took once. No lie. I would've run, but I couldn't. It was like...my feet were glued to the floor or something."

"I couldn't move either... Do you think this guy held me and Tommy because we were going to be next?" Mike shuddered.

Marvin turned his gaze to Mike. "Why would he do that?"

"Because we tried to help you, Brody."

Tommy nodded in agreement. "That's got to be it."

"But, then why weren't we put through the same as Marvin? Why did he let us leave?" Mike wondered aloud.

"I don't think he *let* us do anything. Didn't you

hear him say 'Get out?' "

"No, all of a sudden my feet were able to move and I was out of there. When I turned around, you were right behind me Tommy."

"Well, I never heard him say anything to anyone but me. I knew he and Nancy were talking, but I couldn't hear all their words. Maybe he figured he'd scared you enough," Marv suggested. "But I'll tell you this: you better kiss his feet if you ever run into him again. Because, trust me, you never want to see what I did." He shook his head and covered his face with his hands for a moment. "Anyway, I think Nancy changed his mind somehow."

"So, what did happen? What did he do to you? Come on, Brody, are you gonna tell us or what?"

Marv looked from Mike to Tommy. "You talk about a bad acid trip? This was worse than any acid trip you've ever been on. It was black as coal and the stuff I heard…the things I saw come up out of that…" Marvin remained silent for a few moments and then apologized. "I'm sorry, I just can't do it."

"Okay, Brody. Maybe some other time."

Marvin shook his head. "No. Never." He picked up his coffee and stood at the window looking down to the pool; his entire body shook. "All I want to do is get those images and sounds out of my head."

Mike and Tommy waited for Marvin to compose himself.

"Okay, then." Marvin turned back into the room. "I've put up with you hanging out in the breeze long enough. How about you two get some clothes on and we hit the deli?" He looked at Tommy. "Think you could rustle me up one of those corned beef sandwiches? I'm starved."

Tommy beamed. "You bet."

Marvin added as he watched Tommy and Mike head to get dressed, "And a knish? I could really go for a knish."

Chapter 51

The deadheads in the restaurant turned to stare when Mike, Tommy, and Marvin came through the window of the deli. Within seconds, as recognition lit their expressions, they dropped their cups and scattered. Tommy yelled, "Where's everyone going?"

Tina-I'll-Be-Your-Server-Today stopped in her tracks, her shoulders slumped, and she took a deep breath and muttered, "I am not losing my mind. But I swear, I'm beginning to think this place is haunted." She took a quick surveillance of the tables where cups and glasses had appeared out of thin air. "I swear to God, if this crap doesn't stop, I'm outta here."

"I don't want to be within five-hundred yards of him." A woman pointed at Marvin. "He's bad news."

"Yeah, me either," her companion chimed in. "I was here when..." She trembled and then steadied herself and stood tall. "I was here."

"I'm sorry"—Marvin swept his arms around the room while Tina-I'll-Be-Your-Server-Today dumped dishes from the tables into a bus tub—"everyone. Really, I...I apologize. But it's okay now. It won't happen again, I promise."

The crowd of deadheads looked at him in distrust.

"No, really. Look at him," Mike offered. "Do you see any black edges? Does he look blurry to you at all anymore?"

Tommy spoke up. "It's true. I saw the old man yesterday afternoon and he told me. Well, he didn't *tell* me, but—"

An old regular from Sunday mornings interrupted him. "He told you, but he didn't tell you? Come on, Tommy—"

"Really, Dixon. I saw him standing across the street from here yesterday afternoon. He assured me Marvin would be fine. No more trouble." Tommy turned to the woman who'd said she witnessed it. "Did you hear him say anything on Monday?"

The woman shook her head. "I can't recall any exact *words*, but he didn't have to say a thing. He landed those eyes on me, and I knew he meant for me to get the hell out. And I did, in a right hurry, let me tell you."

"You see? That's how he told me everything's okay now. There's no reason to be afraid of the old guy. Or Marvin. So, come on, sit back down. You can relax. And I'll even get you fresh drinks. Marvin here will help, won't you, dude?"

Marvin grabbed an order pad and pencil. "Absolutely. Here, I'll start with you—Dixon, was it?"

Dixon stood his ground but nodded. "Uh…just a black coffee."

Marvin smiled and wrote it down as he confirmed the order, "One black coffee." He turned to the next deadhead with an inquisitive look and waited. As soon as Dixon retook his seat the rest of the orders came at Marvin faster than he could write them down.

Tommy and Mike helped fill and deliver the orders, and the newly emptied coffee pots sent Tina over the edge. She let out a frustrated scream, pulled her apron off, threw it across the room, and ran out. Tommy laughed and set to brewing more while Moe, the owner of the deli, went after her. By the time she'd calmed down and allowed herself to be convinced to come back in, the coffee pots were full.

"I could swear to you, Moe, I *swear*," she said as he held the front door open for her. "I had all fresh carafes sitting there. I turned around from bussing the last two tables, and they were empty. You'll see." She stepped aside and pointed to the brewer without turning toward it. "Now you look over there and you tell me I'm full of crap."

The deadheads burst into fits of laughter.

Moe looked at the full pots and a sad look painted his face. "You're not full of crap. But maybe you need a vacation, honey." Moe took her by the shoulders and spun her around.

Tina's body sagged, and she drew in a deep breath. She took timid steps to retrieve her apron. She tied it on and poured herself a cup of coffee. A strange vibration ran through her when she sat down at one of the tables.

The crowd of deadheads laughed when the woman she sat in let out a yelp and scampered across the diner. "Pay attention, Betty, they can move mighty fast when you're not looking," one of them hollered out to her amid the chuckles.

Tina shivered. "Fine, Moe. But I'll tell you what, tonight on my way home, I'm buying a great big bottle of whiskey. And I'm drinking it all."

Chapter 52

Over the following weeks, Marvin changed his living arrangement to the suite at the Hilton, but his routine never varied. When they returned home from the distraction or entertainment they'd chosen for the day, Marvin would sit for a few minutes to watch the evening news and then rise from his chair. "See you in a little while. Anybody want anything while I'm out?"

"Where ya going, dude?"

"Just out for a walk. I'll be back."

At first Mike and Tommy tried to get him to explain his nightly meandering, even though they knew what he was doing. Marvin would only mutter a quiet, "Nothing." But Marv needed to know Jenna was doing all right. He would stand across the street from the condo, wait for her to round the corner from the bus stop, and watch her walk up the street and into the building. Then, unless it was her Thursday night out with Colleen, he'd patiently wait for her to emerge on the balcony with her nightly glass of wine. He'd nod, whisper a soft, "Okay, kiddo. I love you. I'll see you tomorrow," and head back to the hotel.

On Thursdays he waited until he figured the two women would be on their way home from dinner, make his statement to the guys, and head out. He'd watch Colleen carefully pull the car around to the back and keep his sentry until Jenna appeared on the balcony.

Once in a while Marvin could've sworn he heard her say, "I love you, Marv. I miss you so much." But he figured it was all in his head. Wishful thinking.

September twenty-second turned out to be a beautiful Indian Summer evening. Marvin stood in his usual spot with a full glass of wine in his hand, waiting. He glanced at the lowering sun and wondered what was keeping her. "Working late, probably. Maybe I should catch a bus to the office. Just to make sure everything's okay." Five minutes later, he was walking toward the bus stop when Jenna came strolling around the corner carrying two large shopping bags. He could see wrapping paper and bows sticking out, smiled and went back to his place, leaning against the storefront to wait.

She emerged on the balcony with the phone in hand, already talking.

Marvin crossed the street to stand below, looked up at her, and listened to her end of the conversation.

"Oh, Colleen, you should see the things they gave me. I think I may have finally solidified my place in the firm." Jenna paused, listening. "No, it had to be JoAnne's idea. They catered in a ton of food, had a cake made, and it was really fun. But, I'm bushed now. Well, maybe it's from the wine; one of the partners actually brought it in from his own cellar." Another pause. "Of course we're still on for tomorrow. I wouldn't miss it. Oh, thank you. Goodnight, Colleen. Sleep well."

Jenna turned off the phone and placed it on the table between the deck chairs with a sigh. "The only thing that would've made this day better... Dammit, Marvin. I wish you could've been there to see it and enjoy it all with us."

"Me too, kiddo. I didn't forget though. I'm with you—I'm as close as I can be without causing trouble. I'd ask the guys to help me find you someone, but I think that might be interfering too much. Plus, I'd probably just get crazy jealous anyway." A deep sadness enveloped him, but he raised his glass in salute. "I hope you know I love you, but I think this has to be my last visit. I hope you find a guy, fall crazy mad in love, and…well… That's my present to you. Happy birthday." He took a sip and walked down the street toward home. He dared one more glance over his shoulder. "See ya, Jen."

Chapter 53

A bit longer than two months later, the coffee shop across from the law firm bustled with late afternoon business. Jenna stared out at the street and sipped the latte JoAnne bought her in celebration of beating the latest deadline by a couple of hours.

"You seem down. What's troubling you?" JoAnne asked.

Jenna shook her head and rattled herself back to the present. "I don't know. Just a bit melancholy I guess. It's gotten…I don't know how to explain it, but something's…been different."

"Different how? Where? At the office?"

"No. At home. I don't know if I can explain it, but it's been so…quiet. Until maybe a few months ago I…I kept misplacing things, forgetting if I'd done something, I'd smell coffee or food when I hadn't made either. I know how this is going to sound, but it's like I could sense Marvin. I thought, you know, maybe he was still hovering, watching, doing things to let me know he was still there. I know, it sounds crazy, right?" A short, embarrassed laugh burst from her. "Sometimes *I* thought I was losing my mind. But now…" She shook her head. "None of that stuff is happening anymore and," tears spilled over the rim of Jenna's eyes, "it's like… It feels like he's…gone. Really gone. And I miss him like crazy."

JoAnne tugged some tissues from her purse and handed them across the table. "Is it because of the unveiling of the headstone tomorrow?"

Jen shrugged and wiped her face. "I guess it could be. It all seems so…final, you know? You're going with me aren't you?"

JoAnne sighed. "You know how I hate this shit. But for you, yes. Only for you."

"Thank God." Jenna let out the breath she'd been holding. "I don't think I could handle it alone."

"Isn't the family going to be there?"

Jenna laughed. "Why do you think I don't want to be alone? I mean, David and his dad are fine. But, Madelyn…Madelyn is a force all her own. She scares the crap out of me."

"Still? Jesus Christ, Jenna. Get a grip on the situation and tell her to go fuck herself."

When they finished laughing, Jenna said, "I can't do that. You know I can't."

"I can. You want *me* to tell her? I will, you know I will. 'Cause I don't give a shit what she thinks and I can tell her that too." JoAnne hoisted her glass.

"JoAnne, you are *so* bad."

"I am, aren't I? And that's why you love me."

"You know me too well." Jenna glanced at the clock on the wall. "Oh, hey, I gotta go, or I'll miss the four-thirty. Thanks for the coffee." Jenna stood, slipped her coat on, and leaned over to kiss her friend on the cheek. "I'll see you over there tomorrow."

"Okay. Get home safe."

****

Marvin, Tommy, and Mike stood well away from the small group huddled around the headstone. A cold wind whisked the Rabbi's words away before they could really be heard. When it concluded, JoAnne tugged on Colleen's coat sleeve, and they took a few steps back to give the family a bit of privacy. Then, with the Rabbi gone, Jenna, who had remained stoic, exchanged a hug with Morton. She turned to Madelyn and allowed a tentative embrace.

David hugged her and said softly, "I'll see you, Jen."

"Yeah, David. We'll talk soon."

David took his mother's arm in his, and Jenna watched as they walked off with Morton following. She turned back to the headstone, and her tears flowed.

"Well, go on, Brody." Mike gave Marv a little push. "Go hear what she has to say."

"Eh, what for? She's probably just gonna cuss me out again for dying." But he walked over and stood by her side.

"You're gone, aren't you, Marvin? I mean you're really gone. I'm sorry. I miss you so much. No one could ever replace you, you know that. I wouldn't even try to find another you. It couldn't be done. I love you, you son-of-a-bitch. But, Marv…"

Marvin smiled at the curse and draped an arm around her. "I know, kiddo. I know. I want you to be happy. That's why I've left you alone. Just," he shrugged, "be careful, okay?"

Jenna leaned down and ran her fingers over the letters on the stone. "Goodbye, Marv."

"Not goodbye, Jen. Not really. Someday you'll be here. When it happens, I'll be waiting and maybe we can… That is, if you…you know, if you still want me. See ya, kiddo." He leaned in, planted a soft kiss in the middle of her forehead, and brushed her face with the back of a hand.

With a small smile, Jenna touched her cheek and walked away from the grave.

Marvin went in the opposite direction with his friends' arms around him.

JoAnne took Jenna's hand. "All done? Terrific. Now, let's go; I need a drink. What d'ya say, Colleen? How about it? I hear you like a good belt of scotch once in a while."

Jenna and Colleen exchanged a smile and a wave of the hand. "Oh, go on."

Chapter 54

A little more than a week after the unveiling of Marvin's headstone, Jenna and Mrs. McClaskey came out of the restaurant after their usual Thursday dinner out. The fall leaves that had danced through the glow of the parking lot lights were replaced with large, drifting snowflakes.

"Do you have a driver's license, can you drive, dear? I'm just feeling very tired all of a sudden." The old woman handed Jenna the keys and feigned a sudden weariness. She'd been concerned ever since that accident at the bus stop. She knew Jenna to be a proud young woman, and a small smile spread across her lips. *Much like yourself when you were young.* It had taken a long while to figure out how to talk Jenna into the plan.

"It's been a long time, but I think I can handle it. Just show me how to adjust everything and how to turn on the headlights."

Jenna helped Colleen into the car and then sat behind the wheel and repositioned the seat and mirrors. It had been so long since she'd driven a car, she was nervous, overly cautious, and didn't talk much, only in response to direct questions, and Colleen kept those to a minimum.

"I don't know why, but I thought you didn't have a license. I suppose because you don't have a car. Otherwise, I would've had you driving all along,"

Colleen said as Jenna eased the big car into its parking space behind the condo building and cut the engine.

"I've had a license; I just never saw the need of getting a car, I guess. I mean with the bus stop down around the corner and one right in front of the office building, it was an expense we could do without." Jenna helped the old woman from the car, closed the passenger door, and held out the keys. "Here, you go."

"No. You keep them. It's yours now. I'm giving the car to you."

"But…"

Colleen held up a wrinkled, age-spotted hand. "No buts. I don't even like to drive anymore. It frightens me. Especially at night. These old eyes of mine just don't see things the way they used to."

"Oh, that's not really the truth and you know it."

Colleen ignored the comment. "It's a good vehicle. Patrick kept it very well tended to, and I've tried to do the same."

"I'm sure it's still in very good shape, but…"

"No arguments. I've been meaning to do this ever since that near miss you had at the bus stop a while back. I'd feel better if you stayed away from them."

"I really shouldn't. What will you do if you need groceries, or if you decide you want to go see a movie or something?" Jenna asked as they made their way into the lobby and headed up the flight of stairs.

"How about this, then. When I need groceries, you can take me. If I want to see a movie, I'll wait for the weekend, and we'll go together, my treat."

"Well that's hardly fair. But—" Jenna glanced up at the light fixtures. "Wow, it seems dark in here tonight, doesn't it?"

"It does. It would appear a couple of the light bulbs have burned out. I'll call the maintenance man first thing in the morning and let him know."

Jenna turned her head to the old woman. "Be careful, now," she cautioned her friend.

"Oh, don't you worry about me. I may be old and my sight may be going but I'm still fairly spr—"

Colleen drew a quick gasp when her feet flew out from under her. She tumbled over backward and grabbed out with both hands in a panic. After several flays of her arms, her fists filled with the back of Jenna's coat. The momentum carried them backward, Jenna fell on top of her, and amid surprised yelps, they tumbled down the entire flight. They landed in a heap at the bottom, a tangle of twisted limbs. The toy truck bounced down after them and came to rest upside down, wheels spinning, next to Jenna's head.

Though Marvin had made a valiant attempt to stay away, every so often the urge, the need, to check in on her became overwhelming. Even if all he managed was a glimpse of her through the glass doors of the balcony, it soothed him. Standing in his usual spot, he heard the sharp cries. Not even trying to dodge traffic, he rushed across the street, through the front door of the building, and stopped in his tracks to see Jenna and Colleen trying to untangle themselves.

"Goddammit, those kids are going to kill one of us someday. Colleen, are you—" Jenna forgot all about Mrs. McClaskey and stared up at him. "Marvin?"

"Oh, shit."

Chapter 55

Jenna shook her head in confusion. She looked from Marvin to the old woman sitting on the steps to a vision of her still lying on the floor. She turned to help Colleen up. "Mrs. McClaskey? Colleen? Are you okay?"

"Jen...honey..." Marvin started out in a soft, even tone.

"Marvin, don't just stand there, help her."

"What do you want me to do? Don't you see, Jenna?"

Jenna turned on him. "Don't I see what, Marv? I see an old woman lying on the floor, in pain, who needs help. Why are you just standing there? Help me get her up."

Marvin sighed and moved to Jenna as she leaned over the mass of twisted flesh. He watched her attempts to grab an arm. "Jenna, stop. Look what happens when you try to move her."

Jenna paused for a second, tried again, and watched her hand wash right through. "What the hell..." She stood up and looked at her hand. "Why can't I pull her up?"

Colleen stood up from the stair and put an arm around Jenna's shoulder. "Jenna, dear, I think your Marvin is trying to tell us we're...we've..."

"Oh, my God. I'm *dead*?" Jenna stood, stunned. "I

can't be dead."

"Oh, my. I'm sorry, dear, and I'm afraid it's all my fault. I shouldn't have grabbed onto you."

Jenna turned to look at her friend and blinked vacant eyes. "Nonsense. We're fine. We're both fine. See? You're standing there, I'm standing here. We're talking to one another." She addressed Marv, her voice full of panic. "Tell her, Marvin."

"Uh, Jen... If you're both fine, who's that on the floor? And, why after all this time can you see and hear me?"

Jenna looked down and studied the features, looked at the clothes, and compared them to what she and the old woman wore.

Colleen turned and climbed the stairs. "I think I want a nice cup of tea." She stopped and asked Marvin, "Would that be possible, do you think? Can I make some nice tea?"

Marvin looked up and smiled at her. "You can do anything you want to now."

The old face scrunched up into a flurry of happy wrinkles and she nodded. "Then I think that's what I'll do; have a soothing cup of tea and wait for Patrick. Do you think he'll come?" She turned her eyes to Jenna. "You two come up when you're ready, dear, and we'll all have a nice cup of hot tea to calm our nerves."

As Colleen neared the top of the steps they heard her say, "I'm going to make some tea, Patrick. Would you like to join us for some tea?"

Marvin and Jenna both peered up into the dimness, and though they didn't see anything but a pair of feet, they heard a man's voice say, "I've missed your tea almost as much as I've missed you." They exchanged a knowing smile.

Jenna looked down at the bodies on the floor and sighed. "Dammit, Marvin."

"I know."

"I was just getting my shit back together. Is this your idea of a joke?"

"What? What the hell are you talking about?"

Jenna turned to him and swung the back of her hand through his upper arm. "You son-of-a-bitch."

"Ow. What the hell was that for?"

"You did this, didn't you?"

"Did what?"

Jenna pointed to the truck on the floor. "That. You put that on the stairs just hoping we'd fall."

"Are you crazy? Of course not. I wasn't even in the building."

"I swear to God, Marvin, if I find out…"

Marvin shrugged, turned, and walked through the closed door out to the street.

"Marvin? *Marvin*?… How did you…" Jenna walked to the door, stopped, and raised her voice. "Does it hurt?"

"Does what hurt?"

"Walking through things like that."

"Come through and find out. Come on… It doesn't hurt, I promise. It just…tingles a bit. You'll get used to it."

She poked a hand through and waited. "It vibrates."

Marvin shrugged. "I guess, yeah. Come on."

She moved the rest of the way through and stood next to him. She looked down the street in both directions. "It's weird. I can sort of see through you."

"A lot of things will seem weird at first." Marvin watched her as she tried to adjust to the new sights, sounds, and feel of being a deadhead.

After a few minutes, she smiled. Then she grabbed him in a hug and kissed him. "I missed you. It was tough."

"I know."

Jenna gaped at him. "What do you mean you know? How could you know, you weren't there."

"Oh, but I was. Every step of the way."

"Really? You've watched over me this whole time? That was sweet." The smile left her face. "Wait a minute… Every step of *what* way?"

"Every step of *every* way." Marv watched her expression change to one of confusion. "The missing sodas, the smell of food, the coffee, the wet towels."

The frown on Jenna's face proved her dawning understanding. "The soda can that flew past my face— that was you?" Marv nodded. "The broken window?" He nodded again. "The food on Mrs. McClaskey's table on your birthday?"

"Yeah, that too." A big grin spread across his face. "God, I loved that you had a party for me with all my favorites. The fact Larry was there and didn't know the real reason for the dinner sweetened the pot."

"Then Larry didn't… Wait. What really happened to him?"

Marv shrugged and grinned. "I punched him."

Jenna walked away, and Marv ran to catch up to her. They appeared like any couple, well, to other deadheads anyway; side by side, out for an evening walk. "So, then, let me get this straight. The shit on the golf course… That was you? *You* hit Larry with the golf

351

balls?"

Marvin laughed at the memory. "Yeah. What a big wuss."

Jenna swung a fist through him.

"Ow. What the hell are you doing?"

"You asshole."

"What?"

"That hurt like hell." Jenna stared at him. "And *now* look what you did."

"No. Wait a minute. I didn't do this, I swear. Honest, Jenna, you have to believe me." Marvin smiled at her. "I missed the hell out of you, though."

She peered into his eyes for the truth then linked an arm through his, and they strolled down the block. "You know, if I find out you put the truck on those steps and killed that sweet old woman…"

"I didn't. I swear I didn't."

She gave him a sideways glance. "Yeah, well, I wouldn't put it past you."

Marvin stopped walking and tugged on Jenna's arm. "Oh, Jesus H. What time is it?"

"I don't know, why?"

"The guys are gonna wonder what happened to me. I told them I'd be right back."

"Guys? What guys?"

"Tommy and Mike."

"Who are Tommy and Mike?"

"New friends. Well, *Tommy's* a new friend. Mike and I—you remember Mike, right? Mike Hamilton, my buddy from Harvard?"

"Now why would I know any of your friends from Harvard?"

"Oh, that's right. Anyway, let's head over there so

I can let them know everything's okay."

"I'm not really in the mood for meeting anyone right now, Marvin."

"You have to meet them at some point, it might as well be now."

"Why?"

"Because you're gonna love them. Tommy's a goofy, sweet kid and Mike's…well, Mike. And because that's what I think we should do right now. And I'm sure they're concerned about me."

Jenna laughed and started walking again, but turned back in the direction of the condo. "Why would they be concerned about you?"

"Because I told them I'd be back in a little while and I've been gone for—I don't know—a couple of hours at least."

"You've been gone for two hours, and that makes you think someone's worried about you?"

"Yeah. What, you don't think I'm worth worrying about?"

"Marvin. I just got here, can't we spend a little time alone? You know, you can be such an arrogant prick sometimes."

"And you can be a petulant bitch."

They stopped in their tracks, turned to one another, and laughed. Then, arm in arm, they walked back into the building.

Jenna looked down at the bodies. "Huh, I wonder how long it'll be before someone discovers us. Isn't there something we can do?"

"Like what?"

"I don't know—bang on someone's door, ring a doorbell. Rattle some pots and pans. I don't know how this stuff works."

"What difference would it make, you'll still be just as dead."

Jenna slugged him. "That's a shitty thing to say."

"Why? It's true."

"Screw you, Broudstein." Jenna started up the stairway.

"You better be nice to me, or—"

"Or what?"

"Or, I won't teach you the ropes around here."

"Oh, yeah, like I need your help. I can learn how to do things on my own, you know."

Marvin paused. "Yeah, I know." He smiled at her and took her hand, "But it'd be a lot more fun together, wouldn't it?"

When they reached the top of the stairs, Marvin stopped and gave a small tug on Jenna's hand. He nodded toward Colleen's door. "What do you think, should we stop in, see how they're doing?"

"That'd be sweet. But, let's wait. I think we should give them some time to be alone. You know Patrick has been gone a long time. I'm sure they have some catching up to do." Jenna shifted her gaze from the door across the hall to Marvin. "Since when did you become all…"

"All what?"

"I don't know. Such a… What's the word your mother always used…a *mensch*?"

Marv shrugged as he passed through the door to their place. Memories of his experience at Jason's hands flooded his mind, and a slight frown crossed his lips. "Trust me, you really don't want to know how that came about."

"Fine. Don't tell me."

A broad smile broke out. "I have no intention of it." He uncorked a bottle of wine and poured some into the glasses Jenna had pulled down from the cupboard. Marvin handed her a glass and led her out to the balcony. "Besides, I'm not *that* different, am I?"

"On second thought, it might be better if I don't question it and just enjoy it." She clinked her glass against his in a toast. Marv heard a small, contented sigh escape from her before she said, "Yeah, it would…"

"What would be what?"

"It would be a lot more fun to learn things if we're together." Jenna smiled and looked out over the city. She didn't see Marvin wave his hand in greeting to the two men moving in the direction of the building.

A word about the author...

Paul Atreides turned writing for his own amusement into a career as a theatre critic and columnist for the *Las Vegas Review-Journal*.

He's had several short stories published in anthologies and is also a playwright. His two-act comedy-drama, "Phallusies," premiered in Las Vegas, Nevada, to good reviews, received Las Vegas City Life's "Pick of the Week," and most recently played to sold-out houses in Nashville, Tennessee. He was invited to post his ten-minute play, "Fusion," to the National September 11 Memorial & Museum in New York City to the Artist's Registry in written form until filming can qualify it for installation as an exhibit within the museum.

He is a member of the College of Fine Arts Advisory Board, University of Nevada—Las Vegas.

~*~

www.paul-atreides.com
Twitter: @atreides_paul
Facebook: paul.atreides.391
Facebook: WorldofDeadheads